Madarach's Secret

D. J. Mitchell

Published by Alma James Publishing LLC
Harrisonburg, Virginia

For Ethan, with love.
May you follow the dance.

Prologue

In the beginning there was only blackness. The blackness was all, and it had no opposite. Then the spirit of life moved through the blackness. The blackness felt joy in the spirit of life, and the blackness began to dance. It danced and danced until it rended itself, and light appeared.

Now blackness had an opposite to dance with, and together darkness and light danced the universe into existence. They danced space and matter, push and pull, motion and rest, sound and silence, energy and entropy, until all the framework of the world had been laid in place. And the spirit of life moved through it, for it was the spirit of life that caused the dance.

We can still see the dance of the blackness and light in the rhythm of day and night, in the circles of birth and death, in the melodies of joy and sadness, in the rising and falling of creation and destruction.

The dance between light and darkness is eternal, and we are all part of it.

From "The Song of Creation"
Translated by Benji Haight

Chapter One

Benji Haight was twelve Earth years old, and a gifted young man. He lived on a planet called Parisa with his sister and his adoptive family. He did well in his lessons, and was a good athlete. He could understand new languages quickly and easily. He could communicate telepathically with his sister, Lisa. But his most important gift, at least to his own mind, was his ability to communicate with a spacecraft named Madarach.

He had found Madarach two years before while exploring the land around his new home on Earth. Behind the house had been an ancient well. When Benji looked into the well, stars had appeared, and when he touched the stars, he'd found himself floating in space enclosed in a bubble.

That bubble was a sophisticated spacecraft that communicated with Benji through telepathy. By shifting just outside the fabric of space, it could take him anywhere in the universe very quickly. His first trips to the earth's moon, Saturn, Pluto, Alpha Centuri, and the Horsehead Nebula had astounded him. The Horsehead Nebula was 1,500 light years from Earth, yet he had reached it in a matter of minutes.

Two years later, the novelty of such rapid travel had worn off, but Benji's fascination with space had not. As often as possible, he liked to take Madarach on adventures. He enjoyed finding new places to see and new people to visit. He also enjoyed having friends on other planets, and he visited them often. He even had a girlfriend named Aelbreth who lived on a planet called Hadrun.

Today, though, he was visiting one of his favorite places which had no people at all. The planet was known in the Parisan star charts as D429-3, but his sister Lisa had named it Summerland. It had a mild climate, no land-based vertebrates, clean water, and so far as Benji could tell, no threats on land of any kind apart from some poisonous plants.

He didn't dare swim in the water. Madarach had told him that the planet's fish were far more developed than its land creatures, and that some of them were quite large and carnivorous.

Still, it had beaches that had never been walked on by another person. Benji enjoyed walking the soft sand barefoot, watching strange creatures skittering away from him, and listening to the wind and the soft waves at the waterline.

Today, Benji had seen a sea worm three feet long and about an inch in diameter. It had emerged from a burrow at the waterline, twisted its head around quickly in search of food, and receded again when it sensed Benji's presence.

He had also picked up a shell that was bright red in color, unlike anything he had ever seen before.

He had seen a crab with twenty legs, a giant seaweed flower washed up on the beach, and a fish with wings skittering over the waves.

Benji never tired of these discoveries. He was, he thought to himself proudly, an explorer.

Now, though, his legs were tired from walking for miles through soft sand. As he walked, he watched the landmarks on the land side of the beach. Eventually, he saw what he was looking for, two giant palm trees taller than the rest. He turned away from the beach, crossed the sand, and found the bubble. Because it was transparent, he had to pay close attention to where he parked it. True, Madarach had the ability to come to him if called, but Benji considered it a point of pride to not to lose his spacecraft.

He put his hand on the side of the bubble and felt the surface give. Then he climbed in.

"Madarach?" he thought.

"I'm here," the bubble replied in his mind.

"I saw some amazing things today," Benji said. "But I think I'm ready to go home."

"Parisa?" Madarach asked.

"Yes," Benji confirmed, aware that he had more than one home these days.

Instantly, the bubble lifted off from the surface and began to rise. Soon it was sliding through the stars at an incredible rate. In a matter of moments, Benji was back on Parisa, six light years from Summerland. He barely noticed the familiar landing place next to an ancient, intricately-carved well. He walked to the street and began to make his way along the now-familiar course home.

Benji had lived on Parisa for the past two years. It boasted an ancient civilization that prided itself on peacefulness and sustainable communities that did not harm the environment. The streets were safe, lined with small houses with gardens in front. They looked like they were made of stone, but Benji had learned that all of their building materials were recycled. The people on Parisa were friendly, and the food was good.

But what Benji enjoyed most about Parisa was that his gifts did not make him different. Everyone on Parisa communicated telepathically. In fact, most Parisans had given up language, except for singing. Benji's teacher and mentor, a priest named Nahum, still spoke. He learned languages quickly like Benji did. And though Benji couldn't telepath with people other than his sister, he felt that he fit there.

He'd spent his first ten years on Earth. They'd been okay, Benji thought, until his family moved to a small town to escape the city.

Benji's family had gifts. His father sometimes knew things without being told. His mom could sometimes see the future. And Lisa, back in those days, could sometimes read minds.

Their move to the small town coincided with the development of Lisa's gift and Benji's discovery of his own gifts. Some of the people in town sensed these gifts, and they didn't like them. The town's founding family, the Thompsons, had been rooting out "witches" for hundreds of years, and to the Thompsons, Benji's and Lisa's gifts made them witches.

The Thompsons had burned Benji's family's house in the middle of the night. Benji and Lisa, whose bedrooms were on the second floor, only escaped because Madarach was able to come get them. Benji's parents, who slept on the first floor, had gotten out, but not without injuries. Mom had gotten cuts and bruises when Dad had thrown her out a window. Dad had been badly burned, and had spent months in the hospital.

Madarach had taken Benji and Lisa to Parisa, where some friends had adopted the two children as their own. It had taken time for the two kids to adjust to their new life. Now, Parisa seemed more home to Benji than Earth.

Benji missed his parents, of course. He'd been able to see them a few times after the crisis was over. The legal matters had been resolved, and his parents had been able to move somewhere else. Only then had Mom decided it was safe for her children to visit. Mom and Dad had even come to Parisa for a few days. But because they couldn't communicate with other people, they decided they were more comfortable on Earth. Benji and Lisa, who were thriving on Parisa, stayed. Besides, they were safer on Parisa than perhaps anywhere else in the universe.

Now, Benji navigated the streets of Parisa and approached his adopted home. He opened the door and stepped in.

Tamar, Benji's adoptive mother, was cleaning the kitchen when he entered. He walked over to her and put his hand on her arm. Unlike the Parisans, and unlike his sister Lisa, Benji needed contact with another person in order to communicate nonverbally.

"Hi, Umma," he thought.

He had never been comfortable calling her Mom because he already had a mom, but the Parisan word Umma, which carried the same meaning, suited her well. She was, after all, Benji's Parisan mother.

"Benji," Tamar acknowledged. "Did you have fun?"

"I did," Benji replied. "I went to Summerland and walked on the beach."

Tamar nodded.

"Good," she said. "Lisa was asking for you. She and Tobin went to the park. Maybe you'll join them there?"

Benji smiled.

"I would," he said, "but I walked a long way in the sand. My legs are pretty tired."

Tobin was the first friend Benji had made when he found the portal. It had been Tobin's job to watch the well in case anyone came through it, so he'd been the first Parisan

Benji had met. At first, communication had been difficult, since Benji was not yet able to use telepathy. But Lisa had helped, and Tobin had become first a friend, and then a brother.

Tobin was even more to Lisa, who had fallen in love with him almost from the moment they first met.

Tobin's older sister, Miriam, had also come to love her new siblings very much. But from Benji's perspective, Miriam was much older and they had little in common.

"Why don't you take a nap?" Tamar suggested. "I'll have Lisa wake you when she comes home."

"I think I will," Benji agreed.

He made his way down the hall and into the bedroom he shared with Tobin. There, he lay on the bed and closed his eyes. In moments, he was asleep.

Chapter Two

Benji?" said a voice.

Benji opened his eyes and saw Lisa standing over him. It would have to be Lisa, he realized, since Parisans didn't communicate with language. On the entire planet, only his sister Lisa and his teacher, the old priest Nahum, had the ability to communicate verbally.

"What's up?" Benji asked, sleepily.

"Did you hear?" Lisa asked him, telepathically. "Someone else came through the well!"

Benji's eyes shot open.

"Really?" he exclaimed, aloud. "Who? Where are they from? Are they like us?"

"I don't know," Lisa replied. "They just came through this morning. They're still talking with Nahum. No one knows anything yet."

"Was Tobin watching the well when they arrived?" Benji asked, thinking that Tobin might have some information.

"No," Lisa replied, sadly. "He was doing school. Someone else, a younger boy, was watching."

Benji thought for a moment.

"But if they're talking to Nahum, we could go in," Benji suggested. "He said we're always welcome at the temple."

"Actually," Lisa corrected, "he said *you* were always welcome at the temple."

"But he won't mind if you come along," Benji said, grinning.

Lisa grinned back.

"I was hoping you'd say that," she said.

Benji jumped out of bed and slipped on his sandals. Then he and Lisa ran though the streets to the ancient stone temple. They slowed to a walk as they traversed its courtyard and walked between its huge stone pillars. The pillars had amazed Benji when he'd first seen them, but after two years of daily visits, he now barely noticed them.

The watcher, a boy about Benji's age, sat on a stone bench just outside the main temple door. He smiled when he saw Benji and Lisa approach. He knew them, as everyone in the city knew them. Probably everyone on the planet had heard of them, because Benji and Lisa were the first visitors to come through the portal in a hundred years.

Lisa communicated with the boy telepathically, and nodded.

"He says the visitors ate lunch, but they're still talking to Nahum," Lisa said, for Benji's benefit. "He says we can go in."

Benji and Lisa stepped softly through the main temple to the side room where they had first eaten lunch with Nahum, over two years before. Benji peeked around the door and caught Nahum's eye.

Nahum, an old man with white hair growing over his ears, broke into a smile and gestured for Benji to enter. He did, and Lisa followed.

At the table with Nahum sat two strangers. They were human in appearance, though smaller in stature than Earthlings or Parisans. They looked young, about Benji's age, a boy and a girl. Both were at least a foot shorter than Benji.

They wore their blonde hair long, tied in ponytails that hung halfway down their back. And their clothing shined, as if made from some sort of plastic. Their gestures and voices seemed quite familiar, though their language was unrecognizable. But the truly remarkable feature of the two was a subtle blue glow to their skin.

Nahum explained something animatedly to his guests, apparently in their own tongue, and Benji guessed that their host was explaining that Benji and Lisa had also come through the portal.

The two children turned to greet Benji and Lisa, and their eyes widened.

The boy spoke first.

"He says his name is Quanda, and his sister's name is Queelie, and they are pleased to meet us," Lisa said, relaying Nahum's telepathic translation.

Benji's mind had already begun matching words with thoughts, picking up rhythms and patterns, and formulating his reply.

"Benji I am and sister Lisa this," he replied in the newcomers' language. "We are pleased also to you meet."

The grammar was tortured, but Benji's reply was understandable, and Quanda grinned in amazement.

"You have the gift of languages, like our host," Quanda observed.

"I do," Benji agreed. "Do you have gifts?"

"There will be time for that," Nahum interrupted. "These two come from a planet they call Hassyr. They discovered the portal some days ago, and just today decided to seek out its source."

Benji grinned.

"The same as us," he replied. "We made some visits in our own system, and went to see some of the spectacular sights before we thought to ask where the portal came from."

Benji's grammar was improving by the sentence, and Quanda smiled at him, approvingly.

"What did you see?" Queelie asked. "Did you see the Helix Nebula?"

"We did," Benji replied, "but later. The first thing I wanted to see was the Horsehead Nebula."

Queelie frowned.

"I do not know it," she said.

"Let me show you a picture," Nahum suggested. Apparently he was able to project the image into Queelie's mind, because she smiled.

"The Eternal Flame!" she exclaimed.

"Ah," Quanda added, "that is spectacular."

"Yes," Benji agreed. "And that's what first amazed me about the bubble. The nebula is 1,500 light years from my planet but I got there in minutes."

"It is astounding," Queelie said.

"I hope to learn how that works," Quanda said, nodding at Nahum.

Nahum explained the basics of how the bubble was able to move slightly sideways in time, so that distance was no longer a concern.

"That is *farchedan*," Quanda said. "We have nothing like that on our planet."

"Ask them what their planet is like," Lisa suggested to Benji, telepathically. She was able to follow the conversation through Nahum's thoughts, but couldn't say anything the newcomers would understand.

Benji did.

"It's very beautiful," Queelie replied. "We have many mountains, and many oceans. Most of us live in the lands between them."

"How many people are there?" Nahum asked.

"A lot," Quanda said. "More than half a million."

Benji couldn't stifle his laugh.

"What?" Quanda asked. "That is funny?"

"Parisa has two billion people on it," Benji explained. "My planet, Earth, has eight billion. We have cities with ten million people in them."

Quanda's eyebrows went up.

"I don't know where we'd put that many people," he said. "Our planet must be smaller. It's very crowded."

"I think there is less habitable space," Queelie said. "We struggle with overpopulation because there is nowhere for people to go. All the land we can live on is crowded."

"Like one big city?" Benji asked.

"Yes, it is city," Quanda confirmed. "People live in cities, no?"

"On my planet, people also live in small towns and villages," Benji said. "A lot of people don't like being so crowded together. And that's where our food comes from. But I prefer the city."

"Our food comes from the oceans," Queelie said.

"And the mountains?" Benji asked. "Do people live there?"

Quanda laughed.

"No," he said. "They are much too cold and dry. There's nothing to eat but rocks. But they are beautiful to look at."

"You must come visit," Queelie said.

Then she glanced at Lisa.

"Both of you," she said, insistently. "Lisa, too."

They chatted for hours. When they finally stopped, Benji felt as if he'd known their language forever, and as if Quanda and Queelie had been friends for years.

"We should get home," Quanda said. "Our parents will be expecting us for lunch."

"Lunch?" Benji exclaimed. "But you've been here all day."

Queelie pulled a small electronic device from the pocket of her shiny pants and glanced at the screen.

"This is my companion," she said, to Benji's curious look. "It's a computer. It says it's only been half a day on Hassyr. We'll be home in time for the noon meal."

They said goodbye to Nahum, and together the four kids left the temple. The watcher guided them back down the street toward the well as Benji chatted and laughed with the other two.

Then Lisa stopped.

"Benji," she said, "I feel left out. I want to see if I can communicate with them."

Benji nodded.

"My sister wants to take your hand and see if she can communicate," he explained to the two newcomers.

Quanda shrugged.

Queelie stepped forward and held out her hand.

Lisa took it.

Then Queelie's eyes lit up.

"*Farchedan!*" she exclaimed. "I can hear her!"

Quanda looked skeptical, but held out his hand as Queelie had done.

"*Farchedan* indeed!" he agreed, as he grinned widely.

"What's *farchedan*?" Benji asked.

Quanda and Queelie looked at each other, but it was Lisa who spoke.

"It's something they say when they are amazed," she explained in English, reading their thoughts. "It seems to literally mean 'dancing.'"

Benji wrinkled his brow.

"Dancing?" he asked, in their language.

Quanda looked confused.

"Yes," he agreed, tentatively. "But it's just a word we say."

"It's from the old language," Queelie added. "It has to do with the old religion. We don't really think about its meaning. It's just *'farchedan,'* you know?"

Benji thought.

"I guess we have words like that, too," he said. "I mean, our people say stuff like 'righteous' or 'cool' when something is really great, but it doesn't mean anything about the thing's morality or temperature."

They continued walking, with Lisa now between Quanda and Queelie, holding their hands.

"It's been great to meet you," Quanda said.

"I really hope you'll come visit," Queelie added.

"Farchedan," Benji replied, and they all laughed. "But how would we find you? It sounds like you live in a big city."

"We do," Quanda confirmed. "And the well isn't in the city. You'd never find us."

"What if we came back for you?" Queelie suggested. "You could even bring your own bubble, so you can leave when you want."

"That would work," Lisa said, telepathically. "Will I be okay if I can't speak your language?"

"Of course," Quanda said. "Benji does, and besides, we won't let anything happen to you."

"I'd really like it if you came," Queelie said. "Can we come for you in a few days?"

"Your days or ours?" Benji asked.

They all laughed.

"It gets complicated, doesn't it," Quanda observed.

"Give me a time here, and I'll put it in my companion," Queelie said, pulling out the black electronic device again. "It will do the conversions."

They agreed on a morning a few days away, and Quanda and Queelie approached the well. To Benji's surprise, it was Queelie who summoned the stars. He didn't know why that surprised him. Until now, Benji himself was the only person he knew who could do it. He also knew that his great-uncle James could do it, and he just assumed that of the two, it would be the brother, Quanda, who had the ability.

He'd been wrong.

Benji and Lisa watched as the two newcomers disappeared into the stars.

"So that's what it looks like from this end," Benji commented.

Lisa looked troubled.

"What?" Benji asked her.

"Does it bother you that they really wanted me to come to their planet before we could even communicate?" she asked.

"They were just being friendly," Benji suggested. "They were very friendly people."

Lisa thought about this.

"Maybe," she said. "It just felt like there was something else. Maybe I was imagining it."

Benji gazed at his sister's face. She was sixteen years old now, in Earth years, and very beautiful. She also seemed very wise to him, when she wasn't chattering on about love and stuff. If she felt something was wrong, maybe it was.

"Something else like what?" he asked. "Can you be more specific?"

"No," she said.

She seemed annoyed, though whether with herself or with Benji's questions, Benji wasn't sure.

"Okay," Benji said. "But let me know if anything else comes to you."

Chapter Three

For two years, Benji had been tutored by the priest Nahum. He'd learned math, Parisan history, and science. He'd also begun Parisan emotional training to manage his anger. Nahum had modified a game controller so that Benji could interface with the computer, which native Parisans did telepathically. He'd done well in his studies, and had now begun to join some of the classes with other Parisan kids his age.

Today, Benji sat in a comfortable room with a dozen other kids. The teacher, Kareah, was a small, bald man. He was nice enough, but had very little sense of humor.

"Let's discuss violence," he said.

He spoke telepathically, but Benji could hear him through his computer interface.

"We all know," Kareah said, "that our civilization was brought to the brink of destruction because of violence. And we know that violence is no longer part of our culture. But what causes violence?"

"Anger," suggested one boy.

"Wanting something someone else has that they don't want to give," suggested a girl.

"Very good," Kareah agreed.

"Ignorance," said Benji, through his interface.

"Ignorance," Kareah repeated. "Thank you, Benji. Can you elaborate on that?"

"Well," Benji began, "when people don't understand someone they think is different, they are afraid, and that makes them want to get rid of the person they find different."

Kareah nodded.

"You've experienced that, haven't you, Benji," he suggested.

"Yes," Benji said. "When I lived on Earth, we moved to a small town. My family had abilities that are not common on my planet. My sister's telepathy was not very developed, but it still scared people, and they thought we were witches."

"What's a witch?" one of the girls asked.

"A witch, as I understand it," Kareah explained, "is someone who uses magical powers to get what they want. I think on Benji's planet they call it the 'dark arts.' Am I right, Benji?"

"That sounds right," Benji confirmed.

"And what would they do with people they thought were witches?" Kareah asked.

"They burned them," he said. "That used to only happen hundreds of years ago. There were some famous trials where a lot of people were accused of being witches, and they were all burned at the stake."

"Alive?" one boy asked.

Benji nodded, and he could almost feel a shiver run through the class.

"But that doesn't happen anymore, right?" Kareah asked.

"No," Benji said. "Being a witch is no longer a crime. There are no trials. But the people in this town were afraid of us, so they burned down our house."

"That's terrible!" said a girl.

"Barbaric," agreed a boy.

"The same thing happened in the same town a hundred years ago," Benji added. "My great-uncle was killed. But we didn't know that when we moved there."

"Okay," Kareah said, changing the subject. "Ignorance can be a cause of violence. And fear. So what do we do about violence?"

"We teach," said one of the girls.

"Exactly," Kareah said. "If we teach enough, violence becomes unacceptable."

"What happens if you encounter violence even though it's unacceptable?" Benji asked.

The other kids looked confused.

Kareah thought about this.

"That's almost unthinkable," he said. "We so rarely have any violence that we can deal with the violent individuals on a case-by-case basis."

"But suppose that you, Kareah, are faced with a violent person," Benji suggested. "Do you defend yourself?"

"No," Kareah said. "We've been trained that violence begets only violence. For me to defend myself would be to promote further violence."

"So you'd let them hurt you?" Benji asked.

Kareah cocked his head.

"I would," he said. "It's what makes our society what it is."

"Would you let them hurt your wife, or your child?" Benji pressed.

"If I could," Kareah said, "I would put myself between the violent person and my family. I would rather be hurt myself."

Benji thought about this.

"Like Jesus," he said.

"Jesus?" Kareah asked.

"He's the founder of the religion most people belong to where I lived," Benji explained. "He said, 'If someone slaps you on your right cheek, turn the other to him also.' He let them kill him for something he didn't do."

"He sounds like a wise and moral man," Kareah agreed. "I apologize, Benji, I often forget that the society you come from is quite different from ours. For you, violence is not unthinkable."

"No," Benji agreed. "And I've been to other planets that are more violent than mine. I can see how this would work on Parisa, where there's no conflict. But what about other places? How do you respond to violence in a place where violence is common?"

Kareah smiled.

"Most of us will never leave Parisa," he said. "For someone with your exceptional experience, I suggest you consult a priest rather than a teacher. For now, let's move on."

Benji enjoyed Parisa because he usually didn't feel different from everyone else. But at moments like this, he felt very different. Today, he was glad the school day only lasted three hours.

When Kareah dismissed the class, Benji headed straight for the temple. He found Nahum pruning the flower beds and picking flowers for the altar.

"Nahum," he said. "Can I talk to you?"

"Of course," the old priest agreed.

Benji told him about the day's lesson at school, and how he felt so different from everyone else.

Nahum listened patiently, nodding occasionally. When Benji had finished, Nahum thought for a long moment.

"Benji," he said, "you *are* different from everyone else. That's because of your unique experience, which most Parisans will never have. They can't understand what you've seen. But that's a good thing, not a bad thing. It makes you useful in a way they will never be."

"Useful?" Benji repeated.

"The society we have on Parisa was not easy to create," Nahum explained. "We chose nonviolence because we had seen violence. The people who created what we have today were not like the Parisans who have grown up in it. They suffered, and they struggled, and they knew from first hand experience what they *didn't* want. To be honest, there's no one alive on Parisa today who has the experience necessary to do what they did.

"Except you," he concluded. "You've seen violence, and you've experienced persecution. You will be able do things that none of us can. You *are* different. You're special."

Benji sighed.

"I'm sick of being special," he said. "I just want to fit in."

"That would be easier, wouldn't it?" Nahum suggested. "But it would also be harder."

"What do you mean?" Benji asked.

"Well, you wouldn't have anything to say to Quanda and Queelie, for starters," Nahum observed. "You wouldn't be going to visit them on their planet. You wouldn't have a girlfriend on another planet. You'd have never seen the Horsehead Nebula. You wouldn't have Madarach. You wouldn't live here on Parisa, and you wouldn't travel to another planet to see your parents. Would you give all that up?"

Benji sighed.

"No," he admitted. "It's just hard."

"Being different always is," Nahum said. "But believe me, it's also rewarding."

The days passed slowly as Benji waited for their trip to Hassyr. He did school in the mornings, and spent his afternoons with Nahum, or playing computer games with kids from his neighborhood. He desperately wanted to take Madarach to the planet Hadrun and see his girlfriend Aelbreth and her brother Offsa, but Nahum had suggested limits on his space travel, and Hassyr would be his next adventure.

He thought about Aelbreth often. She was one Earth year younger than him, and lived on a planet that was peaceful but very primitive. It seemed odd to Benji, with his earthbound sensibilities, that he should have a girlfriend at his age. But on Hadrun, boys and girls chose each other early. And Aelbreth was funny, cute, easy to talk to, and understanding. If he was going to have a girlfriend, Benji was glad it was Aelbreth.

He wished he could talk to her now.

When the day finally arrived for Benji and Lisa to visit Hassyr, Benji woke excited. He always enjoyed his trips to new civilizations, and this time he would already have two friends and be able to speak the language.

He waited impatiently as Lisa woke up late and took a leisurely shower.

"We have plenty of time," Lisa told him. "Getting to the well early won't speed up the clock."

"I know," Benji said. "I just really want to go."

Lisa sighed and continued brushing her long, dark, wet hair.

When they finally left the house, Benji tried to speed his sister along, sure they were going to be late. Lisa, however, refused to be hurried. .

Despite their leisurely pace, they still had to wait several minutes before Quanda and Queelie appeared beside the well.

"Are you ready?" Quanda asked.

"Absolutely," Benji replied.

"We were thinking that I could go with you, and Lisa could go with Queelie," Quanda suggested. "That way, if there's any timing problem on the other end, you'll both have one of us with you."

Benji glanced at Lisa and relayed what Quanda had said, and Lisa nodded her agreement.

"*Farchedan!*" Benji told him, and they all laughed.

Queelie went first, summoning the stars from the well and taking Lisa's hand. In a moment, both girls were gone, and Benji had a moment of panic. He'd often been places without Lisa, but Lisa had never left *him* before.

Benji glanced at Quanda.

"Are you ready?" he asked.

Quanda grinned.

"Let's go," he said.

Benji put his hands on the wall of the well, and in moments, stars began to swirl around the exterior of the wall. He put his right hand into the swirling stars, and took Quanda's hand with his left. Instantly, they were floating in space.

"Madarach," Benji thought.

"I'm here," Madarach replied.

"Do you know where we're going?" Benji asked.

"Yes," Madarach replied. "I interfaced with their container and obtained the coordinates."

By now, Benji had gotten used to Madarach's use of the term "container" to describe himself, even though it was obvious Madarach was much more than just a container. So he wasn't surprised to hear the other spacecraft referred to as a container, too.

"Okay," Benji said. "Let's go."

They began shifting through the stars.

"When we get there," Quanda said, "have your bubble slow down. I want to show you something on the way in."

"Can you be more specific?" Benji asked.

"Have him take us past the seventh planet," Quanda said. "You'll like what you see."

Benji relayed the request to Madarach. Soon, they approached a yellow star, and Madarach began to slow.

Quanda looked intently through the transparent shell of the bubble.

"There!" he pronounced, pointing.

In the distance, but getting closer, they saw a yellow and red planet with rings around it.

"Like Saturn," Benji thought.

But as they approached, Benji saw that it was not like Saturn after all. Saturn's rings were flat and static. The rings around this planet were rippling, like water.

"Wow," Benji said. "What makes it do that?"

"It's dancing," Quanda said. "The whole universe is dancing."

"Do you know why it does that?" Benji thought to Madarach.

"I really don't," Madarach replied. "My best guess would be some kind of harmonics emanating from the planet."

"Harmonics?" Benji repeated.

"A sound wave pattern," Madarach said. "We can stop here and analyze it if you like, but it will take a while."

"No," Benji decided. "I want to catch up with Lisa. Maybe we can do it on the way back."

"As you wish," Madarach said.

"But if it *is* caused by sound, then maybe it really is dancing," Benji suggested.

"To dance is to move rhythmically to sound," Madarach observed. "Or in some cases, less than rhythmically."

Benji thought about that. His own experience at a school dance when he was nine hadn't been very rhythmic.

Then he thought about what Madarach had just said.

"Did you just make a joke?" Benji asked.

"Humor is where you find it," Madarach replied, cryptically.

Benji wrinkled his brow. Madarach was a computer, yet today he seemed to be displaying a sense of humor. Or maybe Benji was reading too much into his words.

"Isn't it beautiful?" Quanda interrupted, verbally.

"It is," Benji agreed.

"It's very holy to us," Quanda said. "Our people have been watching it through telescopes for centuries. Ever since it was discovered, it's been the symbol of the dance. Now, Queelie and I have been able to see it up close!"

"That's pretty cool," Benji replied.

"It's *farchedan*!" Quanda corrected.

Chapter Four

As they approached Hassyr, Benji found himself oddly nervous. What if Lisa wasn't there when he landed? What would he do?

"Queelie's waiting for us, right?" he asked.

Quanda smiled.

"She'll be there," he assured Benji. "She would never leave without me."

Benji nodded, reassured.

They descended, and Benji found himself standing on a rock floor surrounded by a circle of high rock walls. At the center of the circle stood the walls of an ancient well.

Quanda stood to his left. No one else was in the circle.

"Where are they?" he asked, panic building in his chest.

"Not far, I'm sure," Quanda said. "Come."

Quanda led the way to the far side of the circle where a narrow gap in the rock allowed them to exit. The path remained narrow for several yards. Then it opened onto a wide cliff, below which Benji could see thousands of buildings forming a huge city.

"Welcome to Hassyr," Quanda said. "We all live down there. That's why Queelie won't leave without me. It's a long walk."

"Then where is she?" Benji asked, looking around.

"Over here!" he heard a voice call.

Benji looked over, and saw Queelie and Lisa at the mouth of a cave.

Benji began to run, and Quanda, with his shorter legs, had difficulty keeping up.

"This was an ancient temple," Quanda said, between gasps. "It celebrates the Dance of Creation."

"It's beautiful," Lisa told him. "Come look!"

Together they entered the cave. Torches along the walls illuminated a huge cavern, its walls carved with figures of dancers. Some appeared human, some animal, and in some scenes even plants joined the dance.

At the center of the cavern, a huge carving depicted the planet with the dancing rings. Around it, their star danced with several other planets.

"That's the same planet," Benji observed. "Lisa, did you see it on the way in?"

"I did," Lisa replied. "Queelie insisted that we pass it. Apparently it's very holy to them."

"That's what Quanda said, too," Benji agreed.

An older woman approached them from the interior of the temple. She was short, like Quanda and Queelie, and had long, gray hair. She wore a threadbare robe, and her skin was strikingly blue, darker than the two teens. She smiled at the visitors as she approached.

"Darkness and light," she said, by way of greeting. Then she bowed her head.

Quanda and Queelie both inclined their heads, and Benji and Lisa both copied the gesture.

"Thus has it come to pass," the old woman said. "For the spirit of life is inspiration, and the dance is the means. I welcome your steps, for they lead thither."

"Thank you," Quanda said.

Then the old woman fixed her gaze on Lisa.

"The spirit of life is inspiration," she said, again. "And though darkness and light dance, never do they create grey. When grey appears, we see not clearly, and must return to the dance, for the dance is the means. Go softly, child, for you are the spirit of life."

Benji relayed these words to Lisa as best he could, though they made no sense to him. He could tell by Lisa's expression that she didn't understand them either.

The old woman bowed again, and then retreated.

"What was she talking about?" Benji whispered to Quanda.

"I have no idea," Quanda replied. "I think it was a blessing, but these priestesses don't talk the same as the rest of us."

Benji nodded. "I'm good with languages," he said, "but I have no idea what she meant."

"Don't let it trouble you," Queelie advised. "The priestesses speak in riddles."

Benji nodded, and tried to put the strange words out of his mind.

"So what now?" he asked.

"Let's go down to the city," Quanda said. "We'll see our home and meet our parents, and then we'll go see some sites."

"That sounds good," Benji agreed.

Lisa once again walked between Quanda and Queelie, holding their hands so she could communicate. Benji followed behind.

The path down the mountain from the temple wound through rocks and canyons, occasionally giving them a fantastic view of the city below or the mountains above.

"I've never seen mountains this high!" Lisa commented. "I don't think we have anything like this on Earth."

"This is a well-worn path," Benji observed. "Have your people known about the well for a while?"

"We've known it was there," Queelie replied, "but not what it was for. Our people thought it was attached to the temple, kind of a holy well for the priestesses. When we go to the temple, we stop at the well and dip our hands in. It's supposed to bring luck."

"Let me guess," Benji said. "You went to the well and dipped in your hand, but stars came out instead of water."

Queelie grinned.

"Something like that," she agreed.

"Do you have any other gifts?" Benji asked.

"I don't," Queelie replied. "But most of my family does. Quanda sometimes knows things. And both my parents can sometimes see the future."

"It was the same with me," Benji said. "My dad sometimes knows things. My mom sometimes sees the future. Lisa could read minds. But I didn't have a gift. Until I found the well. I was the only one who could work it."

"Yes, exactly," Queelie said, smiling. "I used to think there was something wrong with me. But now I know there isn't."

"Later on, I got the gift of languages," Benji added. "Maybe you will, too."

"That would be *farchedan*," she replied. "Right now, we go places and neither of us can communicate."

"Do many of your people have gifts?" Benji asked.

"Many of them have 'The Gift,'" Queelie said. "That's what we call it. The ability to see the future. Clairvoyance."

"That's cool," Benji said. "But it must make things strange. Why play sports if you already know who's going to win? Doesn't it take the mystery out of things?"

Queelie laughed.

"We believe," she said, "that much of the future is not yet set. The universe is in an eternal dance, shifting and swaying. So we can't see everything that's going to happen. But when we do see something, that's a gift from the Creators, and we take it seriously."

Then she blushed.

"I should say 'they take it seriously,'" she added. "Since I don't have the gift."

Eventually, the path emerged onto the plain below, where it met a cobblestone street. A sheer cliff wall blocked one side of the street, and buildings lined the other. Some of the buildings were obviously shops, open for business. Others appeared to be homes. The street teemed with people, all with the same distinctive blue tint to their skin. Benji noticed that the older people seemed to be a darker blue.

An occasional cart made its way slowly among them. The carts seemed to be driven by electric motors, and carried a variety of boxes, barrels, and produce. There were no other vehicles in sight.

"How do your people get around?" Benji asked.

"We walk," Quanda replied. "Isn't that how everyone gets around? That's why we have two feet."

Benji laughed.

"I guess that's the basic mode of transportation everywhere," he agreed. "But Parisa has monorails for getting from city to city. On Earth, most people have automobiles, and we use jet planes or trains to get from city to city."

"Most of our intercity travel is by boat," Quanda said. "Our land is narrow, and nearly everything is close to an ocean. Plus, boats use much less energy than land transportation. So we don't need to produce as much electricity this way."

"That's smart," Lisa interjected.

Quanda jumped as he heard her thought.

"I still can't get used to that," he said. "I forgot you used telepathy."

They made their way through a maze of city streets. Neighborhoods changed from poor to wealthy and back again.

At one point, Quanda pointed out a temple to their left.

"There's someone there who wants to meet you," he said.

Queelie looked at him strangely.

"Do you know anyone at that temple?" she asked.

"No," Quanda replied.

Queelie nodded.

"Okay," she said, as if this explained everything.

They crossed the street through throngs of people and entered the temple grounds. Benji saw almost an acre of well-tended flower gardens, which seemed huge in a city where space was at such a premium.

Then he saw the snakes, and gasped.

Quanda followed his gaze, and laughed.

"They're carved from stone," he said. "They're not real."

"I know," Benji said. "But on our world, the snake is the symbol of treachery."

"Really?" Queelie interjected. "Here, they're a symbol of creation, because they dance."

"Perhaps they could be both," Lisa said. "Sometimes creation doesn't look like what you expect."

Quanda shrugged.

"Don't let them bother you," he assured them. "They're a holy symbol among our people."

Quanda led them to the main temple shrine, a large room in which everything was plated with gold, including a giant statue of a dancing snake that appeared to be the main object of worship.

He gestured to a young boy who was sweeping the floor. The boy dropped his broom and approached them, and Quanda whispered in his ear. The boy scampered out a side door as if he'd been scolded.

Some minutes later, an old man appeared from the same side door. His skin had a dark blue tint, and he was completely bald save for a pair of bushy white eyebrows. His wrinkled face crumpled into a toothless grin when he saw his visitors.

"Ah, you have brought her," he cackled. "I knew you would."

"But we don't know you," Queelie protested. "How could you know we would come?"

"I know many things," he replied. "For the dance continues, and he who follows its rhythm knows much."

He turned to Lisa, but did not speak.

Lisa gasped.

"What?" Benji asked.

"He knows my mind," Lisa whispered. "I mean, it's not just that he can hear me. He can see inside it."

"What do you want with her," Benji asked the priest, firmly.

"Rest your mind in the sun, as the snake does," the old man said, cryptically. "It is not what I want from her, but what we need from each other. The spirit of life is the motivation, and the dance is the means."

"What does that mean?" Benji asked. "The priestess said the same thing."

"Ah, the old women," the old man cackled. "They speak much but know little. They confuse the spirit of life with the creation, and follow not the dance."

The old man approached Lisa, his hand raised, palm toward her.

Lisa's eyes widened, but she didn't resist as he put his hand on her forehead. He rested it there for nearly a minute.

"It is as I thought," the old man said. "Our worlds have much to gain from one another."

Then he turned and left through the same side door he'd come from.

"What was that?" Benji asked.

"I don't know," Quanda said. "I only know he wanted to meet her."

"Lisa, are you okay?" Benji asked.

"Yes," she said, tentatively.

"What happened?" Benji asked her.

"I don't know," she said. "He showed me things."

"What things?" Benji pressed.

"I'm not sure," she said. "It's very confusing. I saw Tobin, and children, and war. But the war was not on Parisa. I saw Mom in a cemetery, crying. And I saw you with a crown on your head. None of it makes any sense."

"Not to me," Benji agreed.

He turned to Quanda and Queelie.

"Does it make sense to you?" he asked.

Quanda shrugged.

Queelie, however, took a deep breath, and then spoke.

"There is a prophecy," she began. "A white woman with long, dark hair. She will come from a place no one knows. She will not be of the future, but she will become the future. And she will bring a gift that should not fall into the wrong hands."

"What does that mean?" Benji asked.

"I don't know," Queelie said.

Then she turned to Lisa.

"I thought of that prophecy the moment I saw you," she said. "You don't have the gift of clairvoyance, do you?"

"No," Lisa confirmed. "Just the gift of telepathy."

"Do you think," Benji suggested, "that she just gave the gift of telepathy to that old man?"

"It's possible," Quanda said. "I don't know why I was led here. I knew that someone wanted to meet Lisa, but not why. It was just one of those things I know."

"Are those the right hands for the gift to fall into?" Benji pressed.

"He is a priest," Queelie assured them.

"A priest of the snakes," Benji observed.

Quanda's face grew dark.

"I don't know," he said. "I don't like him. Maybe I was manipulated. I don't know."

Now Queelie frowned.

"Brother," she said, using a formal title Benji had never heard before. "Let us return up the mountain and consult with the priestesses. We know their hearts. They will not lead us astray."

Quanda nodded.

"That may be best," he agreed.

"Wait," Benji said, annoyed. "You mean to tell me that we came to your planet, and within an hour my sister became part of some religious conflict?"

"I hope not," Quanda said. "It was not my intention."

Chapter Five

They made their way through the crowds to the edge of the city and hiked up the path to the temple. Going up was much more difficult than coming down had been.

When they reached the temple, Queelie called for the elder priestess. Eventually, an ancient woman came hobbling from somewhere in the depths of the temple. She looked very old, with dark blue skin and thin, white hair. But her robe was not threadbare, as the other priestess's has been. The robe's background was the same dark blue as the woman's skin, and it was covered with strange designs embroidered of white, scarlet, and gold thread.

"Darkness and light," she said, as the other priestess had, and they all bowed their heads.

"How may I help you, my children?" the priestess asked.

Queelie explained what had happened at the snake temple.

The priestess nodded. Then she turned to Lisa.

"You can speak in thoughts?" she asked.

Benji translated her words for Lisa.

"She can if she is in physical contact with you," Benji explained.

"Then may I take your hand?" the priestess asked, bowing her head.

Again Benji translated.

"I'm a little worried after what happened with the priest," he told her. "I'm not sure that's a good idea."

Lisa nodded, and then smiled.

"She asked permission," Lisa observed. "It will be fine."

The priestess held out a small, frail hand, and took Lisa's in it. She closed her eyes for a long moment. Then she nodded.

"The blackness dances with the light," she said. "It is always thus."

"This man," she continued, "has much ambition but little talent. What he sought to take, he could not. And yet he may have given. Whether he has lost, I cannot say, but do not be surprised if you begin to know things that you should not know."

"What of the prophesy?" Queelie asked.

"Child, do not trouble yourself with such things," the priestess replied. "For both motion and rest are one. This may well be the woman spoken of. But of the future, I cannot say, for the dance is never complete. Today, what she carries is safe. Let that be the rhythm to which you step."

"That sounds encouraging," Benji said. "Though I don't really know what she said."

"Nor do I," Queelie agreed. "Except that Lisa is safe, and we did not do any harm to the religious balance."

"Not today," Lisa said. "But I think we should go now, and I will need to be careful if I come back."

"I hope you will," Queelie said. "Come back, I mean. I've grown quite fond of both of you."

"It doesn't make much sense for you to go back down the hill to our house, does it," Quanda observed. "I'm sorry I messed things up. But, like Queelie says, I hope you'll come back."

"I think we will," Benji said.

They exited the temple, and Quanda led them back to the well. Benji put his hands on it, summoned the stars, and soon he and Lisa were on their way home.

"Are you okay?" he asked her, as they slid through the stars.

"I think so," Lisa replied. "I'm just really tired. Whatever that guy did took a lot out of me."

"Apparently he tried to take something out of you," Benji reminded her. "But he couldn't."

"Well, his trying exhausted me," Lisa said. "Let's go home. I need some sleep."

They arrived back on Parisa in the late afternoon.

"I had no idea we'd been gone this long," Benji observed.

"It's deceptive when the days on Hassyr are so long," Lisa agreed.

They walked home in uncharacteristic silence. When they arrived, Lisa went straight to bed.

"Is she okay?" Tamar asked Benji at dinner.

"I think so," Benji replied. "I think the day exhausted her. She'll be fine in the morning."

But Lisa was not fine in the morning. Miriam couldn't wake her, and Lisa had a high fever. In her sleep, she muttered unintelligible phrases that Benji tried to understand, but couldn't.

"I don't think it's a language," he said. "If it is, I can't understand it."

Tamar put ice on Lisa's neck to cool the fever, but it didn't help. By mid-morning, her husband Jachin decided they should call the doctor.

Benji had never seen a doctor on Parisa. With their healthy diet and exercise, few Parisans got sick. The occasional flu, to which Benji and Lisa were immune, wasn't life threatening. So doctors were rarely needed.

About noon, Dr. Tebeth came from the local hospital to examine Lisa. He was a young man, and Benji hoped he was qualified, especially since Earthlings and Parisans were not identical in physiology.

Tebeth looked Lisa over, checked her glands and vitals, and drew some blood. Then he started her on intravenous fluids.

"I see no obvious cause," he said. "You say she was off-world recently?"

"Yesterday," Tamar confirmed.

"These blood tests will detect any pathogen," Tebeth assured them. "If we find one, at least then we can talk about a treatment. For now, I have nothing to offer, except to keep her hydrated and watch her fever."

He left again, and Benji sat on the floor next to Lisa's bed for the rest of the day. He didn't sit still easily. He liked to run and play, as most boys his age did. But with Lisa sick with some unknown illness, he didn't dare leave her.

Lisa did not improve. By evening, she began moaning and twitching.

"What's wrong with you?" Benji pleaded, silently. "Why can't you tell me?"

But Lisa gave no clues.

Tebeth returned in the morning, performed a cursory examination, and pronounced that Lisa had not improved, a diagnosis that surprised no one.

"There are no pathogens in her blood," he told Tamar. "We need to move her to the Ministry of Science facility. They are better equipped to diagnose her."

Benji wasn't happy with this decision. His older sister, his only sister, was about to be taken out of his sight. He realized there was little he could do for her, but he also wanted to be near her.

"Will they let me stay with her?" he asked Tamar.

"No, honey," Tamar replied. "She'll be at a research facility, where the doctors are most up to date about medical developments. Visiting hours are strictly limited."

Benji sulked. But he stayed with Lisa until the transport came. Two orderlies knocked on the door, a man and a woman. They loaded Lisa onto a stretcher. To Benji, his sister seemed small and frail as he watched them move her.

After they loaded the stretcher into the back of an electric vehicle, Benji put his hand on the arm of the woman.

"Please take care of her," he pleaded.

The woman smiled, reassuringly.

"The Ministry of Science has the best doctors on Parisa," she said. "Your sister will receive excellent care."

Then she and the man got into the front of the vehicle and drove away.

Benji stared after them, feeling more alone than he had ever felt in his life. Lisa's familiar presence in his head had been gone since she went to sleep the day before. Now her physical self was gone, too. Before Benji had discovered Madarach, he and Lisa hadn't been very close, but they'd never been separated, either. Lisa had been a constant part of Benji's life since he'd come home from the hospital after his birth.

When the ambulance was out of sight, Benji remained in the street, watching just in case the orderlies changed their minds and brought her back. He knew that was unlikely, but something in him hoped it would happen. But it didn't, and eventually he went back inside the house.

He felt restless all afternoon. He tried to distract himself with computer games and music, both of which he had on the small computer in his room. But nothing worked. He couldn't stop thinking about Lisa.

Every few minutes, he left his room to see what Tamar was doing. She had finished the kitchen and was cleaning the bathrooms.

"When can I visit her?" he asked her, over and over.

"They'll let us know," she told him each time.

Benji wasn't alone in his distress. Tobin, too, was upset when he came home and learned what had happened. The woman he loved had been unconscious for a full day for no apparent reason, and she showed no sign of improving. Now she had been taken to the hospital.

"Tell me what happened when you guys went to the planet," he insisted, when he and Benji were alone in their room.

Benji told him the story.

"Do you think that old priest caused this?" Tobin asked.

"There's no way to know," Benji replied. "I guess we have to wait for the doctors to tell us."

But the more Benji thought about it, the more certain he became that the old priest's assault, whatever its nature, had caused his sister's illness.

Dinner was a somber gathering, with each member of the family acutely aware that one of their number was missing.

"We should go to the priest," Jachin said. "We should ask him to pray for her."

Miriam snorted aloud.

"Do you think that will do any good?" she asked.

"It can't hurt," Tamar agreed. "Benji, what do you think?"

Benji shrugged.

"As you say, it can't hurt," he agreed.

But he was less than enthusiastic. He had spent enough time with Nahum to know that the purpose of prayer was not to make Lisa well, but to help those who loved her accept whatever the outcome might be.

Benji was not ready to accept whatever outcome. He wanted his sister back. He wanted her healed. No other outcome was conceivable.

He woke in the middle of the night with visions of Lisa's twisted face and twitching body.

"What is wrong with you, Lisa?" he asked again, into the darkness. "Why won't you talk to me?"

The relationship between Benji and Lisa had developed over the years to the point that they could communicate telepathically over great distances. In some sense, they were always connected, never apart. To have his sister entirely out of contact troubled Benji deeply.

He woke in the morning feeling tired and irritable. He missed his Lisa.

"When can I visit her?" he asked Tamar again at breakfast.

"This afternoon," she replied, taking Benji by surprise.

"Awesome!" he exclaimed, aloud.

Tamar, who had become accustomed to Benji's occasional verbal outbursts, smiled. She loved her adopted son, despite his idiosyncrasies.

Benji could barely pay attention through his classes that day. Kareah, who knew the basics of Lisa's condition, understood. He didn't push Benji the way he normally would a distracted student.

After class, Benji rushed home and ate lunch. When he'd finished, he approached Tamar once again.

"When can I see Lisa?" he asked.

"We can go now," she replied.

They walked from their house to the monorail station. Benji had never ridden the monorail, which Parisans used to go from one city to another. He and Tamar ascended the stairs just as the monorail car pulled into the station. It made a soft whooshing noise as it docked with the platform, which Benji found cool. Besides that, the car made no sound at all.

When it came to a stop, Tamar took Benji's hand to board the car. Unlike trains and buses Benji had seen on Earth, the monorail had no doors or windows.

"Do people ever fall out?" Benji asked, looking at the ground twenty feet below.

"Not that I ever heard," Tamar replied. "We're taught to be careful. There's no danger unless someone does something dangerous on purpose."

Benji and Tamar took seats together where they could look out the glassless window at the passing scenery, and the monorail slowly began to move. It picked up speed, and soon they left the city and were passing through lush forest.

"This is beautiful," Benji commented. "Does anyone live here?"

"No," Tamar replied. "This land belongs to all of us. No single individual can use it. That's part of what keeps our planet healthy."

The train moved quickly now, and Benji enjoyed the rush of air against his face. Then it began to slow again, and another city came into view. The monorail coasted to a stop at the station, and Tamar led Benji to the exit.

"It's not far from here," she said.

Chapter Six

Benji and Tamar descended the stairs and followed the main street, which looked much like the main street in their home city. Businesses lined both sides, and people bustled between them. There was also a temple that looked much like the one where Nahum lived.

Ahead of them, Benji could see a huge, white building that dwarfed those around it.

"That's the Ministry of Science facility," Tamar told him. "They do a lot of research here, and they also have a medical facility."

The building seemed to grow even larger as they approached, and Benji could see that it was more of a complex than a facility, with multiple buildings and even its own streets connecting them.

Tamar led them through the maze of streets. Eventually, they arrived at a white building that looked much like the others, except for a sign above the door in intricate Parisan script that read, "Medical."

They entered, and Tamar interfaced with a computer to locate Lisa's room. She led them down a series of halls, and finally arrived at what looked to Benji like a hospital ward.

Tamar nodded at one of the nurses, and Benji realized they were communicating about Lisa's whereabouts and condition.

"She's just down here," Tamar told Benji. "They say her condition hasn't changed."

They turned left into a room, and Benji saw Lisa lying in bed. Her face was contorted and her body twitched occasionally.

"What's wrong with you, Lisa?" he asked, again. As before, he got no answer.

A doctor appeared, and he and Tamar communicated for a long moment. Then the doctor turned to Benji and held out his hand.

Benji took it.

"Tamar tells me that we can communicate this way," he said.

"Yes," Benji said. "How is my sister?"

The doctor sighed.

"Unchanged, I'm afraid," he said. "I'm sorry to say that we don't know why she is sick."

Benji frowned.

"How can you not know?" he asked. "Look at her! Something serious is happening to her. But you don't know why?"

The doctor sighed again.

"Let me tell you what we do know," he said. "Her condition stems from a problem in her brain. It's not related to any other system. But we can't identify why her brain is malfunctioning."

"Why not?" Benji pressed.

"Brain chemistry is extremely complex," the doctor explained. "And her brain chemistry, and presumably yours, differs from what we see on Parisa. Many of the chemicals are the same, but they appear to play different roles in your brain than in ours. So we don't have the knowledge to determine what's normal, and therefore we have no idea what's not normal."

"What about mine?" Benji asked. "If you checked mine, that should show you what normal is, right?"

"It would show us what is normal," the doctor said, "for a young man who is just beginning puberty. But we don't know how similar that would be to a young woman who has already reached biological adulthood."

"So what do we do?" Benji asked. "You're saying you can't treat her?"

The doctor sighed again, his expression pained.

"That is what I'm saying," he confirmed. "And it's not an answer I'm happy with, but I'm afraid we just don't have enough knowledge about her biology. I would suggest that you take her back to your home planet, where they are familiar with what normal brain chemistry looks like for someone from your planet."

Benji felt his heart sink. On the one hand, he welcomed the chance to go back to Earth and see his parents. But on the other, he knew that his own people's knowledge of brain chemistry was limited. His mom had often warned that psychiatrists threw medicines at a problem rather than trying to understand it. They had no ability to measure brain chemistry. Instead, they used trial and error, as if each patient was a guinea pig. Compared to Parisa, Earth was extremely primitive when it came to psychiatry.

But it didn't look like he had much choice. Lisa needed help, and the doctors on Parisa couldn't help her.

"Can I spend a few minutes alone with her?" Benji asked the doctor.

The doctor glanced at Tamar, and then back at Benji.

"Of course," he replied.

Then he and Tamar left the room, closing the door behind them.

Now alone with Lisa, Benji went to her side and took her hand.

"What is wrong with you?" he asked yet again. "And what do I do about it?"

He began to cry, deep sobs that made his chest heave.

"How can I help you if I don't know what's wrong?" he lamented.

Then he heard a voice, though whether it was Lisa's or his own, or someone else's, he wasn't sure.

"You're not listening," it said.

Benji stopped in mid sob.

"Listening to what?" he wondered.

"You're asking a question, but you're not listening for an answer," the voice said. It sounded very far away.

"Okay," Benji said in his mind. He asked again: "What is wrong with you, Lisa?"

He listened hard.

At first, he heard nothing. Then, gradually, he began to hear a whisper in his mind. As it grew louder, he recognized the voice as Lisa's. But he couldn't understand the meaning of her words.

"Black and white, grey and red," Lisa said. "What happened has not happened. What I saw I did not see. What I did not see I will see again. Red and grey, white and black. Backward or forward, it is all the same."

"Lisa?" Benji called, his mind to hers. "Lisa?"

"Benji," she replied. "Thank God. I only can hear you a little through the noise, and I can't see you through the colors."

"What colors?" Benji asked.

"Black and white, grey and red," she repeated.

"I don't understand," Benji said.

"Neither do I," she replied. "Can you help me?"

Benji choked back a sob.

"I'm trying, Lisa," he assured her. "I'm trying. But I don't know what to do."

"*Farchedan*," she replied.

That struck him as an odd expression for her to use.

Benji emerged from the room to find the doctor and Tamar conversing together telepathically. He approached them and took their hands.

"You're right," he told them. "If there's nothing you can do for Lisa here, then I should take her home. Our psychiatry is primitive compared to yours, but at least they'll be familiar with her brain chemistry. And I don't know what else to do. Maybe my parents will have some idea. I'm sure they'll want to be with her, even if they don't know how to help her. So I'm going to take her back to Earth."

"I think that's wise," the doctor agreed.

Tamar nodded.

"I feel so helpless," she said. "I consider myself your mother, both of you, but there's nothing I can do, and it breaks my heart. Take her home, with my love. And return when you can."

Benji nodded.

"I'll call Madarach," he said.

Madarach arrived moments later, landing on the grass outside Lisa's room. Benji went out to meet him. He entered the bubble, and began to cry.

"Lisa is unconscious," he relayed to Madarach. "We have to take her home. She's in a bed in that room over there. How can we get her?"

"The room isn't large enough for me," Madarach replied. "Can you have them carry her here?"

Benji went back to the ward and asked the doctor to have someone carry Lisa outside.

"My container is there," he explained, pointing to the grass where Madarach had landed. "I can take her to Earth."

The doctor agreed, and went off to make the arrangements.

Benji kissed Tamar on the cheek.

"I love you," he said. "You've been a wonderful mother to both of us, and we'll be back as soon as we can."

Tamar had tears running down her cheeks.

"I will miss you both," she said. "Take care of her."

"I will," Benji replied. "As best as I know how."

Then he went outside to wait with Madarach.

"Do they know what is wrong with her?" Madarach asked.

"No," Benji replied. "They have no idea."

"How soon after we returned from Hassyr did this start?" Madarach asked.

"Well," Benji replied, "she was really tired when we got back. She went straight to bed when we got home. She slept through dinner, and she never woke up."

"Really?" said Madarach.

He paused for a moment.

"Tell me everything that happened on that planet," he instructed.

Benji did.

Madarach seemed especially concerned with the prophecy and the priestesses, making Benji recall every word.

"What does it mean?" Benji asked him. "Do you know what it means?"

Madarach said nothing for a long time.

The orderlies arrived, carrying Lisa on a stretcher, and Benji helped them load her inside the bubble. Then he waved to Tamar, who was watching through the window, and stepped inside Madarach to join his sister.

"Shall we go?" Benji asked Madarach.

"There is an ancient saying," Madarach said. "I don't think it is said much anymore. 'If you dropped your purse in the water, do not look for it on the hillside.'"

"What does it mean?" Benji asked.

"It means," Madarach said, "that if the problem began on Hassyr, you will likely not find the solution on Earth."

Benji paused.

"You think we should take her to Hassyr?" he asked. "What for?"

"Because that's where the problem started," Madarach replied. "It makes sense that the solution would be found there."

"Where?" Benji asked. "Surely not with the old man who did this to her."

"Surely not," Madarach agreed. "That would be a hostile encounter, not likely to be fruitful. But the priestess sounds like she knows much about these things."

"What things?" Benji asked. "Do *you* know what's wrong with Lisa?"

"No," he replied. "But that is the point. Whatever this is, is known to her, but not to us."

Benji sighed.

"This started on Hassyr," he repeated. "It's a dangerous place for her."

"It may also be her only hope," Madarach pointed out. "I've seen your earth medicine, and it won't help her. Your people are very good at weapons. They're not bad with healing the body. But where the mind is concerned, they know almost nothing. They cannot help her."

Benji thought about this for a long moment. He knew Madarach was right about Earth. He hoped Madarach was right about Hassyr as well.

"To Hassyr, then," he instructed.

Chapter Seven

They shifted through the stars, once again passing the planet with the dancing rings as they approached Hassyr.

"How should we do this?" Benji asked.

"You won't be able to carry Lisa if I go to the portal," Madarach observed. "I will take you to the mouth of the cave temple, and wait while you get help."

"Okay," Benji said. "What should I tell them?"

"Tell them your sister needs help," Madarach replied. "The priestess already knows what happened. I suspect she knows better than we do. Once she sees Lisa, she will know whether or not she can help."

Benji sighed.

"And if she can't?" he asked.

Madarach paused.

"If she can't," he said, finally, "we go back to the original plan and take her to Earth. But I pray that is not the case. Your Earth doctors do not understand the brain. I fear they will make things worse."

Benji felt the anguish in Madarach's thoughts. It was comparable to when Madarach had once spoken of being unable to help as Benji's great uncle, young James Partridge, had burned alive inside his home. These seemed strong feelings for a machine. Madarach was a sophisticated spacecraft, but he was still a machine, wasn't he?

Yet Madarach felt deeply. And he occasionally made jokes. What kind of a machine was he?

Benji didn't know, and his thoughts returned to Lisa.

"You love her, don't you," he asked Madarach.

"Yes," Madarach replied. "But not as much as you."

Benji nodded. He loved Lisa more than anyone else in the world, maybe even more than his mom.

It didn't occur to him until later that Madarach could have been saying that he loved Lisa, but not as much as he loved Benji.

Madarach set them down on the cliff in front of the cave temple. Benji exited the bubble and dashed inside.

One of the attendants looked up as the sound of Benji's rapid footsteps echoed through the cavern. She was young for a temple attendant, but older than Lisa, and much older than Benji.

"Young man," she said, in the formal language of Hassyr, "may I remind you that you are in a holy place worthy of respect?"

"I am sorry," Benji said, using the familiar version of the language he had learned from Quanda and Queelie. "My sister needs help. I have come to ask the elder priestess."

The attendant surveyed Benji, noting his youth, his panic, and his white skin.

"Your sister," she guessed, "is the young woman with white skin and long dark hair?"

"Yes," Benji confirmed. "She is unconscious, and no one on our planet can help her."

The attendant nodded, gravely. Then she turned, and broke into a run.

Moments later, the old priestess appeared from the depths of the cave, hobbling as quickly as she could on her ancient legs.

"The young woman is ill?" she asked Benji as she approached.

Benji nodded.

"She is unconscious," he said. "She's been unconscious since a few hours after we left here."

"Where is she?" asked the priestess.

"Outside," Benji replied. "I need help to bring her in."

The priestess nodded, and then shouted orders in a formal language that Benji could not understand.

Four women appeared, all of different ages. The young attendant was one, and the oldest looked little younger than the old priestess herself.

"Show them," the priestess instructed Benji.

Benji led the way outside, where Lisa appeared to hang suspended in air above the ground inside the transparent bubble. He placed his hands through the wall of the bubble and grasped Lisa's arms, easing them through the bubble so the women could take them. Two of them grabbed her arms, and Benji helped them move Lisa until she was fully outside the bubble and the other two attendants could grab her feet. Once they had her firmly, they hustled inside the temple and laid her before the priestess.

"Hmm," the priestess said, as she bent her gnarled body over Lisa's to examine her. She pried Lisa's eyes open and looked at them. She looked inside her ears. She opened Lisa's mouth and looked inside.

"Hmm," she said again. "Has the girl said anything?"

"No," Benji replied. "But I can sometimes hear her thoughts, and I heard some this morning."

"What did she say?" the priestess demanded.

Benji thought back and struggled to remember the exact words.

"She said, 'Black and white, grey and red," he began. "'What happened has not happened. What I saw I did not see. What I did not see I shall see again. Red and grey, white and black. Backward or forward, it is all the same,'" Benji recalled. "I called to her, but she said she couldn't hear me through the noise and the colors. I asked her what colors, and she said the same thing, 'Black and white, grey and red.' I told her I didn't understand, and she said she didn't understand, either, and she asked me to help her. I told her I was trying, and she said, '*farchedan*.' I thought that was an odd choice if what she meant to say was, 'awesome' or something like that, because this doesn't seem very awesome."

"Hmm," the old woman said again. "She told you what the problem is. It's good you didn't wait longer before bringing her."

"So what's wrong with her?" Benji asked.

"She told you," the priestess replied. "There are too many colors and too much noise."

"What does that mean?" Benji asked.

The old woman gazed at Benji for a long moment.

"You are new to our language," she observed, as if Benji's inability to understand her stemmed from his misunderstanding her words.

For a moment, Benji couldn't think what to say next. Then he realized he needed to ask a different question.

"Okay," he said. "There are too many colors and too much noise. Why?"

The old woman nodded approvingly, as if this question was a better one.

"Because she can see more than she is used to," she replied. "She sees more than she can understand."

"What does she see?" Benji asked.

"*Farchedan,*" the woman replied. "She sees *farchedan.*"

Benji considered this. Lisa had said the word literally meant "dance." He wrinkled his brow.

"She sees the dance?" he suggested.

The priestess smiled.

"Yes," she agreed. "And she cannot yet understand it."

What had the other priestess said during their first visit to Hassyr?

"The spirit of life is the source, and the dance is the means." Benji didn't understand it then, but he thought it made a little more sense now.

"So she sees something about the workings of the universe that is too much for her to comprehend?" he suggested.

The old woman cocked her head.

"That is close enough," she replied.

"So can you help her?" Benji asked.

"Yes," she said. "But you must trust me completely, and I think that you do not."

"No," Benji agreed. "I don't. Not completely. I barely know you."

"If your people could heal her, you would not be here," she observed. "I have told you I can heal her. If you did not believe that, you would not be here. But you must let me, do you understand?"

"What does that mean?" Benji asked.

"Leave her with me," the priestess said. "There must be no outside interference if her mind is to know peace."

Benji hesitated.

"If I wished her harm," she continued, "I could have done so at our first meeting. But though she is not of the future, she may become the future, and that is sacred to me. I would not harm her."

"For how long must I leave her?" Benji asked.

"Eight days," the woman replied. "It is the holy number, and it will be sufficient."

Benji did some quick calculations. The days on Hassyr were long. Eight of them lasted nearly three Earth weeks. For three weeks, Lisa would be in the hands of this strange priestess, and Benji would have no way to know what was happening.

But he had no other options. The priestess was right. If the Parisans could cure Lisa, she'd be on Parisa. If he thought Earth medicine could cure her, he'd have taken her there instead.

"Fine," he agreed. "Where shall I go in the mean time? Where can I stay?"

The old woman shrugged.

"It matters not," she replied. "Only that you return in eight days."

Benji thought about this. The only people he knew on the planet were Quanda and Queelie, but he never got to their house so he didn't know where they lived.

"Do you know the two people I came here with last time?" he asked the old woman. "Do you know where I can find them?"

"The two children?" she confirmed. "They are not known to me, and I could not say where they may be found."

Benji nodded, disappointed. But, he considered, Madarach might know.

"Thank you," he said. "Please take care of my sister. I love her more than anything."

"Yes," the old woman agreed. "You love deeply. For a man."

Benji exited the cave and found Madarach still waiting outside. He entered the bubble.

"Tell me," Madarach insisted. "What took place in the temple?"

Benji told him everything, including his having to leave Lisa there, undisturbed, for eight Hassyri days.

"I don't know where to go," he said. "I don't know where Quanda and Queelie live. Do you?"

"I do not," Madarach replied. "And neither does their container, for they have only been using it a week and she has never been to their home."

"She?" Benji asked.

Madarach ignored the question.

"You should go, I think," he said, "to a place where you can be loved in this difficult time. To whom will you go?"

Benji thought.

He wanted his mother, but he didn't want her to worry about Lisa while they had no information. Plus his mother liked to take matters into her own hands. Benji doubted he could restrain her from going straight to Hassyr and confronting the priestess herself. Obviously she would need Benji to pilot Madarach, but he doubted he could deny her. If the priestess was right, that wouldn't help Lisa recover. Three weeks was a long time for a mother to worry about whether her daughter was dying.

For the same reason, he didn't want to return to Parisa. Tamar and Tobin would be heartbroken and worried. Miriam and Jachin would be, too. Tobin, too, might insist on coming to Hassyr. Better for the moment, he decided, if they believed Lisa had returned to her people on Earth for treatment.

There was only one place for Benji to go for the comforting he needed, he decided. He would go to Hadrun and spend the time with Aelbreth, who loved him almost as much as Lisa did.

Chapter Eight

Madarach landed them in a clearing outside the village. Benji exited the bubble and ran as fast as he could down the path.

Aelbreth lived with her family in a small, primitive village called Korby. The sun had just risen on Hadrun, and women in the village were grinding their large, purple, corn-like grain, which they called *ustro*, in the cool of the morning. He knew the men would be in the fields, and most of the children would be tending the *patret*, small dairy animals that, along with *ustro*, formed the bulk of their diet.

Several of the women waved at Benji as he ran past, for he was now well-known in the village. He gave a half-hearted wave in return, but didn't slow until he reached Aelbreth's house.

Outside, Aelbreth's mother, Aedred, was grinding *ustro* in a stone mortar. She stopped and smiled when she saw Benji.

"Greetings, young traveler," she said, as she almost always did. "You are well?"

"Yes, Mother," he replied. "And you?"

It was appropriate on Hadrun to call any older woman "mother," especially when he was so close to the family. And Aedred treated him like part of that family, so she really was like another mother to him.

"All is well here," she informed him. "You'll find Aelbreth and Offsa at the *patret* pen. But I suspect that Aelbreth can spare some time from her chores this morning."

She grinned, showing a mouth full of teeth reddened from the tea the villagers customarily drank.

"Thank you, Mother," Benji replied, and sprinted away through the village.

The *patret* were kept on the edge of the village where the smell and droppings would not intrude into the huts. They were small animals with sharp teeth, but they gave good quantities of milk and were also tasty to eat. They had thick fur, making their skins useful for warmth and comfort.

Eight or ten children worked in the pen today, feeding and watering the animals, raking the droppings into a pile for fertilizer, and milking the lactating does.

Benji spotted Aelbreth with a rake on the far side of the pen.

"Aelbreth!" he called.

All the children looked up, and he saw Offsa on the other side of the pen milking a *patret*. They all waved, and Aelbreth made a show of leisurely putting her rake down and walking slowly across the pen toward Benji.

"You haven't come for a while. I thought you'd left me for good," she said, in mock disgust.

"Of course not," Benji replied. "You are the most beautiful girl in the galaxy. I could never stay away."

This was a game they played when Benji was unable to come for a week or more, to remind each other how much they were missed.

"Well," Aelbreth said, "you might as well come over here so I can look at you. It's been so long, I've almost forgotten your face."

"Have you grown so old your memory fails?" Benji jibed. "I wasn't gone that long!"

Aelbreth laughed.

"It's good to see you," she said, and kissed him on the cheek.

Then she took his hand.

"Shall we go somewhere we can talk?" she suggested.

"I'd like that," Benji agreed.

They walked out past the irrigation canal where they sometimes swam, and into the forest. Soon they reached a small clearing with a large boulder in the center. They'd come here before, many times. It was a private place where they could talk about anything they cared to.

Benji scampered up the side of the rock to its flat top. He turned to offer Aelbreth his hand, but she scampered up right behind him.

"You've grown," he observed. "You used to need help."

Aelbreth grinned.

"You noticed," she replied. "I'm not a little girl anymore."

Benji examined her more closely. Her long, wavy hair was about the same length and the same amber color. Her face and button-shaped nose hadn't changed. But her curves, which had just begun to show the last time he saw her, were beginning to blossom. No longer did she have the thin, flat figure of a little girl.

For some reason, this stirred mixed feelings in Benji that he didn't understand. His body felt a thrill of excitement, but his brain became anxious. He'd known Aelbreth for more than two years, and had always felt comfortable with her. Why would he now feel something different?

He didn't know.

Aelbreth threw her arms around him and hugged him tightly, and Benji felt his other feelings recede. This was the same Aelbreth, his closest friend and confidante.

"How are you?" he asked her, telepathically. His connection with Aelbreth required physical contact, so it wasn't as strong as his connection with Lisa. But he and Aelbreth had a lot of physical contact, so they communicated through telepathy as much as they did words.

Aelbreth smiled up at him.

"I'm good," she answered. "Nothing ever changes here. I would never tell Father this, but it gets boring sometimes. I'm so glad you're here. Maybe we could go somewhere?"

Benji smiled back at her.

"I'd like that," he agreed. "It's been a difficult time for me."

"Why?" Aelbreth asked. "What happened?"

She gazed at his face for a moment.

"Something happened to Lisa?" she suggested.

"Yes," Benji confirmed.

He told her the story of the two children who came through the portal from Hassyr, and how he and Lisa had traveled back to their planet and Lisa had become ill.

"I can't go get her for three Earth weeks," he lamented.

"How many days is that here?" Aelbreth asked.

"Almost thirty," he replied.

"Oh, Benji," Aelbreth gasped. "That's a long time! You must be worried to death."

"Yes," Benji whispered.

Then he grasped her shoulders tightly, buried his face in her neck, and began to cry.

He realized now that he'd needed to cry for a long time, but had held it in. Now, in the comforting presence of his closest friend, he let it all go: his fear for Lisa, his loneliness from not being able to sense her presence, and his anger at the old man for hurting her.

"I miss her," he whispered to Aelbreth. "She's my sister, and our minds are always connected. Now she's gone."

"Only for a while," Aelbreth said. "The priestess promised to heal her."

"I hope so," Benji replied. "I'm so afraid I'll never get her back."

Aelbreth squeezed him tightly and held him unto his tears stopped.

"I'm sorry," Benji said, later. "I didn't mean to cry. I've been holding that in for a while."

"Benji," Aelbreth scolded, "you never have to be sorry for being you around me. I'm your friend and your partner. And I love you."

She had said those words before, but today they stirred something in Benji that he couldn't identify, as if this girl he'd known for two years was not the same person, as if she was an imposter, a stranger.

"What?" Aelbreth asked him.

"I don't know," Benji replied. "This just somehow feels different than it used to."

"What does?" she asked. "You and me?"

Benji nodded.

"I don't know why," he said.

"It *is* different" she confirmed. "But it's also the same. Because *we* are both different, but we're still the same."

"What do you mean?" he asked.

"We're growing, both of us," she told him. "We're changing. We're growing up. But I'm still Aelbreth, and you're still Benji. We're going to go through changes, but we'll still be who we are."

"Will we?" he asked.

"Of course," she said. "We won't be children anymore, but we'll still be the same people we were as children. We'll outgrow our childhood, but it will still be part of us."

Benji nodded, tentatively.

"Benji, I love you," Aelbreth said. "Do you love me?"

"Very much," he confirmed.

"Then trust who we are," she said. "Trust *us*."

Then she kissed him on the lips, and Benji's head began to spin. He'd never kissed a girl before, and felt like he didn't know what to do. It felt strange, but it felt good. And he felt excitement racing through his body again, which scared him.

Aelbreth broke off her kiss and looked into his eyes.

"Was that okay?" she asked.

Instead of answering, Benji kissed her again. And then again.

Chapter Nine

Benji and Aelbreth spent hours sitting on top of the rock. They talked, they laughed, and they kissed often. Benji felt closer to her than he'd ever felt to another person. In some ways, even though his telepathic connection with Aelbreth wasn't as strong as what he had with Lisa, he felt closer to Aelbreth than to his own sister.

As the shadows began to grow, Aelbreth announced that it was time for them to return to the village.

Benji sighed.

"I really don't want to," he said. "I could sit here with you forever."

"Or until the *fortule* got us," she reminded him, referring to a carnivorous animal that hunted at night on Hadrun. "Besides, Offsa will want to see you."

Aelbreth's older brother Offsa was almost Benji's age, and was his closest friend besides Aelbreth. He did want to see Offsa. But he didn't want to leave this moment with Aelbreth.

He also didn't want to get eaten by a *fortule*, so he reluctantly stood and jumped off the rock. This time, he didn't offer Aelbreth his hand.

"Some gentleman you are," she scolded.

Then she grinned and jumped down next to him, and they sprinted for the village.

Offsa was sitting in the shadow of the house when they got back.

"Benji," he said, getting up. "How are you?"

"I'm okay," Benji said.

He told Offsa about Lisa.

"But spending a little time with Aelbreth helps," he added.

Offsa nodded.

"I thought maybe you came to see me," he said, and grinned.

Benji laughed.

"You're still my best friend," he reminded Offsa. "Aelbreth is just my special friend," he said, using the term they used on Hadrun for girlfriend.

They went inside the tiny hut, where Aedred greeted them.

"It's time for dinner," she said.

"Excellent," Benji said. "I've been missing your cooking."

Aedred's husband, Fennel, came in from the fields as Aedred and Aelbreth were putting dinner on the table, and all five of them sat on primitive stools for the meal. They talked as they ate, catching up on events on Hadrun and Parisa. They talked at length about what had happened to Lisa. Fennel said it was a reminder of why it was better to stay close to home.

"But Dad," Aelbreth protested, "that's boring."

He laughed.

"My little wandering heart," he said, using his pet name for her. "Except not so little anymore."

They talked for a long time, until Aedred announced it was time for bed. As usual, the three children laid thick blankets of *patret* fur on the dirt floor and rested on them.

And, as usual, once their parents had gone to sleep, they continued talking.

"How long will you stay with us?" Offsa asked Benji.

"I don't know," Benji said. "I can't go back for Lisa for almost thirty days, but I think your parents might object if I stayed that long."

"Are you joking?" Offsa asked. "They love you. We all do. They hope you'll be part of the family soon."

"Seriously?" Benji asked. "They want their daughter to marry someone from another planet?"

"They want her to be happy," Offsa said. "Dad wasn't too crazy about the idea at first, but he knows Aelbreth has a wandering heart, and that she'd never be happy married to a *patret* farmer. So he's good with the idea now."

"But not yet," Aelbreth added. "He still thinks I'm his little girl."

Benji laughed.

"No, not yet," he agreed. "I'm still in school. I'm not nearly ready."

"You'd be old enough next year," Offsa reminded him. "We marry young on Hadrun."

"I wouldn't be old enough on my planet," Benji said. "I need to be able to support a wife. Where would we live?"

"You could stay here," Offsa suggested.

"And farm *patret*?" Benji replied. "That's what Aelbreth *doesn't* want, remember?"

"I'm in no rush," Aelbreth said. "I'm happy with the way things are. But I do miss you when you're gone."

"I wish I could take you with me," Benji said. "But I don't think your parents would like that at all."

"No," Aelbreth agreed. "They wouldn't. They don't even like our short trips much. My dad worries about all the things that could happen out there."

Benji laughed.

"But nothing ever happens," he said. "We always come back safe."

"Lisa didn't," Offsa reminded him.

Benji had nothing to say to that, and fell silent.

"I'm sorry," Offsa said. "I didn't mean to make you sad."

"It's fine," Benji replied. "You're right. Let's go to sleep."

They all lay quiet, but Benji's mind wouldn't let him sleep. He kept thinking about Lisa and wondering what the priestess was doing.

Some time later, he felt Aelbreth's small hand on his arm.

"I love you," she said, telepathically. "And I'm not afraid. And Lisa will be okay, you'll see."

"Thank you," Benji replied. "I love you, too."

He wished he could kiss her again, but didn't want to with Offsa right there.

Instead, he fell asleep.

His dreams confused him. Lisa and Aelbreth intertwined, changing from one to the other and back. In one dream, Aelbreth lay unconscious and Benji was powerless to help her. In another, he sat on top of the rock in the clearing and kissed Aelbreth, but when he finished he was horrified to discover that it was really Lisa he'd been kissing. In some of the dreams he felt he had to choose between them, an impossible choice.

Benji woke feeling tired, but rose with his friends anyway. He had an unspoken rule for himself. He would work with his friends, and he would contribute twice as much work as he caused Aelbreth to miss. This seemed like a fair contribution. He was older, larger, and stronger than Aelbreth, but she'd been raised working in the village and seemed never to tire. Benji worked faster, but in spurts punctuated with many rests. Aelbreth worked slower, but constantly.

He shared a breakfast of *ustro* bread with the family. He drank *patret* milk rather than the tea the rest of the family sipped. He'd learned the hard way that the tea acted as a hallucinogen to Earthlings, and he didn't like what it did to him.

After breakfast, the three children sprinted to the *patret* pens to start their day, feeding, milking, and cleaning with the other children of the village as they did every day. They worked hard, but doing it with friends helped lighten the burden.

After lunch, they helped the men carry the *ustro* harvest from the fields to the village, and then helped the women with the threshing, which removed the husks from the kernels of grain. The grain would dry overnight, and in the morning, the women would grind it as the whole process started over again.

This was life in a farming village. Every day required the same tasks, except special holidays or the occasional major project. Raising a new home, for example, required the help of everyone in the village, so many of the daily chores might be postponed, except the milking, which had to be done every day so the *patret* wouldn't stop producing milk.

Benji enjoyed village life for short periods. In the village of Korby, Benji felt that his differences didn't matter. He need not worry about what others thought of him.

But after a while, he tired of the unchanging routine. He would never, he knew, be able to live full-time on Hadrun.

On this trip, he also felt restless. Lisa was never far from his thoughts. Though he knew he couldn't go to her for many more days, he desperately wanted to move, to somehow hurry the time along.

After four days, he told Offsa and Aelbreth that it was time for an adventure.

"I need to go somewhere," he said.

"Where do you want to go?" Aelbreth asked, eagerly.

"I don't know," he replied. "Somewhere new."

"People or no people?" Offsa asked.

"I think no people," Benji said. "Will you come?"

Offsa thought for a moment. He didn't enjoy space exploration as much as Benji or Aelbreth. But an uninhabited planet sounded good to him.

"Sure," he agreed.

"Swimming or climbing, or something else?" Benji asked them.

"Definitely swimming," Offsa said.

Aelbreth glanced at her brother, then at Benji.

"Swimming sounds good," she agreed.

At dinner that night, Offsa told his parents that they'd be taking a break from work the next day.

In the morning, as soon as it was light enough to be safe from the *fortule*, they made their way to the clearing where Madarach waited. Benji helped his friends inside.

"Can you take us somewhere we can swim?" he asked Madarach.

"Of course," Madarach said. "Lake, river, or ocean?"

"Ocean!" Benji replied, excitedly. "Someplace with sandy beaches, like Summerland, but safe to swim."

Madarach consulted his database, and soon they were shifting through the stars.

They approached a bluish star, and a bright blue planet came into view.

"That's beautiful!" Aelbreth exclaimed.

As they came closer, they realized that the bright blue coloring was the reflection of its star's blue light. The planet's surface was mostly green. It had more land than water, but it did have a large sea located near its equator.

Madarach set them down at the edge of the sea.

"Is there anything we need to worry about?" Benji asked.

"Nothing," Madarach replied. "Animal life on this planet is not very developed, and is too small to hurt you. I wouldn't eat the plants, because I don't know if they are safe. And you probably shouldn't drink the water, just in case."

They exited the bubble onto a broad beach covered with fine sand. A few yards away, gentle waves broke on the sand.

"Last one in is a *patret*!" Offsa shouted.

They all quickly began stripping off their clothes. Offsa and Aelbreth, who wore the loose clothing of their village, finished first and began running. But Benji quickly caught up with them. He and Offsa began pushing at each other, trying to gain the lead. Offsa tripped, and Benji stumbled, and Aelbreth scooted past them both.

"You're both *patret*!" she called to them.

Offsa and Benji got up, laughing.

"I'm not a *patret*," Offsa shouted back. "*Patret* can't swim!"

Benji splashed into the water right behind him.

"I can swim," he called, as he dove under the water and passed his friends.

He surfaced at a spot where the bottom was just out of reach, and treaded water. Offsa and Aelbreth stood a few yards away, waist deep in the gentle surf. They turned toward Benji and began to splash in his direction.

Suddenly, Benji noticed Aelbreth's naked body. They always swam without clothes, so this wasn't the first time he'd seen her. But her body had changed. Her chest, which had never looked much different than Offsa's or Benji's, now had small breasts.

Benji felt sick to his stomach. He lost his concentration, stopped treading water, and went under, swallowing salty sea water.

He recovered and swam to the surface, coughing.

"It's just Aelbreth," he told himself, over and over. "It's just my friend Aelbreth. Nothing has changed."

But something had changed. Aelbreth was no longer a child. She was becoming a woman. And Benji, apparently, was becoming a man, because he couldn't keep his eyes off of her.

He willed his mind to focus on the water, on his friends' voices, and on the fun they were having.

It wasn't easy.

They spent hours swimming and playing, occasionally wandering up on the beach to lie in the sand.

Eventually, Benji heard Madarach calling.

"It will be dark on Hadrun soon," he told Benji.

Benji relayed this to the others, and they rinsed the sand off their bodies in the ocean, retrieved their clothes, and dressed.

Chapter Ten

When they reached their home, Aelbreth ran inside to help her mom prepare dinner. Offsa leaned against the wall of the hut and watched the sun dip behind the trees.

Benji paused, and then joined him.

"I had a lot of fun today," Offsa said. "Did you?"

"Yes," Benji said. "It was a blast."

"But something was bothering you," Offsa said. "I could tell. Was it Lisa?"

Benji considered this. He'd had so much fun that he'd been able to put his worries about Lisa out of his mind for a few hours. But it would be so much easier to say that's what was bothering him, because he didn't know how to explain the truth.

"No," he said, finally. "I actually forgot about Lisa for a while. Is that terrible?"

"Of course not," Offsa replied. "That was sort of the point, wasn't it? Do you think Lisa wants you moping around every second worrying about what you can't change?"

"No," Benji agreed. "I suppose not."

"So what was bothering you?" Offsa asked.

Benji shook his head.

"I don't know how to explain it," he said.

Offsa gazed at his friend for a moment.

"Do you trust me?" he asked.

"Of course," Benji replied.

"Then take my hand," Offsa said. "Let me feel what you feel."

Benji hesitated, embarrassed.

"I'm your friend," Offsa reminded him. "I won't judge you."

Benji held out his hand. And he out let his excitement, fear, embarrassment, and all the other feelings he couldn't understand.

Offsa laughed.

"It's Aelbreth," he suggested to Benji.

Benji blushed.

"Why are you laughing?" he asked.

"Because what you're feeling is perfectly normal," Offsa said. "I feel that way all the time. But not about Aelbreth. There are two girls in the village, one older than her and one about her age. When I see them, I get all weird and embarrassed."

"But why?" Benji asked. "This never happened before."

"Because," Offsa explained, "your body is almost old enough to mate, and so is hers."

"Mate?" Benji repeated, shocked. "With Aelbreth?"

"Your body doesn't care who it mates with," Offsa said. "That's biology. Like with the *patret*. A male *patret* will mate with any female. Most males in nature are that way. But not people. Your heart is attached to Aelbreth, and she's the one who makes you crazy."

"So when I see her, I get all weird?" Benji confirmed. "Will it always be that way?"

"I don't think so," Offsa said. "My dad doesn't seem to get weird around my mom. At least, not very often. I think it passes as we get older."

Benji thought about this.

"Am I supposed to mate with her?" he asked. "Is that what you do on Hadrun?"

Offsa laughed again.

"There is no 'supposed to' on Hadrun," he said. "People mate when they are comfortable doing it. I don't think Aelbreth is quite old enough, and I don't think you are, either. I know I'm not, because I tried. But even then, some people wait and some people don't. The only requirement is, once you've mated, you're committed to each other. You're going to get married. We don't mate with someone we don't love enough to marry."

"Okay," Benji said. "But there are two girls that make you feel that way?"

"Yes," Offsa said. "Crazy, isn't it. But the older one isn't someone I would marry, so I won't mate with her."

"Oh," Benji said.

"Is it different on Earth?" Offsa asked.

"I think so," Benji said. "Boys and girls never see each other naked. But Lisa told me once that the boys who wanted to hang out with her only wanted one thing, so I guess they wanted to have sex with her. It doesn't sound like they only have sex with someone they want to marry. In church, they tell us that's what's supposed to happen, but I think a lot of boys don't follow that."

"Oh," Offsa said. "That's very different from here. What about Parisa?"

"I don't know," Benji said. "It's very private on Parisa. I don't even know if Lisa has done it with Tobin, even though she's biologically old enough and they've been together for two years."

Offsa nodded.

"You need a dad to talk to," he said.

"Yeah, but which one?" Benji asked. "Mine, Tobin's, or yours? I'm kind of in a cultural mix-up here. Where I come from is not where I live, and where I live is not where my girlfriend lives."

"That must be confusing," Offsa agreed. "Your people sound very different from ours, and you're caught in the middle."

"Yes," Benji said. "I'm not sure what to do. Aelbreth and I have been friends for a long time, and now all of a sudden I feel so weird when I'm around her. I don't like it, but I can't seem to change it."

"Tell her," Offsa counseled.

Benji laughed.

"Seriously?" he asked. "I can't tell her. She'll think I'm crazy."

"No she won't," Offsa said. "I learned a secret. Girls feel weird, too. Trust me, you can tell her. That way she'll understand why you've been strange this trip."

Benji sighed. He couldn't imagine telling *anyone* how he felt. He couldn't believe he just told Offsa. Now Offsa wanted him to tell Aelbreth, the very person who made him feel so awkward? This really was confusing.

"Maybe," he said. "But what if you're wrong?"

Offsa laughed.

"Then she'll think you're a *patret*-brain," he joked. "Not really. She'll think you're honest and sensitive, which girls like."

Benji scrunched up his face.

"They do?" he asked.

"They do," Offsa assured him. "It's just that some don't like to admit it."

Just then, Aelbreth appeared in the doorway.

"Come in for dinner," she instructed.

They did, and the five of them sat around the table for the usual dinner of *patret* and *ustro* bread.

"How was your trip?" Aedred asked.

Offsa and Aelbreth told them about swimming on the planet. Benji remained uncharacteristically quiet.

About half way through the meal, Fennel reached across the table and took Benji's hand. This surprised Benji, because Fennel preferred verbal communication.

"You can hear me?" Fennel confirmed.

"I can," Benji replied.

"I know you're not from Hadrun, so you don't know how things work here," he began. "I also know you don't see your father much, so you may not know how things work on your home planet. So I want to tell you two things. First, what you're feeling is completely normal. I felt it when I was your age. It's confusing, and it's disturbing, and sometimes I thought the world had gone crazy. But it's normal and every boy goes through it as he becomes a man. I'm pretty sure every girl goes through something like it, too, although they hide it better. The second thing is, I will talk with you any time you want. I know I am not your father, but I am a father, and I'm a man. I would be honored to guide you."

"Thank you," Benji said. "Is it so obvious?"

Fennel smiled.

"It is to me," he said. "But I've been through it. I bet Aelbreth has no idea."

But Aelbreth did have an idea. Later in the evening, she took his hand so they could communicate privately.

"What's wrong?" she asked. "What's going on with you?"

Benji sighed.

"I really don't want to talk about it any more today," he said.

He'd already talked about it to Offsa and Fennel, and that seemed enough.

But Aelbreth, who hadn't talked about it at all, frowned and pulled away. She didn't say anything, but Benji could feel her anger. He sensed he wouldn't be kissing her that evening.

Chapter Eleven

The days passed quickly, partly because they were shorter on Hadrun. Still, Benji found himself impatient. After two weeks of milking *patret* and threshing *ustro*, he missed Lisa desperately. But only half the time had elapsed.

"I've got to go somewhere," he told Offsa and Aelbreth. "I can't sit still."

"You're not exactly sitting still here," Offsa observed. "You work all day."

"I know," Benji said. "But I need a change."

"I could go with you," Aelbreth suggested. "I don't want you to be alone."

Benji thought about that. He'd smoothed things over with her, but they still hadn't talked about what was going on with him. Maybe some time alone would be good for them.

"Okay," he agreed. "Let's leave in the morning. And let's bring some food, so we don't have to go to an inhabited planet right away."

The next morning, they packed *ustro* bread and dried *patret* meat, along with a good-sized skin of water and two changes of clothes. Benji found the irony striking: they would be boarding a sophisticated spacecraft with an old-fashioned skin filled with water. But he didn't find it surprising. His life had become a mixture of cultures, primitive and advanced.

"Where shall we go first?" Benji asked Aelbreth, when they had entered the bubble.

"I want to surprise you," she said.

"Okay," he said. "But how can we do that if I have to tell Madarach where we're going?"

"Let me think," she said.

She closed her eyes in deep concentration, and Benji wondered what solution she would discover.

Then came the real surprise: Madarach lifted off the ground and began to ascend.

"Where are we going?" he asked Madarach.

"It's a surprise," Madarach replied.

Benji's jaw dropped. He opened his eyes and stared at Aelbreth.

"You?" he asked, almost an accusation.

Aelbreth grinned.

"Yes," she said.

"For how long?" he asked. "And how did you know?"

"When we went to the beach," she explained, "I found I could hear some of what Madarach was saying. I wasn't sure if he would be able to hear me, but I thought it was worth trying."

"Apparently he can," Benji observed.

"Yes," Aelbreth said. "Though he isn't comfortable taking orders from me. He only did it because I wanted to surprise you. He still belongs to you."

"I don't know that 'belongs' is the right word," Benji said. "He's pretty sentient for a machine. He has feelings, and makes jokes."

"He makes jokes?" Aelbreth repeated. "Really?"

"Not often, and not very well," Benji added. "But I think maybe he's out of practice. He didn't have anyone to talk to for a very long time."

By now, they were approaching a bright orange star. Soon, they saw a planet below them. It was brown and green and blue, much like earth, but with only two small continents visible.

As they descended, they saw that the surface beneath them was covered with dense, green jungle. Madarach found a clearing to land in, and they got out.

Trees and thick foliage surrounded them, nearly blocking out the light of the sun. The smell of wet air mixed with the scent of fruits, flowers, and rotting vegetation, creating a powerful but not unpleasant aroma.

"He says it's safe here?" Benji wondered.

"He does," Aelbreth confirmed.

She led the way into the jungle, stepping around giant ferns and over muddy puddles.

In a moment, they entered what appeared to be a cathedral in the trees. The clearing was huge, but covered with a roof of dense foliage, creating a giant, green room.

Before them grew a variety of giant flowers. Some looked like daisies, and others resembled lilies. Their colors varied from white to orange to red. All towered over Benji's head. And most of the blooms were more than three feet in diameter.

Benji felt like a pixie, a tiny creature among flowers bigger then he was.

"How did you find this place?" Benji asked Aelbreth.

Aelbreth grinned.

"I didn't," she said. "I asked Madarach too take us someplace romantic, like with unusual flowers. He picked this."

"Wow," Benji said, not sure which was more impressive: that Madarach knew of this place, or that Madarach understood what romantic meant.

"Do you think it's romantic?" Aelbreth asked.

Benji gazed around them at the giant explosions of color. He looked back at Aelbreth, whose face betrayed how much she wanted this place to be special for him. And it was special. He'd never seen anything like it.

Benji didn't reply. Instead, he stepped forward and kissed Aelbreth on the lips.

She kissed him back.

"Will you please let me know what you're feeling?" she begged, telepathically. "Please don't shut me out."

Benji hesitated.

Then he decided that it was better to know if she thought he was crazy than to constantly worry about it.

He let his feelings go.

"I'm afraid I don't know how to kiss right," he began.

"Me, too," Aelbreth agreed. "But it feels good, so I think we are."

"It does feel good," he agreed. "But it makes me feel weird, and that scares me."

"Me too," she agreed.

"I know you're the same person I've known for so long," he continued. "But I feel different around you a lot of the time."

"Me too," she agreed. "But it's not bad different, just unfamiliar."

"Yes," Benji agreed. "But it scares me, because I feel drawn to you in a way I never have before."

Aelbreth sighed, audibly.

"Me too," she said. "I feel excited when I'm near you, and warm inside."

"Mine is a little different," he told her. "I feel excited when I see you, and nervous."

"Why nervous?" she asked.'

"Because," he said, and then stopped. "I don't know. I want something from you that I don't understand, and I don't know if you want it too."

"I do," she said. "But not yet."

"No," he agreed. "Not yet. I think I need to understand a little more."

"Me too," she agreed.

They didn't communicate in sentences after that. They stood in the shade of the giant flowers, arms around each other, breathing in the fragrance and enjoying the closeness of their bodies. What passed between them was pure feeling, something Benji had never experienced before. Lisa had almost always kept her feelings to herself, and Benji had never felt feelings from anyone else, except occasionally Madarach. What he felt now was blissful and intimate in a way he had never imagined.

He felt her love for him, and reflected it back to her in his love.

He felt her kindness and compassion, and reciprocated with contentment and protectiveness.

"This is the Garden of Eden," Benji thought at one point. "This is paradise." Because how could he ever feel any better than he did at that moment?

"I'm hungry," Aelbreth said, after a long while.

"I guess I am, too," Benji agreed. "I hadn't noticed."

They made their way back to the clearing where Madarach waited, and they ate *ustro* and dried *patret*.

"Now it's your turn to choose," Aelbreth told him. "Where shall we go?"

"Summerland," Benji said. "I've always wanted to sleep on the beach under the stars, but I never had anyone to share it with."

"Summerland it is," Aelbreth agreed.

Benji realized he could hear Aelbreth's voice even though they were not in physical contact.

"Am I hearing you through Madarach?" he asked her.

"I think so," she replied. "This is new for me, too, so I'm not sure."

"Madarach?" Benji asked..

"It would appear so," he replied. "I, too, have never been in this situation, with two operators who could not telepath. But yes, it appears that the three of us can converse all at once. And I will take you to Summerland."

Chapter Twelve

Benji spent the night curled up on the sand with Aelbreth, watching the stars. The air was warm and moist, so they didn't need a campfire. With no moon in the sky, they could see millions of stars sparkling above them in unfamiliar constellations.

"Do you ever dream of exploring every one?" Aelbreth asked.

Benji laughed.

"On Earth, I could expect to live about another seventy years, which is a little over 25,000 days, which is a little over 600,000 hours," he said. "If I started now and spent an hour visiting every star, and never slept or took a vacation, I'd still never see them all."

Now Aelbreth laughed.

"I know that, silly," she said. "But do you dream of it?"

Benji paused, and then grinned.

"Yes," he said. "I dream of it. I dream of knowing every corner of the galaxy, and maybe other galaxies as well."

"Me too," Aelbreth said. "Tomorrow, let's ask Madarach to take us someplace new, somewhere none of us has ever been."

They barely slept that night, with excitement passing back and forth between them. But they felt content, and in the morning Benji woke feeling rested.

"We want to go somewhere new, somewhere you've never been," he told Madarach.

"Okay," Madarach said. "But I have no idea what it will be like."

"That's the point," Aelbreth told him. "We want to explore something new."

Madarach paused for a long moment.

"My star charts cover this entire section of the galaxy," he said.

"Then take us to a different galaxy," Aelbreth suggested. "Take us to the far side of the universe."

In a moment, they began shifting through the stars. This time, they saw entire galaxies in the distance as they passed. Nebulae glowed, and other strange sights flickered and shone.

They approached a double spiral galaxy, homed in on a yellow star, and paused some distance away.

"This star is twice the size of Earth's sun," Madarach told them. "It has twelve planets. The outer three are barren rock. The next three are gas giants. There are three that might support life, and then another three that are too close to the star itself and probably have surfaces of molten rock."

"Let's check out the three that might support life," Benji suggested.

They came close to the first one, which from its white coloring clearly had large areas of ice and snow on it.

"There are some primitive animals here," Madarach told them, "but it is too cold to be comfortable for you."

The next one appeared more Earthlike, with several continents and vast seas.

"This one is inhabited," he said, "though the dominant species does not appear mammalian."

"What are they?" Benji asked.

"I'm not sure," Madarach said. "They seem to be cold blooded and have multiple limbs. Perhaps they are arthropods."

"Spiders?" Benji clarified, and shivered. "I don't think we want to visit a planet of intelligent spiders. They might see us as food."

"There is no way to know," Madarach agreed.

The last planet was mostly land, but very green.

"There are two small colonies of the same creatures that populate the other planet," Madarach said. "There does not appear to be any other intelligent life. And it is very warm on the surface, about 115 degrees Fahrenheit."

"Can we go down and look?" Benji asked. "If we don't get out, we should be safe, right?"

"I sense nothing I can't protect you from," Madarach agreed.

They descended through the atmosphere and landed in a clearing between a rocky shoreline and a jungle. Strange, six-legged amphibious creatures basked on the rocks, leisurely flopping into the water as Madarach approached.

The jungle trees were short, barely taller than Benji, and giant insects flew among colorful flowers blooming in the upper branches.

Then they saw one of the spider creatures. It had twelve legs, six of which had opposable thumbs. It was weaving together some kid of net, which it then cast into the ocean as if fishing. But when it retrieved the net, bracing its body with six lower limbs while pulling the net with six upper limbs, the net was about half filled with crablike creatures rather than fish.

"I wish we had some way to find out if it's friendly without actually touching it, or even getting close to it," Aelbreth lamented.

"Perhaps there is," Madarach said. He dipped down close to the creature, staying carefully out of its reach. Then he projected a sound toward it.

"That is the language of an arachnid species on planet G53-6," he explained. "Let's see how the creature responds."

The creature gazed at them for a moment through two clusters of eyes. Then it raised one hand tentatively toward them, and it spoke.

Benji did not perceive the reply as speech. It sounded like a series of high-pitched clicks and screeches, some of which hurt his ears.

"I can't make anything out of that," he said.

"Madarach, can you slow it down and make the tone lower?" Aelbreth suggested.

Madarach did, and it became clear that much of the creature's language was in pitches above what they could hear. Now it sounded more like a language, and Benji picked up several words immediately.

He replied with a simple sentence, which Madarach recorded and changed into frequencies the creature could understand.

A brief exchange took place, and then Benji tried a longer sentence.

"It asked me where we come from," Benji explained. "I said far away. I explained that we are no threat to it, and asked if it had hostile intentions toward us."

The reply came in a long stream of clicks and screeches. When Madarach had processed it, Benji frowned.

"What?" Aelbreth asked.

"It says," Benji explained, "that it personally has no grudge against us, having never met us before. However the policy of its race is that there are no other intelligent species in the galaxy. I think that's part of their religion. So if our existence became known, we would be hunted and killed."

"That's too bad," Aelbreth said. "I've never made friends with an spider before."

Benji replied through Madarach.

"I told it that we do not wish it harm, and thank it for its warning," he explained. "I also told it we regretted not being able to learn from each other."

The reply was fairly brief.

"It says it also regrets that its people, so forward in some areas, are so backward in others. It says perhaps some day in the future they will have grown more enlightened. And it wishes us the blessings of its goddess on our continuing journey. I think the conversation is over."

"Well," said Aelbreth. "That was interesting, if not quite satisfying."

"I was able to gather and catalog a great deal of information about the creature and the planet," Madarach said. "The creature has no gender. Or more correctly it has three genders at the same time. Apparently they all do."

"So there's no distinction between male and female," Benji observed. "That must make things simpler in their culture."

"And less interesting," Aelbreth added.

"Where to now?" Madarach asked.

"Is there anything else in this general area for us to see?" Benji asked. "As long as we're here, I mean. It seems a shame to cross the universe for one short conversation."

Madarach scanned, and soon they were moving again. This time, they approached a red giant star, and a fairly large planet orbiting the star. The planet glowed red in the light of its sun.

Madarach descended, and soon they hovered above a snowy landscape bathed in red hues.

As they watched, suddenly a geyser erupted not far from them. It shot hundreds of feet into the air, and then exploded into a dazzling display of colors.

"Wow!" Benji said. "What makes it do that?"

"The geyser is primarily liquid methane, along with other trace elements, including some metals," Madarach explained. "The atmosphere contains oxygen. And the sky here is heavily charged with static electricity. When the liquid methane reaches the sky, it begins to boil into a gas and mix with oxygen. Static electricity finds an easier path to ground through the liquid methane mixture than through the atmosphere, and that provides a spark that ignites the geyser. The impurities in the methane produce the variety of colors. It's an unusual combination of conditions that produces an extraordinary display."

"It's beautiful," Aelbreth agreed. "But I think it's even more beautiful when it's mysterious. Don't you think knowing all the details takes something away from its beauty?"

Benji stared at her for a moment.

"No," he replied. "I'm fascinated with what makes it work."

"Women," Madarach said. "Your brains are just a little different, aren't they?"

Benji gasped. He'd never heard Madarach say anything insulting to anyone.

"Yes," Aelbreth agreed, chuckling. "But you shouldn't get so jealous. We need men to do the practical work."

Benji glanced at Aelbreth again. She was smiling broadly.

"Madarach," he said. "That was a joke?"

"As you've observed," Madarach replied, "I'm not very good at it."

"That's not true," Aelbreth insisted. "It was funny!"

Benji sighed. It wasn't just Aelbreth anymore. Even his spaceship was changing.

"I think we've done enough exploring for the moment," Benji said. "Aelbreth, do you remember my friends on Zeblack? I wonder what time it is there now."

Chapter Thirteen

Benji had discovered the planet Zeblack with his sister Lisa not long after they had begun to use Madarach. The planet had been at war for hundreds of years, but Benji had made some good friends there, and he and Lisa had returned several times to play with the boys. He spoke their language well.

The war on Zeblack troubled Benji, and somewhere in his heart he hoped that someday he might help to bring peace. But at twelve years old, Benji knew that was a distant dream.

Madarach set them down in a deserted alley around the corner from the neighborhood where Benji's friends lived.

"If you need me, call me," he reminded them, as he always did when Benji went to a place that could be dangerous. "Either of you," he added, now that Aelbreth could communicate with him also.

"We'll be fine," Benji assured him. "We always have been before."

"Just remember, it is a planet at war," Madarach said. "And war has a tendency to be unpredictable."

Benji led Aelbreth around the corner, where a group of boys played a ball game they called numbfoot.

"Benji!" called a boy named Tak, when he spotted the two visitors. "You came back, and brought your wife!"

"She's not my wife," Benji retorted. "She's my girlfriend."

"The same girlfriend for so many moons?" joked the largest boy, whose name was Dorn. "She does look like a wife."

Benji grinned.

"In that case, I won't need to invite you to the wedding, since you think we're already married," he said. "You'll miss the party!"

They all laughed.

Benji looked around.

"Where's Prag?" he asked. "He always plays with you."

The boys all looked sad for a moment.

"His brother was killed," Dorn explained. "So Prag volunteered to take his place in the unit."

"But he's so young," Benji observed. "They'll let him fight?"

"We must all fight, eventually," said a tough-looking boy that Benji didn't know.

"This is Chorl," Tak said, introducing them. "His family just moved here, and his father has an important position in the faction."

Benji sighed. All of Zeblack was divided into political factions, and they constantly fought with one another. Everyone on Zeblack seemed completely loyal to their faction, and most ended up fighting in the war. To Benji, it appeared that the factions were the problem.

"Nice to meet you," Benji said. "How do you like it here?"

"It's okay," Chorl replied. "We're further from the fighting, which is good. But things are a little different. They don't take the war as seriously here."

"I guess the closer you are to the fighting, the more seriously you'd take it," Benji said.

"I suppose," the boy replied. "But if we're going to win, we need everyone to be fully committed."

"It doesn't seem like anyone ever wins," Benji observed.

"Not yet," Chorl agreed. "But I think we're close. We have a new ally, and my dad says he has a plan."

Benji nodded. He'd never understood the war on Zeblack, and how it could have gone on for so long. Factions shifted alliances, and everyone tried to destroy each other's resources. It seemed not only endless, but pointless as well.

But he'd also learned to keep his thoughts to himself around the kids he played with. To them, the war was their life. They lived in poverty and sometimes fear because of it. Their parents and older siblings fought and died in it. They would never believe that the sacrifices they and their families made were pointless.

"Shall we play numbfoot?" Benji asked.

"You'll lose," one of the kids taunted. "Even if your wife helps."

They called the game numbfoot because it could go on for hours, and your foot could get numb from playing so much. Today's game was no exception. They played all afternoon. New players joined in at random intervals, and some of the original players left because of chores or other duties. Benji noticed that the new kid, Chorl, left after about an hour.

Benji had become fairly good at the game, and Aelbreth, who never slowed while doing chores, played numbfoot just as tirelessly as she worked. They stayed even for a long time, and one point gained the lead. But in the end, they did lose.

"This has been fun," Benji said. "But next time, we're going to beat you."

"That will be the day!" Tak exclaimed.;

"Hey, Benji," called a voice from the sidelines.

Benji looked and saw Chorl beckoning to him, so he went over to talk.

"What's up, Chorl?" Benji replied.

"My mom wants you and your wife to come join us for dinner," Chorl said. "She's never met anyone from another planet, and really wants to meet you both."

Benji thought about this. Madarach had always warned Benji not to stay on Zeblack after dark.

"War is always unpredictable," Madarach often said.

He'd also warned that adults might not be as friendly to outsiders as kids would be. But if Chorl's mom wanted to meet them, that meant she was friendly.

"Can you get us back here afterward so we can go home?" Benji asked.

"Of course," Chorl said. "My brother will walk with us. No one messes with him."

Benji glanced at Aelbreth.

"Chorl wants us to have dinner at his house," he explained. "What do you think?"

"I think that's very nice of them to offer," Aelbreth said. "On Hadrun, we would never decline an invitation like that. Let's do it."

"Okay," Benji told Chorl.

Then he said goodbye to the other boys.

Most of the boys lived with their families in apartments above shops that lined the street. Benji had seen the shops, but had never ventured inside any of the homes.

Chorl led them through a now-closed butcher shop. In the back, they ascended a narrow flight of stairs to the apartment.

The inside of the apartment looked clean and solid, but didn't have much in the way of decorations. On one wall hung photos of men and women in uniform, which Benji assumed were family members who had served the faction. Maybe some of them were still serving. On another wall hung a dark blue flag with a complex design in gold thread and, in the lettering of Zeblack, the name of their faction: Darkly.

The rest of the walls were bare.

There wasn't much furniture, either. A large table made of planks dominated one room, surrounded by wooden benches. The room with the photos boasted two wooden chairs. But there were no carpets on the floors, no couches, no lamps, and no books in evidence. Light came from a candle in each room.

"This is nice," said Aelbreth, whose own home had primitive furniture and a dirt floor.

"Not bad," Benji whispered back. "But your house feels friendlier."

"Come, eat!" Chorl insisted.

The three of them sat at the huge table alone for several minutes. Then they were joined by Chorl's older brother, Chute.

"What do you do?" Benji asked Chute. "Are you still in school?"

"Not really," Chute replied. "I joined the faction. I'm in officer school, but we spend most of our time fighting."

Benji nodded.

"I hear Darkly has a new ally," he said, mostly to make conversation.

"Yes," Chute said, excitedly. "We still have Blue, though they turned out to be pretty useless. Now we've been joined by

Whitestone. They're on another continent, so that will give us a geographical advantage. I think we can win this war soon."

Benji nodded. He knew there were dozens of factions. It sounded like Darkly and Blue were about to part ways, which meant Blue would ally with someone else. He questioned the optimism Chute seemed to feel about Darkly becoming victorious in the near future. It looked to Benji like the war would continue unchanged for a long time to come.

Just then, two women appeared from the other room carrying plates of food.

"This is my mom," Churl explained, gesturing toward the older woman. "Her name is Gayla. And this is my sister, Cheela. My father won't be here, because he's on business for the faction."

"It's a pleasure to meet you both," Gayla said.

Cheela smiled, shyly.

They passed plates of food around the table. Benji wasn't sure what most of it was. One dish contained slabs of some kind of meat. Another resembled potatoes in consistency, though it was green instead of white. A dish of pickled vegetables had a very strong aroma, but tasted okay.

"So tell me about your world," Gayla suggested, as they began eating.

"Actually, we come from two different worlds," Benji explained. "I grew up on Earth, in a country that was very prosperous. But my family moved from a city to a small town, and the people there didn't like us. My sister and I took the bubble to another planet that's very peaceful, where we would be safe."

This sparked a number of questions. Benji explained what the bubble was, and how he and Aelbreth could interface with Madarach. Churl asked what a country was, and Benji suggested it was kind of like a faction.

"So your home planet is at war, like we are?" Cheela asked.

"We have war," Benji replied. "But not as much. I've never seen war first-hand."

"How is it possible for a planet not to have war?" Chute asked.

This sparked several minutes of discussion, in which Chute insisted that war was inevitable, and Benji assured him just as emphatically that Parisa had not seen war in centuries and had no conflict.

Then they asked about Aelbreth's planet. Since Aelbreth couldn't speak the language, Benji explained that it was poor and primitive, but peaceful and very happy.

"I've never seen people who were so content with what they have," he observed.

Aelbreth followed all this by keeping her hand on Benji's arm, so she could hear his thoughts.

"Is happiness better than progress?" Gayla asked.

"Isn't happiness what we all want?" Benji suggested. "On my planet, they always say progress will make us happier. It hasn't."

"I can't imagine being happy in such primitive conditions," Cheela commented,

"Me either," Benji agreed. "At least, not for very long. Short visits are a nice change. But doing the same chores every day with no variation? I'd go crazy after a while. But it works for them, so why do they need progress?"

"Sooner or later they will fight," Chute predicted. "And when they do, they will need progress. Better weapons and better tactics. That's how you win a war."

"Wouldn't it be better to prevent a war than to win one?" Benji suggested.

"At what cost?" Chute asked. "These other factions would take everything we have. We'd have nothing if we didn't fight."

"But what if you could be truly happy?" Benji asked.

Chute smiled.

"Victory makes me happy," he said. "There's no other feeling like it. People fight, so we might as well accept that and fight as well as we can."

Benji shook his head, sadly.

"I really don't understand," he said. "On my home planet, they tried to kill my family and me. On Parisa, we're safe. That seems better. I don't understand war."

"Someday you will," Chute predicted. "War is inevitable."

Chapter Fourteen

They finished dinner, and Benji and Aelbreth thanked Gayla for her generosity.

"The food was excellent," Benji added, exaggerating just a little.

"You are welcome any time," Gayla said, warmly. "Now Chute and Churl will walk you back to your spaceship."

They went down the stairs and exited the shop to the street, where three more young men, all Chute's age, waited for them.

"We want to be sure you're safe," Churl said.

There were no street lights, and Chute warned that hand-held lights might make them a target for aircraft or missiles from another faction, so they made their way carefully through the dark.

Eventually, they reached the corner where Benji and Aelbreth had emerged.

"Madarach is just a few meters down that alley," Benji said. "We can make it from here."

The young men looked at each other.

"That alley isn't safe in darkness," Chute warned. "Can you call your ship to meet you here? We'd feel terrible if something happened when we could have made sure you left safely."

Benji nodded. He called Madarach, and in moments they could see moonlight reflecting off the transparent skin of the bubble.

"Thank you," Benji said.

"No," Chute corrected, "thank you. We're going to take your ship for the faction to use."

Benji gaped for a moment. Then he tried to run for Madarach, to get inside where the boys couldn't touch him. He figured once he'd done that, he could think of a way to rescue Aelbreth.

The boys were ready for his dash. One of them stuck his foot out and tripped Benji, sending him sprawling on the broken pavement. Another grabbed Aelbreth from behind and held her arms.

"But you can't communicate with Madarach," Benji protested. "What good will he do for you?"

"We'll need you to pilot the ship," Chute said. "And if you do as we ask, we won't hurt your little friend here."

"You're going to steal our ship *and* kidnap us?" Benji sputtered. "Now I wish I hadn't thanked your mother for her hospitality."

"She knows nothing of this," Chute said. "It was my father's idea. Imagine how our fortunes in war would change if we had an invisible spaceship that would take us anywhere on the planet in seconds! We could mount surprise attacks, steal technology, and destroy the technology of the other factions. No longer would we need allies just to survive. We would dominate this planet."

Benji shook his head. He sensed Churl watching him in the darkness.

"This is how you treat your friends?" he asked, softly.

"The faction comes first," Churl replied. "Always."

"Fine," Benji said, sulkily. "Let Aelbreth go, and I'll take Chute into the bubble."

Chute nodded to the one holding Aelbreth. He released his grip, and Aelbreth stepped back.

At the same moment, Benji took a step forward.

"No too fast," Chute warned him. "Remember, she can't get home without you and your ship."

Just then, a bright flash blinded all of them. At first, Benji wasn't sure what it was. It looked like lightening, but it didn't come from the sky.

It came from Madarach.

Benji turned to see that one of the boys was lying on the ground, and the others were on their knees. Aelbreth, now three feet behind them, had not been touched. Apparently Madarach had instructed her to step back at the same time he'd warned Benji to step forward. Benji hadn't known why, but he trusted Madarach enough to do as he was told.

A second flash erupted from the surface of the bubble, and then a third.

"Come," Madarach instructed.

Benji turned to make sure Aelbreth was headed in the right direction. She was. She reached him and took his hand, and together they stepped inside the bubble.

One final flash erupted from the exterior. In its light, Benji could see that all five of the boys were already lying on the ground. Their bodies twitched in agony as high voltage electricity ran through them.

Then Madarach began to ascend.

"I am afraid," he said, "that Zeblack is no longer safe for you. I am sorry."

"We need to go somewhere," Aelbreth said. "We need to relax for a minute and talk about this."

"Yes," Madarach said. "But first we need to get away from this planet."

As they rose through the atmosphere, two aircraft came speeding toward them. One hovered above them, trying to force them down. The other circled them to ensure that they did not move horizontally.

"Can you shift sideways in time?" Benji asked.

"Not in the atmosphere," Madarach replied. "But atmosphere has its advantages, too."

A bolt of lightning emanated from the exterior of the bubble and hit the plane above them. It lost control and began a steep dive.

The second plane tried to position itself above them, but a second bolt of lightening disabled that one, too.

"Let's get out of here before they send more," he said. "Sooner or later, they're going to realize that we have weapons, and they'll shoot at us with whatever weapons they have. I don't carry much in the way of armor."

Madarach ascended rapidly. Below them, Benji saw four more aircraft approaching. But they couldn't follow Madarach into the upper atmosphere, and eventually they turned back.

Aelbreth breathed a sigh of relief.

Then they saw two missiles approaching from below, appearing at this distance as tiny cylinders with fire emanating from the rear.

"Seriously?' Benji asked.

"Those are heat-seeking missiles," Madarach told him. "But I have no heat signature. It would be a miracle if they hit me."

They watched as the missiles came closer and then passed by.

"I don't think they have anything else to use against us," Madarach said. "Besides, we're almost out of the atmosphere."

"Let's go," Aelbreth said. "Anywhere but here."

Madarach rose some more, and then began shifting through the stars.

"We are safe now," he assured them. "But I will set down on an uninhabited planet while we catch our breath. Shall we go to Summerland? It is familiar to you, and I think not unpleasant."

"Summerland is fine," Benji agreed. "At least we know it's safe."

Moments later, they landed on the sand of the familiar planet. Benji and Aelbreth exited the bubble. Aelbreth fell to her knees on the sand and began to cry.

Benji stared at the sky for a long moment.

"You think you can pull that kind of thing on me?" he demanded of the empty sky, as if Churl and Chute might be able to hear him. "Well, you can't," he shouted. "We are a team, the three of us, and we stand together."

He shook his fist at the sky.

Then he, too, began to cry.

After a while, Aelbreth choked back her tears, came to him, and put her arms around him.

"When I ran for Madarach," Benji told her through his tears, "my only thought was that I could use him to rescue you. I wasn't going to leave you, I swear."

"I know," Aelbreth replied. "I can feel it in you. You wanted to protect me, and you risked your life trying. I love you for that."

They held each other for a long time. Both of them cried some more.

"I can't believe my friends would do that to me," Benji lamented.

"It was Churl and his brother," Aelbreth reminded him. "You'd never met them before. They weren't your friends."

"No," Benji agreed. "But now I'll never know whether or not I can trust the others."

Chapter Fifteen

Later, they sat cross-legged on the sand, and included Madarach in their conversation.

"Thank you," Aelbreth said. "You saved our lives."

"They wouldn't have killed you," Madarach pointed out. "They needed you to communicate with me. Without you, I would be useless to them."

"At the very least, you saved our freedom," Benji corrected.

"And mine," Madarach added. "It could have been bad for all of us, being forced to fight in a war that isn't ours."

They all reflected on this for a moment.

"I didn't realize you had weapons," Benji said.

"They weren't in my original design," Madarach confessed. "But after what happened to young James, I decided that it would be beneficial to prepare for any eventuality. I was able to repurpose some of my circuits into simple defensive weapons. They are really little more than what on Earth you call a Tesla coil."

"And you never said anything," Benji observed. "You kept them a secret."

Madarach didn't reply.

"They worked really well," Aelbreth said. "I'm glad you did it."

"Thank you," Madarach said. "It was not consistent with my programming, but it was logical."

"You know you didn't have to hurt them like that," Benji said to Madarach. "That last bolt of lightening, I mean. We were already in the bubble, and all five of them were on the ground. It wasn't needed."

Madarach paused before answering. When he did, his thoughts were heavy with emotion.

"I am responsible for you," he replied. "I needed to teach them a lesson."

Benji thought about this.

"There's more, though, isn't there?" he suggested. "They angered you."

Benji felt more than heard Madarach's sigh.

"Yes," Madarach agreed. "They angered me."

Benji thought some more.

"How can that be?" he asked. "You're a machine. And even the people who built you control their anger. How can you get angry?"

Madarach said nothing for a long time.

"Let me take you somewhere," he said, finally. "A place of my choosing. Then we will sit and talk some more."

"Okay," Benji agreed, his curiosity rising.

They passed through the stars until they came close to a bright white sun. Madarach took them toward a planet some distance away. As they approached, Benji could see that the entire planet appeared as if painted in bright colors, shades of red, green, yellow, white, and more.

Madarach set them down on a plain near an overhanging cliff. It looked much like the photos Benji had seen of the American West, except this entire landscape was bright blue.

"Copper," Madarach explained. "Because of the planet's distance from its star, there's a high concentration of transition metals in the crust. The blue comes from copper, red is iron and cobalt, green is from nickel and chromium."

"You've been here before?" Benji surmised.

"This is the planet closest to Parisa," Madarach explained. "It used to be one of my favorite places to come and relax."

That, Benji thought, raised more questions than it answered. How could a machine have a favorite place, and why would it come here to relax? Wouldn't Madarach relax as he recharged?

"Why don't you both get out and sit comfortably," Madarach suggested. "The air is safe to breathe, and there's nothing that can hurt you on this planet, so long as you don't eat the soil or the plants. And don't drink the water, it's saturated with metals."

Benji and Aelbreth exited the bubble. The air had a strange, almost metallic smell, and the scenery seemed eerie with its unusual blue shades. They looked around for a few moments, and Benji dug at the blue sand with his toes.

Aelbreth noticed a flat rock just a few feet from Madarach.

"Let's sit there," she suggested.

Benji followed her, and they sat on the rock and gazed at Madarach intently.

"You've said some confusing things today," Benji observed. "I'd like it very much if you could explain."

For a moment, they all sat in silence. Then Madarach began.

"I'm going to tell you a story," he said. "Parts of it you will have heard before at school. But parts of it you will never hear from anyone but me. I will caution you, should you ask the old priest, he will probably tell you I am exaggerating, or perhaps even lying. I am not."

"Okay," Benji said, tentatively.

"This is my secret," Madarach said. "I have never shared it with anyone. But it is about to become our secret, the two of you and me. No one else can know. Do you understand?"

"Yes," Benji said. "But Lisa will know. She can read my thoughts."

Madarach sighed again.

"Yes, Lisa," he agreed. "Lisa has a good heart, and a strong mind. But she is blinded by love. That's natural, but it sometimes causes people to make poor decisions. Especially young people. You will need to impress upon her the need for silence."

"Will Tobin be able to read it in her thoughts?" Benji asked.

"Not unless she reveals it," Madarach said. "Her bond with you is special. It is stronger than the bond that forms between my people."

"Okay," Benji agreed. "Tell us the story."

Madarach paused, as if gathering his thoughts.

"Many centuries ago," he said, "Parisan society looked much like Earth's does today. We had diverse nations and cultures. Our population was over eight billion people. We farmed and consumed as if the resources would never end, and we dumped our refuse as if the whole planet was our personal trash heap. We fought among ourselves. We were greedy, the strong becoming rich while the poor lived in squalor. I know that you have never seen the slums on your planet in Delhi, or Bangkok, or even Tijuana, so you may not realize how many people on Earth live in poverty you cannot imagine. Parisa looked like that, too.

"I cannot say it was all bad," he said. "We made great advances in technology. We could cure almost any disease, created amazing electronic advancements, and our space program took us everywhere in our star system. The leaders impressed themselves, and their supporters. But they did little for the majority, who would never fly in space and couldn't afford access to hospitals.

"We polluted the planet, and we even changed its climate," Madarach continued. "Some small groups demanded change, but they were like whispers on the wind compared to the way we had always done things. Still, as things got worse, more and more people began to realize that our survival was at stake. There came a point at which that group represented a majority. But they did not have the necessary power to make change because, as with your own planet, a very small group makes the most important decisions.

"But this group became a threat to the status quo," Madarach explained. "They gained power. They influenced some of the leaders. The established order felt threatened. So these leaders contrived various means to eliminate the loudest voices opposing them. They used violence when it suited them.

"Of course, the other side resorted to violence also," Madarach said. "Soon Parisa was in chaos. On the one hand, people wanted order. On the other hand, they needed change. So both sides had something to offer, but neither had the solution."

"Imagine, if you can, being faced with that choice," Madarach suggested. "Imagine a teacher, for example, who sees his world dying and his students being killed. He wants to change it, but he has nowhere to turn. What would you do?"

"I don't know," Benji said. "Do you embrace order, and hope that change will follow, or do you embrace change and hope that order will follow?"

"Exactly," Madarach agreed. "But, as teachers, their primary concern was the wellbeing of their students. So they chose order. They were convinced that the violence must stop. Many stopped teaching and joined with the governments, hoping to restore relative peace.

"They chose the losing side," Madarach said. "It took decades, but eventually the rebels, for those who sought change had become rebels, triumphed. By that time, these teachers had become leaders themselves, and advisors, and even generals. They dedicated their lives to the idea that through order the killing could be stopped. And in the end, that was true, but it was the other side that brought us back to order.

"When the governments fell, these teachers were captured and tried for crimes," Madarach continued. "They were convicted, of course, because the loser is always guilty. Had the rebels been just a little less committed to change, the teachers would have been sentenced to death, even though their true crime was caring about the lives of children. But they were not sentenced to death. They were given a much more difficult choice."

Madarach stopped for a long moment.

"What happened?" Benji asked. "What was the choice?"

"We were some of the best minds on Parisa," Madarach replied. "We were given the option of life imprisonment, or we could let our minds work for the future of the planet."

Benji wrinkled his brow. Madarach had just switched pronouns from "they" to "we." He was one of the teachers who opposed the rebels. But the choice he described, what did it mean?

"My mind was separated from my body," Madarach explained, "and transferred to a computer. That was in the early days, when we were just beginning to interface with computers and each other. It was primitive. For generations, I was stuck in a small room, working on societal problems like agricultural production and emissions sources. Then the sickness came, and we all worked on a cure."

"The sickness?" Aelbreth asked.

Madarach sighed, deeply.

"It was a plague, the likes of which my planet had never seen, not even before the development of medicine," Madarach explained. "There had been nothing like it in all of history. We couldn't treat it. And billions of people died. We all joined together to work for a cure, even those of us who had been banished to electronic imprisonment. It took years, but eventually we succeeded."

He sighed again.

"But not before three quarters of our population perished," he added.

"You helped save the planet after all?" Benji suggested.

Benji could feel Madarach's bitter humor as he replied.

"Yes," he said. "Ironic, I think."

"Why?" Benji asked.

"Because I had been a general in the war," Madarach said. "For decades, I killed people in the name of peace. At the time, I truly believed I was doing the right thing. But in hindsight, I was wrong. I couldn't see the future, and I made the wrong choices."

"But if you were a teacher," Benji wondered, "how did you become a general?"

Madarach's sigh carried a lifetime of sadness in it.

"Because I had once been an astronaut," he replied. "I was trained by the military, and I completed several space missions. I was the first person to set foot on this planet. I was once a hero to my people. When I retired, I became a teacher because I wanted to transmit the wonder of the things I'd seen.

"Look at it!" Madarach exclaimed. "Have you ever seen anything so beautiful?"

Benji could almost imagine him gesturing with arms, as a teacher would.

"And I was the only person ever to visit it," Madarach continued. "Until today, I was the only person to have seen this with my own eyes. I wanted to transmit that wonder to the children!

"Instead, I became a merchant of death," he lamented.

Madarach's voice was anguished. If he had eyes, Benji was certain, Madarach would be crying.

"When I rejoined the government, they needed military leadership," Madarach continued, bitterly. "I thought I was being of service."

"That's why you thought to create weapons for yourself," Benji suggested. "Because you were a general."

"Yes," Madarach agreed. "I was wrong in my choices, but not entirely unwise. We do need order, and we do need the ability to defend the ones we love."

Benji's thoughts spun, questions and insights confusing his mind.

"So you were once a person," he summarized.

"Yes," Madarach confirmed. "I like to think that I still am. I still have feelings and emotions. I still have the ability to think and reason. But I'm trapped in this container forever, and on Parisa I am considered a machine."

Benji thought some more.

"Did your work on the cure balance against your crimes?" he asked. "Is there any way you can be pardoned?"

Again Benji felt Madarach's bitter humor.

"I ceased to be considered a person when my mind was transferred," Madarach replied. "There is no way to transfer my mind back into a body, so my personhood is gone forever. But yes, we did regain some trust after we helped with the cure. Until that time, those who controlled us feared that we might somehow work against them. Our access to the outside world was severely limited."

"So you earned the transfer to the bubble?" Benji guessed.

"You could say that," Madarach agreed. "When the space program reached the point that it needed intelligent controllers for its vehicles, we were the obvious choices."

"Is this better?" Benji asked.

"Better?" Madarach repeated. "Yes, it's better. There has been a lot of waiting, a lot of boredom. But during those times when my vehicle has been used, I've been able to see and experience a great deal. And it has been good to interact with people when I've been able to."

Benji looked around the blue landscape.

"You said you came here to relax," he observed. "When was that? Surely not before the war. Your people didn't have the technology yet to take a day trip to a planet. And I doubt your first trip, an experimental space mission, would have been very relaxing."

"No," Madarach agreed. "It was later. I was in stasis a long time on Earth from the time I was installed until your great-great-uncle James Partridge found me. After I was activated, I found that I could improve myself. After James was killed, I developed the ability to activate myself. It was over a hundred years from James's death until you found me. I would occasionally take a vacation. I returned to this planet early on, and have been here probably a dozen times over the years."

Benji shook his head, overwhelmed with new information. But one fact resounded in his brain above all the others.

"You're a person!" he exclaimed to Madarach. "You're a person!"

Chapter Sixteen

Aelbreth had said little through the conversation. When Benji glanced over at her, he saw that she was crying.

"I'm sorry," Aelbreth said. "It's just so *sad*! A man trapped inside a machine because he made bad choices."

She shook her head.

"I can't imagine that happening on Hadrun," she added.

Benji went to her and put his arms around her.

"You don't have to be sorry for crying," he told her, repeating what she'd told him a few days before. "You don't ever have to apologize to me for being who you are."

Aelbreth cried a bit more.

"This world," she said. "The world outside Hadrun. It's beautiful and fascinating. But it's not always nice. Someone tried to kidnap us today, and then they tried to kill us. Now we've heard a story so sad I don't have words to describe it.

"Madarach, did you have family?" she asked.

Madarach paused a long time before answering.

"I did," he replied, finally. "A wife, and three children."

"What happened to them?" Aelbreth asked.

"My wife was also a teacher," Madarach said. "In fact, I met her at school, and we fell in love and married. Her specialty was math. She, too, supported the government. She was transferred into a computer, as I was."

"What happened to her?" Benji asked. "Where is she now?"

Madarach did not reply. Instead, after a moment, waves of emotion emanated from him: sadness, anger, joy, bitterness, and more sadness.

Long moments passed. When he finally communicated, his thoughts were faint, as if he could barely speak.

"I never knew," he said. "Until the day we went to Hassyr."

Benji thought about this, and then gasped.

"You wife is in their bubble?" he suggested.

"Yes," Madarach said. "I hadn't seen her in over six thousand years. And there she was, living a life much like mine."

Now Benji began to cry.

"What about your children?" Aelbreth asked, breathlessly.

"My son and my two daughters did not join my wife and me," Madarach said. "My son, in fact, joined the rebels. He was killed in the war. We hadn't spoken in a dozen years. I have had a long time to regret that.

"My daughters did not choose sides," he continued. "They married and had children. They grew old and died. I have long ago lost track of their descendents, for they now number in the thousands."

"Thousands?" Aelbreth repeated.

"Yes," Madarach confirmed. "In six thousand years, they would have produced millions of offspring. But not all of them had children, and not all survived the sickness. Yes, there are thousands of men, women, and children who carry my genes."

"It must be very sad," Aelbreth said. "To have that much family, and yet you don't know them and they don't know you."

"Right now," Madarach said, "I have all the family I need. You and Benji and Lisa are my family. I don't know my descendants, and they would have no idea who I am. So you are the only family I have. Though it was good to speak to my wife after so much time alone."

"I bet," Benji agreed.

Then he thought.

"If I were in your position," he said, "and I could activate myself and take a vacation, I think I would visit her quite often. Have you visited your wife again, Madarach?"

Nothing happened for a moment.

Then Benji and Aelbreth felt waves of energy coming from him that were different from anything they had felt from him before. They felt joyous and uplifting. And they had almost a physical quality to them, as if the waves impacted their physical bodies.

Benji looked at Aelbreth in amazement.

"He's laughing!" Benji exclaimed.

"Yes," Madarach confirmed. "For you seek to know all my secrets, you clever young man. Let us say that certain things ought to remain private, shall we?"

Benji and Aelbreth laughed, now.

"Very well," Benji agreed. "I won't ask about your relationship with your wife."

They sat in silence for a long time. Eventually, Madarach spoke.

"We should go somewhere," he suggested. "Where would you like to go next?"

"Home," Aelbreth said, emphatically. "I've had enough traveling for now."

"Benji?" Madarach asked.

"Hadrun it is," Benji confirmed. "What time is it there?"

"It's the middle of the morning," Madarach replied. "We've been gone all night. Hopefully Aelbreth's parents won't be worried."

A few minutes later, they landed in the clearing near the village of Korby, and Benji and Aelbreth got out.

"Thank you, Madarach," Aelbreth said. "For keeping us safe, and for sharing your secrets with us."

"You are very welcome, young Aelbreth," Madarach replied.

Benji looked surprised. He'd always thought of Madarach as a machine, and it had never occurred to him to say thanks.

"Madarach," he said, "I didn't know until today that you are a person. It's going to take some getting used to."

"Don't worry," Madarach said. "I am still what I was. Nothing has changed but your understanding."

The two children walked slowly down the path. But Aelbreth stopped, took Benji's hand, and turned to face him.

"Some frightening things happened on our trip," she said, telepathically. "I don't ever want to lose you. Will you promise to be safe when you travel?"

"I'll be as safe as I can be," Benji said. "But eventually, I will have work to do."

"I know," Aelbreth replied. "But do it safely."

"I'll do my best," Benji agreed. "But it may not always be safe. You know what my dream is, right?"

"You want to end the war on Zeblack," Aelbreth said.

"Yes," he confirmed. "More than anything else I can think of, besides getting Lisa back."

"Even after they betrayed you?" she asked.

"Now more than ever," Benji replied. "My friends didn't betray me. One boy and his family did. And they did it for the war. I want that war to end, so that my friends don't have to grow up that way."

"Does it have to be dangerous?" Aelbreth asked. "Is there a way to end a war safely?"

"I don't know," Benji said, softly. "I really don't know. I've learned a lot about what causes war, but I've learned nothing about how to end one. And besides, I'm only twelve years old."

Aelbreth grinned.

"You're sixteen years old on Hadrun," she reminded him."

Chapter Seventeen

The day on Hadrun lasted just over fourteen Earth hours. Though they were shorter and filled with hard physical labor, they passed very slowly for Benji.

It wasn't that he disliked his time there. He enjoyed it as much as he could enjoy time anywhere while waiting to return for his sister. He worked hard with kids he knew and liked. He played hard with them when the chores were done. And he spent time alone with Aelbreth, kissing and enjoying the telepathic exchange of emotions. He had no complaints, apart from the waiting.

One night after dinner, he lay on a *patret* fur mattress on the dirt floor alongside Offsa and Aelbreth as usual, chatting with them.

"I've been thinking about that spider creature we almost met," Aelbreth said. "Something bothers me."

"What?" Benji asked. He'd almost forgotten about the encounter.

"It said that it had no problem with us," she recalled. "It said that the policy was that any other intelligent species must be destroyed, because their religion said they were the only one. But it also called that policy backward, so clearly it didn't agree."

"Yes," Benji agreed. "It seemed more enlightened than the rest of its kind."

"And yet it still wouldn't meet us," she observed. "I think it wanted to, but it put the archaic rules of its society above what it believed was the right thing to do. Why?"

Benji thought about this. The question intrigued him, because he'd seen his best friend on Earth, Timmy Reynolds, abandon him and join the crowd that claimed Benji and Lisa were witches. Timmy had even broken his vow of secrecy and told them about the well. Benji had never understood why Timmy had done that. And he wasn't sure if the same thing might have happened on Zeblack. As much as he wanted to believe that it was the new kid, Churl, who'd betrayed him, he couldn't be sure that his friends wouldn't put the faction above their friendship with Benji.

"I don't know," he told Aelbreth. "I think it's important to belong."

"But that creature was on another planet, in the wilderness by itself," Aelbreth pointed out. "No one would have ever known."

"Maybe they have telepathy," Offsa suggested.

"That's possible," Aelbreth said. "But none of us got that impression. They still use language."

Benji laughed.

"If you can call it a language," he joked.

"It seemed very sophisticated," Aelbreth said.

"It was," Benji agreed. "And you're right, people on Parisa, which is the only planet I've seen that has telepathy, gave up the ability to speak because they didn't need it anymore."

"So something caused that creature to stick to a belief it thought was wrong," Aelbreth summarized. "Even though no one would have ever known if it hadn't. Don't you find that interesting?"

"A little less interesting than the dreams I plan to have," Offsa interjected.

"You hope you'll dream about Elvina again," Aelbreth suggested.

Offsa fell silent, and Benji was certain he was blushing in the dark.

"Why not?" Benji said. "She's cute!"

"Cuter than me?" Aelbreth asked, with mock dismay.

"Maybe a little," Benji replied.

Aelbreth punched him in the ribs, playfully.

"I only meant that Offsa finds her cuter!" Benji protested. "I've barely noticed her at all!"

"Is that so?" Aelbreth taunted. "You're saying that Offsa finds her only a little cuter than he finds me?"

"Well, you *are* awfully cute," Benji pointed out.

Aelbreth snickered.

"Go to sleep," she said.

But Benji couldn't sleep for a long time. He was fascinated by the question Aelbreth had raised. Why do people, in the absence of supervision or coercion, follow a rule that they believe to be wrong instead of doing what they believe to be right?

In the morning, before chores, Benji sprinted to the clearing where Madarach waited.

"Is it time?" Madarach asked.

"No," Benji replied. "I wish it was. I have a question."

He explained what Aelbreth had observed about the arthropod creature, and how that related to Timmy Reynolds' betrayal.

"Why do people who are not being watched follow a rule that they believe to be wrong, instead of doing what they believe to be right?" Benji asked.

Madarach paused.

"That is a very large question," he observed. "I'll give you a short answer to think about now, and we can discuss it in depth another time."

"Okay," Benji agreed.

"The greatest social desire of most intelligent species is to be part of the largest group, where it's safest," Madarach said. "To be part of the group means to conform to their ways of thinking and doing. So that creature may have been alone, unobserved. But it would have been afraid, perhaps so deeply it was not even aware of that fear, that someone from its group might see what it did and report back to the larger group."

"I see," Benji said. "When I was on Earth, I desperately wanted to belong, but I never did."

"And how did that affect your experience of life?" Madarach asked.

"They made fun of me, and treated me like an outcast," Benji recalled, bitterly.

"So you can see why a person who is in the group would want to avoid being expelled at any cost," Madarach summarized.

"Hmm," Benji said, as he thought. "Does the belief being part of its religion make a difference?"

"Absolutely," Madarach replied. "Religion is literally 'that which binds us together.' It is a set of shared beliefs so powerful that in most instances, even questioning them sets you apart from the group. And because they cannot be questioned, their factual correctness, relevance, or morality can never be discussed. They are what the group believes, and to be part of the group you have to believe them, too."

"Wow," Benji said. "So religion is very powerful."

"It is," Madarach agreed. "Now go do your chores. We'll talk more about this another time."

Benji headed for the *patret* pen and picked up a rake. But he couldn't stop thinking about what Madarach had told him.

He recalled what he knew of religion in the history of Earth. The Crusades had been about religion. The wars in Ireland and Palestine had been about religion. He vaguely remembered that the English Civil War had been about religion. So religion was powerful enough to motivate people to fight and die for what seemed like very stupid reasons.

But at the same time, he recalled some very important people from Earth's history, people who had risked their lives to change things for the better, who had been motivated by religious beliefs. Jesus was the most obvious. And Mahatma Gandhi, who had brought independence to India. Bishop Desmond Tutu, who had worked for freedom in South Africa, had belonged to the Anglican Church. Dr. Martin Luther King, Jr, who had fought for equal rights in the United States, had been a Baptist minister. Former President Jimmy Carter, a Baptist, had worked for peace and human rights around the world. Sister Theresa, who fed the hungry in India, had been a Catholic nun, and Dorothy Day, who fed the hungry in the United States, had been Catholic, too. So religion could be a force for good as well as violence.

He wondered if the arthropod creatures would some day use religion to move beyond their prejudice against other intelligent species.

"Hey Benji," Offsa called, interrupting his thoughts. "You haven't said a word in hours. Are you still with us?"

Benji grinned, weakly.

"Just thinking," he said.

"Well, think faster," Offsa said, tossing a large *patret* dropping at him.

Benji dodged, and laughed.

"I can think faster than you," he said.

He picked up a pile of droppings with his rake and tossed them at Offsa.

Offsa dodged them, all but one. But another hit Aelbreth in the head. She spun around.

"Benji! You hit me with that!" she accused.

"Sorry," Benji said, his face reddening with embarrassment.

"No, I'm sorry," Aelbreth said, as she picked up a large dropping and threw it overhand at Benji. It hit him in the chest.

Now the other kids had stopped working and gathered around to watch the show.

"And you, too," Aelbreth said, throwing another dropping at Offsa. It missed him and hit another boy standing nearby.

Soon, they were all throwing manure at each other. Most of their pitches missed, but some didn't. By the time one of the men wandered by to see what the commotion was, most of the kids had stains on their clothes, droppings in their hair, and filthy hands. Some had obviously been hit in the face.

"What is this?" the man protested. "You're supposed to be cleaning the pens, not making them worse! Off to the canals, all of you. Wash your bodies and your clothes, and then get back to work!"

All the children did their best to look chastised. But as soon as the man was out of sight, Offsa and one of the other boys began to laugh. Soon they were all laughing as they walked single file along the path to the irrigation canal.

When they reached it, they all stripped off their clothes and jumped in.

Offsa put his hand on Benji's arm and gestured with his chin toward the girl named Elvina.

"See?" he said, telepathically. "She's the one who makes me feel weird."

Elvina was taller and slimmer than Aelbreth, but had the same long, amber hair. She also had curves that Benji couldn't stop looking at.

"I can see why!" he told Offsa. "She makes me feel weird, too!"

Why, he wondered, would he feel weird looking at Elvina when he loved Aelbreth and felt weird looking at her, too?

Elvina dove gracefully into the water, and Offsa and Benji looked at each other for a moment, commiserating.

"I'm not sure I like growing up," Benji said. "It's confusing."

Chapter Eighteen

It had been eight days since Benji and Aelbreth returned from their trip to Zeblack. To Benji, it seemed like a month. Each day seemed the same, and it was difficult to keep track of the passage of time. Perhaps, he thought, that's why on Hadrun they keep track of seasons and years rather than weeks.

With regular physical labor, Benji's body had grown stronger, and his muscles had developed. He no longer took as many breaks during the work day.

"You're working like one of us, now," Offsa commented.

Aelbreth seemed to like it, too. When they were alone, she often ran her hands over Benji's growing biceps and shoulders.

Aside from these slow changes, there was little to distinguish one day from another. They worked, they played, they ate, and they slept.

But Benji slept poorly. He woke often, having dreamed that Lisa had called him.

He would lie awake on his *patret* blanket, waiting for her voice in his head.

But it never came.

On this night, Benji woke again. He'd been dreaming that Lisa was calling, but he couldn't go to her because it was dark and the *fortule* were out.

Now he lay on the blanket, thinking of Lisa and wondering what the priestesses were doing to her.

"When will you call me?" he wondered.

"Benji?" he heard in his head. "Benji?"

The voice sounded weak and distant. But it was Lisa's.

Benji bolted upright.

"Lisa!" he replied, urgently. "Are you okay?"

"I think so," she said. "This is still very strange, but at least I can see and hear."

"I'm so glad," Benji replied.

"Benji," Lisa said, urgently. "Listen. This is important. Do not go to Zeblack. They will try to trick you. Do you understand?"

"Lisa," he replied, "I already went to Zeblack. They tried to trick me, but I'm okay. We got away."

"It already happened?" she asked. "This is so confusing."

"What is?" Benji asked.

"I need to rest some more," she said. "But you can come here now. I miss you."

Then she was gone.

Now Benji stood. Lisa was ready to see him!

But he couldn't go yet, because it was dark and the *fortule* were on the prowl.

Just like his dream.

He wanted to pace, but there wasn't space in the tiny room with Offsa and Aelbreth sleeping there.

He sat back down. He desperately wanted to leave immediately, but he couldn't. He couldn't go anywhere.

He wondered how many hours of darkness remained. There were no clocks in the village, so there was no way to tell time at night, without the sun.

Benji tried to figure it out in his head. The night was about seven hours long, and they had eaten at sunset and then talked for a while.

How long had they talked? An hour? Two? He didn't know.

How long had he slept? One hour, or four? He didn't know.

He sat in the darkness, alone, in what seemed like the longest night of his life.

A very long time later, or so it seemed, the first light of dawn leaked in around the window shutters.

"It won't be much longer," he told himself.

Still, it seemed like hours before Aedred rose and began making breakfast.

Benji joined her in the kitchen.

"It's time for me to go to Lisa," he said.

"You heard from her?" Aedred asked.

"Yes," Benji confirmed. "In the middle of the night. She said I could come right away."

Aedred considered this.

"You've been awake most of the night?" she asked. "Oh, my poor dear. The night can be very long, can't it."

"It can," Benji agreed.

"It will be safe to travel soon," she said. "But wait a moment and I'll have some food for you to break your fast before you travel."

"Thank you," Benji replied.

"Will you take Aelbreth this time?" she asked.

Benji considered this.

"I've thought a lot about it," he admitted. "I love Aelbreth, and I enjoy it when she's with me. But I think I need to be alone with Lisa right now."

Besides, he thought to himself, it would be ironic if they had a prophecy on Hassyr about his girlfriend as well as his sister! He didn't want to put Aelbreth in danger.

Aedred nodded.

"Fennel will be pleased," she observed. "He accepts your journeys, but always worries."

"And you?" he asked Aedred. "Do you worry?"

"Not much," Aedred replied. "The *fortule* is dangerous, but not if we take care to avoid it. I trust you, Benji, and I trust my daughter in your hands."

Benji recalled the treachery on Zeblack, in which they would not have escaped except for Madarach's secret weapon, and he felt guilty.

"I will try to be worthy of your trust," he said.

"I know," she replied. "Now go wake Aelbreth and say goodbye. I'll have some bread and milk ready for you in a moment.

Benji went to Aelbreth and shook her shoulder,

"What?" she asked, sleepily.

"I'm leaving to go get Lisa," he replied.

"Leaving?" she asked. "Now?"

"As soon as I've eaten," he said.

Aelbreth shook her head to clear the sleepiness.

"When will you be back?" she asked.

"I don't know," Benji told her.

"Okay," she said. "It's just that I miss you."

"I haven't even left yet," Benji replied, testily.

"I know," she said. "Benji, what's wrong?"

Benji didn't know what was wrong. He missed Lisa, and he couldn't wait to see her. And for some reason, Aelbreth was annoying him.

"Nothing's wrong," he said. "I just need to leave."

"Okay," Aelbreth said. "I didn't mean to make you angry."

"I'm not angry!" Benji snapped.

Aelbreth gazed at him for a moment.

"Okay," she said. "Go and get Lisa. I'll miss you."

Benji huffed.

"We've been together every moment for days," he replied. "It will be good to spend some time apart."

Benji's voice sounded harsh even to him, but he felt as though he couldn't control it. He watched in shock as his body and mouth behaved without his consent, almost like he was watching someone else.

"Are you mad at me?" Aelbreth wondered.

"No, I'm not mad," he snapped. "I just need to be alone."

"For how long?" she asked.

"I don't know," he replied. "I'll be back when I come back."

Then he turned and stalked to the kitchen.

Aedred, who couldn't avoid hearing their exchange in such a small house, gave Benji a questioning look.

He ignored it.

"Thank you for breakfast, Mother," he said, as he began eating *ustro* bread.

Aelbreth, wisely, chose to let him eat alone.

When Benji finished, he returned to the living room, where Offsa was now awake.

"I'll see you soon," he told Benji.

"I guess," Benji said, as he turned toward the door.

"Wait," Aelbreth said.

She ran to him and took his hand. She said nothing, but Benji could hear her thoughts.

"I know you miss Lisa," she thought. "If I angered you, I'm sorry. Just know that I love you, and I'll be waiting for your return, no matter how long that may take."

Benji didn't reply. He stalked out the door and headed for the clearing.

"Women!" he said to Madarach, when he had entered the bubble.

"Indeed," Madarach said. "They are infuriating and captivating. What did she do?"

Benji thought for a moment.

"I don't even know," he replied. "I think I just spent too much time with her, and now it's time to go."

"And where are we going?" Madarach asked.

"Hassyr," Benji replied. "Lisa contacted me last night. She's better now."

"Hassyr it is," Madarach said. "As you can imagine, it's a destination I rather enjoy."

"Because your wife is there," Benji guessed.

Madarach didn't answer.

"What's your wife's name?" Benji asked.

"In life, she was called Jael," Madarach replied. "But our names were taken from us along with our bodies."

Benji thought about this. He realized that Madarach was not his real name. He had told Benji once that the word meant "teacher."

"And what was yours?" Benji asked him.

Madarach did not answer as they lifted off the ground and began to shift through the stars. Only as they approached Hassyr did he reply.

"I was called Zebul," he said. "But that was in a different life. I have not heard that name spoken in so long that it no longer seems to belong to me. Please, continue to call me Madarach."

"I will," Benji assured him.

Madarach set Benji down near the well.

"Call me when you need me," he said.

Chapter Nineteen

Benji glanced around the clearing, located the path, and headed for the cave temple. As he reached the cliff top open area, he began to run, and was out of breath by the time he reached the temple.

He entered, trying to walk more respectfully than the last time. But his excitement overcame him, and he sprinted toward the altar.

The same young woman swept the floor, stopping as Benji approached. She gazed at Benji, and then nodded.

"I will call the priestess," she told him.

She put down her broom and headed deeper into the cave.

Benji couldn't stand still, his anticipation was so strong. He shuffled his feet, and then walked in circles. In desperation, he finally picked up the broom and began to sweep.

"You do women's work?" asked a gravelly, old voice behind him.

He turned, and found himself facing the priestess.

"I do whatever work I find," he replied. "Where is Lisa?"

"Come," she said, beckoning. "She awaits."

The old woman led Benji back into the cave and down a narrow passageway lit with torches. Benji noticed rooms on either side of the corridor. Instead of doors, the entrances were covered with blankets of what appeared to be burlap. Some had their coverings pulled aside, and Benji could see that the rooms contained a simple bed, a wooden table, and two primitive chairs.

Eventually, the priestess stopped before a covered door.

"She awaits," she repeated, gesturing for Benji to enter.

Benji pushed the blanket aside and walked into the room. It was furnished like the others he'd seen, and lit with torches.

On the bed sat Lisa, paler than Benji remembered, and looking very tired.

"Lisa!" Benji shouted, and ran to her.

"Benji," she replied, smiling weakly. "I am so glad to see you!"

"Are you okay?" he asked. "You look tired."

"I'm fine," Lisa said. "But it was very difficult. And I'm still not used to it."

"Used to what?" Benji asked.

"The noise, and the colors," Lisa replied. "That old man awakened something in me, and now I can see much more than I'm used to. A lot of it doesn't make any sense. And there's no sense of time, so I can't tell right now whether what I'm seeing is past, present, or future."

"The gift of clairvoyance?" Benji suggested.

"More or less," Lisa agreed. "Except that means literally 'clear sight,' and what I have is not always the future, and it's rarely clear."

Benji nodded. He didn't really understand, but he'd heard enough to realize he wasn't going to comprehend what she saw any time soon.

"Are you ready to go?" Benji asked.

"Yes," Lisa replied. "But we need to wait for the priestess. No one is supposed to wander the halls alone, unless you're a member of the temple."

Benji nodded.

"How did you know I was in danger on Zeblack?" he asked.

"I don't know," she replied. "I just knew. I think it's like what you experience with languages. It just came to me, with no apparent reason."

Benji nodded.

"Have you seen Quanda and Queelie?" he asked.

"No," she replied. "I haven't seen anyone except the priestess and the woman who brought me broth and bread."

"Broth and bread?' Benji asked. "For a whole month?"

Lisa grinned.

"That's all I could eat when I first came out of it," she explained. "You have no idea what I'd give for a cheeseburger right now!"

Just then, the priestess entered the room.

"You find her well, I trust?" she asked Benji, gesturing at Lisa.

"Much improved," Benji agreed. "She says she's still seeing the colors and hearing the noise. How long will that last?"

The priestess laughed.

"*Farchedan!*" she said, with a cackle. "So long as the dance lasts."

Benji thought about this. Were the noise and colors part of the Gift of Clairvoyance, so that Lisa would never be without them?

"That is so," said a voice in his head.

Benji's eyes widened. The voice belonged to the priestess.

"She gave me her gift," the priestess explained. "I did not take it from her. She examined my mind, and chose to fulfill the prophesy."

"Lisa?" Benji asked.

"It's true," Lisa confirmed. "This woman has one of the kindest hearts I have ever met. If anyone on Hassyr was to have my gift, I wanted it to be her."

"And what will you do with it?" Benji asked the old woman.

"I follow the dance," the priestess replied. "It will tell me."

Benji nodded.

"What of the old man, the snake priest?" he asked. "He wants the gift."

"That he does," the old woman agreed. "But he shall not have it. What little conflict we have on this planet is disguised as religion. The priest is blinded by lust for power. From what Lisa has told me of your new home, the gift and peacefulness go hand in hand. Which precedes the other, I do not yet know. I will watch the dance and see where it leads. My hope is that *farchedan* will yet bring us peace.

"But for now," she said, "I imagine you want to bid us goodbye. It has been a long time since you two had your connection."

"It has," Benji agreed. "I missed her terribly."

The old woman smiled.

"You love deeply, for a man," she said again. "Your heart is strong. Use it well. There is much good you can do in the world."

Then she turned toward the door.

"Come," she instructed. "You may take your leave."

They followed her back down the long corridor to the temple cavern.

"Wait," the priestess said. "Young man, you came here accompanied by your teacher. Would that I might meet him."

"My teacher?" Benji repeated.

"An old soul, he is," she added. "It is right that we should speak a few words."

Benji glanced at Lisa, who shrugged.

"My teacher is not in human form," Benji told her.

"Wisdom is found where it lies," she replied. "You can call to him, can you not?"

"I can," Benji agreed.

Then he thought of Churl and Chute, and their attempt to steal Madarach. How could he be sure this priestess wouldn't do the same?

"It's safe," Lisa assured him, telepathically. "This woman has no desire to steal him."

Benji gazed at Lisa, then at the old woman.

"Okay," he said. "I'll ask him to meet us outside."

They made their way to cave's entrance, and found Madarach waiting there.

"I think you will need to communicate through me," Benji said.

The priestess nodded.

"The dance is the means," she said.

This struck Benji as odd. She had once spoken as if Lisa was the spirit of life. Now she seemed to be suggesting that Benji was the dance.

For a long while, the old woman said nothing. She just stood, as if in thought.

"You are wise," she said, finally. "Wisdom born not only of age, but of experience. Your mistakes have been painful."

Benji wasn't sure to whom she was speaking, but she gestured for him to relay her words to Madarach.

Benji did.

"I have made mistakes," Madarach replied. "I carry their cost. But all who live long choose badly at times."

"What you did, you did for love," the old woman said. "Though it looked not like love at the end."

Benji felt Madarach sigh, sadly.

"You have lost much," the priestess continued. "Yet you have gained much. You have survived longer than a person can imagine, seen much, and known much. You are nearly immortal. But tell, me, if you would, if you could return to human form, would you do so?"

Madarach said nothing for a long moment.

"This life I have today is satisfying," he replied, finally. "I have grown to love these children. But there is one I love above all others. If I could be with her in human form, or any other, I would choose that form."

The priestess nodded.

"You, too, love deeply for a man," she observed. "It is well that you are this one's teacher, for his guidance should not come from one who loves less deeply than he. Care for him, nurture him. It may be that he shall do that which cannot be done."

"Thank you," Madarach said. "It is an excellent task."

"And you," she said to Benji, "shall nurture your heart. For it is the heart that accomplishes what is truly worthwhile. You are welcome here any time. It may be that you have something to learn from us."

"Thank you," Benji said.

"Now go," the old woman said. "The young woman desires food, and it must be something that comforts her. The spirit of life is the source."

They all thanked her, and Benji helped Lisa aboard Madarach.

"Shall we go?" Benji asked.

"Not yet," Madarach said. "I have a surprise for you."

He lifted off the ground slightly, and took them to the clearing where the well stood. From the bubble, Benji could see Quanda and Queelie leaning against the well.

"There they are!" he exclaimed. "I wondered how we'd ever find them."

Chapter Twenty

B enji!" Quanda shouted.

"Lisa!" shouted Queelie. "We were so worried about you."

Benji and Lisa had exited the bubble, and now the four friends hugged each other.

"We went to Parisa to see you," Quanda explained. "But the priest said you'd both gone to Earth to get Lisa some help."

"We didn't know how to find you there, so we came back here," Queelie added. "We were quite surprised to learn you were here already!"

"Madarach told you?" Benji suggested.

"No," Queelie corrected. "Jael did. That's the name of our bubble. You know, until I heard you call your bubble Madarach, it never occurred to me that ours might have a name."

Benji smiled. He now knew that Madarach had far more than a name. He had consciousness as well. But he couldn't tell Queelie that.

Yet, as he thought it, he felt Lisa tense., and he saw that she was looking at him strangely.

"Later," he said, telepathically.

"Why did you bring Lisa here?" Quanda asked.

"I thought maybe the priestess could help her," Benji explained.

"Did she?" Queelie asked.

"Yes," Lisa replied. "She is a kind, generous, and amazing woman."

"What happened?" Quanda asked. "How did you get sick?"

"When that old priest touched me," Lisa explained, "he gave me the gift of clairvoyance. But my mind couldn't understand what it saw. I got lost."

"You have the Gift?" Queelie asked, enviously.

Lisa chuckled, sadly.

"It's not a lot of fun," she said. "I still have trouble understanding what I see."

"You'll get used to it," Quanda said.

"But there's just so much, all at once," Lisa added. "Colors and sounds and images. It's too much to comprehend."

Quanda thought about that.

"You've got it really strong," he said, his voice serious. "I've never met anyone who had it like that."

"I always said you were special," Queelie said.

"I don't feel very special right now," Lisa replied. "Just exhausted."

No one had anything to say to that, and they fell silent for a long moment.

"We were just going to get Lisa something to eat," Benji said, finally. "Why don't you come with us?"

"Where are you going?" Quanda asked.

Benji glanced at Lisa.

"She wants a cheeseburger," he said. "And I only know one planet where we can find one. We're going to Earth."

"Oh, yes!" Queelie squealed. "Can we come?"

Soon all four of them were in the bubble, and Benji gave Madarach instructions. They shifted through the stars, and then approached the planet Benji and Lisa both recognized as their original home. They watched as the bubble approached North America, and then the region east of the Great Lakes. There were no state lines visible, of course, but Benji knew they were headed to a place between the St. Lawrence River and Long Island.

Madarach set them down in a deserted alley in Manchester, where Benji's family had lived before they moved to the small town, and they all got out.

"Follow me," Benji said.

He led them to a busy street, and halfway down the block. There they found a small restaurant with a sign that promised the best burgers in New England.

"What's a burger?" Quanda asked.

"It's ground meat, cooked over an open fire and served on round bread," Benji explained.

Queelie made a sour face.

"Trust me," Benji continued. "There's no way to describe it that explains how good it tastes!"

They entered the restaurant and perused the menu, which listed a dozen or so variations on the basic burger, as well as chicken sandwiches, grilled cheese, a list of side orders, and sodas and shakes. Benji could smell the burgers cooking, and felt his mouth start watering.

"I want the cheeseburger with mushrooms," Lisa announced.

"Me, too," Benji agreed.

"I guess we'll try that, too," Quanda said.

"And some onion rings and French fries," Lisa added. "I'm starving!"

"And a milk shake," Benji added. "Chocolate."

Lisa glanced at Quanda and Queelie.

"Better make that four," she said.

It was the middle of the afternoon, so the restaurant wasn't busy. They took a table in the corner, away from the handful of customers already eating.

"Will they notice we're speaking a different language?" Quanda wondered.

"I doubt it," Lisa replied. "They're all thinking about their own problems. But if anyone asks, we'll tell them you're friends from Europe. The Czech Republic, maybe. No one here will know what the Czech language sounds like."

"Besides," Benji added, "there are a lot of immigrants here, and they speak a lot of different languages. They're more likely to notice your blue skin, but we can tell them it's a style of make up where you come from."

They chatted until the waitress brought their burgers.

"This smells amazing," Quanda commented, as Queelie lifted the top of the bun to inspect the inside.

"It's better than amazing," Benji suggested, "It's *farchedan!*"

They all laughed at that.

All four children were getting ready for their first bite when Lisa, who was facing the door, squealed.

"Mom!" she cried. "Dad! You came!"

Benji looked up to see his parents crossing the room toward them.

"Of course we came," Mom said. "I got Lisa's message. We weren't going to miss a chance to see the two of you. Who are your friends?"

Benji did the introductions, and told his parents about Hassyr. He decided not to mention what had happened to Lisa, and Lisa didn't mention it either.

"Do you want a burger?" Lisa asked their parents.

"We've already had lunch," Dad said. "If it's alright, we'll just sit with you."

"That's fine, Dad," Benji agreed.

He looked his parents over carefully. Mom looked older, and tired. Dad looked happy, though he still bore the scars he'd gotten when their house burned down. Benji still couldn't get used to the shiny swath of skin that ran from Dad's left ear, down his cheek and neck, and under his shirt.

Benji cringed. His dad's scars were a potent reminder of why he and Lisa no longer lived on Earth.

"So tell us what you've been up to," Mom suggested.

They talked about the places they'd visited, and school, and Jachin and Tamar and their family. Benji told them about Aelbreth and her family. Then, with Benji translating, they talked about Quanda and Queelie's family, and how life was on their planet. Then they talked about burgers, fries, and milk shakes, which Quanda and Queelie agreed were delicious.

"What about you, Dad?" Benji asked. "How are you doing?"

"I'm fine," Richard Haight replied. "I found a new job. It doesn't pay much, but I enjoy doing it."

"That's wonderful, Dad," Lisa said. "What are you doing?"

"Driving a bus," he replied. "I get to spend my whole day out with people, seeing what's going on."

Benji smiled, but inside he thought how difficult that must be for his dad. Before the fire, Dad had worked in the Governor's office at the State House. Now he was driving a bus.

Mom chattered about their new house, which was smaller than the old one, she said, but very cute and easier to keep clean. She played cards with her neighbors, and worked part time at a convenience store. They were, she insisted, very happy, though they missed their children.

Benji felt sadness creeping into his heart. Mom had never had to work before. All these changes, Dad taking a menial job, Mom working, a smaller house, all this happened because of the fire, and the fire had happened because Benji and Lisa's gifts became known.

"It's not our fault," Lisa said to him, telepathically. "We didn't do this. The Thompsons did with their witch hunt. It was ignorance and bigotry, not us."

"It *was* because of us," Benji insisted.

"No, it wasn't," Lisa insisted. "We were just being ourselves."

Benji nodded.

"Mom, Dad," he said, "I miss you so much. I'm sorry we have to live on another planet."

"We miss you, too," Mom said, answering for them both.

Dad just nodded.

Chapter Twenty-One

They chatted for hours. Finally, Dad said they had to go. "Today I have to work at five o'clock," he explained. "But I'm glad we got to see you. You're both growing up so fast, and becoming remarkable people."

"Take your friends someplace special before you leave," Mom suggested. "It will still be light at the Grand Canyon for a couple of hours after it gets dark here."

"That's a great idea," Benji agreed. "Let's take them sightseeing!"

They left the restaurant and returned to the alley where Madarach waited.

"Let's see a couple of things before we return to Hassyr," Benji told them. "The Grand Canyon, obviously. Then, maybe the Himalayas. Let's see how they compare with the mountains on Hassyr."

"And the pyramids," Lisa cut in. "From the pictures I've seen, those are pretty spectacular, too."

Neither Benji nor Lisa had actually seen any of these in real life, only in photographs. Both were at least as excited as their friends to see these wonders up close.

Madarach didn't ascend through the atmosphere. Instead, he took them cross country, a few thousand feet off the ground. He couldn't shift in the atmosphere, but he could travel very fast, and they got there in fifteen minutes. Quanda and Queelie gawked at the vast plains of open space they flew over.

"There's nothing like this on Hassyr!" Queelie exclaimed. "I've never seen so much space!"

"This is called the Midwest," Lisa explained. "It's mostly agricultural land. They grow a lot of corn and wheat. Those are the grains we eat," she added, to Quanda's mystified glance.

They crossed the snow-capped Rocky Mountains, which Quanda and Queelie agreed were not quite as big as the ones on Hassyr, but were much more beautiful. Then they crossed the high desert and the Grand Canyon came into view.

Queelie gasped when she saw it, but said nothing.

Madarach started by descending slowly into the canyon and suspending them between its walls. The view was astounding, far better than the photos Benji had seen. People had told him that photographs could never really show its beauty, and now he understood. It was too big to fit in a photo. And now they were literally floating inside it!

"This is amazing," Queelie exclaimed. "It's really natural? Your people didn't somehow carve this?"

"It's all nature," Benji assured her. "That little river down there did it over millions of years."

They hung there for a long time, awed at the beauty nature had created.

Then Madarach began to move again, and in a few moments they approached the Himalayas.

They flew along a river lined with bright green rice paddies. As the altitude increased, the river ran at the bottom of a deep canyon. Rice paddies terraced the hills, with deep forest surrounding them on the steeper slopes. Tiny villages of mud huts dotted the more level areas, though one or two villages seemed to hang out over the river, defying gravity.

"Those fields are amazing!" Queelie said. "What do they grow?"

"It's called rice," Lisa explained. "And what's really amazing is, it has to be underwater to sprout, so all these paddies are connected to a stream. They flood them in the spring."

"All the way up here on the hillsides?" Quanda marveled. "That *is* amazing."

Then the mountains came into view, towering majestically over the foothills. Benji had seen photos of the Himalayas, but again, nothing compared to the real thing.

Madarach rose above the mountains, and they crossed a maze of sharp ridges and rocky peaks, all covered with snow. Benji had never seen the Himalayas from above, and the view was amazing.

"These are the highest mountains on the planet," Lisa told them. "The tallest is Mount Everest, which is over 8,800 meters high."

"It's beautiful!" Queelie said. "A few of our mountains are taller, but they aren't nearly as striking. And the snow!"

"Ours are smoother," Quanda added. "These sharp ridges are amazing. I can't imagine anyone trying to climb these."

"People do it," Lisa said. "But they need oxygen. Over 8,000 meters, there's not enough oxygen to breathe."

"I bet it's dangerous," Quanda said.

"It is," Lisa agreed. "Over a hundred people have died trying to make the climb."

"Then why do they do it?" Queelie asked.

"Because sometimes you have to challenge yourself," Benji said. "I can't imagine climbing Everest, but I can imagine doing something dangerous if it was important enough."

They hovered over the mountains, exploring harsh valleys and rugged terrain, for almost an hour.

"What time is it in Egypt?" Lisa wondered.

Benji consulted Madarach.

"We'll get there just about sunrise," he relayed.

"Perfect!" Lisa said. "There are so many things I want to see on Earth, but the pyramids are high on my list. Shall we go?"

They crossed mountains and deserts, and came into Egypt from the north. The city of Giza was more modern than Benji expected. He'd had images in his mind of camels and vast tracts of mud huts, but the buildings were mostly modern. There were even a few skyscrapers.

They could see the pyramids long before they passed over the city, the sun just rising behind them.

"Those are amazing," Queelie squealed. "How old are they?"

"About 5,000 years," Lisa said. "I did a report on them for school. The big one is called the Great Pyramid. It was the tomb of one of the pharaohs, the kings of ancient Egypt. It was originally 481 feet tall, and was the tallest structure on Earth for almost 4,000 years. They built them with no machines, no pulleys, and no winches."

"How?" Quanda asked.

"No one knows," Lisa replied. "Those are 80 ton blocks of granite that came from 800 kilometers away."

"How many miles is that?" Benji asked.

"About 500," Lisa said.

"Wow!" Benji exclaimed. "With no machines to move them with?"

"But this is even better," Lisa said. "The Great Pyramid is aligned with True North, not Magnetic North. How did they know where the North Pole is?"

They gawked at the ancient structures, the Great Pyramid and its two smaller copies.

"What's that over there?" Queelie asked. "It looks like a statue of some kind of animal."

"It's a sphinx," Lisa explained. "It's the body of a lion, with the head of one of the Pharaohs. It was built almost 5,000 years ago."

"It's huge!" Quanda exclaimed.

"It is," Lisa agreed. "It's 74 meters long and 20 meters high."

"What happened to it's nose?" Queelie asked. "Didn't it have one?"

"I think I read that it was shot off with a cannon by Napoleon's troops," Benji said, proud of his knowledge.

"Who was Napoleon?" Quanda asked.

"He was an emperor in France who tried to take over Europe in the early 1800s," Benji said.

"And his troops shot off the statue's nose with a cannon?" Queelie asked. "That seems rude."

"That's a popular myth," Lisa corrected. "But its nose has been missing for 600 years, long before Napoleon. They think a Muslim leader had it removed to punish the locals for worshipping the statue."

"That seems rude, too," Quanda suggested.

"Apparently the Egyptian Caliph thought so too," Lisa continued. "The man who ordered the nose removed was executed for it."

"Hey look!" Benji exclaimed, looking out over the pyramid complex toward the city, where a very modern strip mall faced the ancient ruins. "There's a Pizza Hut! Anyone hungry?"

Lisa looked.

"An American restaurant chain at the edge of a 5,000 year old archeological site?" she observed. "That almost spoils the experience. Besides, I'm still full from lunch."

"Me, too," Queelie agreed.

"Where else should we go?" Quanda asked. "These are great, but I think we've seen as much as we're going to."

"How about a waterfall?" Benji suggested. "What's the highest waterfall on Earth?"

"I don't know," Lisa admitted. "Ask Madarach."

Benji did, and relayed the reply.

"It's Angel Falls in Venezuela," he said. "They're 979 meters tall." He quickly converted that to feet for himself and Lisa. "That's over 3,000 feet! But it's just after midnight there. We won't be able to see anything."

"I've heard there are some beautiful waterfalls in Iceland," Lisa suggested.

"Madarach says it won't be light there for a couple of hours," Benji relayed. "We're pretty much limited to Eastern Europe, Eastern Africa, and Asia. He suggests Victoria Falls, which are considered the largest falls by flow rate. They're in Zimbabwe, in the same time zone as Egypt."

"Sounds good to me," Quanda said.

Queelie and Lisa both nodded.

Madarach took them high enough to not be seen from the ground, but beneath a layer of high clouds so they could see the scenery. They followed the Nile River south through vast stretches of desert, until it gradually became greener and wetter. In places, they saw small villages packed in on small areas of high ground, surrounded by water and greenery.

"Your planet is so diverse!" Queelie marveled. "Ours is mountains, plains, or water. Yours has more variation than I've ever seen!"

"It is beautiful," Lisa agreed. "Especially when you're traveling like this."

They passed over a series of huge lakes, all tall and narrow.

"Those are fresh water?" Quanda asked, amazed.

"I guess so," Lisa said. "They're along the river."

Eventually, they passed over a range of rugged mountains. Then Madarach descended over what appeared to be a vast lake with a lot of swampland around it. He moved slowly south.

"Where are the falls?" Benji wondered.

As they came closer to the southern end of the lake, Queelie gasped.

"The lake!" she exclaimed. "It just ends! There's no edge in that direction."

They all looked. Sure enough, the lake disappeared as if into the end of the world.

They could hear and feel the falls before they saw them. Then they came to the edge, and Madarach dropped them into the spray. All four children gaped in awe at the sight. Water dropped more than 35 stories into a huge gorge. Yet the drop was dwarfed by its length, which was more than a mile long. Massive amounts of water flowed over the edge and into the chasm, where it flowed through a relatively small gap on the opposite side from the falls.

Madarach rose again, until they could see that several long canyons channeled the water nearly a mile west, and then back east again.

"*Farchedan!*" Queelie exclaimed. "It's like the dance!"

They hung there for a long time, soaking in the incredible beauty.

Finally, Quanda spoke.

"We should get back," he said. "Our mother wasn't expecting us to be gone long. This trip was a surprise to us, and it will be to her as well."

"But I want to come back," Queelie added. "I bet we haven't seen a fraction of the beauty of this planet."

"No," Lisa said. "Not even a tiny fraction. I miss it. But Parisa is safer for us."

Chapter Twenty-Two

They landed next to the well on Hassyr and exited the bubble, but they continued to chat in amazement about what they had seen, as if the two sets of siblings could not be parted.

"We have to get home," Quanda said, finally. "Mom will be worried."

Queelie sighed.

"I guess we've kept her waiting long enough," she agreed. "But Benji and Lisa don't know how to find us. Why don't we invite them home for dinner, so they can see our house?"

Benji glanced at Lisa, and heard her voice in his head.

"We'd love to," Benji said, "but Lisa has just recovered from her illness, and we need to get her some rest. You'll have to find us on Parisa. I think we'll be there for a while."

Queelie looked disappointed.

"Can Nahum contact you," she asked, "if we go to the temple?"

"Yes," Benji said. "And I go to the temple almost every day when I'm home."

It occurred to Benji that Parisa really was his home now, and that made him feel sad. He missed his parents, and he missed Earth culture, and he missed cheeseburgers. But it wasn't safe for them on Earth, and he couldn't stand Hadrun for any length of time, so Parisa was his home.

Lisa gave him a sharp glance, but said nothing until they had said their goodbyes and climbed back aboard Madarach.

"What's going on with you and Aelbreth?" she asked.

"What makes you think there's something going on?" Benji asked back, trying to deflect the conversation.

Now Lisa fixed him with a steady gaze.

"Really?" she asked. "Has it been so long you forget how well I know you?"

Benji sighed.

"I don't know what's going on," he replied. "I don't think it's her. It's me. And it's like my mouth has a life of its own, beyond my control. Sometimes I don't know who I am."

Lisa nodded.

"And talking to Tobin or Jachin won't help," she said. "Parisans are so controlled that they don't go through it like Earthlings do. Have you talked to Offsa?"

"Yes," Benji replied. "But he doesn't understand this any better than I do."

"You should talk to Dad," she suggested. "Next time we go to Earth, pull him aside, and you two have a conversation."

Benji huffed.

"*Awkward!*" he pronounced.

"If we lived with him," Lisa said, "he would have talked with you already. But we don't. And who else is there?"

"Fennel offered to talk to me," Benji said. "But it's his daughter I'm mad at."

Lisa considered this.

"I think," she replied, "that Fennel will talk with you because you are both men. The bond between men is strong, even if it *is* his daughter that's causing you the problem."

"Maybe," Benji allowed. "But he still sees her as his little wandering heart."

"Trust me," Lisa insisted. "He'll talk to you."

They landed on Parisa next to the ancient well. The sun had already dropped low in the sky, and shadows shrouded the path to the street.

"I know we should hurry," Lisa said. "Tamar won't know to expect us. But I am so tired!"

"It will be fine," Benji assured her. "They'll all be glad to see you, no matter what time we get there. Especially Tobin."

Lisa smiled.

"I've missed him," she said, sadly. "But I've missed you more."

They arrived at their adopted home as dusk was growing. The family had just sat down to dinner. But, as Benji predicted, they were overjoyed to see Benji and Lisa return. Tamar jumped up and made them both plates of food. Tobin jumped up and hugged Lisa.

"We were so worried," Miriam said, putting her hand on Benji so he could be part of the conversation. "They helped you on Earth?"

"We ended up going back to Hassyr," Benji explained

He told the story from his perspective.

"You took her back to the planet that made her sick?" Tobin exclaimed. "Why would you do that?"

"'If you lost your purse at the water, don't look for it in the hills,'" Benji quoted.

"What does that mean?" Tobin asked, accusingly.

Jachin, however, nodded.

"That is an old proverb," he said. "There is much truth to it. Tell Tobin how it applies."

"Earth medicine is primitive," Benji said. "I was afraid they'd make it worse. But the priestess seemed to know something about this, so I took a chance."

"A big chance," Tobin clarified.

"But he was right," Lisa pointed out. "The priestess was able to help me."

"We're just glad to see you back and doing well, honey," Tamar said. "But you look like you need rest. Let's eat, everyone, so Lisa can rest."

They finished dinner with little more conversation. Then Miriam and Tobin helped clear the table and do the dishes while Benji and Lisa sat at the table with Jachin.

"Benji," Jachin said, "you are becoming wise. It is good to see."

Benji blushed.

"It was Madarach's idea," he admitted.

"We are all grateful that you two have Madarach to watch over you," Jachin said.

After dinner, Lisa and Tobin sat outside for a long time, leaving Benji alone with his thoughts. Benji often enjoyed time alone, but at the moment his thoughts confused him, and he wished to be anything but alone.

He thought about Aelbreth. How had the cute little girl he'd known for two years grown into such a complicated and confusing person? How could Benji, who understood languages and had friends on a dozen worlds, who called three different planets home, be so unable to understand their new relationship? The intricacies of male-female interaction confused him and made him feel stupid, and Benji didn't like that at all. No wonder he'd been so angry with her when he left. He didn't understand what was going on, and for a smart kid that was intolerable. It made him feel like he was riding the bus to school with the other kids teasing him for no apparent reason.

It made him feel alone. And if he was going to feel alone, he might as well *be* alone.

On the other hand, the feeling he had when he and Aelbreth connected was beyond anything imaginable, and he didn't want to give that up.

Was it worth the price of feeling like an idiot much of the time?

He wasn't sure.

Benji thought about his friends on Zeblack, and his betrayal by Churl and his brother. That angered him. Friends were supposed to stand by you. But they didn't. Timmy Reynolds hadn't, and the kids on Zeblack hadn't either.

That wasn't quite true. Benji didn't know whether they were even aware of Churl's plot. And he couldn't go back to find out, because he didn't know whom he could trust.

That seemed to be a recurring theme. He didn't know who to trust with his feelings. He didn't know who he could trust as a friend. Did he even have any friends?

There was Offsa, of course. He trusted Offsa like he'd trust his own brother.

And maybe Quanda and Queelie.

And Madarach. Madarach, he realized, was probably his closest friend of all.

His best friend was a machine! It couldn't play games, or fantasize about the future, or even talk about girls.

Except Madarach wasn't really a machine. He was a person with a machine for a body.

And Benji knew he could trust Madarach absolutely.

Finally, Tobin came back in the house. He looked relieved.

He approached Benji, and put his hand on Benji's shoulder.

"She wants to talk with you for a minute," he said.

"Thanks," Benji replied.

He sprinted for the door, stepping outside and finding Lisa in the garden in front of the house.

"How are you feeling?" he asked her.

"It's good to be home," she replied. "But I am so tired!"

"You should rest," Benji said. "Let me walk you inside."

"Wait," Lisa protested. "Tell me about Madarach."

"What about him?" Benji replied.

Lisa sighed.

"I'm too tired to have you mess with me," she said. "On Hassyr, I heard you thinking about a secret he has. Tell me."

"Okay," Benji agreed. "But you can't tell anyone else, ever. Not even Tobin."

Lisa hesitated.

"Okay," she said. "It must be really big."

"He's a person," Benji explained. He told her the story about how Madarach had once been a teacher, and his part in the war, and his punishment and transfer to the bubble.

When he finished, Lisa didn't say anything for a long time. When she did speak, her voice was tired.

"I guess I'm going to have to think about that for a while," she said. "But not tonight."

"Let's get you inside so you can rest," Benji said again.

"Wait," Lisa said. "I have something to tell you."

"Okay," Benji agreed, feeling a little apprehensive. He wondered what could be so important.

"Dorn," she said.

Dorn was the name of one of Benji's best friends on Zeblack. But without a verb or some kind of context, Lisa's pronouncement made no sense.

Benji waited, but Lisa said nothing more.

"Is that all?" he asked her, finally.

Lisa twitched her head, as if startled.

"Yes," she confirmed.

"But what does it mean?" Benji asked.

"I don't know," Lisa replied. "It's just what I had to tell you. Let's go inside, now. I'm ready to sleep."

Chapter Twenty-Three

Benji lay in bed in the darkness and thought.

"Dorn," Lisa had said.

Dorn was the biggest kid in the group he played with on Zeblack. At first, Dorn had seemed like a bully. But after Benji had gotten to know him, they'd become friends.

What did Lisa's message mean? Was Dorn trustworthy? Was it safe for Benji to go visit him? And how would Benji visit Dorn without the other kids knowing? They all traveled in a pack, inseparable.

Benji decided to talk to Madarach about it in the morning. For now, he too was tired.

But his sleep was restless. He woke feeling like he was about to do something important, but he didn't know what.

"Let's welcome Benji back to class," Kareah announced, as school began. "His sister, Lisa, was sick for a while, and that must have been very difficult for him."

"Welcome back," all the kids said.

But Benji didn't pay much attention in class. All he could think about was Dorn.

When class finished, Benji sprinted to the temple to see Nahum. They greeted each other warmly, and Nahum asked about Lisa. Benji told him everything, and then he told the old priest what had happened on Zeblack.

"That is troubling," Nahum agreed. "It sounds like that planet is no longer safe for you."

"But I have friends there," Benji said. "I don't want to lose them."

Nahum sighed.

"War causes people to lose much," he said. "Your friend Tak lost his brother. Now you have lost your friends."

Benji paused. He recognized that his loss was nothing compared to what some of his friends had lost. But it still hurt.

"How does someone end a war?" he asked Nahum.

Nahum gazed at Benji, appraisingly.

"That," he replied, "is a very good question. The truth is, no one knows. Wars have been ended, but there is no single formula for doing so. The key is, the leaders must be convinced to stop fighting. They must believe that peace is in their best interest. But where is the leverage to convince them? It depends on what they want, and every war is somewhat different."

Benji nodded.

"I was afraid of that," he said. "Besides, I'm only twelve years old. I doubt there's much I could do."

Then he told the priest about Lisa's message the night before.

"She knows things," Benji said. "She has the gift of clairvoyance, even though she's not very good at it."

"And all she said was your friend's name?" Nahum confirmed.

"Yes," Benji replied. "She seemed to think it was important, but she couldn't tell me why."

"Hmm," Nahum mused. "It could be a message to go to him, or that he is in danger, or something else entirely."

"If he is in danger, shouldn't I go to him?" Benji asked. "He's my friend. That's what friends do."

"Even if it puts you in danger?" Nahum countered.

Benji thought about this.

"Yes," he said. "There has to be a way to minimize the danger. I bet Madarach can help me think of something."

Nahum wrinkled his brow.

"Don't do anything rash," he warned. "The message is cryptic. Don't risk your life on something that you aren't sure of the meaning."

"Okay," Benji agreed. "I'll talk to Lisa again. And I'll talk to Madarach."

Benji walked home from the temple, his thoughts spinning.

When he arrived, he found Lisa in her room, resting.

"Can you tell me anything more about Dorn?" he asked. "Is he in danger? Does he need me?"

Lisa thought for a long moment.

"I'm sorry," she said. "This is still so confusing for me. I saw a door, and it was locked. There were a lot of people waiting to go inside. Dorn opened the door."

"He had the key?" Benji clarified.

"I guess," Lisa replied. "I don't remember seeing a key. But I guess he must have had it."

"So Dorn can open a door no one else can open?" Benji summarized.

"I'm sorry, Benji," Lisa said. "I don't know what it means. I only know what I saw."

Benji nodded.

"Thank you," he said.

"Benji," she said, before he turned to go. "You have another gift that we don't see yet. I don't know what it is. But it's important. And Dorn has something to do with it."

"How?" he asked.

Lisa shook her head.

"I don't know," she said.

Benji took a step forward, leaned over, and hugged his sister tightly.

"I love you," he said.

If she replied, he didn't know, because suddenly his mind was filled with noise and colors. Black and grey, red and white. And he heard a deafening sound, like a cacophony of voices, but unintelligible, and some not even human.

"*Farchedan*," he muttered. "That's what you live with? No wonder you were sick!"

He pulled back. As he did so, he saw two distinct images. One was of Lisa with two children on her lap, a boy and a girl. The other was of himself, with Aelbreth standing next to him. In it, Benji wore a crown on his head.

He gasped, and shook his head.

"Are you pregnant?" he asked Lisa.

She smiled.

"No," she assured him. "Definitely not. But that image is with me every day. It brings me joy and hope."

"And the other?" he asked. "Me with the crown? What is that all about?"

Lisa shook her head.

"I have no idea," she said. "I think it may be metaphorical."

"Do you know what will happen if I go back to Zeblack to see Dorn?" he asked.

She paused for a moment, concentrating.

"No," she replied. "But you should be very careful. Zeblack is dangerous."

Benji nodded.

"I need to sleep now," Lisa said. "I'm sorry. I didn't mean to be this tired."

"I've seen what goes on inside you," Benji replied. "I'm not surprised you're exhausted."

He left the room and closed the door so Lisa could sleep. Then he walked back to the main street and headed for the well.

Benji summoned the stars, and in moments he was floating in the bubble above Parisa.

"Where are we going?" Madarach asked him.

"It doesn't matter," Benji said. "I just wanted to talk to you."

"Talk to me?" Madarach repeated.

"You have thousands of years of experience," Benji said. "Plus, I realized that you're my best friend."

Madarach paused.

"I am honored," he said. "But you realize that your best friend is trapped inside a machine?"

"I do," Benji replied. "Is that sad?"

"Some might think so," Madarach said. "I do not. I will endeavor to be the best friend that I can. But we won't be able to play numbfoot."

Benji laughed.

"I know," he said. "And I wish we could. But that brings up what I want to talk to you about."

He explained to Madarach about Lisa's message and vision, and about his desire to see Dorn. He conveyed Nahum's message about not being rash.

"Is there any way we could sneak in so I could talk to him?" Benji asked.

Madarach though about this.

"The challenge," he observed, "would be getting Dorn to leave the group so you can talk to him alone."

"Yes," Benji said. "I can only communicate with him telepathically if I'm touching him. And it's not like I can shout his name without anyone else hearing me."

"No," Madarach said. "But I think I can."

"How?" Benji asked.

"Have you heard of subliminal messages?" Madarach asked.

"Yes," Benji said. "That's like when you're watching a movie and they slip in one frame of a soda and popcorn, and everyone gets hungry and thirsty even though they didn't consciously see it."

Madarach chuckled.

"That's one example," he said. "The principle is the same. It's a sound or image that is not consciously perceived, but your subconscious perceives it and starts thinking about it."

"And you can do that?" Benji asked.

"In theory," Madarach said. "I can transmit a sound on a frequency so low that no one will notice it, but I believe Dorn will hear it subconsciously and react to it."

Benji thought about this.

"That's worth a try," he said.

Then he thought for another moment.

"Madarach," he said, "do you know how to end a war?"

Madarach paused.

"You mean the one on Zeblack?" he suggested.

"Yes," Benji replied.

He could almost hear Madarach's sigh.

"That war will never be won by military means," Madarach began. "At least, not while all sides have comparable weapons and tactics. In my experience, a war like that cannot be ended until a significant portion of the population gets fed up with the violence. Even then, it's not easy."

"But it can be done?" Benji pressed.

"Yes, my friend," Madarach said, slowly, "it can be done. On Parisa, the rebels negotiated a victory because everyone was tired of the fighting and the fear. The rebel leaders were able to harness that exhaustion. I have studied your history on Earth, and there are not many examples of war coming to an end without victory, but there are some. In each case, there has been significant opposition to the war, and a charismatic individual has been able to harness that opposition to force the leaders to stop fighting. Often religious leaders or mothers are mobilized.

"But then comes the hard part," Madarach continued. "Left to their own devices, those same leaders will return to war if they can. So in most instances, to be successful, both sides need to have their leadership replaced. And that is another challenge entirely."

"Because no leader wants to give up power," Benji suggested.

"Exactly," Madarach agreed. "Too often, the leaders use war to gain and keep power. So they oppose peace. Even if peace is forced upon them, they will do their utmost to keep their power, and start the war up again if they can."

"So how did they do it?" Benji asked.

"Most often, they followed peace with elections, and elected the peacemakers to be leaders," Madarach replied. "The advantages of peace for the majority are many, and if the majority chooses their leaders while experiencing peace for the first time in many years, the peacemakers can gain power and make lasting change."

"Is that what happened on Parisa?" Benji asked.

"Yes," Madarach replied. "The rebels really did want peace, and they were accepted as leaders. But they forced their way in. A more appropriate example is El Salvador, or Nicaragua, or Sri Lanka, or East Germany. Because peace is not just the absence of fighting. Bridges must be built, and injustices must be righted. True peace is a long and difficult process."

"But to begin it," Benji observed, "the fighting has to stop first, right?"

"Yes," Madarach said. "And I feel the need to point out that you are only twelve years old."

"I'm sixteen on Hadrun," Benji observed, grinning.

Chapter Twenty-Four

Benji spent the next few days on Parisa. He went to class in the mornings, and then spent the evenings with Lisa and the rest of the family. He still worried about Lisa. She tired easily, and had not returned to her former playful personality.

"I'm fine," she assured him, over and over. "This is just going to take some time."

Benji spent his afternoons with Nahum, quizzing the old priest on what he knew about ending wars.

"You are ambitious," Nahum said, "for one so young."

"I'm motivated," Benji corrected. "I care about my friends."

Nahum nodded.

"Your love is deep," he commented.

Where had Benji heard that before? The old priestess on Hassyr had said something similar: "You love deeply, for a man."

She had said something else, too. She'd said that Benji might have something to learn from her, and she'd invited Benji back to her temple.

Parisa observed a day of rest every eight days, so on the next day off, he boarded Madarach once again.

"Let's go back to Hassyr," he said.

"As you wish," Madarach agreed. "It is my favorite planet to visit."

"Please give my regards to your wife, Jael," Benji added.

He could almost sense Madarach smiling.

As they entered the Hassyri system, Benji saw the planet with the dancing rings.

"Slow down," he instructed. "I want to watch that planet for a minute."

He gazed at the rings in fascination as waves rippled through them in a clockwise direction. Maybe Aelbreth was right, he decided. He really didn't care why they behaved that way. The mystery somehow enhanced their beauty.

Eventually, Madarach set Benji down near the well on Hassyr. Benji walked along the narrow path to the cliff top, and then to the temple entrance. This time, he entered reverently.

The same young woman was tending the altar as he made his way into the relative gloom of the cave. She spotted him, and disappeared into the depths of the cavern without a word.

Benji had reached the altar by the time the priestess appeared. She looked, if anything, even older than just a few days before.

"You have come," she observed, telepathically. "I knew you would, but not when. Please, come and sit with me, and we shall have tea."

"Thank you," Benji replied, bowing his head slightly.

They retreated into the cavern where the priestess led them to a small room furnished as Lisa's had been, with a table, two chairs, and a bed. She gestured for Benji to sit, and she took the chair opposite him.

"What shall I call you?" Benji asked.

"You may call me Yorga," she replied. "I am pleased you have come."

"You told me I might learn something from you," Benji said.

"Indeed," Yorga replied. "You may learn much. Though I have only one thing to teach."

"*Farchedan?*" he suggested.

She smiled.

"You are indeed quick," she said. "Tell me, what is it you wish to learn?"

"I want to learn to end a war," he replied.

The old woman laughed.

"Is that all?" she asked. "You might as well ask to learn to fly! But then, you already have that ability, do you not?"

Benji didn't understand for a moment. Then he realized that he flew through space using his ability to communicate with Madarach.

He laughed.

"The impossible sometimes seems normal," he said.

Yorga nodded.

"They are easily confused," she agreed.

The young woman brought them tea, which Benji sniffed suspiciously. His experience with tea on Hadrun had left him cautious.

"It will not hurt you," Yorga assured him.

Benji tasted it, and found it quite soothing, both to his palate and his nerves.

"Destruction and creation are the same," Yorga said. "Do you realize that?"

Benji frowned. That didn't make sense to him.

"Matter and energy cannot be destroyed, they can only be transformed," she continued. "Everything that is, was once something else."

"Okay," Benji said, tentatively.

"To build a house, you must destroy a tree," she continued. "To build a monument, you must destroy a mountain. Even the tea you drink, which creates in you, was once a living plant that was destroyed in the picking. There can be no creation without destruction. And there can be no destruction without creation, for everything that was, is now something else."

Now Benji nodded.

"I can see that," he said.

"To end a war requires perception," the old woman said. "For war is the process of destruction, and therefore also creation. But what is being destroyed, and what created? It is not always clear."

"So how does one know?" Benji asked.

"Come," the old woman said, standing and beckoning.

She led him to the other side of the room, to a shelf on which sat a wooden box.

Yorga lifted the box, and underneath it glowed a glass orb filled with swirling lights. To Benji, they resembled the stars spinning as they came out of the well when he summoned Madarach.

"Watch," Yorga instructed. "Watch, and tell me what they do."

Benji gazed at the lights, which seemed at first to be spinning clockwise in the orb. Then he realized that only some of them were spinning clockwise. Others spun vertically, some moved back and forth, still others made tiny circles of their own, and some appeared not to be moving at all.

"It's chaos," he murmured.

"Watch," she said again.

Benji did. The patternless movements continued, with some lights changing direction and course.

Benji frowned. He glanced at Yorga, then back at the orb.

Then he saw it. The directions varied, but there was pattern to it. Each light changed course as it bounced off other lights. Some of the lights that at first appeared to be moving independently were actually revolving around other lights. The rhythm was complex, but it was there.

"I see it!" Benji exclaimed. "They're all moving together!"

"Yes," Yorga agreed. "That is the key. When you see how all are moving together, then you understand the why. But you must yet learn the what. Now, touch the orb and bring it into harmony."

He glanced at Yorga, and she nodded.

Benji tentatively reached toward the orb. It felt cool to his finger. And where he touched it, the lights changed direction, some deflected and some attracted to his touch.

He touched it again in another spot, and watched the lights change course. Then he used two hands, touching the orb in various places. Eventually, more and more of the lights began to rotate in the same direction. He touched the orb again, and disturbed the flow. It took some time, but finally all the lights moved in the same direction. With no interference from each other, they spun faster and faster, and became brighter and brighter, until suddenly the orb let out a bright white glow.

Yorga nodded.

"Do you understand what you have done?" she asked.

"I got them all moving in the same direction," he replied.

"You destroyed one pattern and created another," the old priestess corrected. "The dance is the means. See the dance, and use it."

Benji thought about this.

"The dance is the means," he repeated. "You've said that before."

"Oh, yes," Yorga agreed. "I say it many times each day, for it is the truth that sets us free. 'We can still see the dance of eternal blackness and light in the rhythm of day and night, in the circles of birth and death, in the melodies of joy and sadness, in the rising and falling of creation and destruction. The dance between light and darkness is eternal, and we are all part of it.' So our ancient text says. And we can see the dance in war and peace. That is what you have come to learn."

Benji thought about this. It made sense to him.

"Please, teach me more," he said.

They talked for hours, though it seemed to Benji that their conversation was more stories and personal observations than it was lessons. Yorga spoke of her youth, and how she had first glimpsed the dance at a river when she was not much older than Benji. She asked about Benji's life, and suggested ways to see the dance in his own experience. He would not be who he was, she suggested, if he hadn't had the experience of being outcast among his peers. Even the burning of their home by the Thompson family was part of it, she suggested.

"For in that act of destruction, something was created," she said. "It is always so. No destruction can occur without creation, and nothing can be created without destruction. Watch the dance. Study it. For the dance is the means. When you can feel the rhythm, then you too shall be part of the dance, creating as it creates."

Chapter Twenty-Five

When Benji returned to Parisa, it was after midnight and he felt exhausted. He made his way through the dark, empty streets to Jachin's house and let himself in.

When he turned on the light, he saw Tamar sitting in a chair in the small living room. Benji went to her and put his hand on hers.

"I'm glad you're home safe," she said. "I was worried."

"I'm sorry, Umma," Benji said. "The time differences make it easy to lose track. But I'm fine. You shouldn't have worried."

Tamar smiled, sadly.

"It's my job to worry," she corrected. "Especially after what happened to Lisa. Which I still don't understand."

Benji shook his head.

"I don't understand it completely," he said. "But maybe if you think about it this way. Imagine someone who can communicate telepathically, but lives on a world where no one else can do it, so they don't know they can. Then they come to Parisa, where everyone can. After silence for so many years, they would hear so many voices in their head, it would be overwhelming for a while."

Tamar considered this. Then she nodded.

"I can see how that could be," she acknowledged.

"When Lisa went to Hassyr," he continued, "it woke something up in her that she'd never known before. Whatever it is she sees was overwhelming to her. It crowded out everything else. Like so many voices, she couldn't hear herself think. But for her, it's images, too. It was all so much, she couldn't function anymore."

Tamar nodded.

"So the priestess helped her control it?" she asked.

"I don't know if she can control it," Benji said. "I think the priestess helped her tolerate it. She's still struggling with it. I touched her the other day, and I could hear and see it. It really is overwhelming. Imagine lots of loud music and lights, like at a concert, while you're trying to carry on a normal conversation with the person next to you."

Benji had seen rock concerts on television back on Earth. Tamar clearly hadn't, and she grimaced at the image Benji's description created for her.

"That sounds dreadful," she said. "But thank you for helping me to understand. Is there anything we can do to help her?"

"I don't think so," Benji replied. "Just let her rest when she needs to. It must be exhausting to have that racket going on all the time."

Tamar nodded.

"You need rest, too," she observed. "Go to bed, now. I'll see you in the morning."

As excited as he was to go to Zeblack, Benji decided to wait until Lisa was better. His routine returned, with school in the morning, his visits to the temple in the afternoon, and evening with the family. Often, he played the Parisan version of video games with Miriam, and sometimes Tobin, though Tobin preferred to spend his time with Lisa.

Benji also made a point to watch for the dance. Sometimes he saw it in his classroom, where what seemed like an orderly class of children actually had a great deal of differing focuses and attitudes. Often he saw it on a busy street, where people did not move in a straight line, nor did they move randomly. Each step they took was affected by others around them. They dodged, set a course for a perceived clearing, and corrected course when the people ahead of them shifted. It was, Benji realized, *farchedan* in action.

On his next day off from school, Benji returned to Hadrun to see Aelbreth. He felt nervous as he approached the village. He'd been so angry when he left, and he'd said some hurtful things. He was afraid Aelbreth wouldn't want to see him.

"Benji!" she shouted, when she saw him, a huge smile breaking across her face.

Then she caught herself and adopted a stern look.

"Where have you been?" she demanded.

But she'd already given away her true feelings, and she couldn't keep a straight face for long.

"I've missed you," she said, hurrying to him and throwing her arms around him. Then, telepathically, she added, "I was worried you wouldn't come back. You were so angry when you left."

"I'm sorry," Benji said. "I have no excuse, except that my feelings confused me, and I felt like I needed to put some distance between us."

"In the future," Aelbreth suggested, "why don't you just say that?"

Benji smiled.

"That would be easier, wouldn't it?" he said. "I'll try. But sometimes I feel like my body and mouth have a mind of their own."

Aelbreth nodded.

"I forgive you," she said. "How long are you staying?"

"Just today," Benji replied. "I have to get back. Lisa is better but still struggling."

He told her what he'd learned of Lisa's new gift, and how it left her tired all the time.

"That almost sounds like a curse rather than a gift," Aelbreth commented.

"I think she'll get used to it after a while," Benji said. "How about you? Can you take the day off?"

Aelbreth gave him a skeptical look.

"I don't know," she began.

Then she laughed.

"Of course I can!" she said.

They spent the day walking in the forest, talking, kissing, and swimming. To Benji, it felt like none of the confusion of the previous visit had ever happened. Once again, they were best friends and confidants, partners, and hopelessly in love.

"So what will you do next?" Aelbreth asked him, as they sat under a canopy of tall trees.

"I need to make sure Lisa's okay," he said. "Then I'm going back to Zeblack to try to talk to Dorn."

"Why?" she asked. "I mean, I know he's your friend and you want to see him. But that's pretty dangerous after what they did to us last trip."

"I don't know, exactly," Benji admitted. "But Lisa said Dorn can open a door no one else can open."

"You're going to try to end the war?" Aelbreth suggested.

Benji sighed.

"I don't know yet," he said. "I have to see where this leads before I know what the door even is."

"I wish I could go with you," Aelbreth said. "But I know you'll need to do this alone."

"I put you in danger last time," Benji replied. "I don't want to risk doing that again."

"Benji," she said, sharply. "Do you imagine that my life is more important than yours? It isn't. Keep yourself out of danger, please!"

"I'll do my best," he agreed, reluctantly.

The shadows had begun to grow in the forest now.

"I'll need to leave soon," Benji observed. "The *fortule* will be out."

"Stay a little longer," Aelbreth begged. Then, with a grin, she added, "If you stay long enough, you'll be spending the night."

"I can't," Benji protested. "Lisa needs me."

So Benji returned to Parisa and his daily routine. He continued his lessons, discussed various aspects of conflict with Nahum, and watched as Lisa slowly grew stronger. She still slept more than normal, but gradually less so. And her sense of humor had begun to return.

"I'm okay," Lisa assured him, a few days later. "It's time for you to go visit Dorn."

Benji waited until his next day off from school. He headed for the well early in the morning, both excited and nervous. He looked forward to seeing his friend again, but he remembered too well the treachery of Churl and Chute during his last visit.

But there was something else. He was about to embark on an adventure, a secret mission to a dangerous planet.

"Sort of like a secret agent," he thought to himself.

"What time is it where Dorn lives on Zeblack?" he asked Madarach, once they had reached space.

"Just after dawn," Madarach replied.

"Perfect," Benji said. "We can catch Dorn as he comes out after breakfast."

Madarach took them to an alley as close to Dorn's house as they could get without being seen. Then they waited, watching down the street for Dorn to emerge.

Eventually, Dorn came out of the house and paused on the pavement.

"He looks sleepy," Madarach said. "That will help. Sleepy people don't question their thoughts as much as those who are awake."

Dorn began to walk down the street, away from them.

"I'm sending him a message now," Madarach said.

If the message had sound, it was so low in tone that Benji couldn't hear it. He suddenly began to doubt that this would work.

"Are you sure about this?" he asked Madarach, as they watched Dorn continue away from them.

"No," Madarach said. "But I've told him there's something in the alley he'll want to find. Let's see what he does."

Dorn walked a few more steps, and then paused. Then he turned and began to walk toward them.

"Here he comes!" Benji said, excitedly.

Dorn entered the alley and looked around, confused.

Benji exited the bubble and hissed at him.

"Dorn!" he said. "It's Benji."

Dorn looked at him in confusion. Then he stepped closer.

"What are you doing here?" Dorn asked.

"I came to talk to you," Benji replied.

"Why?" Dorn asked.

"Because you're my friend," Benji said. "I've missed you."

"We're not supposed to talk to you," Dorn said. "You're considered an enemy of the faction now."

"An enemy of the faction?" Benji repeated. "What did Churl tell you?"

"He said you invited yourself over to his house for dinner," Dorn said. "Then you used that as an excuse to lure Churl and his brother to your spaceship and try to kidnap them. They think you were going to turn them over to another faction, maybe Hobnails."

"What?" Benji exclaimed. "That's ridiculous."

It never occurred to him that Churl might lie about what happened. But of course he would. He would never tell Benji's friends the truth.

"Dorn, you know me," Benji said. "Have I ever given you any indication that I even know another faction, much less might be working for one?"

"No," Dorn agreed. "But spies never let things like that slip."

"Spies!" Benji exclaimed. "But Dorn, you remember that afternoon, right? Churl left early. Then, as the numbfoot game was breaking up, Churl came back and asked Aelbreth and me if we wanted to come to dinner at his house. It wasn't my idea. I've never been invited to any of your houses before, and we almost didn't go. But Churl said his mother wanted to meet us."

"I remember that," Dorn said. "Churl did leave early, and I remember he came back and was talking to you as the game broke up. I didn't hear what anyone said."

"But if he came back to talk to us," Benji suggested, "doesn't it make sense that he invited us to dinner? I mean, relying on the off chance that Churl might come back to the game isn't much of a plan if we wanted to kidnap anyone, right?"

Dorn thought about this.

"I suppose not," he reluctantly agreed. "Well, then, what did happen?"

"They tried to steal my spaceship," Benji said. "Chute said that wars were won through superior weapons and tactics, and having my spaceship would let Darkly win the war."

Dorn nodded.

"That does sound like what Chute would say," he allowed. "But how do I know you're telling the truth?"

"Because I'm your friend," Benji said, "and I have no reason to lie. Churl said, when they tried to steal my ship, that nothing comes before the faction. But for me, it does. I don't belong to a faction. I'm not even from this planet. I'm only here because you're my friend."

Dorn nodded again.

"Yeah," he agreed. "For Churl, nothing comes before the faction, not even friendship."

Dorn thought for a long time, and then nodded.

"I believe you, Benji," he said.

Then he stepped forward and shook Benji's hand.

Benji grinned.

"Do you want to go for a ride?" he asked Dorn.

Dorn's face lit up.

"In your spaceship?" he asked. "Of course!"

Chapter Twenty-Six

They rose above the town, and Dorn gaped at the transparent floor as the ground fell away.

"You can go anywhere you want?" he asked Benji.

"Anywhere," Benji confirmed. "Where do you want to go? Are there things to see on this planet?"

Dorn thought for a moment.

"I've always wanted to see the lava lakes at Mount Storfy," he said. "They're not that far away, but we can't get there because of the war."

Benji relayed this to Madarach, and soon they were moving above the landscape.

They watched the ground below as villages and towns passed by. Then they passed over a devastated city, where all the buildings had been reduced to rubble.

"That's Mardy," Dorn said, sadly. "It used to be our capital. Now it's gone."

Further on, they passed over a battlefield, and they could see the fighting below. Huge explosions rocked the ground, throwing debris skyward and leaving giant craters behind.

Dorn shuddered.

"That's Darkly fighting Fawnscape," he said. "Tak is down there somewhere."

Benji shook his head.

"I'm glad I'm not," he said.

"Me too," Dorn agreed.

Then a range of mountains came into view. Madarach passed over several tall summits, and they could see a smoking peak ahead of them.

"Mount Storfy," Dorn said. "It's an active volcano."

Madarach skirted the mountain, dropping closer to the ground. On the far side, they hovered over a series of pools of molten lava that glowed orange and emitted smoke or steam. Some of them were small, but the largest one was the size of a football field. Strange, twisted rock formations covered the landscape nearby.

"Wow!" Benji exclaimed. "That's impressive!"

"Can we go down?" Dorn asked.

Benji consulted Madarach, and soon they exited the bubble and walked among the volcanic rocks, picking their way between twisted pillars created by the lava. They found an outcropping above the largest pool. The surface of the pool seemed to bubble, like thick gravy on a stove. Benji could feel the heat on his face from the molten rock.

"It's beautiful," Dorn said. "I've seen pictures, but they're nothing like the real thing."

"They never are," Benji replied.

Personally, he found the lava pools striking, but not exactly beautiful.

They gazed at the pool for several long minutes. Then they turned to make their way back to Madarach, and Benji gazed out over the vast field of twisted formations.

He paused.

"*Farchedan*," he murmured.

"What?" Dorn asked.

Benji looked up. He hadn't realized he'd spoken aloud.

"Nothing," he said. "It's just that all these strange formations were created by rock boiling out of the ground.

There was something here before, and now there's something else."

Dorn gave him a bemused look.

"I'm sorry," Benji said. "That doesn't make much sense, does it? But I was thinking about something an old priestess taught me. Nothing can be destroyed without creating something else. And nothing can be created without destroying something else."

Dorn wrinkled his brow.

"We've gotten pretty good at destroying," he said. "I don't know about the creating part."

"You're creating something," Benji said. "Maybe just not what you want to see."

"No," Dorn agreed. "If we're creating anything, it's misery. Thol's sister was killed last week. Now Thol's family wants him to take her place."

Benji knew Thol. They had played numbfoot together many times.

"Oh, no," Benji exclaimed. "Is he going to go?"

"He kind of has to," Dorn said. "It's how we do things. But I wish there was another way."

They stood in silence for a moment, surveying the surreal landscape.

"I hate this war," Dorn said, finally. "But it will never end, no matter what Chute says."

"It will never be won," Benji said. "But that doesn't mean it can't end."

"What do you mean?" Dorn asked. "How can a war end if no one wins?"

"They could just stop fighting," Benji suggested.

Dorn snorted.

"Like that's going to happen," he scoffed. "They've been fighting for two hundred years. Why would they just stop?"

"Why are they fighting?" Benji asked.

"Everyone is afraid that someone else will take what they have," Dorn explained.

"But everyone has less because of the fighting," Benji pointed out. "So that doesn't make sense. It's not the real reason."

Dorn thought about this.

"You're right," he said. "I remember you said that the first time we met you. If everyone destroys everyone else's resources, then everyone has less. That's sort of obvious, but no one seems to think about it. So protecting our resources isn't the real reason we're fighting."

He thought some more, and then he frowned.

"It's a lie," he said, darkly. "So then why are we fighting?"

"I don't have the answer," Benji replied. "But I know the question to ask."

"What question?" Dorn wondered.

"Who benefits, and how?" Benji suggested. "Whoever is making the decisions benefits in some way. If they didn't, they wouldn't keep doing the same thing over and over."

"Who benefits?" Dorn repeated.

He thought for a moment. Then he turned to Benji.

"Let's go," he said. "I want to show you something."

They ran back to where Madarach waited. When they were safely inside the bubble, Dorn gave directions.

"Our new capital is at Denmar," he said. "Let's fly over it and look."

Benji relayed this to Madarach.

"We can do that," Madarach agreed. "But they have radar detection and anti-air defense. I don't know if they'll be able to see us or not, so we'll have to go in close to the ground where we won't be detected."

They rose high above the ground to cross the countryside, and Benji saw rivers and lakes below them. There was some cultivated land, but most was empty. Some had been scarred by the fighting, with craters and scorched vegetation.

"There would be a lot more room if the war stopped," he observed. "Look at all that unoccupied land down there!"

Dorn sighed.

"No one dares live outside a town anymore," he lamented. "There aren't many farmers, and food is scarce. But they tell us it's because of the other factions. That's a lie, too."

As the city came into view, Madarach dropped close to the ground. They approached the outskirts at high speed, and Benji saw vast neighborhoods of tiny huts, mostly made of scrap wood. The people here appeared to be very poor.

Madarach rose a bit as they approached the center of the city. Now Benji could see markets and shops.

Then he gasped. Ahead of them rose a huge complex of very official looking buildings. They were all covered in gold.

"That's the capitol," Dorn explained. "That's where the faction leaders and the government are."

They passed over the complex, which shone brightly in the sun. On the other side, Benji saw what could only be described as a palace. It appeared to be constructed of marble and gold, and was surrounded by intricate gardens and a high wall that was also plated with gold.

"Wow," Dorn said, bitterly. "I've heard about this, but never seen it, not even in pictures."

"What is it?" Benji asked. "Do you guys have a king?"

Dorn laughed, sadly.

"No," he replied. "The head of the faction is General Obedas. That's where he lives."

Benji stared as the palace passed out of sight behind them, and slums again covered the land below.

"Well," he said, "I guess we know who benefits from the war. Are all the factions like this?"

"I don't know," Dorn replied. "But I think so. The leader is entitled to the benefits of leadership, right?"

"While the rest of the people live in poverty and die in his war?" Benji countered. "That doesn't seem fair."

"No," Dorn agreed. "It doesn't seem fair. I bet that's why we never see pictures of the palace. They don't want us to know."

"Now *you* know," Benji pointed out.

"No one would believe me if I told them," Dorn said. "I wish I had a camera."

Benji paused, while he communicated with Madarach.

"Who would you show first?" he asked Dorn.

"That's easy," Dorn replied. "Thol."

"Then let's go find him," Benji said. "Madarach took pictures. There's no way for him to give them to you, but he can show them to Thol."

"Why would Thol believe they're real?" Dorn asked.

"Because," Benji said, "you and I are in them."

They returned to the alley near Dorn's street, and Dorn went to find Thol.

"You're doing well," Madarach told Benji, when they were alone. "You've already got Dorn convinced."

Benji chuckled.

"That was easier than I expected," he acknowledged. "But what good will it do? Even if Thol agrees, that's two kids on a world that's been fighting for two hundred years."

"Two kids in a couple of hours," Madarach pointed out. "You didn't think this was going to happen quickly, did you? But you're making amazing progress."

Benji sighed.

"I can't see what we could possibly do," he said. "But I'm doing what I can."

"Some days, that's the best you can do," Madarach replied. "You will know what to do when it's time."

"*Farchedan*," Benji muttered again. "Watch the dance, and it will show me."

Dorn returned a few minutes later with Thol, and Benji helped them into the bubble.

"This is your spaceship?" Thol asked Benji. "This is awesome!"

Benji smiled, proudly.

"We took it to the lava lakes at Mount Storfy," Dorn said.

"You did not!" Thol exclaimed.

He looked at Benji, and then back at Dorn.

"We did," Benji confirmed. "And then we went to the capital."

"No way," Thol said. "You can't get into the capital. It's restricted."

"Not if you have a spaceship," Dorn replied.

"We have pictures," Benji said. "You want to see?"

Thol looked skeptical, but nodded.

Then, on one side of the bubble, a huge image appeared as if projected there from an unseen source. It showed Benji and Dorn picking their way across the twisted landscape near the lava pools.

"Wow!" Thol said. "You really did go there."

Another image appeared, showing Dorn looking over the precipice at the lava, which glowed orange behind him.

"How did you get this?" Benji asked Madarach, silently. "You were following us?"

"I had to make sure you were safe," Madarach said. "It wouldn't do for you to fall into a lava pool."

There were several more photos, and then Madarach put up a shot of the slums outside the capital.

"That's Denmar," Dorn explained.

"Really?" Thol said. "They look really poor. I thought people in the capital were better off than us."

"Some are," Dorn said, as a photo of the government complex appeared.

Then Madarach put up a photo of the palace.

"What in the name of the faction is that?" Thol asked, amazed.

"That," Dorn replied, "is where our leader, General Obedas lives."

Thol stared.

"That's Obedas's house?" he confirmed.

"Yes," Dorn said. "The benefits of leadership."

Then Madarach put up one last photo. Benji and Dorn stood in the foreground, the slums of Denmar behind them, and the glittering palace of General Obedas shown in the distance. Thol stared at the unmistakable irony. Their leader lived in splendor, while all around him his people lived in squalor.

"That's what they want me to fight for?" Thol asked, disgustedly. "I don't think so. They can keep their war."

Chapter Twenty-Seven

Who decided that General Obedas was the leader of the faction?" Benji asked. "Did he get elected?"

"Elected?" Dorn repeated, with a snort. "We don't have elections. None of the factions do. Obedas was chosen by the Council."

"Who chooses the Council?" Benji pressed.

"Obedas," Thol replied. "Or whoever the leader is. The Council that chose Obedas was chosen by his predecessor."

"So they choose each other?" Benji concluded. "No wonder they want everyone thinking about the war."

Dorn and Thol looked at each other.

"I never thought of it that way," Dorn said. "While we're focused on the war, no one pays attention to the system itself."

"But I bet if anyone complained," Thol added, "they'd be labeled an enemy of the faction."

Benji laughed.

"I was labeled an enemy of the faction," he observed. "Because Churl and Chute lied."

"Yeah," Dorn agreed. "It's a pretty tidy system. No one pays attention, and if they do, they get punished."

"So there's no way to change it," Thol concluded.

"Yes," Benji disagreed. "There's always a way to change it. But it will take a lot of people, and a lot of risk."

Thol laughed.

"Going to the front line is a lot of risk," he said. "Compared to that, what can they do to me?"

Dorn nodded.

"Every one of us has lost a brother or a sister, or a father or a mother because of this stupid war," he said. "How do you think they'll feel when they learn that Obedas lives in a palace of gold?"

"We just have to find a way to show them," Thol said.

"Do any of you have a camera?" Benji asked. "We could go back there and you could take pictures."

Dorn sighed.

"Cameras are expensive," he said. "I think Churl's dad has one, but none of us do."

Benji thought about this.

"What if I gave you one?" he asked, fishing in his pocket. "My dad gave me this one a couple of years ago, and it still works."

Dorn and Thol looked at each other.

"We'd be able to show them photos?" Thol asked.

"Yes," Benji assured him. "It's digital, so whatever you take pictures of you can show on a little screen. It won't be as nice as the ones Madarach showed us, but it will work."

"How will we explain where we got the camera?" Dorn wondered. "They'll think we're working for another faction."

"All your friends know me," Benji said. "Start with them. Except Churl, of course."

Dorn nodded.

"Most of them are going to be very angry when they find out," he predicted. "But what do we do then?"

"One step at a time," Benji told him. "We'll know what to do when the time is right."

They took another trip over Denmar, and Benji showed Thol how to work the camera. Thol, it turned out, had a talent for photography, and his photos were very good. Benji's favorite showed Dorn against the backdrop of the city, the slums below him and the palace behind. It was similar to the one Madarach had taken, but closer to the palace. Even on the tiny camera screen, the contrast between Obedas and his people couldn't be overlooked.

"You're good," Benji told Thol. "I wish there was a way to make those pictures bigger."

They returned to the alley near the street the boys lived on. Dorn and Thol said their goodbyes, and they agreed to meet again in two Parisa weeks, which was twenty-one days on Zeblack.

"I can't wait!" Thol said. "Hopefully there will be more of us."

Benji headed back to Parisa, excitement filling his mind.

"This is really happening," he said.

"It's begun," Madarach agreed. "But keeping it going is hard. Still, Thol is very good with that camera. Images can change the world."

"What do you mean?" Benji asked.

"On your own planet, the images taken by photographers of the Vietnam War helped to build resistance against the war," Madarach explained. "People saw with their own eyes, and they refused to support it. Many refused to fight, even though they might go to prison if they didn't."

"They could be sent to prison?" Benji asked. "In the United States? I thought we were a free country."

"Yes," Madarach said. "But at the time, they had what was called conscription, or the draft. Young men were chosen at random to fight in the army. If they refused, they were sent to prison."

"All young men?" Benji asked.

"No," Madarach replied. "Not all of them went. It was chosen by lottery. But those who went to college didn't have to go."

Benji thought about this.

"Wasn't it mostly rich kids who went to college?" he asked.

"Yes," Madarach agreed.

Benji shook his head.

"The benefits of leadership," he surmised.

"And it was the photographers who brought the war home," Madarach continued. "So many people became opposed to the war that the government eventually gave up. It was the first war your country fought that it didn't actually win."

"Why were they fighting?" Benji asked. "What did we want?"

"I'm not really sure," Madarach said. "The Vietnamese wanted to run their own country. The Americans at first tried to keep them from seceding from France, but then they continued to fight because the Vietnamese chose a communist form of government."

"France?" Benji asked. "Isn't France like thousands of miles away from Vietnam?"

"Yes," Madarach agreed. "Strange, isn't it."

Benji thought for a moment.

"So we were fighting a war that didn't make any sense," Benji concluded. "And the images of the war woke people up to that."

"That's how I see it, yes," Madarach agreed.

Benji thought some more.

"What kind of photos did they take?" he asked. "What kind of photos can change minds like that? Do you have any of them in your database?"

Madarach paused.

"I do," he said. "But I don't think you should see them."

"Why not?" Benji asked.

"Because," Madarach said. "The kind of photos that change minds are shocking, and often violent. You have a peaceful heart, Benji. I think they would haunt you."

Benji nodded.

"Sooner or later, I'm going to have to know," he suggested.

"Yes," Madarach said. "Sooner or later you will. But not yet. You're a boy. Go be a boy for a while."

Chapter Twenty-Eight

Back on Parisa, Benji took Madarach's advice. He went to school in the mornings, helped Nahum at the temple in the afternoon, and played video games with his family. Lisa had recovered enough now that she and Tobin sometimes joined Benji and Miriam in solving the three-dimensional puzzles they enjoyed.

One afternoon, Benji arrived at the temple to find Quanda and Queelie waiting there.

"We stopped by to see you," Quanda said. "If you have time, we'd like you to come to our house for dinner."

"You plural," Queelie clarified. "Both you and Lisa."

"That would be fun," Benji agreed. "Let's go to my house, and we can check with Lisa and see if she wants to come."

"Great!" Queelie squealed. "We haven't seen much of Parisa!"

"These streets are so clean and empty!" Quanda observed, as they made their way through the neighborhoods.

"Most people are doing their jobs right now," Benji said. "Plus, this is a residential area. It's busier in the main part of town."

"The houses are so beautiful!" Queelie added. "And every one has a garden!"

"People try to grow as much of their own food as they can," Benji explained. "They also grow food in the parks. That way they can leave more of the surrounding land to nature."

"They don't have oceans?" Quanda asked.

"They have a couple of smaller ones," Benji replied. "But they don't eat fish. People on Parisa are vegetarian. It's better for the environment."

"That makes sense here," Quanda agreed. "But on Hassyr, we don't have enough land to be vegetarian. If we didn't eat fish, we'd starve!"

They arrived at Benji's home, and Benji introduced them to Tamar.

"This is my mother on Parisa," he explained.

With his hand on Tamar's arm, he relayed a short conversation in which Tamar asked about the two visitors' home planet, and how they liked Parisa.

"Is Lisa here?" Benji asked Tamar, telepathically.

"She's still at the park," Tamar replied. "You can go find her, though. I'm sure she'll be happy to see her friends."

Benji relayed this to Quanda and Queelie in their own language.

"She works in the park every afternoon," Benji explained. "We all work, so we can share what we need."

The walk to the park took only a few minutes, and Queelie gushed at how beautiful it was.

"Everything is flowering and fruiting!" she observed. "Is it good to eat?"

"Almost everything here is good to eat," Benji replied.

He picked three pink fruits from a tree and offered one to each of his friends.

"This is delicious!" Queelie said.

"We don't get much fruit on Hassyr," Quanda lamented. "There's not enough land to grow it."

They found Lisa pruning berry bushes.

"Quanda!" she exclaimed. "Queelie! I was starting to wonder if I'd ever see you again."

"Me, too," Queelie said. "So we wanted to invite you to dinner at our house. Can you come?"

Lisa paused a moment before answering. Then she smiled.

"Of course!" she said. "I've missed you! I haven't seen you since our trip to Earth, and that was weeks ago!"

They decided that Benji and Lisa would take Madarach. That way, Madarach could take them all to the house, and he would know where Quanda and Queelie lived. And Quanda and Queelie wouldn't have to take their two guests back to Parisa afterward.

"We can stay longer that way," Quanda suggested.

They got into their respective bubbles, and they all met at the well on Hassyr. Quanda and Queelie boarded Madarach, and Queelie gave him directions.

"You can set us down in that park," she instructed.

Benji looked. The park she indicated was a dirt lot with a playground.

"You could grow fruit in that park," he suggested. "There's a lot of dirt with nothing growing."

"I think everyone would steal it," Quanda replied. "There are a lot of people, and not much fruit."

"If you grew it for them, it wouldn't be stealing," Benji observed.

He could see Queelie thinking about this, but she said nothing.

They exited the bubble, and Quanda led them down a lane, and through several turns.

"Look," he pointed out. "From our house, that tree lines up with the spire of that temple. That's how you can find us if you forget."

"Except I have almost no idea where we are," Benji replied, with a laugh. "I wouldn't be able to find the temple, much less the tree."

Quanda and Queelie lived in a small flat on the third floor of a five-story building. They took the stairs up, and Quanda led them in through the front door.

Inside, Benji saw that the floor was made of something like concrete, and it was bare aside from a throw rug in front of a sofa-like piece of furniture in what Benji guessed was the living room. Quanda led them into a small kitchen, where an older woman was working over an electric burner.

"Mother," Quanda said, "This is Benji and Lisa."

The woman turned. Her skin was a dark shade of blue, and her hair was white. Benji guessed that she was very old.

"Welcome," she said. "We're happy you have chosen to visit us."

"Mom," Queelie said, "they're from another planet. You don't need to be formal. They don't even know our formal manners."

"Well," Mom said, "that's going to take some getting used to. I've always used formal manners with guests."

"Then pretend they're part of the family," Quanda said. "They practically are."

Quanda showed them the rest of the house. There wasn't much to see. Their parents had a bedroom, and Quanda and Queelie shared a bedroom, which was divided with a heavy curtain so they each had their privacy. There was a small bathroom that consisted of a sink, a primitive shower, and something Benji guessed was a toilet, though it looked nothing like any he'd seen before.

Quanda saw Benji staring at it.

"You squat," he explained. "I've seen the kind you sit on when we visited other planets. But this is actually healthier and more sanitary."

"Really?" Benji replied, skeptically.

He hoped they'd get back to Parisa before he needed to use it.

"Dinner is ready!" called their mom.

They all returned to the living room, where Mom handed them each a plate. Quanda and Queelie sat on the rug, so Benji and Lisa joined them.

Benji looked at his plate. The food seemed to be some kind of meat in a sauce, served over some kind of vegetable. There was no utensil. He waited to see if Mom would give them one, but she didn't. Instead, Quanda and Queelie began mashing the meat sauce into the vegetables with their fingers. They rolled the mixed food into balls and popped them into their mouths.

Benji ate with his hands on Hadrun, but that was meat and bread. Eating sauce with his fingers seemed strange, but he imitated them as best he could.

The meat turned out to be some kind of fish, and the sauce was salty and sour. But the vegetable was unexpectedly sweet, so it all went together well.

"This is delicious!" Benji pronounced.

After dinner, they washed their hands at the kitchen sink. Then Quanda produced a deck of cards.

"Do you play?" he asked.

"We know some card games," Benji replied. "But probably not the ones you know. I'm not even sure our deck is the same as yours."

"It has sixty cards," Quanda explained. "The numbers one through ten, in six different colors."

"That's different," Benji said.

But the game was familiar, very similar to the rummy game Benji's dad had taught them back on Earth.

It moved quickly, and Lisa inched ahead of Queelie, catching Benji and Quanda with a lot of points.

"I always tell Quanda that girls play this game better," Queelie joked.

Quanda scowled, and then grinned.

"Next time," he warned, "Benji and I will obliterate the two of you."

"So you want to play in teams?" Queelie suggested. "I think we'll have the two best players."

Quanda glanced at Benji, who nodded.

"You're on," he said. "Next time."

Benji guessed that it was late afternoon on Parisa, so he and Lisa said their goodbyes to Mom, and the four children descended the stairs to the street. Madarach was waiting for them in the park, and the friends hugged and said goodbye again.

"We really enjoy you guys," Queelie said. "I hope you'll come back soon!"

Chapter Twenty-Nine

As Benji went through his daily routines, his mind wasn't very focused on class or his work at the temple. Instead, he thought about Zeblack.

Madarach seemed impressed that Benji had recruited two boys to the cause of peace in an afternoon. Nahum, too, had been encouraging.

"Imagine if each of them convert two more, and each of them two more, and so on," the old priest had suggested. "There would soon be thousands."

"Maybe so," Benji had replied. "But they would still all be in one faction. How can they affect the other factions?"

Benji still didn't have an answer for this, but he was excited to see whether Dorn and Thol had recruited more people.

He didn't get to visit Zeblack again for two Parisan weeks, which was sixteen days. He didn't have a system for contacting Dorn, so he needed to arrive at dawn again and catch Dorn as he left his house. This time, that meant leaving Parisa in the afternoon.

Madarach took Benji to the same alley near Dorn's house, and this time Benji got out and waited at the corner. When Dorn came out, looking sleepy as before, Benji hissed at him.

Dorn looked up, saw Benji, and smiled. He walked quickly to the alley and shook Benji's hand.

"It's good to see you," he said.

"You too," Benji agreed. "How are things going?"

Dorn sighed.

"Slowly," he said. "Thol and I got about a dozen boys to join us. But then Thol had to leave, and we're not sure what to do next."

"Thol had to leave?" Benji repeated, cautiously. "Did he get sent to the front?"

"No," Dorn said. "They wanted to send him, but he ran away to the mountains instead. I'm a little worried about him."

"Do you have any way to reach him?" Benji asked.

"Not really," Dorn said. "Unless one of us wants to run away to the mountains and join him, but then we wouldn't be able to come back."

"Do you know where he is?" Benji wondered.

"Not exactly," Dorn replied. "But we know he went north, away from the fighting."

"So you'd have to look for him," Benji observed. "I imagine that would be difficult."

"Yes," Dorn agreed. "But it gets worse. No one ever ran away before, so now the faction has patrols to keep us in town. We'd have to avoid the patrols, too."

"Or take Madarach," Benji suggested.

Dorn considered this.

"That would work," he said.

"Do you want to go now?" Benji asked. "We could find him and make sure he's okay."

Dorn hesitated, but only for a moment.

"Yes," he said. "What did you tell me before? Friends come before faction."

"For me they do," Benji agreed. "Let's go."

Benji helped Dorn into the bubble, and then explained to Madarach what they wanted to do. In moments, they were lifting high above the ground and heading north.

"Do your sensors have anything that can help us find Thol?" Benji asked Madarach.

"Of course," Madarach replied. "I can search for infrared signatures, which include body heat. And I can determine fairly accurately whether a signature is a person or an animal. How many people can there be in the mountains if Thol is the first to run away?"

"Not very many," Benji suggested.

But Benji was wrong. As they approached the mountains, Madarach projected a view of them showing infrared signatures for Benji and Dorn to see. There were hundreds of them.

"What do we do now?" Dorn asked.

Benji pointed at the image.

"They seem to mostly be concentrated in these three areas," he observed. "They look like camps. Maybe Thol is in one of those."

"But we don't know who they are, or what faction they belong to," Dorn observed. "What if we go to the wrong one and they attack us?"

Benji thought for a moment.

"If people come here to escape the factions," he suggested, "then they won't care which faction we come from, as long as we're not trying to bring them back. Besides, Madarach has some defensive weapons."

"So I heard," Dorn said, chuckling.

They chose the nearest camp, and Madarach approached to within a few hundred yards and landed in the trees.

"Be careful," he reminded Benji. "I will monitor you, but these thick trees will be difficult for me to navigate."

"I'll be careful," Benji assured him.

Benji and Dorn exited the bubble and made their way through the forest. The trees were indeed thick, and they reminded Benji of the woods out behind their house where he had found the well. He had to be careful to hold the clinging tree limbs so they didn't snap back and hit Dorn in the face.

"Do you think there'll be guards?" Dorn whispered.

"I don't know," Benji replied. "I don't see any, and I doubt they could see us through these trees."

Then they emerged into a clearing filled with about thirty tents. They didn't see anyone as they approached.

"It looks deserted," Benji said.

"There must be someone here," Dorn replied. "Madarach saw infrared images, and there's freshly-washed laundry on that rope. It's still wet."

They wandered between the tents calling, "Hello?"

"There's a cook stove with food cooking," Dorn observed. "Someone lives here."

"Then where are they?" Benji wondered. "Did they hear us coming and hide in the woods?"

"Who are you?" asked a gravelly voice behind them.

The two boys spun around.

Twenty yards away, an old man had emerged from one of the tents. He looked frightening, with long, scraggly, gray hair and a tangled gray beard that seemed to have twigs in it. But he didn't seem to carry a weapon.

"We're friends of Thol," Dorn replied. "We came looking for him."

"I don't know Thol," the old man replied. "And I don't know you. What faction are you from?"

"He's from Darkly," Benji answered. "I'm from another planet."

"Another planet?" the old man scoffed. "A space man?"

Benji chuckled, imagining how he would have felt before he found the well if someone on Earth had announced that they were from another planet. It must sound ridiculous.

"More or less," he agreed. "I mean no harm."

"Are you from Darkly?" Dorn asked.

"I am a citizen of Free Zeblack," the old man replied, proudly. "What faction I was born in doesn't matter."

"Free Zeblack?" Dorn repeated. "I like the sound of that."

"Do you?" the old man asked, sounding like he didn't quite believe it. "But you said you're from Darkly. What are you doing here?"

"I told you," Dorn said, "I'm looking for my friend, Thol. He ran away rather than fight in the war, and he said he was coming here."

"Here?" the old man repeated. "No one knows where here is."

"I mean, he said he was going to the mountains," Dorn said. "I didn't know there were already people here. I was worried about him, and I wanted to make sure he's okay."

The old man looked the two boys up and down. Then he nodded.

"I think I believe you," he said. "My name is Blot. I'm only here because I'm too lame to work. Thol is with the others, working the farm."

"I thought you didn't know Thol," Benji said.

"I didn't know Thol because I didn't know you," Blot replied. "Now I know you, and it seems I do know Thol after all. You never know when the factions will send someone to spy on us."

"Have they?" Dorn asked.

"Have they what?" Blot asked back.

"Sent someone to spy on you," Dorn clarified.

Blot laughed a long, harsh, cackle.

"Sometimes they try," he said. "But most of the spies end up joining us. I'm sure the factions think we're bloodthirsty, since none of their people ever return. The truth is, Free Zeblack wins people over once they see what it means."

"And what does it mean?" Benji asked.

Blot thought for a long moment.

"I was born in Larkspray," he said. "My wife was born in Blue. My neighbor was born in Whitehall. My other neighbor was born in Red Hill, but Torrent took his land and made him fight for them. Your friend Thol is from Darkly. We all live together here as equals, sharing what we have regardless of who might have once been our enemy."

"That," Benji said, "is what I dream of seeing on your whole planet."

"Do you?" Blot asked. "Do you indeed?"

Then he cackled again.

"Then we have the same dream, my friends," he concluded. "Come into my tent and have tea."

Chapter Thirty

Blot's tent barely had room for two cots and a large rucksack. Blot sat on one cot, and he gestured for the two boys to sit on the other. Then he produced three clay cups and a clay flask wrapped in animal skins. He poured, and gave the first cup to Dorn.

The second cup went to Benji, who sniffed it suspiciously. He put his hand on Dorn's arm.

"Is this okay to drink?" he asked, telepathically.

"It's regular tea," Dorn replied. "It's made from bark and flowers, completely harmless."

Benji sipped a tiny bit as Blot took a gulp from his own cup.

"Everyone will be back in a couple of hours for lunch," Blot said. "I imagine Thol will come with them."

"You said they work on a farm," Dorn said. "I didn't see any farm. Is it nearby?"

"Not far at all," Blot said. "But it's disguised, of course, so the factions can't see it from the air. We grow some crops hidden in bushes, and others under the trees, and we've replaced some trees with fruit trees. And we grow mushrooms and some other fungi in a cave. That, plus what the others hunt, keeps us fed."

"The other camps you mean?" Benji asked. "We saw two others on the way in, but this was the closest."

Blot cackled again.

"Oh, there are more than two," he said. "Obviously some are better hidden than others."

"How many of you are there?" Dorn asked. "We saw several hundred on our sensors."

"Did you?" Blot asked. "I'm glad the factions don't have the same sensors you have. We try to stay hidden, but apparently some of us are not doing that so well."

"How many?" Dorn repeated.

"All together?" Blot asked. "Maybe five thousand."

"Five thousand?" Benji and Dorn repeated in unison.

"I had no idea," Dorn said.

"That's the plan," Blot said. "If no one has any idea, they won't come looking for us."

"Just those desperate enough to run away to the mountains," Benji observed.

"Exactly," Blot agreed. "And we'll take as many of those as we can get."

"So you have several camps," Dorn continued. "This one farms. What do the others do?"

"What they can," Blot replied. "One hunts. One manages water and medicine. One mines. One works on technological innovations, like better cook stoves and better ways to work metal. There are two other farming camps."

"How long have you been here?" Benji asked.

"I've been here almost forty years," Blot replied. "But the first camps were here long before that. No one really knows, but it seems like they formed over a hundred years ago. There were deserters and avoiders since the beginning, and at some point enough of them gathered here to form their own community. Now it's grown so much that it's more like a society."

"Who's in charge?" Dorn asked. "Is there a leader, a general, or a president?"

Blot laughed.

"That's what got our planet into this mess," Blot replied. "Our only leader is the Goddess, and she moves each person's heart as she sees fit. We do nothing without a consensus."

"What's a consensus?" Benji asked unfamiliar with the word.

Blot smiled.

"A consensus is when everyone agrees," he said. "Not just a majority, but everyone."

"That must be hard," Benji suggested. "How do you get everyone to agree on anything?"

"We have to," Blot explained. "Otherwise, we die. Everyone knows that. So when a matter comes up, we work hard to reach an agreement. If we can't, we don't do it. There are things that have to be done, so we're used to coming to agreement. Our survival depends on it."

"That's amazing," Benji said. "Where I come from, it's hard enough to get a majority to agree on anything."

"Well, we also leave decisions to those who are best positioned to make them," Blot added. "We let the miners decide how and what to mine, and they let us farmers decide how and what to farm. There's no point in making everyone agree on everything. Let decisions be made at the lowest level by the least number of people."

"Wow," Benji said. "Would that system of government work for the whole planet?"

"It would," Blot replied. "For a while. Until some *flemunk* of a general decided he knew better what crops should be planted and how. Then it would fall apart."

"What's a *flemunk*?" Benji asked Dorn.

"I don't really know," Dorn replied. "My grandfather used to say that word, and I know it's an insult, but I don't know why."

Blot cackled again.

"A *flemunk* was a giant bird," he said. "Almost as tall as you are. They liked to rest on flat, barren ground. When we developed mechanical transportation and built roads, the roads were warmer and the *flemunk* liked the warmth. They would rest in the roads and get run over. They became extinct."

"So a *flemunk* is someone too stupid to get out of the road?" Dorn suggested.

"Exactly!" Blot confirmed.

Then he cackled again.

"Only stupid people pretend to know everything and think they know what's best for everyone else," he said. "And stupid people are too often in charge."

Just then, they heard voices and footsteps outside.

Blot cocked his head.

"They're back for lunch," he noted. "Go out and see if your friend is with them."

Benji and Dorn slipped through the flap of the tent and watched as a crowd of almost a hundred men, women, and children entered the camp walking single file. They split into families and couples as they went to their tents.

"Thol!" Dorn called, as he spotted his friend making his way through the camp.

"Dorn?" Thol called back. "And Benji! I thought I'd never see you again!"

"Well, you were wrong," Dorn replied. "We wanted to make sure you were still alive."

"I am," Thol said. "This place is better than I ever imagined."

They followed Thol to his tent, and Thol held the flap open for them. Inside, another young man was already perched on a cot, eating a meal from a clay bowl.

"This is Prett," Thol said, by way of introduction. "He's my tent mate. And he's also from Turret."

"Turret?" Dorn repeated. "And you two get along?"

Thol laughed.

"We're all citizens of Free Zeblack now," he explained. "We have no allegiance to the faction we came from."

Thol left the tent briefly and returned with two more bowls of food. He handed one to Benji and the other to Dorn, and they all began eating.

"How are things in town?" Thol asked.

"The same," Dorn replied. "There are about a dozen of us who want to change things, but we don't know yet what to do. How's your life here?"

Thol explained how after days wandering alone, he was almost starving and thinking about turning himself in to the faction. Then he'd stumbled onto some members of Free Zeblack. They had fed him and invited him to join them. He'd been assigned to a farming camp. He knew nothing about farming, but they'd been patient with him and he was a hard worker.

"Now it feels like home," he said. "I really like the way they think here."

"I'd like to see Free Zeblack over the whole planet," Dorn said, sighing.

"Me too," Thol agreed. "But I don't know how, and I don't think they do either."

They talked for a half hour, and then Thol said he had to get back to work.

"Is there any way we can stay in contact with you?" Benji asked. "Coming out here every time isn't the best plan, especially since you guys want to avoid being noticed by the factions."

"I don't know," Thol replied. "I've never seen a radio. But you could talk to the guys at the technology camp. They'll know better than I do."

Thol gave them directions, and Dorn and Benji headed back to meet Madarach.

Half an hour later, they approached a different camp, this one much higher in the mountains and mostly in the shelter of caves. The rock walls prevented Madarach's sensors from detecting it, but Thol's directions had gotten them there.

Benji and Dorn stopped outside one of the larger cave entrances.

"Hello?" Dorn shouted.

Nothing happened for a long moment.

Then a young woman of about twenty came to the entrance of the cave. She was dressed in primitive clothes, and her hair was cut short. Even so, she was very pretty, Benji thought.

The woman stared at the two boys.

"Who are you?" she asked.

"We're friends of Thol," Dorn replied. "We want to talk to someone about your technology."

"What about it?" she asked.

She made no move toward them, so Benji and Dorn moved closer to her so they could talk more easily.

"Listen," Benji said, "Thol left Darkly because they wanted to send him to the front and he refused to go. Dorn is his best friend, and we're trying to set up a peace movement inside Darkly. But we want to find out if there's a way we can communicate with Free Zeblack."

"Why?" she asked.

"Why?" Benji repeated. The question hadn't occurred to him.

"Because Thol was instrumental in starting our movement," Dorn said. "We value his advice."

"And because what we want is the same as what you want," Benji added. "But unless we can communicate with you, we have no way to talk about how to accomplish it."

"What is it you think we want?" she asked.

Dorn gestured around the camp.

"I've never seen anything like what you have here," he said. "We want the wars to stop, but until today we had no idea what could replace the factions. I want to see what you have across the entire planet."

"That's pretty ambitious," the woman observed.

"It is," Benji agreed. "And it won't happen overnight. But it can happen. We want to help."

Now the woman gestured around the camp.

"Does it look like we need help?" she asked.

"I meant," Benji said, carefully, "that we want to help the planet. It looks to me like the planet really does need help."

The woman sighed.

"Come on in," she said.

She led the way into the cave.

Benji was surprised to see the interior lit by electric lights instead of torches.

"Where do you get electricity?" he asked.

"There's a hot spot down in one of the caves where lava is close to the surface," she explained. "We have a system that converts heat to electricity using different conductors that we mine. It doesn't generate a lot, but it's enough for us to get by."

"I've never heard of that before," Benji said. "I wonder if they have that on Earth."

The woman stopped and turned to them.

"What's Earth?" she asked.

"It's the planet he comes from," Dorn explained. "He's not from Zeblack."

"So what are you doing here?" she asked Benji. "Why do you care what happens on Zeblack?"

"Because Dorn and Thol are my friends," Benji replied. "Where I come from, friends help each other."

The woman wrinkled her brow.

"Earth must be very different from Zeblack," she said.

Then she turned back and led them further into the cave.

They stopped at a door in the side of the cave. The woman knocked first, and then opened it.

"Flan?" she called.

"I'm here, Mel," came a male voice from inside.

The woman named Mel gestured for the two boys to enter.

"Flan knows more about communications than anyone else here," she told them. "He used to be a communications officer for Blue."

She turned and left, and Benji and Dorn glanced around the crowded room. It was lined with shelves, all stacked with what appeared to be complicated electronic equipment. The middle of the room was piled with crates, boxes, and more equipment.

A young man emerged from behind the crates.

"I'm Flan," he said. "How can I help you?"

Benji and Dorn introduced themselves, and Benji explained that they wanted to communicate with Free Zeblack.

"That's simple," he said. "But not so easy. Do you have a radio?"

"No," Dorn said. "That's why we're here."

"We have one," Flan said. "Only one. I use it to communicate with some of my buddies back in Blue who are sympathetic."

"We have people in Darkly who are sympathetic, too," Dorn said.

"And if we want to get other factions involved, we'll need to be able to communicate with them, too," Benji added.

"Involved in what?" Flan asked.

Dorn and Benji looked at each other.

"We don't know yet," Benji admitted. "But we want to stop the war, and we need something to replace the faction system. Free Zeblack is the only thing we've seen that could do that."

Flan smiled.

"Yeah," he said. "It's not easy, is it? And here's the thing. Radio technology isn't complicated. If I give you my frequency, you could contact me, if you had a transmitter. But you'd have to have one, and we don't have enough parts to make more. I've cannibalized everything I can just to keep this one working."

Benji thought for a moment.

"What parts would you need?" he asked. "Maybe we could get them for you."

"You know a lot about electronics, do you?" Flan asked.

"No," Benji admitted. "But I know someone who does."

Chapter Thirty-One

Flan followed Benji and Dorn back into the woods, and they led him to Madarach.

"What's this?" Flan asked.

"It's a spacecraft, more or less," Benji explained. "And he's sentient. And he knows electronics."

"Can he hear me?" Flan asked.

"Yes," Benji said. "But he doesn't know your language, so I'll need to translate. And he doesn't communicate verbally, so he'll have to reply through me."

"Okay," Flan said. He began explaining the frequencies they used, and then talked about the various parts that they needed.

"Wait," Benji said. "He's not familiar with your units of measurement, so we have to understand those first. He wants to know what your cyclic measurement is based on."

"Wow," said Flan. "No one has asked me that since I was in school, but I still remember. One cycle is defined as the duration of one planetary rotation divided by a hundred thousand."

"Okay," Benji said. "He says he can work with that."

Then they had to find common units for resistance, capacitance, and so forth. Eventually, Madarach said he could make a list of what was needed.

"You can get all that?" Flan asked Benji.

"I don't know," Benji said. "But I'm going to try."

They said goodbye, and Benji and Dorn boarded the bubble.

"Where can we get that stuff?" Dorn asked. "Not on Zeblack. Only the factions have it."

"No," Benji agreed. "It will have to come from somewhere else."

"Parisa?" Dorn suggested.

"I don't think so," Benji replied. "They have the technology, but they don't use radios because they don't use verbal communication. And Hadrun hasn't developed electronics. Somehow, this is going to have to come from Earth."

"Is that difficult?" Dorn asked.

"I bet I can buy everything he needs on the internet in an hour," Benji said. "Plus a dozen radios, if Madarach helps me figure out which ones will work. That part is easy. But I don't have a credit card, or any money to pay for it."

Dorn gazed at his friend.

"I don't understand what you just said," he admitted, "but I hope you find a way to figure it out."

They dropped Dorn back in the alley near his house, and Madarach lifted off into space.

"Where are we going?" he asked Benji.

"I don't know," Benji replied. "I think the only place to get all that stuff is on Earth. I'm sure they have it, but I don't know how to buy it."

"I've been thinking about that," Madarach said. "I have an idea."

"What?" Benji asked.

Madarach paused.

"The biggest challenge is that you don't have any money, right?" he said, finally.

"Yes," Benji agreed. "That's the biggest one, but not the only one."

"So let's focus on that biggest one," Madarach suggested. "How do you get money on Earth?"

"By working," Benji replied. "And I'm too young to work even if I wanted to live there again."

"But that's not the only way," Madarach said. "How else can someone get money?"

"Steal it?" Benji suggested.

Madarach laughed.

"That's possible, yes," he agreed. "But it's not the right way. But suppose you had something someone else wanted."

Benji thought about this.

"Then they would buy it from me," he concluded, "and I'd have money."

"Exactly," Madarach agreed.

"But what do I have that someone would want to buy?" Benji asked.

"Nothing yet," Madarach admitted. "But you have the universe at your fingertips. It's filled with minerals, gems, precious metals, archeological artifacts, technology, strange life forms, and more."

"So I could find something people on Earth want," Benji suggested, "and sell it to them?"

"Exactly," Madarach replied.

"Gold," Benji said. "Everyone on Earth wants gold. I don't know why, but it's very expensive."

"Yes," Madarach agreed. "It always has been. It has beauty, of course, and it doesn't degrade like iron or silver. And it's fairly rare. So gold has always had value on your planet."

"Do you know where I can get gold?" Benji asked.

"As a matter of fact, I do," Madarach replied. "Remember the colorful planet that I took you to? At least one area of it is heavy with gold ore."

"Really?" Benji marveled. "Why didn't you take it?"

Madarach laughed again.

"What would I do with it?" he asked. "I'm trapped inside a machine."

Now Benji laughed.

"Somehow I forgot that," he said. "To me, you're just my friend Madarach."

Then something changed. Benji sensed that Madarach became very sad.

"I wish," Madarach said, "that I could play numbfoot with you. I wish it more than almost anything."

"Me too," Benji said.

Benji felt something he'd never felt coming from Madarach, and realized it was both sadness and love. Madarach had the ability to love, and he loved Benji!

And Madarach was suffering in the awareness of his handicap.

Benji changed the subject, hoping to shift Madarach's focus.

"So we know how to get gold," he said. "But how do we turn that into money, and how do we buy all this stuff?"

Madarach regained his composure.

"Let's go to Earth and do some shopping," he suggested. "We just have to get close enough to access the internet. That will tell us how much gold we'll need."

"But Madarach," Benji insisted, "even if we get gold, how do we turn it into money and get a credit card so we can buy this stuff on the internet? And where will we have it shipped to? I don't even live there anymore, and I can't imagine asking my parents to help. And I'm a twelve-year-old boy, and you're a machine. Even Lisa is only sixteen, and no one will take her seriously. Who's going to do business with us directly?"

"I don't know yet," Madarach said. "One thing at a time. Let's gather information."

So they went to Earth. Madarach hovered over a library and accessed the internet. He put the display up, but screens passed by so quickly that Benji couldn't make sense of them.

"The parts Flan wants are pretty cheap," Madarach informed him. "The most expensive are the antennae, and we can get them for about five dollars. We can buy enough parts to build ten radios for about $350."

"That still seems like a lot," Benji observed.

"For the same amount, we could buy two already-constructed radios," Madarach said. "Now, $350 is a lot of money for a 12-year-old to have, but not so much as to be suspicious. It's not like you'd be walking into a radio store with ten thousand dollars in cash."

"Or gold," Benji added, grimly. "We still don't know how to convert gold into money."

"I think we can figure that out," Madarach told him. "But it's getting late on Parisa, and we should head home."

It was indeed getting late on Parisa, and Benji walked home in the growing shadows. Tamar was just serving dinner as he arrived.

Benji smiled as he sat down between Lisa and Miriam. Tamar had prepared one of his favorite Parisan meals. It was the closest thing to mashed potatoes he had seen on any planet other than Earth, along with the local version of green beans served in a spicy sauce flavored with some kind of nut.

Miriam put her hand on Benji's arm so they could communicate.

"You were gone a long time," she observed. "Did you have fun?"

"Yes," Benji replied. "I got to see my friend Thol, who moved to a different part of Zeblack."

"That's great!" Miriam replied.

"I'm so glad you have so many friends, Benji," Tamar added. "You are a special boy who seems to make friends everywhere."

Benji blushed.

But Lisa furrowed her brow.

After dinner, Lisa invited Benji outside to sit on the porch in the cool of the evening.

"Why didn't you tell them?" she asked.

"Tell them what?" Benji replied, fidgeting.

"Benji," Lisa scolded. "I'm your sister. Don't ever think you can keep secrets from me. I just want to know why you kept them from the rest of the family."

Benji sighed.

"I don't know where this is going," he said. "They're already so worried because of what happened to you. I don't want to worry them any more."

Lisa frowned.

"And you think that if something happens to you, they'll be glad you protected them from the truth about what you were doing?" she suggested.

"Yes," Benji said. "Well, no. But if nothing happens to me, they'll have worried for nothing."

Lisa shook her head in frustration.

"Benji, do you know what love is?" she asked.

Benji paused.

"I think so," he said, slowly.

"If Aelbreth was doing something that could be dangerous, would you want to know about it?" she asked.

"Of course," Benji replied. "I love her, and I want her to be safe."

"And if she didn't tell you, would you feel like she lied to you?" Lisa pressed.

"I guess I would," Benji agreed.

"Well, love is treating others the way you want to be treated," Lisa continued. "If you wouldn't want someone you love to do that to you, don't do it to them."

Benji flushed. He didn't like being wrong, but he could see that Lisa was right.

"Does that mean I have to tell them *everything*?" Benji asked. "They don't know that Chute tried to kidnap me and steal Madarach. If they did, they'd probably make me stop going to Zeblack."

"Yes," Lisa insisted. "Everything."

Then she paused.

"No," she said. "Not everything. You're right, they would make you stop going to Zeblack, and you have something important to do there. I'm sorry, you're right and I was wrong."

Benji stared at his sister.

"Lisa are you okay?" he asked.

"Yes," she said, sharply. "Why?"

"Because you were right, and then you just changed your mind," Benji said.

Lisa shook her head, this time in confusion.

"I thought I was right," she said, softly. "But I wasn't. I forgot *farchedan*."

"The dance," Benji murmured. "The dance is the means."

"Yes," Lisa said. "The dance is the means."

"And the spirit of life is the source," Benji added.

Lisa frowned.

"That's what she said," Lisa agreed. "But I still don't know what it means."

Then she began to cry.

Chapter Thirty-Two

Benji put his arms around his sister. She rarely shared her emotions directly, but now he could feel waves of them coming from her. Sadness, confusion, anger, and despair all rolled through his body as if he felt them himself.

"Lisa," he said, softly. "You've been keeping secrets, too."

She didn't reply. Instead, she sobbed into his shoulder, soaking his shirt and flooding him with feelings.

Finally, her tears began to recede.

"I thought I had to," she said. "I thought no one could understand."

"I don't think anyone can understand," Benji agreed. "But that doesn't mean you have to be alone. I don't understand your experience, but I do understand your feelings about it."

She smiled, briefly, and tousled his hair.

"I should have trusted you," she said. "You're older than I think you are. And you saved my life."

"You can trust me," Benji assured her. "You can share with me whatever you need to. And I won't tell a soul."

"I know," she said. "And I think you're the only person I *can* share this with. Tobin can't understand. He's still so angry about it."

"Tobin is angry?" Benji repeated. "I had no idea."

"He holds it in," Lisa said. "But I can tell."

"It seems like there's a lot of holding it in going on," Benji observed.

Lisa chuckled, weakly.

"Yes," she agreed, "I guess there is. But I can't anymore, and I am grateful to have a brother I can share with."

"Me too," Benji said.

"And you?" she asked. "Who do you share everything with?"

Benji thought about this.

"Madarach," he replied. "He's my best friend."

Lisa wrinkled her face.

"Madarach is a machine," she reminded him.

Benji paused.

"I told you before," he said. "Madarach is not just a machine."

Lisa looked confused.

"You said he used to be a person," she acknowledged. "But how can he still be a person when he's been in a computer for thousands of years?"

"Listen," Benji said.

He told her everything that had happened over the past few weeks, from Madarach making jokes to their conversation on the painted planet, from Madarach's confession of love for his wife, who was also a machine, to Madarach's anger at Chute and his gang, to Benji's realization that Madarach actually loved Benji the way a person would.

"The priestess told me that I love deeply for a man," Benji confessed. "And she said the same about Madarach."

Lisa said nothing for a long while.

"Madarach can love?" she asked, finally.

"Yes," Benji confirmed. "He's a person, and he has all the emotions of a person, even though he's trapped in a machine."

"That's really sad," she said. "And no one knows?"

"Just Aelbreth and me," Benji replied. "And now you. But like I said, you really can't tell anyone, not even Tobin."

"Why shouldn't everyone know?" she asked. "This is really sad."

"They shouldn't," Benji said. "Madarach told me what happened. It's not the same as what they teach in school. He was an enemy, and his punishment was to be transferred to a computer. If they learned he had emotions, and even anger, they might fear he's still an enemy. But maybe worse, Madarach's story contradicts history handed down through hundreds of generations. And he was there. He saw it all. He admits his mistakes, and he feels bad about them. But his story threatens the entire Parisan culture."

Lisa thought about this.

"Okay," she said. "I won't tell a soul. You can trust me like I trust you."

"Not even Tobin," Benji reminded her.

"Not even Tobin," Lisa agreed.

They sat a while in silence. The night was pleasantly cool, and the insects were humming in the trees nearby.

"It's nice here," Benji observed. "And there aren't any *fortule* to eat us."

Lisa laughed.

Then she turned serious.

"Did you meet an old man on Zeblack?" she asked.

"Yes," Benji replied. "His name is Blot. He lives in the Free Zeblack settlement. Why?"

"He's the key," Lisa said.

"The key?" Benji repeated.

"Dorn can open the door, but the old man is the key," she said.

Benji thought back to the vision Lisa had described a few weeks earlier. Dorn had been able to open a door that no one else could. But at the time, Lisa had said she couldn't see the key.

"You saw it?" Benji suggested.

"Not exactly," she replied. "I just know it."

Benji thought about this. Then he nodded.

"I thought maybe it would be Thol," he said. "Thol is a great photographer, and Madarach told me that photographs can change minds."

"I'm not saying Thol isn't important," Lisa said. "I don't know about that. But this old man has some special part to play."

Benji nodded. He knew better than to ask what that part was. If Lisa knew, she would tell him.

They sat a while longer, and then went inside. Benji, who'd had a long day, got ready for bed.

But his mind wouldn't let him sleep for a long time. He kept thinking about Zeblack, and Dorn and Blot and Flan, and about how he and Madarach could get radio parts, and what Free Zeblack might do with them.

But nothing would happen the next day. Instead, Benji returned to his routine of class and visiting the temple.

Benji found it hard to concentrate on his schooling. Parisan school focused on math, history, and science. Benji excelled in math, even though it was a little different on Parisa. On Earth, he'd be in the seventh grade doing pre-algebra, but on Parisa his classes were tailored for him by the computer. As he mastered one topic, the computer would advance him to another. He had already mastered algebra and beginning geometry, and was learning the Parisan equivalent of conic sections.

He loved science, though he found physics more interesting that chemistry or botany. Parisans began the study of botany at a young age because so much of their work involved tending the plants that fed them, but Benji's job at the temple had little to do with plants.

At first, Benji had found Parisan history irrelevant. Why should he, an Earth child, care about the development of a society light years from his home? Now, though, Parisa was his home, or at least one of his homes. And Parisa had been through a war and ended it. That fascinated Benji. Between his classes, which taught the "official" version of history, and his discussions with Madarach, who had seen what really happened, he was learning a lot about Parisa's successful struggle to overcome violence.

Benji wished they would spend more time on the mechanics of peace, so that he could apply it to Zeblack. But Parisans seemed to have lost interest in other worlds. They focused only on what had happened on their own planet, the goal of which was to prevent it from happening again.

"I think you're looking for a class in interplanetary sociology," Lisa told him one day. "And I don't think that's been invented yet."

"What's sociology?" Benji asked, puzzled.

"It's the study of societies and their problems," Lisa explained.

"Yes," Benji agreed. "That's exactly it."

"But no one has studied the societies of other planets," Lisa observed. "No one knows yet whether the problems on one planet can be solved by solutions from another planet."

"You and I have studied other planets," Benji objected.

Lisa sighed.

"Yes," she agreed. "But I think we're the first."

Benji thought for a moment.

"Maybe you could become a teacher and invent interplanetary socio-whatever," Benji suggested.

Lisa laughed.

"Interplanetary sociology," she said again. "Maybe I could. Or maybe you could. But who would be interested in it?"

"I would," Benji replied.

Chapter Thirty-Three

On his next day off, eight days after his previous trip to Zeblack, Benji leapt out of bed as soon as his eyes opened. He dressed quickly in a blue jumpsuit of the style favored on Parisa. Then he rushed to the kitchen to see what leftovers he could eat for breakfast.

To his surprise, Tamar and Miriam stood over the electric range cooking. Miriam glanced at Benji and smiled. She reached out for his hand.

"Breakfast will be ready in a few minutes," she said.

"Okay," Benji said.

Usually Tamar only made breakfast on special occasions, like a graduation or recognition, a new job, or a guest. Benji wasn't aware of any special occasions. There must be a guest coming that he didn't know about, he decided.

But when they sat down at the table, no guest joined them. It was just Benji and Lisa, Miriam and Tobin, and Tamar and Jachin.

Miriam uncovered the platter of food, and Benji stared. On the platter sat small fried circles that looked a lot like pancakes.

He looked at Miriam.

Miriam grinned, and put her hand on Benji's arm.

"Lisa gave us the recipe," she explained. "We did the best we could with the ingredients we have here. I hope they're okay."

"Lisa had you make them?" he asked.

Then he turned to Lisa.

Lisa blushed.

"It's a bribe," she said. "I know you haven't had pancakes in almost two years, and you miss them. I was hoping you'd be willing to take me to Hassyr for the day."

Benji's mind went through several changes in a matter of seconds.

"You had them make pancakes for me?" he asked Lisa, his disbelief mixing with gratitude. "That's sweet."

Then he darkened.

"But it's a bribe?" he added. "You knew I wanted to go to Earth today and get radio parts, right? So you bribed me so I'd do something else that you wanted?"

Then he put his hand back on Miriam's arm.

"Thank you," he said. "I can't wait to try them."

Miriam smiled.

"And Umma says it would be good for you to forget about Zeblack today. That can wait a week. Take some time off," she said.

"Miriam," Benji protested, "people are dying on Zeblack. Some of my friends are in danger."

Miriam sighed.

"I know," she said. "But you're a boy. We know you have these abilities, and that you want to help. But you need to do something fun, too."

Benji sighed. Tamar rarely insisted that he do or not do any particular thing. She seemed to feel strongly about this. And she had made him pancakes.

"Fine," he agreed, reluctantly. "We'll go to Hassyr. Do you want to come?"

Miriam smiled again.

"Yes," she replied. "I've never been to another planet, and I like your friends and would like to see where they live."

"Really?" Benji asked.

Miriam had always listened attentively to Benji's and Lisa's adventures, but had never shown any interest in leaving Parisa.

"Why not?" Miriam replied. "I want to see a whole planet of blue people!"

Benji shrugged.

"Okay," he said.

"Now eat your pancakes," Miriam replied. "I made fruit syrup to go with them because we didn't have anything like marble syrup here."

Benji squinted in confusion for a moment, and then laughed.

"It's maple syrup," he corrected. "Maple is a tree. Marble is a rock."

He took some pancakes and poured syrup over them. Then he took a bite. He wasn't sure what to expect. Parisa didn't have wheat or sugar cane, so the flour and sugar they used was quite different from Earth. They didn't eat eggs, either, and Benji had watched his mom make pancakes often enough that he knew you needed an egg. He had no idea what else went into a pancake, and whether they might have that on his adopted planet.

The pancake was actually quite good. It was cakier than an Earth pancake, but nicely sweet. The fruit syrup added just a little tartness, giving almost the reverse effect of his mom's pancake breakfast where the cakes were slightly bitter and the syrup gave the sweetness.

He reached his hands out to both Tamar and Miriam.

"These are really good," he said. "Thank you."

After breakfast, Benji waited impatiently as the girls got dressed. Eventually Miriam appeared, and finally Lisa emerged.

"Shall we go?" Benji suggested.

"Yes," Lisa agreed. "And Tobin is coming, too."

"Tobin?" Benji repeated. "He hates Hassyr because of what happened to you there!"

"I convinced him he should see it and meet our friends," Lisa explained, as Tobin joined the procession. "He's ready to let it go."

They left the house and walked through the streets to the well, hidden in the trees. Benji summoned the stars and helped the other three children enter. Then he told Madarach to take them to Hassyr.

"But go slowly past the dancing planet," he instructed, telepathically. "I want Tobin and Miriam to be able to see it."

Moments later, the planet with the dancing rings came into view.

"What is that?" Miriam asked, clearly fascinated.

"They call it *farchedan*," Benji explained. "It means 'the dance.'"

"Is that like their god?" Tobin asked.

"Not exactly," Benji replied. "They look for the dance in all things, but there seems to be no god or goddess that causes the dance. The dance is the means of creation."

"That's a nice way to look at it," Miriam commented.

They approached Hassyr and Madarach took them in over the mountains, which neither Benji nor Lisa had seen up close before.

"I can see why no one lives there," Lisa said. "It's all dry and rocky. Nothing could grow there."

"But it is beautiful," Miriam said.

Then they passed over the coastal strip, which looked like one giant city.

"They all live near the coast," Benji explained. "Their food comes from the sea."

Then Madarach passed out over the ocean, a vast expanse of water that appeared bluer than any ocean Benji had ever seen before.

"Do you think something in the ocean causes their skin to be blue?" he wondered.

To his surprise, Madarach answered him.

"That is exactly right," Madarach replied. "There are small creatures in the water, similar to what you call plankton on Earth. They contain a deep blue pigment. They are the source of food for many fish and mollusks, which then contain the pigment. Everything the predator fish eat has the pigment in it. So any creature harvested from the sea contains the pigment, and it passes to the people who eat it."

"So if we stayed on Hassyr for a while, we'd turn blue too?" Benji asked.

"Yes," Madarach confirmed. "Though I'm not sure how quickly, or how long the effect would last."

Benji relayed this to the others, who were amazed.

"Tobin," Lisa asked, "would you still love me if I turned blue?"

Tobin made a face.

"This is why I like Parisa," he said. "Everyone stays their original color."

An island came into view. It appeared to be fairly large, with a mountain in the center that Benji guessed was once a volcano. He could see lush vegetation in the lowlands, and it appeared to be surrounded by wide, sandy beaches.

"It looks like Summerland!" Lisa exclaimed.

"It does," Benji agreed. "Madarach, what is this place?"

"It's a sanctuary," Madarach explained. "It's similar to your national parks on Earth. It's owned by the people, and kept for public use. There are only a few primitive buildings, and they want to keep it that way."

"How do people get here?" Benji wondered.

"There's a ferry that brings people out for the day a couple of days a week," Madarach replied. "This isn't one of those days."

"So it's deserted?" Benji surmised.

"We're only here because we have alternate transportation," Madarach said. "Would you like a closer look?"

"Yes!" Benji exclaimed in his mind.

They dropped lower and approached the beach, and Madarach began a slow tour around the perimeter.

The beaches looked lovely. The sand was wide and obviously very fine. But it was a darker color than Benji was used to seeing, almost a blue-black. Perhaps, he guessed, the sand was from volcanic rock, tinted with pigment from the sea.

Then he saw people. A small group sat on the beach in the shadow of something that looked a lot like a palm tree.

"Madarach," he said, "I thought you said this place was deserted."

"I didn't say that," Madarach corrected, as he approached the group. "I said we're here because we have alternate transportation. I never said we were the only ones who had it."

Now Benji could see the people more clearly. Only one was facing them, and it was a girl about Benji's age.

Benji stared for a moment.

"It's Queelie!" he shouted.

Madarach set down on the beach, and Benji helped his family exit the bubble. As they did, Queelie came running toward them, followed at a more leisurely pace by Quanda.

"Queelie!" Lisa shouted. "Come meet my family!"

They did the introductions through telepathy and translation, which seemed awkward at first until they fell into a rhythm.

"Who else is with you?" Benji asked.

"Friends," Quanda said, grinning. "Come and see."

They did, though in deference to Lisa and Miriam, both of whom seemed to find running undignified, they moved at a walk.

As they approached the shade of the tree, Benji saw a boy a little older than him and a girl that appeared a little younger. The boy reminded Benji of Dorn in size and shape, and he thought sadly of Zeblack and what he might otherwise be doing that day. But Tamar was right. Benji was, after all, only twelve. He wasn't ready to be an adult yet.

As they stepped out of the bright light and into the shade, Benji's eyes needed to adjust for a moment. When they did, he glanced at the boy again. Quanda's friend wasn't blue. But that didn't make any sense. Everyone on Hassyr got their food from the sea, didn't they? Or were some people immune to the pigment?

He stared, as his brain tried to make sense of what he was seeing. The boy looked remarkably like Dorn.

That's because he *was* Dorn.

"What are you doing here?" Benji asked, incredulously.

"You're not happy to see me?" Dorn asked back.

"Of course I am!" Benji protested. "It's just, well, how? Why?"

Dorn grinned.

"He's easily confused," said a familiar female voice just behind him. "I bet he doesn't even know what day it is."

Benji spun around.

Aelbreth stood there almost close enough for him to touch. Benji gawked, completely confused, wondering briefly if this was some kind of trick.

"You're not glad to see your wife?" Dorn joked. "I'll take her if you don't want her."

Benji turned to look at Dorn, and then back to Aelbreth.

"I don't understand," he said, weakly.

"Oh, shut up and kiss me," Aelbreth instructed. "You think I came halfway across the universe to watch you act like a *patret*?"

It was definitely Aelbreth, Benji realized.

He stepped forward and kissed her, feeling the exquisite joining of their emotions.

"What are you doing here?" he asked her, telepathically. "What's this all about?"

He felt Aelbreth's internal laughter.

"You really don't know what day it is," she observed, "do you?"

"It's 32," he replied. "It's the last day of month Seven."

"Not on Parisa, silly," she communicated back.

"I don't know the calendar here on Hassyr," he replied. "And I'm sorry, but I lose track of the calendar on Hadrun because even you guys don't pay attention to it. Did I miss something? Is it your birthday?"

Aelbreth broke off their kiss and laughed.

"You really are a *patret* brain," she said, aloud. "Today is June 27 on Earth. It's *your* birthday!"

Chapter Thirty-Four

Benji stared at Aelbreth.

"Today is June 27?" he asked. "I wasn't even paying attention. But how did *you* know? I can't even keep track of it without a computer."

"I didn't," Aelbreth confessed. "But Madarach did. He put this all together. Isn't he sweet?"

"Madarach?" Benji exclaimed. "Madarach threw me a surprise party?"

"I think Lisa helped," Aelbreth added. "You might want to go thank her."

Benji turned. He shook hands with Dorn, and then approached Lisa and threw his arms around her.

"You and Madarach conspired against me?" he joked. "Thank you."

Lisa smiled.

"I wanted to do something special for you," she said. "But really, it was Madarach's idea. And guess what? You're not twelve anymore. You're a teenager."

"Really? A teenager?" Benji asked, even though it was obvious that thirteen years old was a teen.

Benji's parents always talked about teenagers as if they were some kind of alien creature, but he didn't think he felt any different than he had the day before.

Or did he?

"Come on!" Quanda shouted from nearby. "Let's swim!"

He stripped down to a pair of shorts and ran for the water.

Aelbreth had slipped out of her clothes and was already running.

"Last one in is a *patret!*" she yelled.

Benji laughed. They'd already established that he was a *patret*.

"Wait," Benji said, puzzled.

"What?" Lisa asked.

Benji looked around at his friends. Aelbreth had already reached the water, and Quanda was right behind her. Dorn wasn't far behind, because he hadn't bothered to take off his clothes. Queelie and Tobin trailed by a dozen yards, having stopped to strip down to their shorts as Quanda had. Miriam trotted along behind, though she showed no indication she planned on getting wet. They were all laughing and joking and having a good time, as friends should.

"What's the matter?" Lisa asked.

"How?" Benji asked. "They are from four different planets with four different languages, one of which isn't even spoken. How do they understand each other?"

Lisa smiled.

"Did you know that Quanda and Queelie are twins?" she asked.

"Yes, but what does that have to do with it?" Benji wondered.

"Their birthday is today, too," she continued. "Their year is different than Earth's, so it won't be the same every year, but this year, you share a birthday with them."

Benji scrunched up his face, trying to figure out what any of that had to do with his question.

"So?" he said, hoping to prompt her to continue.

"I just thought it was cool, that's all," Lisa replied. "So I gave Queelie a gift."

"You gave..." Benji began.

But he didn't finish, because he realized what she was telling him.

He thought about the Hassyri prophesy, and about the old priestess's warnings.

"You gave Queelie telepathy?" he asked.

"I did," she confirmed. "But I talked to the priestess first. She agreed that it would be okay."

Benji puzzled about this for a moment.

"When?" he asked. "When did you have time to do all that, and how did you get to Hassyr?"

Lisa laughed.

"Do you think I sit around all day and pine while you're gone, like Aelbreth?" she asked.

"Aelbreth doesn't sit around," Benji protested.

"And neither do I," Lisa replied. "Queelie came and got me, and we had a lot of fun together. And in her, the gift is a little different. She seems to act as a conduit, almost like a universal translator from that space show we used to watch on TV."

Benji turned and looked at Queelie, who was now splashing in the shallows with Aelbreth while the boys played in the waves farther out.

Then he turned back to Lisa.

"She lets everyone understand each other?" he asked. "Is it a choice, or does it happen automatically?"

"I don't know yet," Lisa admitted. "But for the moment, we should join our friends. It's your party, and you should be there. Last one in is a *patret*!"

Lisa sprinted for the water, fully clothed in deference to her physical maturity.

Benji threw off his clothes and followed, but Lisa had longer legs and Benji couldn't catch up. Lisa did a perfect running shallow dive into the water and came to the surface near Queelie.

"Hey, *patret*-brain," Lisa called. "Get in here!"

Benji did a running shallow dive as Lisa had, and surfaced next to Aelbreth.

"Anyone want to body surf?" he asked, gesturing at the waves breaking a few yards further out.

"*Patret* can't surf!" Aelbreth insisted. "They can't even swim."

"Well, maybe you'd better stay here, then," Benji joked, dunking her head under the water.

Aelbreth came up sputtering.

"Let's go," she said. "We'll see who the *patret* is!"

"I want to try, too," Queelie said. "I've never been out here before, so I don't know how to surf."

"It's easy," Aelbreth assured her. "Even Benji can do it!"

Benji splashed her, and then headed toward the waves.

They played in the water for hours, body surfing in the waves and splashing each other. Lisa joined them at times, though she spent most of the day in the shallow water where Miriam waded up to her knees.

Queelie had fixed a lunch for them, so they stopped once to eat spicy dried fish with their fingers, and then returned to the water.

Eventually, Madarach called Benji to let him know it was getting late on Parisa.

"We have to go," Benji told his friends.

"I wish we didn't," Dorn said. "I've never had this much fun in my life! I've never been swimming in anything bigger than a small pond."

"Doesn't your planet have oceans?" Quanda asked.

"It does," Dorn said. "But I've never seen one before. We can't travel because of the war."

"That's sad," Queelie said. "I hope you and Benji find a way to end the fighting."

"Me, too," Dorn said. "Though it's hard to imagine. No one alive on my planet has ever seen a time without war."

"We'll find a way," Benji said. "I know we will. And I'm not just twelve anymore. I'm a teenager."

"You're almost seventeen on Hadrun," Aelbreth reminded him.

They swam ashore and let the wind dry them. Then those who weren't already dressed replaced their clothes. Quanda and Queelie boarded Jael, and the rest of them boarded Madarach.

"We'll take Dorn home," Madarach told Benji. "But it's dark on Hadrun, so Aelbreth will have to stay on Parisa."

Benji relayed this information to the others.

"How terrible for me," Aelbreth joked.

"I'd like to see Parisa some day," Dorn said, sadly. "I want to see more planets that don't have war."

"Another time," Benji said. "I promise."

They set down in an alley on Zeblack to let Dorn off, and then returned to Parisa. Aelbreth had stayed with them before, and Tamar seemed to be expecting her this time. She had kept dinner warm, and they all ate bread with a kind of soup made from a local version of a bean. Tamar made up a bed for Aelbreth to sleep on the couch, as was appropriate on Parisa.

Benji hugged Aelbreth tightly before they went to bed.

"I've missed you," he said. "I'm sorry I haven't come to see you."

"It's okay," she replied. "I miss you, of course. But today I met Dorn, and I heard his sadness. I know how important this work is to you."

"It is," Benji agreed.

"Benji?" Aelbreth said, as he was about to release her.

"Yes," he replied.

"Just don't forget that even though it was your birthday, you're just one day older than you were yesterday," she cautioned. "Reaching a birthday doesn't create magical changes. So be careful, okay?"

Benji smiled.

"I will," he promised.

Chapter Thirty-Five

Two Parisan weeks after Benji and Madarach priced radio parts, Benji finally got a chance to buy them. First they went to the painted planet, where Madarach set them down on a sandy white plain that was littered with gold nuggets.

"We only need about an ounce," Madarach told Benji. "They are very close to pure."

"Why don't we get some extra?" Benji suggested. "Then we'd have more money in case we need something else."

"But we don't need anything else," Madarach reminded him. "Getting more just because there *is* more doesn't make logical sense. You don't even live on Earth. Why would you need Earth money?"

"I guess," Benji agreed, reluctantly.

On Earth, everyone wanted more. Then again, Benji realized, on Parisa and Hadrun, they didn't want more, and they were much happier, and on Zeblack they wanted more and they were fighting each other to get it. But Benji was from Earth, and wanting more seemed to be part of his makeup.

He gathered some nuggets and showed them to Madarach.

"That's about right," Madarach said, apparently measuring them with some kind of sensor.

"Now what do we do?" Benji asked.

"We go to Earth and find someone who will buy them," Madarach said.

They set down in an alley in Manchester. It was a relatively small city in a relatively small and mostly-rural state, so Madarach guessed it would be safer than, for example, New York City or Los Angeles.

"There is a store just around the corner that buys gold," Madarach said. "Go in and tell them you went on vacation to Arizona with your uncle, and he took you to hunt for gold. Tell him your dad is outside in the car."

"What if he wants to actually meet my dad?" Benji asked.

"He won't," Madarach said. "But if he does, bring him here. I'll make sure he doesn't take advantage of you."

"How do I know he's paying me enough?" Benji asked.

"You won't," Madarach said. "But it doesn't really matter, as long as you get enough money to buy the parts. You know how much we need, right?"

"Yes," Benji agreed.

"But we might need some extra, so make sure he gives you at least five hundred dollars," Madarach instructed. "This gold is worth more than that, even at the retail buying price."

"What does that mean?" Benji asked.

"It means," Madarach said, "that the published price of gold is what gold sells for under ideal conditions. But people who buy it want to sell it for a profit. So they may pay you anywhere from twenty percent to fifty percent less than the listed price."

"Fifty percent!" Benji exclaimed. "You mean they might pay me only half what it's worth?"

"As I said," Madarach explained, "they are in business to make a profit. But if they offer you less than five hundred dollars, say you'll go somewhere else."

"Okay," Benji said. "I've traveled all over the universe. I've talked to reptiles and arachnids. I have a girlfriend on another planet. I can do this."

"Yes, you can," Madarach assured him. "Remember, if anything happens, you call me."

"I will," Benji said, as he exited the bubble.

He walked down the alley and around the corner. As Madarach had said, there was a store halfway down the block that had a big yellow sign in the window.

"We Buy Gold," it said.

Benji walked down the sidewalk and pushed open the door to the shop. A bell rang as he entered.

Inside, a kind-looking old man sat at a desk. His hair was gray, and he squinted at Benji through thick glasses.

"How may I help you, young man?" he asked.

"I have some gold to sell," Benji replied.

"Do you indeed?" the old man asked. "Let's take a look."

Benji pulled the nuggets from his pocket and set them on the desk.

The man's eyebrows went up.

"Those are quite nice," he said. "Where did you get them?"

"I went on vacation to visit my uncle in Arizona," Benji said. "He took me looking for gold, and he let me keep the ones I found."

"Really?" the old man asked. "How did you like Arizona?"

"It was okay," Benji said, trying to recall quickly anything he knew about the state. "It was hot and dry. I like it better here."

"Did you see the Grand Canyon while you were there?" the man asked.

Benji grinned. He had indeed seen the Grand Canyon while he was there, though not exactly on vacation with his uncle.

"I did," Benji replied. "It's amazing. I've seen photos before, but it's too big for photos. It's really something."

"Yes, it is," the man replied.

Apparently satisfied with Benji's story, he turned his attention to the gold.

"Let's see what we have here," he said.

He picked up a nugget and examined it closely. Then he set it down and examined another.

"These are quite nice," he told Benji again. "Let's take them over to the bench and see how pure they are."

"How do you do that?" Benji asked.

"We use a measured amount of acid," the man explained. "The purer the gold, the more acid will be required to dissolve it."

"You're going to dissolve the gold?" Benji asked.

The man laughed.

"Only a tiny bit," he said. "We rub it against this board, which is called a touchstone. We make several lines, like this. Then we put different strengths of acid, wait a few minutes, and dip it in a neutralizer."

He rubbed one of the nuggets against the touchstone, making five thick lines like chalk on a blackboard. Then he used five different applicators to put drops of acid on each line.

"Your dad didn't come with you?" the man asked, as they waited for the acid to do its work.

"He's out in the car," Benji lied. "He thought it was important for me to do this myself."

The old man nodded.

"That's good," he said. "It's good to learn responsibility at your age. What are you, thirteen?"

"Just barely," Benji said. "My birthday was last week."

"Well, you're very grown up for your age," the man said.

Benji blushed.

When the time was up, the man dipped the touchstone in a container, and then removed it. He showed Benji the result.

"See how these lines have gaps in them where they've been eaten away by the acid?" the man said, pointing. "But these lines haven't. The first line that didn't get eaten away is twenty carat, which is about 80% pure."

"Is that good?" Benji asked.

"It's above average for gold nuggets," the man said. "I've seen some closer to 50% pure, and others that were 95% pure. These are good quality, but not the best."

Benji nodded.

"How much are they worth?" he asked.

The man weighed them, and punched numbers into a calculator.

"Based on the price of gold, they are worth about twelve hundred dollars," the man said. "We have to refine them and sell them and cover our overhead, so we pay 60% of that. You would get just over seven hundred dollars."

"Okay," Benji agreed.

The man filled out the paperwork, had Benji sign a form, and then counted out the money.

Benji had never held a hundred dollar bill in his hand before, and now he had seven of them, plus some smaller bills. He folded them carefully and stuffed them into his pocket.

"Thanks!" he said, as he headed for the door.

Back in the alley, Benji reentered the bubble.

"Wow!" he said. "That was easier than I thought!"

"You did well," Madarach agreed. "But remember that not everyone is honest when it comes to money," he warned.

Their next stop was an electronics chain that Benji had seen many times. Once again, Madarach set down in an alley around the corner.

"This is going to be more difficult," Madarach said. "I know what we need, but I can't be there to tell them. So I'm going to have to tell you, and you'll have to tell them exactly what I say. But no one is going to believe that you remembered a whole parts list, so find a sheet of paper that you can pretend to refer to."

"Okay," Benji agreed.

He exited the bubble and walked down the alley. This time, the store was on the corner, so he entered through the side door.

"Can I help you?" a young man asked.

"Yes," Benji said. "My dad and I are doing a project, and he wants me to get a list of parts."

Benji pulled a blank sheet of paper out of his pocket and pretended to read it.

"I can just take the list," the man said. "That might be easier."

"My dad doesn't write very well," Benji said. "I doubt you could read it. I'll just read it to you."

The man shrugged.

"Whatever you like," he said.

"Okay," he said, as he heard Madarach's voice in his head. "The first thing I need is a trimmer capacitor, six to forty picofarads."

The man gave Benji an odd look.

"Okay," he said, as he rummaged through a drawer. "How many do you need?"

"Ten," Benji replied.

The man's eyebrows went up.

"We're building ten of them, one for me and nine for my friends, so we can talk to each other," Benji explained.

"Wouldn't a cell phone be easier?" the man asked.

Benji sighed.

"That's what I said," he agreed. "But my dad wants to show me how building something from scratch can be more satisfying."

"Okay," the man said. "So for each part, you're going to need enough for ten radios."

"Right," Benji agreed.

They went down the list, and in about a half hour they had half filled a basket with loose electronic parts. Benji had no idea what they did, but apparently Madarach knew because he approved the list as the man read it back and Benji repeated it.

The man scanned everything into his computer, accepted a good portion of Benji's cash, and printed a receipt. Then he handed Benji the parts in two plastic bags.

"Thanks," Benji said, as he left through the same side door he'd come in.

"It was more than you thought," Benji told Madarach, "but we had enough money."

"That's why we got a little extra," Madarach reminded him. "How much is left?"

"About two hundred dollars," Benji replied.

"How would you like a cheeseburger while you're here?" Madarach asked. "Then we can donate the rest to a place that helps people."

"Donate it?" Benji repeated. "Why?"

"Because we don't need it," Madarach explained. "If we need more money, we can get more gold."

"Okay," Benji said, hesitantly. "It's just, I've never had this much money in my pocket before."

"And what do you think having that money will do for you?" Madarach asked. "Will it make you happy? Will it buy you something you need that you don't already have? You can't even spend it anywhere you usually go."

"That's true," Benji agreed. "It just doesn't seem right to give it all away."

"What did your planet's Jesus say about money?" Madarach asked.

Benji tried to remember.

"He said something about giving it all away to the poor," he acknowledged. "He said it was easier for a camel to go through the eye of a needle than for a rich man to get into Heaven. So I guess you're right. I don't need it."

Madarach took Benji to the same burger place he'd gone to with Quanda and Queelie, and Benji bought a double cheeseburger with mushrooms and onions, along with a chocolate shake. He ate the burger slowly, relishing every bite as the grease dripped into the paper wrapper. Then he sipped the shake until it was gone.

He wished that any of the other planets he spent time on knew how to make a cheeseburger. But they didn't, so he made a point to appreciate this one.

When he was done, he walked down the block to a homeless shelter and gave the manager the rest of his money.

"Thank you!" the young woman gushed.

Then it was time to leave Earth and deliver the radio parts to Flan on Zeblack.

"We have Flan's radio frequency," Benji observed, as they shifted through the stars. "How close do we have to be to contact him?"

"We can't use radio while we're outside normal time," Madarach explained. "And the frequency is what people on Earth would call shortwave, so it can be deflected by atmosphere, clouds, or even dust. On the planet, that's good, because the atmosphere bounces the signal all over the planet. But trying to contact him from outside the atmosphere wouldn't work very well."

They approached Zeblack, and Madarach descended through the atmosphere.

"Now we can try," he told Benji. "You talk, and I'll broadcast the signal."

"Okay," Benji agreed.

"Flan?" he called. "Is Flan there?"

He repeated it several times before an answer came back.

"This is Flan," a distorted voice said. "Who is this?"

"Benji," Benji said. "I have what you wanted."

There was a long pause.

"You have it?" Flan repeated. "Okay, I'll meet you where we met before."

Madarach set down in a clearing near the technology camp, and Flan stepped out of the trees.

"You really got it all?" he asked.

"We did," Benji assured him.

He handed Flan the two plastic bags of parts.

Flan examined the contents. Then he looked up.

"These are very different than I'm used to," he said. "How do I know what they do?"

Benji consulted Madarach, who translated the Earth units into Zeblack units. Benji did his best to repeat the unfamiliar terms exactly as Madarach told him.

Flan looked skeptical.

"I'll see what I can do," he said.

"There are enough parts for ten radios," Benji told him. "I'd like to make sure Dorn has one, and as we find people in the other factions maybe we can give some to them."

Flan nodded.

"This will change things," he said. "Until now, we've been alone and unknown. Now we'll have a network, and that brings both opportunity and risk. The factions will know we exist."

"I think a lot of people will want to join you once they know you exist," Benji said. "Until now, they didn't know there was an alternative."

Flan nodded.

"I've been working on a different kind of transmitter," he said. "I was thinking that if we can get information from inside the factions about what's going on we could broadcast a news program that tells the truth. Two-way radios are hard to come by, but every neighborhood has at least one radio so the factions can broadcast their notices and propaganda to their people."

"Like Radio Free Europe," Benji said, nodding. "I read about that on Earth. They sent out the real news, not just what the communists wanted people to hear."

"Is a communist like a faction?" Flan asked.

"I think it's a kind of faction," Benji said. "But I'm not really sure. There don't seem to be many anymore."

"So your planet is peaceful?" Flan asked.

Benji shook his head.

"No," he said. "There are wars. Mostly they seem to be over money. Like I said, I think the communists were just one kind of faction. When they went away, there were still plenty of other factions."

"Yeah," Flan said. "Even if one set of factions defeated another, the winners would still be factions. The only way to stop this is to get rid of the separation between us all."

"Free Zeblack," Benji affirmed.

"Free Zeblack," Flan said. "Wish us luck, because there are a lot of people who don't want us to join together."

Chapter Thirty-Six

It's hard to let things take their course," Madarach said. "But there's nothing you can do on Zeblack right now."

"How do you know?" Benji asked.

"Because I've seen what you've done," Madarach replied. "You have done everything an outsider can, for the moment. Now it's time for them to do what they can."

"What if they can't?" Benji asked.

He felt Madarach's sigh.

"Then there will not be peace," Madarach observed. "But if they can't, you must realize that you can't do it single-handedly. The failure would not be yours."

"That's easy to say," Benji muttered. "But how will I know I've done everything?"

"*Farchedan*," Madarach replied. "The dance is never a solo performance. You learned this, did you not?"

Benji thought about this.

"Yes," he agreed. "Even when I caused all the lights in the globe to go in the same direction, it was not really me doing it. I was dancing with the lights. I was part of the dance."

"As you are on Zeblack," Madarach observed. "Trust that the dance continues without you."

"Okay," Benji said. "But if we're not going to Zeblack today, where shall we go?"

It was the day off after they had delivered the radio parts to Flan, and Benji desperately wanted to know how things were going. But what Madarach said was true: the dance would continue without him, and perhaps must continue without him. He remembered the globe again, and the process of getting most of the lights spinning in the same direction, then with one wrong touch creating chaos once again.

"Hassyr," he said. "I need to see the priestess."

As they approached Hassyr, Benji asked Madarach to stop.

"I want to watch the dancing planet for a minute," he said.

He watched as the waves rippled through the rings around the planet. They varied in size, and in the light of the system's sun they seemed to change color as well. The crests of the waves appeared yellow where the sun hit them strongly. The leading edge was orange, while the trailing edges faded to blue and then purple in the depths of the troth.

Benji tried to understand the pattern of the sizes, but he couldn't see one. They appeared totally random, and yet they were all the same speed so that no wave ever overtook another. There had to be some pattern, he decided, even if he could not figure it out.

Then he stopped thinking and just absorbed the incredible beauty of the phenomenon.

"Have you ever seen a planet whose waves did anything like this?" he asked Madarach.

"I haven't," Madarach replied. "I've seen some interesting effects where the gravity of a planet's moons interfered with the rings, but never anything like this."

"I can see why they attach so much spiritual importance to it," Benji observed. "It's both amazingly beautiful and apparently miraculous."

Madarach chuckled.

"Like peace," he said. "Shall we go?"

They landed at the well, where Benji was sure Madarach would remain with his wife as long as Benji cared to stay on the planet.

Benji took the path through the rocks to the cliff and approached the entrance to the cave temple. He entered with reverence, walking softly and slowly.

The attendant noticed him as he was about half way toward the altar, and she disappeared. By the time Benji reached the altar, Yorga the Priestess was waiting for him.

"I've been expecting you," she said.

"You have?" Benji asked. "Why?"

Yorga smiled, the wrinkles in her face deepening and her face becoming an even darker blue.

"Because," she said, "most people find that after a time they can no longer discern the dance. They return for another lesson."

Benji considered this.

"I don't think that's my problem," he replied. "I think I still see the dance as well as I did before. But I want to see it better."

Yorga laughed with a shrill cackle.

"As we all do," she replied. "As we all do."

"You see it better than I," Benji suggested.

"I would hope so," she said. "I have been watching it since before your parents were born."

"Yorga," Benji said, earnestly, "for what I want to accomplish, I need to see it better. Please, teach me something of what you have learned."

The priestess considered this.

"You speak of creating a peace," she observed.

"Yes," Benji said. "On a planet on which no living person has ever known peace."

Yorga nodded.

"That is worthy," she said. "Come, let us see if you can learn something of what I know."

She turned and led Benji back into the depths of the cave as she had before. But this time, they took a different passageway that had no rooms along its length.

They traveled downward through the narrow, dark corridor for what seemed nearly half a mile. Then the corridor widened into a large cavern, lit by torches. From the ceiling, giant stalactites hung like icicles. Water ran from them in tiny rivulets, creating the appearance of rain throughout the cavern.

"Sit with me," Yorga instructed.

She sat on a rock, cross-legged, just out of range of the water. Benji took a seat beside her.

"Now, study the dance," she told him.

They sat like that for nearly an hour. Benji watched the water falling from the ceiling, but in the gloom it was difficult to discern even individual streams and drops, much less determine a pattern. He also wasn't sure what he was doing. Would Yorga ask him to change the flow of the water, as she had with the lights in the globe? That seemed unlikely. But if not that, then what?

"The dance is all around us," Yorga said, finally. "But that is not exactly true, for we are in the dance as well. We see ourselves as apart from it, perhaps even able to affect it from outside. But we are not outside, and we are not apart. We are one with it. We are the dancer."

She paused as she struggled to her feet.

"Now watch," she said.

She stepped forward. Except that she didn't quite step forward, she danced forward. Her legs quick-stepped in a strange rhythm, her hips gyrated from side to side, and her shoulders moved in an entirely different rhythm. She danced to the center of the cavern, and there she remained for several minutes, dancing and gyrating. Then she made her way back using the same asynchronous rhythmic patterns.

Then she stood beside Benji once more.

"Touch my clothing," she instructed. "Feel my hair. Is it wet?"

Benji did as he was told, and found no trace of moisture on her clothing or in her hair.

"But how?" he asked.

"*Farchedan,*" she replied.

She grinned.

"Having seen what you have seen, you are wiser than you were," she said. "Is that sufficient for today?"

Benji thought for a moment. He did not understand what he had seen. Somehow the priestess had *danced* around and between dripping streams of water and avoided every drop.

"Can you teach me to do that?" he asked.

Yorga gazed at him sadly.

"No," she said. "There is no teacher for this, none but the dance itself."

Benji thought some more. Then he gazed at the dripping water some more.

Finally, he stood.

"*Farchedan,*" he repeated.

He stepped forward into the water and began to dance. But it seemed every movement he made increased the amount of water that fell on him. He couldn't time his movements with the falling of the water, and he couldn't separate the movement of his legs, hips, and shoulders.

He stopped.

Standing in the midst of the water, he gazed at it. His hair and clothes were now drenched, but he ignored that. He watched the water all around him, as he had watched the waves in the dancing planet's rings an hour or so before.

He noticed gaps in the falling streams, and began to pass his hands through them. Then he began to move his feet to avoid the water. It took some time, but eventually he was able to keep his hips out of the rain as well. And he did it not by thinking, but by knowing.

No matter how hard he tried, though, he could not get his whole body into the dance. When he began to succeed with his shoulders, he would fail with his feet. Getting his feet back into the dance, he would realize that his hips had stopped cooperating.

Yet at the same time, he saw *the dance*, and he was part of it. It didn't matter whether he stayed dry. *He was part of the dance!*

Benji smiled, and he saw Yorga smiling back at him.

"You begin to understand," her voice said in his head.

"How can I understand faster?" Benji asked her, telepathically.

"So impatient!" Yorga chided.

"I need to learn," Benji insisted.

Yorga paused for a moment.

"Do you do a sport?" she asked.

"I play ball on Parisa, and I play numbfoot on Zeblack," Benji replied. "Why?"

"How do you learn to do these things better?" Yorga asked.

Benji thought about this.

"By practicing," he said. "By doing them."

Yorga did not reply, and Benji realized that he had answered his own question. To understand the dance, he must watch the dance and be the dance. The more he watched it, the more he danced, the better he would get at watching and dancing.

Chapter Thirty-Seven

W hat time is it on Hadrun?" Benji asked Madarach, when he returned to the bubble. "I would really like to see Aelbreth."

"It's early evening there," Madarach said. "I would not recommend going when it's dark."

"Nor would I," Benji agreed. "I wish they didn't have *fortule* running around at night."

He thought for a moment.

"Let's go see something new," he said.

"Anything in particular?" Madarach asked.

Benji pointed in a direction just over his right shoulder.

"Go that way," he said. "Let's see what we see."

Madarach began to move in that direction, and Benji watched the stars shift past. There were so many of them! He could see thousands, and knew that there were millions more. He could never see everything in the galaxy, much less the universe.

Off to his left, Benji saw a red giant star come into view, small but bright in the distance. They approached it rapidly.

"Let's go there," he said, pointing it out. "Let's see if there's anything interesting."

Madarach approached the system, slowing as he neared the outer planets.

"Have you ever been here before?" Benji asked.

"No, never," Madarach replied. "These planets are unusually large, even for a red giant system."

"Are any of them habitable?" Benji wondered.

"There does appear to be a habitable zone with two planets in it," Madarach said. "Shall we see what they have to offer?"

"Sure," Benji agreed.

Madarach passed two very large planets that appeared to be barren and rocky. Then an even larger planet came into view, glowing bright red in the light of its sun.

"This is interesting," Madarach said. "There's a lot of methane in the atmosphere, and gravity is enormous compared to what you're used to. But there's some form of life down there."

"Can we go down?" Benji asked.

"You won't be able to get out," Madarach replied. "And I can only partially compensate for the gravity. You're going to want to lie down for this."

"Okay," Benji agreed. "Let's see what it looks like."

They descended through a thick, reddish atmosphere, though Benji wasn't sure whether that was its actual color or if it was caused by the light of the star. As they dropped, Benji began to feel heavier, until he couldn't lift his arms or legs or head from the floor.

"How far to the surface?" he asked, beginning to get worried.

"Not far," Madarach replied. "You should be able to see it any moment now."

Then it came into view. Benji saw a landscape of red, twisted rock surrounded by swirling clouds of gas. But the clouds weren't the only thing moving. The rocks were covered with large, wormlike creatures. Each appeared to be about a foot in diameter. They were looped around and through each other, so Benji couldn't quite make out how long they were, but they appeared to be at least ten feet and maybe longer.

The rocks all had holes in them, too, about a foot in diameter, just large enough for the worms to take shelter in them.

Benji gazed across the landscape, seeing worms as far as he could see in every direction.

"There are no plants," Benji observed. "What do they eat?"

"It appears that they eat rocks," Madarach replied. "They seem to convert carbon into energy through a sort of digestive process."

"Are they intelligent?" Benji asked.

"They've created massive cities of tubes in these rocks," Madarach said. "But if you mean can they communicate, I have no idea."

"What's the temperature out there?" Benji asked, curiously.

"About ninety degrees Fahrenheit," Madarach replied. "But you wouldn't be able to breathe out there."

"I know," Benji said. "But remember how you let me pick up a rock on the Moon? Earth's moon, I mean?"

"I remember," Madarach said. "You want to slip your hand through the bubble and touch one of these creatures, is that it?"

"Yes!" Benji said, excitedly. "If I can communicate, I would know at least what goes on in their minds."

Madarach paused.

"If you stick your hand through, you won't be able to pull it back," Madarach observed. "Gravity is too strong. I'll have to rotate so gravity works in your favor, and that will cause you to roll around in the bubble. You understand that, right?"

"Yes," Benji said.

But in reality, he could not imagine being so weak he couldn't retrieve his own hand.

"Okay," Madarach said. "Let's try this."

He descended to a spot only inches above the cluster of worms.

"Don't put your hand out any further than you have to," Madarach instructed. "We don't know how these creatures will react."

Benji gently eased his hand downward through the bubble until he could touch the nearest worm. It felt warm and dry to him, and hard like a shell.

For a moment, he heard nothing.

Then something happened. What Benji perceived was not verbal thought, but feelings. He felt comfort, and peace, and connection to others. In particular, there was one object of connection and love. He couldn't see any images associated with this object, but he smelled something that to him seemed both acridly bitter, and at the same time comforting. And he felt desire, the same kind of desire he sometimes felt for Aelbreth.

"This worm has a single mate," he relayed to Madarach. "And he loves her."

"I don't think they are either him or her," Madarach replied. "They seem to be asexual. They reproduce by exchanging DNA. So that level of emotion is quite remarkable."

Benji grew bolder, and sent a thought to the worm.

"I am a visitor," he said. "I mean you no harm, I just want to understand you better."

He felt the worm jump under his hand.

"Other?" it asked. "There is no other. All is the same."

"I am not the same," Benji replied. "I come from another place."

"All is the same," it said again. "All eat the land, all live in the land. The land sustains. We come from the land and return to the land. There is only land and us."

Benji thought about this. He wanted to tell the creature that he was indeed from another place, from the sky, and that he was different. But what if that created some kind of religious upheaval when this worm tried to explain to others what Benji had told it. A creature from the sky that did not eat rocks? Seriously?

Benji said nothing. Instead, he let his hand linger on the creature's segmented shell, enjoying the feel of its peacefulness and comfort, and its love for another worm that Benji could not imagine being able to recognize among the hundreds of seemingly identical worms in view.

"Okay," Benji told Madarach, finally. "Let's go."

He tried to pull his hand back inside the bubble. As Madarach had warned him, he was unable even to budge it. He couldn't even move his wrist, much less pull his own hand toward him.

Madarach rose a few feet above the ground. Then he rotated the bubble about ninety degrees, so that Benji's hand was above the centerline. It easily slipped back inside, and at the same time, Benji's body slid downward to what was now the lowermost point inside the bubble.

Then Madarach began to rise.

"That was a weird experience," Benji said. "The gravity was so strong, and these creatures were so simple in their thinking, and at the same time, so content."

"Does your thinking make you content?" Madarach asked. "It seems that only when you are *not* thinking do you become content."

Benji thought about that.

"Maybe that's true," he acknowledged.

"Do you want to see the other planet?" Madarach asked.

"Sure," Benji said. "We might as well, since we're here."

They'd risen now to where Benji could sit up, and soon they were back in space.

The next planet was a little smaller, but even more red. Benji lay down again as they descended, but he found that he could move at least a little as they approached the surface.

"This planet has a breathable atmosphere," Madarach said. "But you won't be able to walk, there's too much gravity."

The planet was quite different than the other. It had water, for one thing. In the red light of the star, its vast oceans appeared a deep red. They passed over land that looked much like the deserts of the American Southwest, except for the ubiquitous red tint. There were scraggly plants, and what looked like some kind of reptile, but they were shorter and thicker than anything Benji had ever seen, even in dinosaur books.

"This is kind of cool," Benji said. "But they don't look like they're very intelligent."

Then they passed over a forest and a river. In the river, Benji could see what appeared to be small boats.

"What are those?" he asked.

Madarach dropped lower, so Benji could see.

They weren't boats at all. They were creatures, though of what type Benji couldn't imagine. Their bodies, which were long and cylindrical like a log, appeared to be inflated with air, and they floated on the surface of the water. Above their strange bodies, each one had two tiny torsos, each with four long arms that could reach into the water. Above this, on a tiny neck, they had large heads with giant eyes. Benji guessed that they were black in color, but in the red light it was hard to know for sure.

"What are they?" Benji wondered.

"I have no idea," Madarach replied. "I've never seen anything like them."

They dropped even lower, and one of the creatures spotted them. It began to chatter, and soon all the creatures were looking at Benji suspended in the air in a transparent bubble.

"Can you amplify what they're saying?" Benji asked.

Madarach did, and a stream of low, mechanical sounds filled Benji's ears.

"Try bringing the pitch up," Benji instructed.

Madarach did, but all Benji heard now were high mechanical sounds.

"I can't make heads or tails of that," he said. "Do you think I can touch one?"

"I don't detect any poisons," Madarach said. "But I can't guarantee they won't bite."

"They seem more curious than threatening," Benji observed.

"Anything with teeth will bite if it feels threatened," Madarach reminded him.

"I suppose," Benji said. "But let's try it."

Madarach dropped down close to the water, and one of the creatures came close to them. Benji guessed it had some means of propulsion underneath its body, maybe legs or flippers.

Benji extended his hand through the bubble toward the creature. To his surprise, the creature extended one of its arms toward Benji. Its hand was made up of three claws that Benji guessed were useful for catching fish or whatever else might live in the river.

Benji touched the creature's hand, tentatively. It was cool and covered with shell. Immediately, Benji heard its thoughts in his head.

"What are you?" the creature asked. "Have you come from the sky?"

"Yes," Benji said. "I traveled a long distance. I am an explorer."

"We are also explorers," the creature said. "We travel the waters, everywhere. But we have been waiting for an explorer of the sky."

"Why?" Benji asked.

"Because there must be explorers of the sky, just as there are explorers of water, and of land," the creature replied.

"Do you have a name?" Benji asked.

"Yes," it said. "We are called Tipjlat. We are pleased to meet you."

"Tipjlat," Benji repeated. "That is the name of your kind?"

"No, no," the creature corrected. "Our kind is called Watermen, and we are of the Blidnot tribe. Our name is Tipjlat."

"You are plural?" Benji asked.

"Yes, of course," Tupjlat replied. "We are mature, and we have mated and become one. We were Tip and Jlat. Now we are Tipjlat."

"Okay," Benji said. "I am singular. My name is Benji."

"Ah," Tipjlat replied. "We are pleased to meet you. You are not yet mature?"

"No," Benji confirmed. "Although I am close. But my kind does not become one when it mates. We remain separate beings."

"How strange," Tipjlat commented. "That is the way of lower beings, but we can see that you are not a lower being. What is your kind called? What can you tell me about it?"

"We're called human," Benji answered. "We are mammals, which means we are warm-blooded, have hair on our bodies, and produce milk to feed our young."

Tipjlat considered this for a moment.

"You are very different from us," it observed. "You have two genders?"

"Yes," Benji confirmed. "Male and female."

"And do you lay eggs, or give live birth?" the creature asked.

"Live birth," Benji replied.

"Maybe you are not so different," it said. "But you do have fewer limbs and more digits."

Benji smiled.

"Yes, I suppose I do," he admitted. "How many limbs do you have? Do you have more beneath the water?"

In reply, Tipjlat rolled over in the water to display its underside, which looked like two rows of many oars. Benji couldn't count them that quickly, but he guessed there were fifteen or twenty in each row.

Tipjlat rolled right side up again.

"You are well equipped for the water," Benji observed.

"It is our domain," it replied. "Only the largest sea creatures pose a danger to us, for we move quickly and defend ourselves well. But you, you are not well equipped for the air. Where are your wings? How do you travel? What keeps you in the air?"

Benji laughed.

"I am a land creature," he said. "But our kind have developed machines that allow us to fly."

"What is a machine?" Tipjlat asked.

The question stumped Benji. How could he explain a machine to a creature that seemed to have evolved with everything it needed?

"Do your people ever use tools?" he asked.

"Tools?" the creature repeated. "We do occasionally use rocks to open difficult shellfish."

"Imagine if you had a very large and difficult shellfish," Benji said. "The rock you would need would be too large to move. But you might instead use a tool that had a handle, to give you more speed and leverage. You might combine materials and knowledge to create something new. Though it doesn't look like you have much need for that."

"No," Tipjlat agreed. "This is a very difficult concept for us to understand. We have been given what we need by the Great One, and if we do not have it, we cannot imagine needing it."

"May I ask you," Benji began, "if Tip and Jlat are joined, are you entirely one? Do you think the same thoughts? Do your brains work in unison?"

"Oh, it is much better than that," Tipjlat replied. "We have the benefit of both, working cooperatively for the survival of our joined being. Tip, being formerly female, takes the lead in all things. Jlat, who was male, has knowledge to contribute. But the joining is nearly complete. Our thoughts occur in coordination. We retain two reservoirs of knowledge, but one stream of consciousness. We are one in all things, and complete in a way neither of us could be alone."

"Interesting," Benji said. "Could you be separated?"

"Only in death," Tipjlat said. "For we share a body, and all our critical organs. We are one so long as we live."

"That sounds like the ideal our mating rituals aspire to," Benji commented. "But we don't do it biologically."

"So you remain separate but somehow joined by emotion?" Tipjlat wondered. "Even though you are separate, you do not mate with other than your mate like the lower beings do?"

"It's physically possible," Benji allowed. "But the idea is that we don't."

"Interesting," Tipjlat said. "For it seems the Great One has given you one nature, yet you choose a different nature."

"Our given nature can be violent," Benji said. "We work hard to change that nature also."

"Violence is required for survival," Tipjlat said. "We eat these river creatures under the water. They must die so that we can live. But we do not kill them all, or we would have none for ourselves."

Then it paused.

"Wait," it continued. "You mean something else, don't you? You commit violence against your own kind. How does that promote survival?"

"Not all of us do," Benji explained. "In fact, some planets of us have evolved beyond that. But some haven't. And to be honest, I don't understand how it promotes survival. I can see that some humans justify violence because they want what others have, or are afraid of them, but I don't understand why that's in our nature. It just is. And that's why we try so hard to change it."

"You are strange creatures," Tipjlat said. "Have you come here to do violence?"

"No," Benji assured it. "I came as an explorer. I wanted to see what was here. And I probably will never be back. There are too many things to explore to keep coming back to the same places over and over."

"That is true," Tipjlat agreed. "Though we are fond of this river. We will miss it when the season is over."

"Are there other intelligent beings on this planet?" Benji asked, curiously.

"We have not seen any," Tipjlat replied. "Nor have we heard of any. There are only lower creatures."

Benji couldn't think of anything else to say.

"Well, thank you," he said, finally. "I guess I'll be going now."

"May the Great One go with you," Tipjlat replied. "May the one who is both female and male, who sees all and knows all, guide your journey."

"Thank you," Benji said. "And yours."

Chapter Thirty-Eight

Back on Parisa, the days passed slowly for Benji. It had been just over a week since he delivered the radio parts to Zeblack, and Madarach and Nahum both counseled patience. But Benji did not feel patient. He wanted to go see what was happening there.

Instead, on his next day off, he returned to Hadrun.

He arrived there at daybreak, and joined Aelbreth and her family for breakfast.

"It is good to see you, my young traveler," Aelbreth's mom, Aedred, told him. "You have been having many adventures, I hear?"

"A few," Benji acknowledged. "I was grateful for the birthday party Lisa and Madarach scheduled. I'm glad Aelbreth was able to come."

"My little wandering heart would not have missed it," Fennel assured him. "She is quite fond of you, you know."

"I guessed," Benji replied. "Though you know women. It's hard to understand what they're thinking most of the time."

"Indeed," Fennel agreed, laughing. "Though in this regard, her thinking is quite obvious. At least to me. But perhaps you spend too much time with the *patret* during your visits."

"Father," Aelbreth scolded. "I'm sitting right here. If this *patret*-brain wants to know what I'm thinking, he has but to ask."

"And would you tell him?" Fennel wondered.

Aelbreth blushed, which surprised Benji.

"I would," she said, shyly.

Benji stared at Aelbreth, who stared at her plate. This was unlike her, Benji thought. Aelbreth never feared expressing herself. Unlike Benji, she voiced both her opinions and her feelings without hesitation. What, he wondered, could have her so flustered that she wouldn't even look at him?

"Oh, no," Benji thought. "She probably wants to break up with me, and she's afraid to say it."

Benji had always feared this would come to pass. Aelbreth, after all, lived on a primitive planet in a village that farmed *patret*. Though she enjoyed space travel, she always loved coming home. And she knew, as they all did, that Benji's future was not as a *patret* farmer. She must have finally realized, Benji thought, that Benji was not the right partner for her.

"Aelbreth?" Benji asked, tentatively.

"What?" she asked, sternly.

Did he really want to know what she was thinking? He decided that it was better to know than to not know.

"What are you thinking?" he asked.

She didn't look up from her plate as she began to speak.

"Benjamin Haight," she said, sternly.

Benji felt his heart constrict in his chest. Was he losing his dear friend and only love, Aelbreth? What would he do without her? Would anyone ever want a culturally-confused young space traveler as a boyfriend? But he didn't want anyone else, he wanted Aelbreth.

"Yes," he answered, sadly.

"How long have we been special friends?" she asked.

The question confused Benji. He knew it was a little over two Earth years, and maybe a year and a half on Parisa. On Hadrun, he'd lost count, and right now he was too distressed to even guess.

"Since we met," he replied, avoiding the calculations.

"And in all that time," she said, her voice accusing him, "have you never thought to ask me to commit to you?"

Benji looked around, confused.

"I thought I was committed to you," he said.

Fennel placed his hand on Benji's and spoke telepathically.

"There's a ceremony to make it official," he explained. "She's asking you to become engaged."

Benji stared at Fennel. Then he stared at Aelbreth, who seemed to be holding her breath.

"I didn't know I was supposed to," he said. "But I will ask you now."

Of course he would! Hadn't he just spent the last few moments, which had seemed like an eternity, realizing how much he loved her?

Aelbreth looked up from her plate and turned to him, obviously relieved.

"Then ask," she instructed, her voice still stern.

Benji remained flustered for a moment, realizing slowly that this was all part of a cultural pageant that people on Hadrun were very familiar with. Benji wasn't, and it took him a moment to think of words to say.

"Aelbreth, my love," he said, "I want to commit to you and I ask that you do me the honor of allowing me a public demonstration of my commitment."

Fennel reached out his hand to Benji's once more.

"Close enough," he told him.

"It's about time," Aelbreth huffed. "I'm getting old, you know?"

"Aelbreth, you're only fifteen on Hadrun!" Benji protested.

She grinned.

"At least you remember my age, if not how long we've been together," she scolded, mockingly.

There seemed to be relief all around the table. Aedred was smiling broadly, and Fennel looked quite satisfied. Offsa's face was glowing.

And so was Aelbreth's. Benji suspected he had just made her very happy.

Then Fennel banged his fist on the table.

"Tonight, we feast!" he announced, "To celebrate the betrothal of my daughter to a man of honor. Tell everyone in the village! There will be no chores today, aside from the milking."

They stared at Fennel, all except Aedred, who smiled.

"Go!" she commanded. "Offsa, Aelbreth, go tell everyone!"

Offsa and Aelbreth jumped to their feet and ran out the door.

Benji sat in his chair, mouth hanging open.

"What does this mean?" he asked. "What happens?"

"They'll go tell the other families that today is a feast day," Aedred explained. "Then they'll come back. The women will gather outside and we'll make our arrangements for food and such. The men will build a tent for the celebration, and a bonfire to keep away the *fortule*. Offsa will help the men, and of course Aelbreth and I will get her prepared."

"So what am I supposed to do today?" Benji asked.

Fennel smiled.

"Normally, you would spend the day with your father, being groomed for this evening," he said. "The father passes on wisdom, and helps the son dress properly. But I think what you're wearing is fine."

"What about the wisdom?" Benji asked. "Would you be my father today?"

Fennel bowed his head.

"It would be my honor," he replied. "Though for the ceremony itself I will stand with Aelbreth. Offsa can stand with you."

"Do you have a commitment gift for her?" Aedred asked.

"I don't know," Benji said. "What should it be? A ring?"

"No, not a ring," Fennel said. "Rings catch too easily while working. It could be a pendant, if the chain is not too long. But most prefer a hair pin."

"This is mine," Aedred said, proudly, removing a small object from her hair.

She handed it to Benji. It was a copper leaf, inlaid with gold veins. Benji had noticed it before, but had never gotten a close look at it.

"Fennel gave this to me when I was Aelbreth's age," she said. "I treasure it even now."

"I don't have anything like that," Benji said. "But I could go get something."

"You mean from another planet?" Fennel asked, frowning. "That's a lot of trouble."

"Not for Aelbreth, it isn't," Benji said. "Besides, I think Lisa would want to be here for this. I could go get her at the same time."

Fennel smiled.

"You're right," he said. "You love her a great deal, as I have loved my Aedred. Go, then, and hurry back. The ceremony will begin two hours before nightfall, and you and I should talk before then."

Benji paused for just a moment. Then he sprinted for the door, and down the trail to where Madarach waited.

"Madarach!" he exclaimed, when he had entered the bubble. "I'm getting engaged to Aelbreth today!"

"Really?" Madarach asked. "The culture here is so different. You know that your sister didn't become engaged to Tobin until she was three Earth years older than you are, and even that was considered early."

"I know," Benji agreed. "It's a little scary. But that's not the point. There's a ceremony today. I have to get her a gift, and I want Lisa to come."

"What kind of gift?" Madarach asked.

"Fennel gave Aedred a hair pin that was like copper with gold veins in it," Benji explained. "They prefer hair pins to rings because they are less likely to get caught on something when they work."

"That makes sense," Madarach said. "Let me consider for a moment."

Benji waited, impatiently, while Madarach did whatever he was doing. Benji guessed that he'd be checking his database for something.

"Let's go," Madarach said, as he began to ascend. "I think I can help you."

Chapter Thirty-Nine

Where are we going?" Benji asked. "Parisa?"

"No," Madarach replied. "Parisa is not known for its decorative metalwork. First we need raw materials, and then we need a smith. Neither will be found on Parisa."

Benji watched the stars shift past, until he saw a cluster of stars that he thought looked familiar.

"Gold," he said. "We need gold."

"Indeed we do," Madarach agreed. "Not only is it precious in almost every culture, but it is easier to work with than silver or copper, especially on short notice."

They approached the painted planet, and landed at the same white sand plain they had found gold at before.

"Now go get some nice nuggets," Madarach said. "We won't need as many this time."

Benji got out and picked up several good-sized nuggets. He had to restrain himself, because his instinct told him to grab everything he could find. But what would that accomplish? If he brought back a hair pin that weighed a pound, Aelbreth wouldn't be able to wear it!

He returned to the bubble.

"So what's a smith, and where do we find one?" Benji asked.

"A smith is someone who works with metal," Madarach explained, as they began to ascend. "You know what a blacksmith is on Earth, right?"

"Someone who works with iron," Benji answered.

"Right," Madarach said. "Because the result was black, they were called blacksmiths. There are also silversmiths, coppersmiths, pewtersmiths, and goldsmiths, as well as others on other planets where they use other materials."

"So we need a goldsmith," Benji observed. "Where do we find one?"

"There's a culture on a planet not too far away that is renowned for its goldsmithing," Madarach said. "Let's go there and see what they can do for you."

The planet turned out to be very Earthlike in appearance, with two major continents and a lot of ocean. But when they landed, Benji realized it was not much like Earth at all, at least not the parts Benji had seen. They set down in a clearing in a thick jungle, and Madarach directed Benji to follow the path to a village.

"This village is filled with goldsmiths," he said. "They will all want your business, so look around and see whose work you like best."

Benji got out and followed the path. It was well worn, but surrounded by foliage so thick that it might as well have been walls and ceiling. The air smelled heavily of wine and flowers, and Benji began to feel that he was in a dream.

The path led him to the edge of a village of several dozen buildings. Each building seemed to be made of trees, living trees that grew together to form shelter.

And it was raining. The foliage apparently was so thick that no rain penetrated to the path, but in the open space of the village it was coming down pretty hard.

Benji smiled as he watched the rain fall. He paused for a moment. Then he began to dance.

He danced his way to the first building, which turned out to be a home. Then he danced to the second, which was the shop in which the smith from the house worked.

Benji glanced at himself. He had only a few wet spots on his clothing, and none at all in his hair.

"*Farchedan*," he murmured, and smiled. He was learning.

The smith, meanwhile, had looked up from the bench.

Benji gaped. For some reason, he'd expected the culture to be human, more or less. But this creature was covered with thick, black hair from head to toe, like some kind of ape, and stood maybe three feet tall.

The creature addressed him in a guttural language.

Benji replied by holding out his hand as if to shake. The creature looked at Benji, and then at his hand. Then it tentatively reached out its own hand and grasped Benji's.

Its hand was furry on the back, but the palms and fingers were covered with wrinkled, black skin. It had only three fingers, but it had a very strong grip.

"Can you understand me?" Benji thought to the creature.

"I can," it replied. "You are not from around here."

"No," Benji agreed. "I'm from very far away. But I was told that this village does exceptional work in gold."

The creature made a sound that Benji guessed was laughter, though it sounded more like a diesel truck starting.

"Indeed we do," it said. "You are welcome to look around the village, but I must suggest that the men do clumsy work that is more bold than delicate. I'm guessing that you are male, looking for something special for your female. Am I right?"

"You are," Benji replied, blushing.

"Then look around," it said. "But my work is more feminine, for obvious reasons."

Benji tried to examine the creature more closely without being obvious.

"I'm not familiar with your people," he said.

"Ah, of course!" said the creature, laughing again. "Then you might not realize that I am the only female goldsmith in the village! My name is Ikthar, and I would be proud to show you my work."

"Ikthar," Benji repeated. "My name is Benji. I would be honored to see your work."

"Come" she said. "Through here."

She led Benji past the bench, past a furnace on which sat a pot of liquid gold, and into a back room.

Inside, Benji gasped. The walls were covered with gold art, all intricately worked and some inlaid with different colors. Some were containers, perhaps goblets for wine. Others were rings for fingers or arms. Still others were round or square plates with scenes carved into them.

"What are you looking for?" Ikthar asked. "A ring, perhaps?"

"Not a ring," Benji replied. "Something fairly small that she can use as a hair pin."

"Ah, yes," Ikthar said. "I love hair pins, myself. See?"

She turned toward the wall, and Benji could see that the back of her head, her shoulders, and her back were all adorned with gold pins.

"My daughter helps me put them on," she explained. "I wear them on my back so they don't interfere with my work. How many would you need? Perhaps a set of six?"

Benji gulped.

"My female has somewhat less hair," he said, carefully. "She's more like me."

Ikthar turned back to him and looked from Benji's feet to his head.

"I see," she said. "Pity. Well, look around and see what suits you. And as I said, you're welcome to visit the other smiths, but I guarantee that if you're not looking for tableware or ceremonial weapons, you'll come back."

"Could I see your back again?" Benji asked.

Ikthar nodded and turned, and Benji examined the pins she wore. Some were in the shape of flowers, animals, birds, and insects. Some of the leaves were quite nice, but since Aedred already had a leaf, Benji wanted to get something different for Aelbreth.

"Thank you," Benji said.

Then he looked at the artwork on the walls.

A dragonfly caught his eye. At least, it was similar to a dragonfly, though it had eight wings instead of four. The detail on it amazed him, with veins in the wings and tiny lines on its skin. It was about three inches long, and had two green jewels set into its face for eyes, which Benji thought would look good on Aelbreth.

"This," he said. "This is a pendant?"

"It is," Ikthar confirmed. "But if you have a few moments, it can be a hair pin."

"The jewels," he asked, "are they precious?"

"To some," she said. "They are rare in some places, but I have a source. You can see that these are very smooth and clear. They are exceptional quality, even though they are small."

Benji nodded.

"How much does this cost?" he asked.

Ikthar tilted her head, as if calculating. Benji wasn't sure if she was calculating her cost, or how much she thought Benji would be willing to pay.

"You're paying in gold?" she asked.

"Yes," he acknowledged.

"Let's see," she mused. "Four for the piece, and two and a half for the gems, plus resetting it on a pin. Let's say six and a half."

"Six and a half what?" Benji wondered.

"Six and a half times its weight," she explained. "I measure the purity of your gold, and calculate six and a half times the pure weight."

"Okay," Benji agreed, tentatively.

She laughed.

"You don't haggle where you're from?" she asked.

"What's that?" Benji asked.

She laughed again.

"You should offer me three," she said. "I would counter with five, and we'd settle on four and half."

"I don't know how to do that," he said. "Is it six and a half, or four and a half?"

She laughed harder.

"It's four and an half, my friend," she said. "Is there anything else I can help you with?"

"No," Benji said. "I don't think so."

Then his eye caught a glimpse of something on the wall. He took a step toward it, and couldn't believe what he saw. It was a pendant formed in the shape of a sphere, and around the sphere was formed a wavy ring. It looked exactly like the dancing planet in the Hassyri system.

"Wait," he said. "Tell me about this."

Ikthar looked to where he was pointing.

"Oh, that," she said, dismissively. "That was a mistake I made when I first started smithing."

"A mistake?" he asked.

"Yes," she said, sadly. "It was many years ago. Someone asked me to make it, and I failed to get payment in advance. They never returned for it."

"Who?" he asked. "What did they look like?"

"They looked much like you," she said. "They had a hair shortage, as you do. Though her cranial hair was much longer than his. She was able to speak to me, and they asked to have it made for her. They were going to pay in gems. But as I said, they never returned for it."

"Did they give you a name?" he asked.

"If they did, I have forgotten it," Ikthar said. "I remember only that they came from a place called Arth. I thought it was an odd name for a place, and I so remembered it."

"Arth?" Benji repeated. "Could it have been Earth?"

Ikthar shrugged her woolly shoulders.

"It could have been," she said. "That was nearly eighty summers ago, and my memory isn't what it used to be."

Could it be, Benji wondered, that his great-uncle James and his sister had been to both Hassyr and this planet? He supposed there was no way to be sure.

But of course, there was. Madarach would know.

"I'll take that, too," he said. "For my sister."

"As you wish," she said. "I'll charge you only two for that, because it's been here so long."

They returned to the front room, where Ikthar examined the gold Benji had brought.

"This is quite good," she said. "I'd put it at eight parts out of ten."

"That's what I've been told before," Benji agreed. "But you can tell just by looking at them?"

Ikthar laughed her growly laugh again.

"Not by looking," she said. "But when you've been doing this as long as I have, you can tell by the feel, the weight, and the smell."

"I didn't realize gold had a smell," Benji said.

"Oh, yes," she replied. "And I smell different qualities every day."

She weighed the two finished pieces Benji had selected. Then she moved some beads around in a bowl, which Benji guessed was some sort of calculator. Then she began putting Benji's gold nuggets on the scale, one at a time.

"These four will do it," she said, selecting various sizes. "You still have some left. Are you sure I can't help you with anything else?"

"No, thank you," Benji replied. "But I think I will wander around the village while I wait for you to remount the one piece."

"As you wish," she said. "I'll be here until dark."

Chapter Forty

The rain had stopped, and Benji made his way through the rest of the village. Buildings alternated between homes and smiths, as apparently every smith kept a separate work building next to his home.

Ikthar had been right, the rest of the smiths were all male. They were larger than she was, and sported great manes around their necks. Their work was very different from hers, too. Benji saw lovely goblets, plates, boxes, small cages, daggers, and even swords. But none did the small and intricate work he'd seen in Ikthar's shop.

On the other side of the village, though, he found himself fascinated by a ring. Its shank was smooth gold, and on its head was carved a bird that looked like the doves Benji had seen on Earth. The bird was descending onto a broken sword that extended over the ring's shoulders. It was a sturdy ring, but not gigantic, and Benji thought it might suit him.

Though the local language was difficult, Benji had learned enough of it by now to carry on basic conversations.

"Can I try this on?" he asked the huge, hairy smith behind the counter.

"Certainly," the smith replied. "It's a small ring. It may suit you."

Benji glanced at the smith's hands. They were at least twice the breadth of his own, and very thick. The ring wouldn't have come close to fitting on even the smallest of the creature's three fingers.

Benji tried it on his own hand. It was slightly large on his ring finger, but fit perfectly on his index finger.

"What can you tell me about the design?" he asked.

"It's my mate's work," he replied, scowling. "She has romantic ideas. Some bird can come and end war. I think she heard it from a storyteller."

"Interesting," Benji said.

But in his mind, he thought about himself and Madarach coming down from the sky to end a war on Zeblack. The ring represented that perfectly.

"How much?" he asked.

The smith gazed at Benji for a moment.

"I shouldn't do this," he said, "but I'll let it go for four."

Benji thought about this. He'd paid four and a half for the dragonfly, which was far more intricate and also had two gems set into it. He remembered what Ikthar had said about haggling. He guessed he was supposed to offer two, and they'd settle at three.

Then again, he wasn't sure how much gold he had left compared to what this piece weighed.

He pulled the remaining nuggets out of his pocket.

"Would you weigh these, please?" he asked.

The smith nodded, and held out his hand for Benji to drop them into his massive palm.

The smith examined them.

"Not bad," he said. "Six parts out of ten, I'd say."

"I believe you'll find they are eight," Benji corrected him.

"Perhaps," the smith said.

He bit one, and nodded.

"Tastes like seven," he said.

"Smells like eight," Benji insisted.

"Perhaps you're right," the smith agreed.

He set them on the scale, then weighed the ring. Then he moved stones around in a dish, as Ikthar had, making his calculation.

"This is just under three," he said. "You have more?"

"Sorry," Benji said. "That's what I can give you."

"Ach!" lamented the smith. "I could let this ring go for maybe three and a half. But less than three? This is my mate's work, after all."

Benji shrugged.

"I had the impression you didn't like her work much," he said. "This is all I have left."

"I said it was romantic," the smith corrected. "I never said I didn't like it. She's my mate, after all, right? I could go three and a quarter."

"That's everything," Benji said. "If you don't want to sell the ring, I understand. I'll just take my gold back and be out of your hair."

Then he realized what he'd said, and hoped he hadn't offended the woolly, thick-maned creature.

The smith laughed. But Benji noticed he kept his hand protectively next to Benji's gold nuggets.

"Too bad you came to a goldsmith village," he said. "Down river, there's a village that makes body wigs. You should get one! But since you're here, and since you want the ring so badly, I'll take what you've given me. You drive a hard bargain, hairless one. My mate will be disappointed."

"I'm sure you'll find a way to make it up to her," Benji said.

He accepted the ring, put it on his finger, and headed back toward Ikthar's shop. As he moved away, he heard one of the other smiths growling.

"Can you believe it?" he moaned. "Klep got three for that bird ring his mate designed! I never thought he'd get even two!"

"Well, you never know what a stranger wants," his companion replied. "That's why we call them strangers, because they're strange."

Ikthar had finished her work, affixing a pin to the dragonfly so it could be used in Aelbreth's hair.

"It's finished?" Benji asked.

"You have learned our language so quickly," Ikthar observed. "Yes, I have finished. I trust you find it acceptable?"

Benji picked up the piece and examined it closely.

"It's perfect," he agreed. "Thank you."

"And what did you think of the males' work?" she asked.

"It's nice," Benji said. "But most of it is not my style. I did find a ring I liked."

He showed it to Ikthar, holding out his hand palm down so she could inspect it.

"Ah," she murmured. "Klep's bird ring. His mate, Ungor, designed it. I've always liked it, but the males of course laughed about it. I'm glad it found a suitable home."

"Thank you," Benji said. "Your work is amazing, and if I need more I'll come back."

"Please do," Ikthar replied. "It is always a pleasure, and we do not discriminate against the hairless."

Benji turned and left the shop. Then he located the path and sprinted for the clearing.

But Madarach wasn't there.

"Madarach?" he called. "Madarach?"

He wondered if he had chosen the wrong path, and was now lost. But would another path have a clearing about the same distance from the village? He didn't think so, but he couldn't be sure.

"I'm coming," he heard Madarach reply in his head. "There were a lot of passersby, and I didn't want to be discovered. Imagine a crowd of primates stumbling into a transparent bubble in the middle of the jungle! It would surely upset them, and I might have to hurt them."

"We don't want that," Benji replied. "They seem like nice people. Or whatever they are."

"They're nice enough unless they get angry," Madarach replied.

He descended into the clearing, and Benji climbed aboard.

"You found what you needed?" Madarach asked.

"I did," Benji said. "I got Aelbreth this dragonfly hair pin."

"That's very nice," Madarach agreed. "Did you know that the eyes are emeralds?"

"Emeralds?" Benji repeated. "Aren't they really expensive?"

"Those are very good quality," Madarach said. "On Earth, I imagine they'd be worth several thousand dollars. They're more common on some planets. But I doubt someone in a tiny village on Hadrun will have ever seen one. You picked a queenly gift for the daughter of a farmer!"

He remembered Lisa's vision of him wearing a crown, and wondered briefly if Aelbreth might indeed some day be a queen.

"But she won't be the wife of a farmer," Benji replied.

"Indeed she won't," Madarach said. "I cannot imagine you being happy as a farmer."

"I also found this ring for myself," Benji added. "I like to think it represents making peace."

"Also very nice," Madarach commented.

"And I found this," Benji said, holding up the pendant of the dancing planet. "I wondered if you might know anything about it."

Madarach said nothing for a long moment. Then Benji felt him begin to sob, and huge waves of emotion washed through Benji's body.

"I brought them here," Madarach said, finally. "It was their last trip before James was killed."

"And they'd seen the dancing planet?" Benji surmised.

"They had," Madarach confirmed. "We found it by accident. They wanted to see all the worlds on which the Parisans had placed wells. And Agnes was quite taken with the planet, so James wanted to make her a pendant of it. We came here to have it done. But she was never able to pick it up."

"Because James was dead," Benji finished.

"Yes," Madarach said.

"I'm sorry," Benji said. "That must be so hard for you. But now Lisa will have it. That must be something."

Madarach began to cry again.

"It is something," he said. "I hope she will cherish it, as I cherish the two of you."

"I think she will," Benji said. "Let's go get her now."

Chapter Forty-One

They arrived on Parisa, and Benji sprinted through the streets until he couldn't run anymore. He arrived home breathless.

"Are you okay?" asked Lisa, who was sitting on the couch with Miriam.

"Yes," Benji gasped. "I just ran all the way. You need to get ready to go."

"Go where?" Lisa asked, furrowing her brow.

"Hadrun!" Benji exclaimed. "They're having a feast tonight. I'm getting engaged to Aelbreth!"

"You're getting engaged?" Lisa repeated. "Really? But you're only thirteen!"

"I know," Benji said. "But that's how they do things there. And I feel like I'm engaged to her already. I love her, and she's my best friend."

"But Benji," Lisa protested, "you're still growing up. What if you change your mind later?"

"What if you change your mind later about Tobin?" he countered. "Age has nothing to do with that. We make choices, and then we live with them. Isn't that what Dad always told us? I've chosen the culture of Hadrun for this. And we don't have time to argue about it. The feast starts in a couple of hours, so you need to get ready."

Lisa glanced at Miriam.

"Miriam thinks we should all go," Lisa said. "It's a big day for you, and she says they will all want to be there. Is that okay?"

"Sure," Benji said. "I just didn't think they'd want to."

"Of course they would," Lisa said. "They love you. Tamar is in the kitchen. Go tell her."

"First, I want to give you this." Benji said, producing the pendant of the dancing planet. "There's a story behind it, but we don't have time now."

Lisa accepted the gift and examined it.

"Benji, it's wonderful!" she exclaimed. "Where did you get it?"

"Later," he insisted. "Go get ready."

Then he headed for the kitchen, where he placed his hand on Tamar's arm so she could hear him as he told her about the reason for the feast.

Tamar's eyes lit up.

"I am so happy for you!" she replied. "Of course I want to come! Jachin will, too!"

"We have to hurry," Benji told her. "The days are shorter on Hadrun."

Tamar rushed out of the room to inform Jachin and Tobin.

That left Benji alone in the kitchen with nothing to do but wait. It was the first time since breakfast that he'd stopped moving, and he began to think.

He thought about Aelbreth, and how much he cared for her.

He thought about breakfast, and how Aelbreth had primed him to say yes by pretending she was angry with him. Fennel had said that was how they did it on Hadrun. And it had worked. Benji had jumped at the chance to make her happy.

He thought about what Lisa had just said, about the possibility of changing his mind. And he began to wonder if he was indeed moving too fast. What if Hadruni culture was just too different? What if Aelbreth would never be happy anywhere else, and Benji ended up as a *patret* farmer? What if they ended up hating each other over some stupid thing?

He wandered out to the living room, where Tobin and Jachin sat waiting for the women. He sat down next to them and put one hand on each of them.

"How do I know if I'm making the right choice?" he asked.

Neither man replied for a moment. Then Jachin, as the father, went first.

"Don't follow your head," he said. "Follow your heart. A man can try to figure out the best choice, but he'll decide based on all the wrong reasons. Trust what your heart tells you."

"How did you and Tamar get together?" Benji asked.

Jachin smiled.

"She was my next door neighbor," he said. "We used to play together. When I started to consider women, I never thought about her, because I saw her as the child I always played with. I looked for the right woman. I met many in school and at work. Some were very beautiful, but none were a good match. All my friends were matching, and I was getting older, and I began to feel anxious that I would never find the right woman. I worried that I would either become a priest, or I would have to choose a woman that did not suit me. Then one day I was talking to Tamar, and I noticed that she was not a little girl at all. Our relationship began to change, and I realized that she had been the right woman for me all along, I just wasn't willing to see it."

"Are the two of you happy?" Benji asked.

"Very," Jachin replied. "Happier, I think, than most couples. We're very lucky."

"Do you argue?" Benji wondered.

"Of course," Jachin said. "No two people think the same. If they did, one of them would be unnecessary. But we argue with love, and we rarely get angry, and when we do, we remember that we love each other, and our children, and that our family is more important than anything else."

Benji nodded.

"Tobin," Benji said. "How soon did you know Lisa was the right woman for you?"

Tobin laughed.

"I knew the moment I saw her," he said. "Even though we couldn't communicate. But of course I didn't believe it. I thought it was silly, falling in love with someone from another world who couldn't even telepath. But then she could. And things just fell into place after that."

"You two are happy?" Benji asked.

"I would think you'd know the answer to that from your connection with Lisa," Tobin suggested.

"She keeps her feelings to herself," Benji observed. "But that wouldn't tell me your feelings, anyway."

Tobin smiled.

"I love your sister with all my heart," he replied. "She makes me very happy. And this is my advice to you. Stop thinking! It's your heart that needs to make this decision. If I had listened to my head, I wouldn't be with Lisa. It would have seemed impossible."

"Stop thinking?" Benji repeated. "You make it sound so easy!"

They sat there, waiting for the women, for what seemed to Benji like hours. He felt restless and anxious. He wanted to go.

"Benji," Jachin told him, "there is something you must learn. Woman is like a river. No matter how much you push, they cannot be hurried."

Tobin laughed.

"I sometimes think woman is like physics," he corrected. "If you push, there is an equal and opposite reaction."

"They defy physics," Jachin added, "for the reaction is often disproportionately larger!"

Benji laughed. Though he had nothing to add, he liked feeling like one of the men.

Eventually, the women appeared. Tamar came first, then Miriam, and finally Lisa. All were dressed in their finest Parisan outfits, and they had each clearly spent some time on their hair. Lisa had put the pendant of the dancing planet on a chain and now wore it around her neck. Benji wouldn't have noticed, but Parisan women didn't use makeup, and their dress clothes were not appreciably fancier than their daily wear, but to him they all looked beautiful.

"Shall we go?" Tamar suggested.

They filed out the front door and down the street to the well.

"What is it like, traveling in the bubble?" Jachin asked. "Does it feel like you are high above the ground?"

"Not at all," Benji replied. "It feels like you're floating on a sea of space."

Jachin nodded.

"High places make me nervous," he explained.

They reached the well, and Benji summoned the stars. They all held hands, and were quickly floating in space.

Benji looked over at Jachin, who appeared disoriented for a moment. Then he looked around, realized that he was safe, and nodded.

"Let's go," Benji said to Madarach.

Minutes later, they landed in the clearing on Hadrun, and Benji led them to the village.

The men had been busy. In the center of the village, a structure had been erected of tree limbs and thatch.

The women were still busy, tending open fires over which they roasted *patret* on spits.

Benji led his family to Aelbreth's home, where Fennel greeted them.

"This is my family," he told Fennel, introducing them all, except Lisa who had been there before.

Fennel bowed.

"I am honored that you would come," he said. "It is a pleasure to meet the family of such a fine, upstanding young man."

Benji blushed at the praise.

"I have little to offer," Fennel said. "We will be feasting soon. I would normally offer tea, but I know it disagrees with some people from other places. Would you care for water, or *patret* milk?"

They all chose water, which Fennel served them in copper cups.

"Please, make yourselves at home," Fennel instructed. "I regret that I have one more duty to perform before the ceremony. As Benji's surrogate father here, and with no disrespect to my honored guest Jachin, I must speak with him and pass on to him what wisdom I can."

Benji translated Fennel's words, which Lisa then relayed to the family.

"Jachin understands," she said, "and is grateful for your care of his adopted son."

"I wish Mom and Dad could be here," Benji said. "There just wasn't time to make the arrangements."

"I know," Lisa agreed. "They'll be sad they missed it. But there's no way to contact them in time."

Fennel led Benji to the edge of the village.

"I am honored that you will be part of my family," he said. "And if there is one thing I can teach you, it is this. Man is head of the family, but woman is head of the house."

Benji wrinkled his forehead.

"What does that mean?" he asked.

Fennel laughed.

"It means," he explained, "that as man, it is your duty to head the family. Final decisions must be yours, for you are responsible for the wellbeing of all. There will be times when you must curb your woman when she is defiant or disobedient. However, it also means that the woman rules the house, and there will be times when compromise is necessary to maintain a peaceful home."

"I've heard my dad say that if Momma ain't happy, ain't nobody happy," Benji observed.

Fennel nodded.

"That is true," he agreed.

"But how do I know which times are which?" Benji wondered.

"Trust me," Fennel said. "Some of those times you will learn very quickly. And others, you may never learn. It is a delicate balance. We're taught that man is the king, and that he has all authority. But any man can tell you that the queen has her ways of overpowering the king."

Benji shook his head.

"This is confusing," he said.

"Yes," Fennel agreed. "It is. But work together, and conflict will be uncommon. When there is no conflict, there is no confusion. It is better to sacrifice for peace than to lose all in war. For if it comes to war, I cannot say that woman always wins, but it is certain that man always loses."

Benji nodded.

"Tell me what happens next," he said.

Fennel smiled.

"In a short time, the food will be cooked," he explained. "Then we will all gather at the tent. You and Offsa will wait at the front. Jachin may join you if he wishes, though I know he has no way to communicate, so he may be more comfortable remaining with Lisa. Aedred is now preparing Aelbreth. You know how women are. She will be the most beautiful star in the sky on this day. When she is ready, I will bring her to the tent where you are. You will ask me for her hand, and I will give it to you. Then you will present her with a gift worthy of her love. If she is satisfied, she will accept your engagement."

Benji nodded.

"What if she's not satisfied?" he asked.

Fennel laughed.

"Then she will probably compare you to a *patret* and leave the ceremony," he replied. "But I doubt that will happen."

Chapter Forty-Two

Back at Fennel's house, Benji waited impatiently with the rest of his family. He felt nervous, and he wanted to run, and he also wanted to just get it over with. Why, he wondered, did everything have to move so slowly? It gave him too much time to think, and to worry.

"Benji," Lisa said. "Why don't you tell us the story behind the pendant?"

Benji snapped back into the present.

"Madarach took me to a planet of apelike creatures, to a village where they make things out of gold, so I could buy a gift for Aelbreth," he explained. "The goldsmith was a woman, or actually a female ape I guess, and she was very old. I saw this pendant on one of her shelves, and I asked her about it. She said that when she first started smithing, two people came from far away and ordered this special. They were brother and sister, she said, and they came from a place called Arth. But they never came back to pick it up."

Lisa thought about this for a long time.

"It was James," she said. "James and his sister, before he was killed. Benji, you bought me my great-grandmother's pendant! That is incredibly sweet!"

Benji blushed again. He felt like he'd been blushing a lot. But then, people had been saying a lot of nice things about him lately, and he wasn't sure he deserved it.

"I also got this ring," he said, displaying his index finger.

They all leaned forward to examine it.

"That's amazing," Lisa said. "It's a ring for a peacemaker!"

"That's what I thought," Benji said. "I wouldn't have bought it otherwise. I don't wear jewelry."

"What did you get Aelbreth?" Lisa asked.

Benji blushed yet again, somehow afraid that his gift was inadequate. What if Aelbreth actually did walk out of the ceremony? He'd never be able to show his face here again!

He produced the dragonfly pin, which shone in the sun.

Everyone made oohing noises, even Jachin.

"That is gorgeous!" Lisa exclaimed.

Miriam put her hand on Benji's arm.

"It's very beautiful," she said. "If you ever see another like it, think of me!"

"Thank you," he said. "I hope Aelbreth likes it."

"If she doesn't, she doesn't deserve you," Miriam replied.

Finally, Fennel summoned them to the tent. Jachin chose to wait with Lisa and the rest of the family, so she could relay to them what was going on. Benji waited at the front of the tent with Offsa at his side.

Meanwhile, the rest of the village gathered in the tent, until there were almost a hundred people present to witness the daughter of Fennel, a village elder, becoming engaged to a boy from another planet.

"She's going to make you wait," Offsa warned. "They always do."

"Oh, great," Benji replied. "Like I'm not already nervous enough? If I get more nervous, I won't be able to talk!"

But Aelbreth didn't make Benji wait for long. With Fennel at her side, she approached the tent. The crowd parted for her, and Benji gasped as he saw her. Aelbreth was absolutely, stunningly beautiful. She wore a white dress that set off her tanned skin and amber hair. Unlike most of the dresses he had seen on Hadrun, which hung straight with little shape or style, this one had been fitted across the waist and bust to hint at Aelbreth's blossoming figure beneath.

The dress was adorned with pink and purple ribbons. And Aelbreth's hair, normally untied and untamed, had been braided and woven around the crown of her head, with pink and purple flowers in it, which matched the ribbons.

Benji felt like he couldn't breathe. Aelbreth seemed to glow as she approached. She was, Benji realized, the most beautiful woman he'd ever seen. No, she was the most beautiful *thing* he'd ever seen. Her beauty was greater than the painted planet, the dancing rings, or even the Horsehead Nebula!

And he was about to become engaged to her.

He didn't know whether to laugh or cry, so he did neither. Instead, he just stared as Aelbreth reached the front of the tent, escorted by her father.

They stopped about two feet from Benji, and Fennel waited expectantly.

"Honorable Fennel, Elder of Korby," Benji said. "I humbly ask for the hand of your daughter Aelbreth, that we may be committed from this day forth to marry."

Fennel thought about this, appearing as if he had never considered the matter before. Benji guessed that this was part of the tradition.

"Benji of Parisa," Fennel responded. "Do you love my daughter? Will you care for her? Will you protect her with your life?"

Benji gazed at Aelbreth. He wondered if he was supposed to pretend he had never considered these questions. But he couldn't. As he looked at Aelbreth, he couldn't wait to get the words out fast enough.

"I will," he said.

Fennel nodded. His expression seemed to be telling Benji that Fennel knew Benji spoke the truth.

Then Fennel took Aelbreth's hand and extended it toward Benji.

"I accept this commitment," Fennel replied. "If my daughter also accepts it."

Benji took Aelbreth's hand.

"Will you have me?" he asked.

"What have you brought me?" she countered.

The abruptness with which she spoke took Benji aback, even though Fennel had warned that the gift was an important part of the ceremony. He fished in his pocket, retrieved the hairpin, and held it out to her.

"There is nothing I have ever seen that compares with your beauty," Benji said. "But this small token is the most worthy gift I could find."

Aelbreth took the pin. She made a show of holding it up and examining it. Then she frowned.

"A bug?" she asked. "You give me a bug?"

Benji felt his stomach clench, and suddenly felt like he was falling.

Some in the audience chuckled.

"It's made of gold and emeralds," Benji observed. "And I thought it was very pretty. Queenly, even."

"Why, yes," Aelbreth replied. "I shall be the Queen of Bugs."

More laughter erupted, and Benji realized this, too, was part of the tradition.

"You shall be queen of my home," Benji corrected. "Unless you're saying that I'm a bug."

Aelbreth made a great show of looking Benji up and down.

"No," she decided. "Not a bug. More like a *patret.*"

Now everyone was laughing.

"*Patret* can't swim," Benji reminded her. "Perhaps the emerald eyes were unnecessary, for you seem to be a blind queen."

"I can see enough to recognize the man who asks for my commitment," she retorted. "And I accept. From this day forth, I shall be known as Aelbreth, Queen of Bugs!"

Cheers and applause erupted. Then, to Benji's surprise, Fennel produced a crown, which he set on Aelbreth's head. It wasn't made of gold, but of some gold-toned wood that had been polished to a shine. It was very beautiful.

Then, from behind, Benji felt Offsa put something on his head, which Benji guessed was also a crown.

"May you be king and queen of each other's worlds!" Fennel announced.

Benji glanced at Lisa, who looked unusually pale.

"The crown," he said to her, telepathically.

"It's as I saw it," she replied. "It's exactly as I saw it. But I didn't know what it meant."

"Is that bad?" Benji asked.

"No," Lisa said. "It's just... *farchedan.*"

"I think I know what you mean," he agreed.

Meanwhile, the crowd had erupted into applause and cheers.

"Kiss her!" Offsa told Benji.

Benji did.

"Isn't this grand?" Aelbreth said, telepathically. "I've never been so happy!"

"Me too," Benji agreed.

"Now let the feasting begin!" Fennel announced. "And the King and Queen shall be served first!"

Offsa hustled them outside, where the women began serving up slabs of roast *patret*, *ustro* bread, and some other dishes Benji had never seen before. The sun had begun to set, and the men lit the bonfires to keep the *fortule* away.

As people finished their meal, they began singing, with several drums beating a rhythmic accompaniment.

"Nothing is more sacred than the joining of the two," they sang.

"Let peace rule your home, and the land," went another song.

"With love, we need little else," began a third.

"You're supposed to dance," Offsa told Benji, as the song came to an end. "No one else can dance until you dance with Aelbreth."

"But I don't know how," Benji protested.

"It's easy," Offsa said. "Just take her hand, and do what she does. Now go!"

He shoved Benji toward Aelbreth, who was standing less than a foot away. She caught his hand and began to jump from foot to foot. Benji copied her movements as best he could.

"Now twirl me," she instructed.

Benji attempted a twirl like he'd seen in the old movies his parents watched, spinning Aelbreth while holding her hand over her head. That was clearly not what she expected, because she stumbled. Benji caught her in his arms and dipped her.

The onlookers clearly didn't know this was unscripted, because they all cheered. Then Fennel grabbed Aedred's hand and joined them. Then Benji saw Offsa dancing with Elvina, and several more couples spinning and twirling as well. Lisa was even trying to coax Tobin to dance, though he looked as uncomfortable as Benji felt, his moves stiff and ungraceful.

The festivities went on for hours. Finally, the crowd began to break up, and Benji breathed a sigh of relief. Aelbreth was as tireless dancing as she was working, but Benji felt exhausted.

Jachin, Tamar, and the rest of the family gathered near one of the fires, which the men had kept well-stoked.

"Shall we go home now?" Tamar asked.

"You can't," Benji told them. "It's not safe away from the fires. The *fortule* would get you. You'll need to stay in the village tonight. But it will be light again in a couple of hours, I think."

Lisa, who had brought her pocket companion, confirmed this.

"Come! You can sleep at our home," Fennel said. "The children can sleep with the neighbors."

"Which neighbors?" Benji asked Offsa, greatly looking forward to sleep.

"We'll stay with Aelfreth and Mabli," Offsa said, clearly excited.

"And who else?" Benji pressed.

Offsa blushed.

"And their daughter, Elvina," he replied.

"Ah," Benji said. "Such a hardship for you."

"We do what we must for our honored guests," Offsa replied, grinning.

"So your parents have enough blankets for five people?" Benji wondered.

"No," Offsa said. "I expect Lisa and Tobin will have to stay with Gruffud. But he's right next door."

They all went to their respective places of rest. Aelfreth's home was comparable to Fennel's, if more sparsely furnished. He brought out three of the best *patret* fur blankets for his guests, and made Elvina sleep on a worn one.

Benji suspected that Elvina would soon be sharing Offsa's anyway, once the adults had gone to bed.

He curled up with Aelbreth. They were both too tired to talk, and fell asleep as soon as the candles had been put out.

Chapter Forty-Three

Dawn came much too soon, as far as Benji was concerned. The sun streamed through the window, and he groaned.

"Already?" he muttered.

He looked around the room. Aelbreth was already sitting up, but Offsa and Elvina, as he'd expected, were curled up together, still asleep on a single blanket.

"Rise and shine," Aelbreth told them. "We have a day's chores to catch up on."

Offsa moaned and stirred. Elvina didn't.

"I have to take my family home," Benji said. "But I don't want to leave you. Will you come with me?"

"I can't silly," Aelbreth said. "There's a day's chores to catch up on. And if you're going to be lazy and not help us, I can't exactly take the day off, now, can I?"

Benji grunted.

"I suppose not," he said. "I wonder how my Parisan family liked the accommodations. This isn't exactly what they're used to."

"I'm sure they were fine," Aelbreth said. "*Patret* fur is soft."

"I hope so," Benji said. "They're not accustomed to meat, either. I hope they don't get sick."

"You worry too much," Aelbreth scolded. "They'll be fine."

Elvina had finally awakened now, and Offsa, Aelbreth, and Benji made their way to Fennel's home.

Aedred had breakfast on the table when they arrived, and the rest of the family was already eating.

"Come," Aedred instructed. "Break your fast."

They did, sharing a plate of *ustro* between them while sitting on the ground outside, because there was only one plate left and no room at the table.

Then it was time to say goodbye. Jachin thanked Fennel from the bottom of his heart on behalf of his whole family. Tamar and Miriam hugged Aedred, and then Aelbreth. Lisa hugged everyone, while Tobin shook hands.

"I'll miss you," Benji told Aelbreth.

Then he turned to Fennel.

"Thank you," he said. "For everything. I'll miss all of you."

Fennel bowed.

"Just remember," he said, "that you only wore the crown for an evening. Be careful as you travel."

Benji grinned.

"I have Madarach," he reminded Fennel.

Benji's Parisan family gathered and headed for the clearing. Aelbreth accompanied them, and when they reached the clearing Benji kissed her for a long time.

"I love you," he whispered.

Then he turned and began to help his family board Madarach.

"How did you like Hadrun?" he asked them, once they began to ascend.

"These people are wonderful!" Tamar exclaimed.

"I see now how Aelbreth came to be so sweet," Miriam added.

"It was quite an adventure for us, though," Jachin said. "We're not used to such primitive conditions. It was a lot like camping, only more fun."

"I've never been camping," Tobin said, "so I have nothing to compare it with. But I'll be glad to get home."

"Did you have any fun at all?" Lisa asked him.

"A little," Tobin replied. "But it's hard to relate to a people who have so little regard for science."

"How was the food?" Benji asked. "Was it okay for you?"

"It was fine," Tamar answered. "There were enough vegetarian dishes to keep us satisfied."

"I must admit that I tried the meat, and found it quite enjoyable," Jachin said.

"You ate meat?" Miriam asked, horrified.

"Yes," Jachin agreed. "It seems to be part of their sustainable economy, so I saw no harm in it."

"But it's animals!" Miriam exclaimed. "You ate animals!"

Jachin shrugged.

"Just because our culture doesn't eat them doesn't mean it is never appropriate to do so," he suggested. "We eat what we are served when we visit someone's home, do we not?"

"But not animals," Miriam said. "That's disgusting."

"Lucky for you, you have your own mouth, and can make your own decisions as to what goes into it," Tamar observed.

It was still dark on Parisa when they landed. Fortunately, Tobin had thought to bring a flashlight. They made their way home in the dark, arriving well before dawn.

"The nights are short on Hadrun," Tamar observed. "And we spent half of that short night dancing. I think we should all go to bed."

They all made agreeable noises, and wandered off to their respective bedrooms.

But Benji couldn't sleep. Things were changing too quickly for him. He had just turned thirteen in Earth years. He was trying to end a war. He was now engaged to be married. And he had begun to understand *farchedan*.

He thought about how he had danced through the rain in the goldsmith village, and had barely gotten wet. In hindsight, it made no sense. He couldn't figure out how he had done it. But he *had* done it.

It seemed like everyone lately had been telling him to stop thinking. His experience in the rain supported that suggestion. But how could he stop? How did you just make your brain stop thinking? That's what a brain did.

He recognized the irony as he lay in bed and thought about that.

In the morning, they all returned to their regular routine. Benji went to class, where he had trouble paying attention. They were studying chemistry, which Benji didn't much care for. Tobin claimed that chemistry was the gateway to the universe. If you understood how things were put together, he said, you could make or unmake anything.

But Benji didn't care about making or unmaking physical things, and especially chemical compounds. He recognized that someone needed to. He had only to look at the difference in the understanding of brain chemistry between Parisa and Earth to understand that. But in the end, Lisa hadn't been cured by brain chemistry. She'd been cured by something else, a deeper understanding of the universe that didn't dwell on details such as how many bonds a carbon atom could make.

And the things Benji wanted to fix wouldn't be helped by an understanding of carbon atoms, either.

After class, Kareah called Benji over.

"You're not paying much attention these days," he observed.

Benji sighed.

"I want to," he said. "But I have so many things to think about, and to be honest, I just don't find chemistry that interesting."

Kareah nodded.

"We're not all meant to be chemists," he agreed. "But a basic understanding is helpful. You should have a basic understanding of all the disciplines, because they support each other."

"How does chemistry support sociology, for example?" Benji asked.

Kareah smiled.

"You have an uncanny ability to ask very difficult questions," he observed. "Chemistry and sociology are two sciences that are quite far apart on the spectrum. Still, did you know that the anger control methods we teach actually change our brain chemistry?"

Benji considered this.

"They do?" he asked. "How do you know?"

"Because," Kareah replied, "a scientist measured the levels of the various brain chemicals before, during, and after the anger management process. Do you want to guess what kind of scientist?"

Benji sighed.

"A chemist?" he guessed.

"Exactly," Kareah, confirmed. "So you see, the two disciplines do have an intersection. You may not be interested in it, but it exists, and you will benefit from knowing something of both."

Benji sighed again.

"I'll try to do better," he assured the teacher.

From class, Benji headed for the temple, where he helped Nahum weed the garden and then sweep the floors. He chuckled to himself just a little, recalling how the old priestess, Yorga, had referred to sweeping as "women's work." In a temple full of women, it surely was. But in a temple of men, who else would do it?

When he finished at the temple, Benji returned home to play video games with Tobin. He found himself getting bored with the games, however. They all involved solving puzzles, and the puzzles seemed to have gotten easier for Benji. He wasn't sure if his observation of *farchedan* might have something to do with this. But lately, he seemed to be able to look at a puzzle and know the solution almost instantly.

Chapter Forty-Four

Benji hadn't been to Zeblack for the past two days off. By the third, it had been twenty-four days on Parisa, and more than a month on Zeblack.

"It's time to see how they're doing," he told Madarach.

"As you wish," Madarach replied. "But I caution you that things move slowly in these situations. Setting up networks, recruiting people one at a time, setting up a broadcast system, all of these take time. You may be disappointed."

"I doubt it," Benji said. "I'll be happy if *anything* has happened."

They landed in the alley near Dorn's house, and Madarach projected his low-level message. Dorn came out a few moments later and approached them.

"How are things?" Benji asked.

"You won't believe it," Dorn said. "We've been able to set up exchanges between the northern factions and Free Zeblack. There are almost hundred people working in Darkly, and more in the other factions. Flan got me a radio, and now I can talk to people all over the planet. It's amazing how sick everyone is of this war. They were just afraid to say so."

"Is Flan broadcasting yet?" Benji asked.

"Not yet," Dorn replied. "But here's something you'll like. Come look at this wall!"

Dorn led Benji around the corner, just into the street, and pointed out the wall of an abandoned building. It was covered with posters in different designs. One showed the flag of the faction and a photo of General Obedas's palace. Underneath, in the local alphabet, it said, "We die while generals get rich." Another showed three young amputees in tattered uniforms sitting on a stone wall. It read, "The cost of war is not just poverty." There were several others.

"Wow," Benji said.

"Thol," Dorn explained. "He's a really good photographer, and Free Zeblack stole a printing press to distribute his photos."

"That's amazing," Benji said.

"What's really amazing is, no one has taken them down," Dorn said. "Chute took some down the first time we put them up. But apparently someone threatened him, and the next time, they stayed up."

"I'm not sure threats are the way to peace," Benji observed.

"No," Dorn agreed. "But like Madarach told us, no one knows what to do about the extremists. This one is in line for the moment. But no one will trust him enough to let him join us."

"Has there been any reaction from the factions?" Benji asked.

"Not yet," Dorn said. "They're still ignoring us, hoping we'll go away. Darkly started a new offensive last week, and they're telling everyone that loyalty is more important than ever. I think they expect that if they can keep people occupied with the war, no one will think about Free Zeblack. That's how they think, anyway. They can't imagine a bigger threat than the other factions."

"They must have noticed people weren't showing up to fight," Benji suggested.

"You'd think so," Dorn agreed. "They did send someone around to ask about Thol, and his parents told them Thol ran away. But they don't seem to realize yet that this is a movement."

"What will happen when they do?" Benji asked.

Dorn sighed.

"I honestly don't know," he said.

"Can you do anything before that happens?" Benji wondered.

"I don't know," Dorn said again.

"What do you want to happen?" Benji pressed.

Dorn sighed, and kicked at the broken pavement.

"I want to see every soldier walk away from the fighting for a day, or maybe even a week. That would get their attention," he said. "How can you fight a war if no one shows up?"

"And then what?" Benji asked.

"I don't know," Dorn replied. "Obviously we need to get the faction leaders in a room to talk. But to talk to whom? And what incentive will they have to step down? If we threaten them or kill them, we're the same as they are."

Benji gazed at Dorn for a long moment.

"Dorn," he said, "is there anything special about your family?"

"What do you mean?" Dorn asked. "What kind of special?"

"I don't know," Benji admitted. "I'm just asking. Is there anything unusual or special about your parents, or grandparents, or anything?"

Dorn laughed.

"My dad says his grandfather was a priest of some kind," he replied. "I don't know if that's true or not. Why?"

Benji thought about telling him Lisa's vision, but decided against it. If Dorn knew how important he was, he might panic.

"I was just wondering," Benji said. "Can you find out if it's true?"

Dorn stared at him.

"You're serious?" he asked. "You think my family might carry the old religion, and that the generals would listen to them because of it? You're crazy. They demolished the temple more than fifty years ago. They have no respect for religion, or royalty, or anything else."

"I suppose not," Benji agreed. "But it would put you in a position to talk to them."

Dorn thought about this, and Benji could see the wheels turning in his head.

"Talk to them about what, though?" Dorn asked. "What could I say to them that would make them change anything?"

"I don't know," Benji said. "But I think I know who does."

Dorn considered this.

"That old man, Blot," he suggested. "He seemed to know more about the history of Zeblack and the structure of Free Zeblack than anyone else I've ever met."

"Exactly," Benji agreed. "Shall we go see him?"

Dorn thought for a moment, and then smiled.

"Yes!" he said, excitedly. "Let's make this happen!"

They returned to the alley where Madarach waited. They boarded, and moved north over the wilderness. They landed near the same camp they'd visited a few weeks before, and Benji and Dorn made their way through the thick woods to the cluster of tents.

Blot was hanging laundry on one of the clotheslines near the edge of the encampment. He finished positioning a shirt on the line, and then turned to face his visitors.

"Greetings!" he announced. "How are things in Darkly, young friends?"

"Good," Dorn said. He told Blot about the progress they'd made in communications and organization.

"But I'm worried," Dorn said. "I think it won't be long before the faction figures out there's a movement against them, and I don't know what they'll do when they realize it."

Blot nodded.

"A valid concern," he agreed.

"We were thinking," Benji said, "that if we could do something before the faction does anything, we'd have a better chance of success."

"Also a valid thought," Blot agreed. "What do you have in mind?"

"We don't know," Dorn admitted. "I envision everyone on the front line going home and refusing to fight. But that's not enough. It would make a statement, but I don't think it would accomplish anything except making the generals angry."

Blot nodded again.

"I see," he said. "You can show your strength, but you can't yet challenge the power of the generals, nor do you have anything to replace them with. In which case, they will respond in the only way they know how, which is with force."

"Exactly," Dorn agreed. "And then we're in another war we don't want."

"We were wondering," Benji began, "if you have any ideas about what we should do?"

"Me?" Blot asked. Then he laughed. "I'm just an old cripple with too much time to think and little energy to do anything about it."

"You seem to know a lot about Zeblack's history," Dorn pointed out.

"Ah, yes," Blot said. "From history, we learn what has happened in the past. If we are wise, we learn how to prevent it from happening again in the future. But who has such wisdom, and who would listen to that man?"

"I would," Dorn said. "We need wisdom if anything is going to change."

Blot considered this, gazing steadily at Dorn, and then at Benji.

"Come," he said. "Let us have tea."

They retreated inside Blot's tent, and the old man put a pot on the oil burner. They sat in silence for the few minutes it took for the water to boil. Only after Blot had poured three cups did he speak.

"Where shall we begin?" the old man asked.

Dorn looked at Benji.

"Can you tell me about religion here on Zeblack?" he asked.

"Religion?" Blot repeated. "Our religion is war. But it was not always so. Once there was a great temple, with a high priest. Priests and priestesses traveled all over the planet teaching and washing."

"Washing?" Dorn asked.

"Yes," Blot confirmed. "This was before your time, of course. They taught that all should be kind and just to one another because we are all created in the image of wisdom, and wisdom is of God. When we fail, as we all do, we must be washed clean of our fault so that our image does not remain soiled."

"So there was peace?" Benji guessed.

"There was peace," Blot agreed. "It took centuries to achieve it. But the priests and priestesses made it happen."

"Then how did it end?" Dorn asked.

Blot shook his head, sadly.

"It began with one governor who decided that his neighbor had more than he did," Blot explained. "His province had a drought, but his neighbor had plenty. He sent his policemen to a city in the neighboring province and took their food. The other governor complained, of course. She called in the priests, and they confronted the offending governor and tried to get him to admit his fault. But he refused. So they refused to wash him. Soon the whole province was refusing the priests, because the priests had refused to wash the governor. And because they refused the priests, the neighboring provinces stopped sharing food with them, and they were in worse shape than before. So they sent their policemen out to steal more. So the neighboring provinces began defending themselves, and soon they were shooting at each other. Then the whole planet went to war, and it never stopped."

"If they were having a famine, why didn't the other provinces help them?" Dorn asked.

Blot chuckled, bitterly.

"That is the irony," he replied. "They never asked. If the governor had just asked for help, he would have received it. But he was a weak man trying to appear strong. He refused to ask for help, and instead took what he needed. Had he but asked, or even if he had admitted fault afterward, or if the other governors had been more patient with him, none of this would have happened. But no one imagined it would become a war, or that the war would go on endlessly."

"And the priests and priestesses?" Benji asked. "What happened to them?"

"You can imagine," Blot said. "They spoke out against the violence at every opportunity. But once the whole planet became involved, they became a nuisance to the generals. They were killed. Eventually, the temple was destroyed. There are no priests anymore."

"What if there were?" Benji asked.

Blot gazed at Benji for a long moment.

"You mean," he suggested, "that there might be a descendent of a priest who would step forward and claim the old religion?"

"What if there was?" Benji asked. "What if all the soldiers went home in response to a call from a priest?"

"Then there would be a leader," Blot said. "That would be very good. And very dangerous."

"If there was such a person," Dorn continued, "how would he learn about the old religion? I've never seen or heard anything about it."

"No," Blot agreed. "Speaking of it is considered treason to the generals. They destroyed every piece of evidence they could find that the religion ever existed."

Dorn frowned.

"So it's lost?" he asked.

Blot chuckled, softly.

"Not exactly," he replied. "Because there are parts of the planet that no general controls. And the records that made their way there have been kept safe."

"Where is that?" Benji asked.

Blot didn't answer for a long moment. Then he stood, pulled a trunk out from under his cot, and opened it. He retrieved an old, leather-bound book and handed it to Dorn.

"This," Blot said, "is the future of our planet. Read it, but do not let anything happen to it. There are very few copies left."

Dorn held the thick book in his hand for a long moment. Then he opened it to a random page and began to read.

"'You cannot harvest fruit by sowing grain. Plant therefore what you wish to reap.'" Dorn read. "'An act of violence will be returned, and an act of kindness will likewise be returned. Knowing this, the wise man chooses his actions based on what he wishes to receive.'"

He flipped to another section of the book.

"This is the history of Zeblack!" he exclaimed. "From long ago, before the war started."

"Yes," Blot agreed. "That is there, too."

Dorn flipped again.

"'And in the darkness, fires burned,'" he read. "'All had been destroyed. But, like winter, destruction cannot last. Creation, too, comes in its season.'"

"*Farchedan,*" Benji muttered.

Dorn turned to him.

"You told me that a few weeks ago," he said. "Destruction and creation are inseparable."

"Yes," Benji agreed. "Apparently I'm not the only one to know that."

"He's reading from the Prophesy of Omnin," Blot said. "Study that book, young man. Learn it. Understand it. Prepare to teach it. We may yet see its prophesy fulfilled."

"But don't take too long," Benji suggested. "I suspect the time to act is coming very soon."

Dorn nodded.

"Blot," he asked, "do you have room for me to stay here for a while? I think it would be safer than if I went back to Darkly."

Blot nodded, solemnly.

"This other cot is currently unoccupied," he said. "Perhaps I could help you with your studies."

"Wait," Benji said. "I have an idea."

The three of them went up to the cave and talked with Flan. He told them he was very close to being able to broadcast, so they came up with a plan.

Chapter Forty-Five

Back on Parisa, Benji couldn't focus on much of anything. Kareah scolded him several times for daydreaming in class, but it didn't help so eventually the teacher gave up. Benji daydreamed through his lessons and didn't learn much that week.

Even Nahum noticed.

"Where is your mind lately?" he asked Benji.

Benji grinned.

"Zeblack," he replied. "I think something is going to happen there soon."

"You think, or you know?" Nahum pressed.

Benji just shrugged.

"Nothing is known until it is known," he replied.

Nahum laughed.

"I think," he said, "that you've spent too much time with that old priestess."

Benji laughed, too.

"You'd like her," he suggested.

"I'm sure you're right," Nahum said, with a grin. "But my place is here on Parisa. And I can tell you don't want to talk about this. Are you afraid I'll try to talk you out of it?"

"Maybe," Benji hedged.

Nahum laughed.

"You and I are more alike than you can imagine," he said. "At your age, I would have felt the same. So keep your secret. Tell me when you're ready."

But Benji couldn't keep his secret from Lisa.

"You're planning something," she accused, as they sat outside one evening.

"I'm not!" Benji insisted.

Lisa gazed at him.

"I'm you're sister," she reminded him. "If you're not planning something, it's because it's already planned. Don't play dumb with me."

Benji scowled.

"What if I was planning your birthday party?" he asked. "I'd never be able to make it a surprise."

"This isn't about my birthday party," Lisa said. "We both know it's about Zeblack."

"Yes," Benji admitted, softly.

"You found the old man?" Lisa asked.

"I did," Benji said. "His name is Blot. He knows more about the history of Zeblack than anyone I've met there, and more than anyone Dorn knows, too."

"How does that help you?" Lisa asked.

"He knows about their religion," Benji replied. "The factions destroyed the religion and killed the priests, but Blot has a copy of their Bible."

"They have a Bible?" Lisa wondered, skeptically.

"It's not the same as ours," Benji said. "But it's their sacred book, like the Bible is sacred to Christians."

Lisa considered this.

"So you need to find a priest," she observed. "Or someone who's willing to become a priest, anyway. Is Blot a priest?"

"No," Benji said. "But Dorn's great-grandfather was."

"Really?" she asked. "That's convenient."

Suddenly, Lisa gasped.

Benji spun toward her.

"What?" he asked. "Are you okay?"

Lisa's face had turned snow-white, and she didn't answer for a moment.

"Lisa?" Benji said, wondering if he should call Madarach. Was she getting sick again? Would he have to take her back to Hassyr?

"I'm fine," Lisa said, finally. But she didn't sound fine. Her voice sounded far away, like her mind was somewhere else.

"Can you hear me okay?" Benji asked, remembering the mental noise that had almost consumed her.

"I can hear you," she said. "This is just a little strange."

"What is?" Benji asked.

"I can see it," she replied. "I can see it happening, just as you planned."

"You read my mind?" he wondered.

"No," she said. "This didn't come from you. It came from... somewhere else."

"*Farchedan*," he muttered. Then, he said, "Tell me. Tell me what you see."

"They're all marching," she said. "They're all leaving. But they're going somewhere. No one knows what's going to happen. But they're going. Oh, Benji, they have so much hope!"

She began to cry.

"Benji," she said, through her tears, "you know this is dangerous."

"I know," he agreed. "And not just for me. For Dorn and Blot, too, and everyone. But I can't stop it now. Everything is moving forward. And I can't abandon them. I have to go."

She grabbed him and pulled him close, so that her tears wet his shoulder.

"Yes," she agreed, softly.

"Yes?" Benji repeated. "I thought you were trying to talk me out of it."

"No," Lisa said. "No, this has to happen. And I need to be there with you."

"You?" Benji asked, skeptically.

"Yes," Lisa confirmed. "You need someone who can read people. There isn't anyone else. It has to be me."

"Lisa, if anything happens..." Benji began.

"If anything happens, we'll be in it together," Lisa concluded. "You're my little brother. You think I won't stand by you when you're in danger?"

Benji thought about this. He knew he would stand by Lisa. He knew, because he had stood by her. Now she wanted to stand by him. How could he refuse?

"Okay," he said. "We'll do this together."

"But Benji?" Lisa interjected. "Don't tell Tobin. He'd have a fit."

Benji laughed.

"Yes, he would," he agreed. "I won't say a word."

They sat in silence for a while, and then Lisa suggested they go to sleep.

"That sounds good to me," Benji agreed. "When I'm sleeping, I'm not thinking about what Dorn and Blot are doing."

The days passed slowly for Benji. By the next day off, he was going crazy with nothing to do but think. But it wasn't yet time to go to Zeblack.

"We need to go see your fiancée," Lisa told him.

"My fiancée?" Benji repeated. "That sounds so weird!"

"I know," Lisa agreed. "And you haven't seen her in weeks. Don't you think it's time?"

"I guess," Benji said, reluctantly. "I can't stop thinking about what's happening on Zeblack."

"I know," Lisa replied. "Your brain is loud right now."

Benji chuckled.

"Sorry," he said. "You want to go, too?"

"Sure," Lisa said. "It would be good to get away. Plus I think you need the company."

"Let's go, then," Benji agreed.

They made their way to the well and Madarach took them to Hadrun. The sun was high in the sky, and Benji sprinted to the village. Lisa tried to keep up at first, but quickly gave up.

Benji found Aelbreth and Offsa at the *patret* pens, as he knew he would.

"Aelbreth!" Benji called.

"Who's that?" Aelbreth said, squinting. "You look familiar, but I don't remember your name!"

"Very funny," Benji replied. "Get over here and greet the man you're betrothed to."

"How do you know I haven't changed my mind?" she called back.

"Because you're wearing a golden bug in your hair," Benji said. "You'd never do that if you weren't in love with the man who gave it to you."

Aelbreth cocked her head.

"You may be right," she said, and grinned. Then she sprinted across the pen and threw her arms around Benji.

"There you are!" Lisa called from the direction of the village.

"You brought a chaperone?" Aelbreth asked. "What did you think I was going to do to you?"

"Last time, you covered me with *patret* dung," Benji reminded her.

"That wasn't last time," Aelbreth protested. "That was a long time ago, and I've grown up since then."

"Have you?" Benji wondered. "That's too bad."

Aelbreth laughed.

"Just wait until you're not looking," she cautioned.

Lisa reached them and took Aelbreth's hand.

"It's good to see you," she said. "I haven't seen you since the ceremony."

"I know," Aelbreth replied. "Your little brother apparently has other important things to do. He doesn't come visit me anymore."

Lisa sighed with mock sadness.

"That's what happens once they get you to commit," she complained. "They forget all about you."

"Lisa!" Benji scolded. "I haven't forgotten about her for a single second!"

"So you say," Aelbreth scolded. "But how do I know that? You don't visit. You don't send me presents. You don't even send a messenger to tell me you're not dead. What am I supposed to think?"

Benji felt flustered, and didn't know what to say.

"You want me to send you presents?" Benji asked. "Really?"

"No, silly," Aelbreth replied, grinning. "I want you."

"Well, here I am," Benji observed. "But so far, all you've done is complain. Maybe you really have changed your mind."

Aelbreth laughed.

"I have something to show you," she said.

Aelbreth led them back to the village, to her father's house. Aedred sat outside, grinding *ustro* into meal. They chatted while Aelbreth went inside.

"We've missed you both," Aedred said. "Lisa, you don't come very often anymore."

"I know," Lisa replied, her hand on Aedred's shoulder. "But Benji has his betrothed, and I have mine."

"He's a nice young man, your Tobin," Aedred observed. "You should bring him once in a while."

Lisa smiled, sadly.

"He prefers to stay at home," she said. "He doesn't like adventures."

Aedred nodded.

"Nor do I," she said. "Nor do I."

Aelbreth reappeared, grinning widely.

"Close your eyes," she told Benji. "And hold out your hand."

Benji did, though he half expected her to play a prank on him.

She didn't. She placed something small and cold in his hand.

"Now look," she said.

Benji did.

It was a gold pendant, shaped like a leaf and neatly engraved with script he didn't recognize.

"It's beautiful," Benji exclaimed. "Where did you get it?"

Aelbreth grinned.

"You think you're the only one clever enough to find a goldsmith?" she asked.

"No, of course not," Benji stammered. "It's just, I've never seen one here."

"There isn't one here," she said. "But there is one in the town a day's walk from here."

"You walked a whole day to get there?" he surmised.

Aelbreth grinned.

"Not exactly," she said.

Now Benji was confused.

"But you said…" he stammered, weakly.

"I said it was a day's walk away," she observed. "I didn't say I walked."

"Then how?" Benji wondered. "Unless you learned to ride a *patret*."

Aelbreth grinned.

"Not exactly," she said. "Madarach helped me. That's how I got the gold."

"Madarach?" Benji repeated. "How?"

"When you guys came for the ceremony, I asked if he would come back in a couple of days," she explained. "He took me to the gold planet, and then to the town."

"You and Madarach are getting a little too friendly!" Benji joked.

"It won't happen again," Aelbreth said. "But I really wanted you to have something from me."

"What does it say?" Benji asked.

"It says, 'Peace is all,'" she replied. "It's our local script. Most people here don't know their letters, but a goldsmith in a town can read and write."

"Aelbreth," Benji exclaimed. "It's perfect!"

Aelbreth beamed.

"If only she knew how perfect," Lisa said in his mind. "You're not going to tell her, are you?"

"Of course not," Benji replied. "She'd only worry."

"Well," Aelbreth said, "shall we go for a swim, then?"

They did, with Offsa, swimming naked in the irrigation canal, as was their custom. Lisa, as usual, stayed clothed, but at least she swam with them. But they couldn't swim for very long, because the day was coming to an end.

"This was a short visit," Benji acknowledged.

"It was," Aelbreth agreed. "But I know you have a lot on your mind. I'm glad I got to see you at all. And Lisa, too. Thanks for bringing her."

"She wanted to come," Benji said. "She loves you, too."

"I think she came because she loves you more," Aelbreth suggested.

Chapter Forty-Six

Benji counted the slowly moving days back on Parisa. There was nothing he could do to make the time move faster, and nothing he could do to help Zeblack get ready. Everything was out of his control. The waiting made him feel anxious, restless, and a little crazy.

Finally the day arrived. He woke Lisa up before dawn, and together they slipped out of the house and made their way through the darkened streets.

"It's early," Lisa observed. "The sky hasn't even begun to get light."

"It'll be daylight on Zeblack soon," Benji replied. "We need to be there as soon as the sun rises."

They went to the well and boarded Madarach.

"Zeblack," Benji said.

"As you wish," Madarach replied. "But aren't you going to tell me what your plan is? I know today is the day, and you haven't said a word."

Benji sighed.

"I didn't want to upset you," he explained. "Besides, you never said a word about taking Aelbreth shopping."

Madarach chuckled.

"Oh, that," he said, dismissively. "It was just a little harmless fun."

"Well, hopefully this will be, too," Benji said.

Then he told Madarach what he had in mind.

As they entered Zeblack's stratosphere, Benji asked Madarach to see if he could pick up Flan's radio broadcast. Madarach scanned and found it, and he put it on audio so they could hear. Benji relayed what he heard to Lisa, who still didn't know the language.

"And in the tenth year of the reign of King Pillum," the broadcast said, "Farnell the priest went to him in peace. 'Oh great king,' Farnell said, 'you have taken much of the wealth of the people, and they are angry with you but they dare not speak.' Pillum replied, 'Am I not the king? Surely I have the right to live better than the rest of the people.' But Farnell pointed to the chair of gold in which the king sat. 'That one chair would feed ten thousand children,' he said. 'Now it is said that you plan to make a palace out of gold. How many will go hungry if you do?' Pillum replied, 'What is that to me? Am I not King?' Then Farnell tore his robe and exclaimed, 'Pillum, you have strayed far from your teaching! For the king is meant to serve the people, and not the other way around. Will you steal from them until they come to you with violence in their hearts? Think, oh King! For that would not only be your end, but the end of peace. For after they kill you for what you have done, will they accept your son in your place? And who, then, would rule? Your greed has the power to destroy not just yourself, but your people as well!' Pillum was angry, but he respected the priest, and so he thought deeply on what he had said. Then his heart was turned. 'You are right,' Pillum said. 'Wash me, and I shall serve my people.'"

"What is that?" Lisa asked.

"It's from their Bible," Benji replied. "They started broadcasting yesterday, reading the whole thing from one end to the other. Most of Zeblack has never heard it before."

"And what does it say" Lisa asked. "Is it all history?"

"No," Benji explained. "There's wisdom, and prophesy, and other stuff, too. I don't know it all. But they're going to read a special part when it's sunrise in Darkly."

They landed near the Free Zeblack camp, and Benji led Lisa to the cluster of tents. Everyone seemed to be up already. They could smell food cooking, and it looked like people were packing for a journey.

Dorn came running when he saw Benji.

"You came!" he said. "I was afraid you wouldn't."

"You thought I'd miss all the fun?" Benji retorted.

Dorn held out his hand to Lisa.

"It's good to see you again," he told her. "I'm glad you're with him."

"Me too," Lisa said. "How are you?"

"Nervous," Dorn replied. "I've never done anything like this before. But then, I guess no one has."

Lisa smiled.

"Someone has to go first," she said.

"Right now, I need to go get ready," Dorn said. "I'll be back in a while. Get some food over there while you wait," he added, gesturing toward a group of people gathered around several tables.

"Food sounds good," Lisa agreed. "We missed breakfast."

Dorn went to join a group of men and women at the edge of the clearing, and Benji led the way to the tables and found Lisa and him two places to sit. A man offered them plates, and a woman followed him with a pot of stew that she ladled onto the plates. Another man handed them each a chunk of some kind of bread.

"This is pretty good," Benji commented, as he ate. "I forgot about breakfast. But I don't think it's good to make peace on an empty stomach."

As they finished eating, Blot came over to them.

"It's good to see you, my young friend," he said. "And who have you brought with you?"

"My sister, Lisa," Benji replied. "She doesn't speak your language, but if you take her hand she can understand you."

Blot raised his eyebrows briefly, and then offered his hand to Lisa. He said nothing for a long moment.

"Well," he said, finally, "that's something I never experienced before. It must be handy at times."

Benji grinned.

"It can be," he said.

Then Benji turned to Lisa.

"What do you think of him?" he asked her, telepathically.

She smiled.

"He's everything I imagined," she replied. "He's the doorway. Now we need Dorn to become the key."

Dorn didn't join them for quite a while longer. When he did, he was almost unrecognizable, for he wore what Benji guessed was the robe of a priest. It was made of course, white fabric and decorated with strips of brightly colored embroidery with symbols that Benji didn't recognize.

But Lisa did. She gasped, and her mouth fell open.

"What?" Benji asked.

"I saw the same symbols at the temple on Hassyr!" she exclaimed. "They are symbols of creation."

"Yes," Dorn agreed. "I don't know exactly what they mean, but Blot told me they symbolize making order out of chaos."

"*Farchedan*," Benji muttered.

Then he thought for a moment.

"I need to take a walk," he said. "Alone."

"Are you okay?" Lisa wondered.

"I'm fine," he replied. "I just realized that I need to prepare, too."

He made his way to the edge of the clearing and into the darkness of the trees. Then he stopped.

"The dance is the means," he said. "The dance is the means."

Then, in the midst of the forest, in the darkness of the night, he began to dance. He could see nothing with his eyes. Yet somehow, he managed to navigate through the trees without running into any. He started slowly, moving his arms and legs in discordant rhythm. He sped up, until he spun furiously in the darkness, leaping forward and sideways and backward. Suddenly, he catapulted forward into a handspring, and then dodged to the side.

He felt invigorated, filled with some strange new awareness, exploding with energy—and at the same time, calm inside. He felt one with the forest, as though he could actually see it. Yet he couldn't see anything, it was too dark.

How could this be?

"*Farchedan*," he muttered.

Then he shouted it at the top of his lungs.

"Farchedan!"

He stopped dancing, and smiled. Then he turned and walked back to camp. He had no idea what direction he had danced, yet somehow he knew exactly which way to go.

Back in the clearing, Dorn spotted him and came running over.

"Are you okay?" he asked.

"I'm fine," Benji said. "I'm ready now."

"What were you doing out there?" Dorn wondered.

Benji smiled.

"Dancing," he replied.

Just then, they heard a commotion in the center of the campsite.

"It's starting," Dorn said. "Let's go listen."

They joined the crowd and pressed in until they could hear the short wave radio someone had set up.

"This is the Voice of Zeblack," the radio said. They both recognized Flan's voice. He sounded very dignified.

"Over the past twenty-four hours, we have read you the Book of the Sacred," Flan continued. "This book is the foundation of our religion. But it was banned by the factions because it threatened them. It tells us that things were not always as they are now. And it tells us that things will not always be as they are now.

"In the Book of Beginnings, we are told that the Great God made order out of chaos, because only in order can there be creation. Plants, animals, and people all came from that order. And the Great God gave us peace.

"In the Book of Farnell, we are told that the priests counseled the kings to make sure that they served the people, and not the other way around.

"And in the Prophesy of Omnin, we are warned that greed will bring about the destruction of our society. And indeed it has. But Omnin also tells us that this is not the end, for Wisdom exists, and it cannot be denied. Always a new priest shall rise to counsel our leaders.

"Today that priest has arisen. He is going to the city of Denmar, where all the generals of all the factions are gathered, and he will counsel them. And he asks you to come with him to witness this great event.

"All of you, every soldier, every merchant, every mother, every man, woman, and child who can walk, you are summoned to Denmar in the name of Zeblack. Stop what you are doing *now*, drop what is in your hand, and join us. Let wisdom return to these lands!

"From this moment forward, there is no faction. There is only Zeblack!

"But be disciplined. As we've said before, for two hundred years we have seen the truth that violence begets only violence. Do not lift a hand against anyone, not even the generals. Do not say a rude word to anyone, not even the generals. Today, we begin a new world, and that requires that we practice new behavior.

"Now I will play a song no one alive has heard before. It is the Anthem of Zeblack, and it celebrates a free, unified, and peaceful people. It has not been played for over a hundred years. But it will be played today, and it will be played every day hereafter!"

"Let's go," Dorn said. "It's time."

Chapter Forty-Seven

They flew slowly over the landscape, amazed to see thousands of people walking in the early light. They were all headed in the same direction.

"We're going to need food," Blot said. "They can drink from the city water and they can use the sewers, but there won't be enough food for everyone."

"It's covered," Dorn replied. "We've been stealing rations from the militias and stockpiling them near Denmar."

"You've really thought this through," Lisa observed, as she monitored the conversation through Benji. "But how did you know all the generals were going to meet today in Denmar?"

"Because we sent the invitation," Dorn replied. "We faked a series of messages convincing the generals that Obedas wanted to talk about the threat of Free Zeblack. They'll be there in about an hour."

"And they believed it?" Lisa wondered. "Weren't they afraid it was a plot by one of them to kill the others?"

"Oddly, no," Blot said. "It turns out they're all on friendly terms. They send armies against one another all the time, but the system serves them all so they don't have any personal enmity."

"That's the craziest thing I've ever heard," Lisa exclaimed. "Enemies who aren't really enemies?"

"You and me both," Dorn agreed.

"And Obedas doesn't know they're coming?" Lisa asked.

"He does," Dorn explained. "But he thinks Blue arranged it, and everyone else thinks it was Darkly."

"There's the city," Benji said, pointing ahead of them. "It looks like there are already people filling the streets."

"By the Great God," Blot said, as the gold and marble palace came into view. "I've never seen it before. That's more obscene than I could have imagined."

"Great God willing, it will belong to the people soon," Dorn replied.

"How will the generals arrive?" Benji asked.

"They'll land at the airfield," Dorn explained. "They'll come to the palace in a caravan."

"And we'll meet them there," Blot added, "when they're all outside. Some of our people will take down the gates so there'll be plenty of witnesses."

"And then what?" Lisa asked.

"And then, we'll see," Dorn said, softly, "what a general does without an army."

They hovered for a while, and then Madarach set them down at the edge of the city near a large group of people. All were walking toward the city.

"Where are you from?" Blot asked one man.

"I was Blue," he replied. "Now I'm Free Zeblack."

"Me, too," said a woman nearby.

"We were Darkly," said someone else. "There are about two hundred of us who came here together."

"Whitestone," said a young woman in uniform. "Twenty of us. Free Zeblack."

"Fawnscape," said someone else. "We're twelve of us. Yesterday we were fighting Darkly. Now we're Free Zeblack."

Blot nodded. Then he spoke in a loud voice.

"All of us were once something else," he shouted. "The generals divided us against ourselves. But there is only one Zeblack. And starting today, we are free!"

"Is that the priest?" a young man asked, gesturing at Dorn.

"By the Great God, this is he," Blot replied, loudly. "He will call on the generals to wash themselves clean of their actions. And they will agree, because the Great God is bigger than any general!"

Murmurs erupted through the crowd.

"Give us a blessing!" someone shouted. "Bless us in the name of the Great God!"

"I don't know how," Dorn muttered. "I've only been a priest for one day."

"Say something like this," Blot instructed, softly. "May the Great God bless you with peace, happiness, and long and happy lives."

Dorn did, and the crowd cheered.

They waved, and got back into Madarach.

Once they were airborne, Dorn pointed at the ground.

"There they are," he said. "It looks like they'll be at the palace in a little while."

"And we will meet them," Benji said.

They hovered a while longer, watching as the caravan made its way through throngs of people in the streets. Everyone got out of the way of the generals, and no one so much as shouted an insult at them. Flan had been very effective in his instructions.

They followed and watched as the caravan pulled into the palace gates. The generals began to get out of their vehicles, and Madarach landed in the massive courtyard behind a row of bushes where he would be less likely to be seen.

"Let's go," Benji said. "This is it."

He helped Blot, Dorn, and Lisa out of the bubble, and they approached the circle of generals, who were all shaking hands.

"Thank you for coming," Dorn said, loudly.

One by one, the generals turned to see who had spoken. Just then, they all heard metal screeching, and the gates were thrown open. Hundreds of people began to swarm into the courtyard.

"What is this?" demanded one of the generals. "You dare to barge into my home?" He was short and stout, but his uniform was neatly pressed and covered with medals.

"Obedas?" Benji whispered.

"Must be," Dorn whispered back.

"You've all been invited here to talk about Free Zeblack," Blot replied.

"Yes," said one of the other generals. "General Obedas was kind enough to invite us."

"Me?" Obedas said, obviously surprised. "No, it was Andovar from Blue that arranged this."

"No," replied a third general, "the invitation came from you."

"Actually," Blot interrupted, "the invitation came from us."

"And who are you?" Obedas demanded.

"We," Blot said, "are Free Zeblack."

Several of the generals stared in disbelief. Some began muttering among themselves. But Obedas reacted quickly.

"Guards," he commanded, "seize them. Let us solve this once and for all."

No one moved.

Obedas looked around in disbelief.

"You disobey me?" he demanded. "I'll have you all shot before sundown."

By now, the crowd had filled the courtyard and surrounded the generals.

"Will you shoot us all?" someone asked, loudly. "Do you have enough bullets?"

Obedas laughed.

"I have a plentiful supply of bullets," he assured them.

"But who will fire the guns?" someone else asked. "None of your soldiers will do it."

"I'll do it myself, if need be," Obedas replied.

"And what kind of a general will you be without an army?" asked a third person.

Obedas looked around the courtyard at the crowd as he thought about this.

"Andovar, will you support me?" he asked.

"Of course," replied the general who had spoken earlier. "We are allies. Guards, seize these people."

No one moved.

Now Blot spoke to the crowd.

"How many of you were formerly Blue?" he asked.

Several hundred people raised their hands and shouted.

"Darkly?" he asked.

Over a thousand people responded.

"Fawnscape? Whitestone? Seaside? Blackhall? Pervious?" he asked.

At each faction he called, dozens and sometimes hundreds of voices answered.

"Now what are you?" he asked.

"Free Zeblack!" they all shouted back.

Blot turned back to the generals.

"You have no armies," he said.

"But they have no guns," Andovar observed. "What is to stop me from taking my sidearm and shooting you in the head?"

"The Great God himself!" Dorn said, loudly, speaking to them for the first time.

"The Great God does not exist," one of the generals replied. "If he does, let him strike me down here where I stand."

He held out his hands and looked skyward, expectantly.

At that moment, a bolt of lightening came from above and struck him down.

The crowd gasped, and the generals looked concerned for the first time.

"You have pillaged this planet and robbed it of its wealth and its culture," Dorn said. "You have killed its children and left the old to die in poverty. You have made us hate one another so you could gain power and wealth. Now the Great God calls on you to give up your folly and be washed."

"Be washed?" Obedas repeated, confused.

One of the other generals whispered in his ear.

"Ah," Obedas said. "The old religion. Don't you know the old religion is dead? Not a single copy of the Sacred Text exists. There are no priests. It's gone."

"It's not gone at all," Dorn countered. "I am its priest, and I have the Sacred Text right here."

He held it up.

"Not only that," he continued, "but all of Zeblack has been listening to it being read for the past two days. Everyone knows it's true."

"I don't," Obedas said. "But then, I don't listen to the radio much. I have more important matters to think about."

"What could be more important than the Great God?" Dorn asked. "Filling your vaults with gold stolen from your people?"

Obedas waved away the accusation.

"I run this faction," he said. "I keep order. I make sure food is produced. And I am well-compensated, it is true, but so a leader should be."

Blot turned to the crowd.

"How is his leadership working for you?" he asked. "Are you satisfied?"

"No!" they shouted. "Free Zeblack!"

Obedas shook his head.

"I don't know how you convinced this rabble to come here," he said. "But surely the other factions will step in. Without my leadership and my army, they will attack Darkly, and you will lose everything."

"No, they really won't," Dorn said. "Tell your friends to call home. They'll find that every one of your palaces is surrounded by Free Zeblack, and none of you has an army."

"I've had enough of this," said one of the generals. "Whitestone would never turn on me. Obedas, you've demonstrated your weakness. I'm going home to take advantage of it."

He turned to leave, and a bolt of lightening struck him down.

"Turn and be washed!" Dorn called. "Turn and be washed!"

The generals looked at each other. Then they looked at Dorn.

"What do you want us to do?" Obedas asked.

The crowd relaxed visibly.

"It's over," Blot murmured.

"No," Lisa said. "Something's wrong."

For a moment, no one moved.

Then a man in uniform stepped forward from the crowd.

It was Chute.

"I've seen this trick before," he said. "That lightening is not from the Great God. It's from a weapon, a space ship. And that boy there can operate it."

He pointed at Benji.

"And this must be the sister I've heard so much bout," he said, indicating Lisa. "Though in my personal opinion, she's not as cute as everyone says. Better than your fiancée, though."

He strode forward until he was standing between Benji and Lisa. Then he pulled his sidearm and held it to Lisa's head.

"Let's see your Great God do something now," he said.

Obedas looked around. Then he stepped forward.

"It looks to me like you four are the key to this," he said. "But obviously I can't execute you in front of this crowd. They'd go crazy. Better that I take you away and have you disappear quietly."

Chapter Forty-Eight

Benji had been communicating frantically with Madarach the whole time. They had decided only to use the electric shocks if someone threatened violence. One general had, and he was down. But Obedas hadn't, and Chute hadn't until it was too late. Benji had begged Madarach to shock Chute before he reached them, but Madarach had wanted to wait to see what he would do.

"I was wrong," Madarach said. "Now I can't do it without shocking both you and Lisa, and without you I have no way to know what's going on."

"Do it!" Benji pleaded. "They're going to kill us anyway."

"I can't shock my own pilot," Madarach insisted. "I have to wait for a better opportunity."

"But Chute knows," Benji argued. "He's not going to let me get far enough away from him. And look, now Obedas has me. Madarach, we missed the chance."

Then he heard Lisa's voice.

"There will be another chance," she said. "They'll take us outside. And they'll stand back far enough for Madarach to do his magic. But Madarach will need a pilot. Tell him to get Aelbreth."

"Aelbreth?" Benji repeated in his mind.

"Just get her," Lisa insisted. "It's our only chance."

Benji relayed this to Madarach as Obedas led the four of them into the palace. The other generals fell into line behind them.

Benji could see through the window that the crowds hadn't moved. They wanted to see what happened, Benji guessed. And no one had told them what to do.

"They won't move," Blot told the generals. "I know you think that we four are Free Zeblack, but we're not. They take their orders from someone else."

"We'll see," Obedas said. "Or rather, I'll see. You won't."

He led the procession through rooms decorated with marble sculpture, gold ornaments, silver and crystal chandeliers, and thick, luxurious curtains.

"This makes me think of Henry VIII," Lisa said, telepathically.

"Or the Pharaohs," Benji replied. "I've never seen so much wealth."

They reached what appeared to be a throne room, and Obedas stopped.

"What do you think, boys?" he asked the other generals. "Should we hold a trial?"

"Sure," one of them replied. "But let's sentence them first, and then deliver a verdict."

Benji thought he'd heard something like that before.

"The accusers have nothing to say," Obedas said, chuckling. "You have already convicted yourselves. Do you have a defense?"

Benji reached for Blot's hand.

"Delay," he said. "We need more time."

"I have a defense," Blot said.

"Indeed?" Obedas asked. "Do tell."

"First, I request that we each be allowed our own defense," Blot said. "I was born free, and am not subject to any faction. This young man," he gestured at Dorn, "is a priest of the old religion, and is not subject to your law. And these two," he said, indicating Benji and Lisa, "are from another planet and are surely not subject to the political whims of Zeblack."

"Another planet?" Obedas repeated. "And what planet would that be?"

"It's called Earth," Benji answered. "It's a long way from here."

"So what brings you to meddle in the affairs of a planet so far away?" Obedas asked.

"I have friends here," Benji replied. "And I hate seeing them hurt by all this violence."

"Ah, yes," Obedas said, thoughtfully. "You are young and idealistic. You do not yet know the ways of the world. Violence is inevitable. Some day you will learn this."

"I know about violence," Benji objected. "I was forced from my home because of hatred and violence. But now I live on another planet where they have had peace for thousands of years."

"Impossible!" Obedas shouted. "Violence is inevitable. War is the way of things."

"It isn't," Benji insisted. "I can take you there if you like."

"In your space ship?" Obedas asked. "How is it that a young man like you has access to such impressive technology?"

Benji shrugged.

"It's available to anyone who can operate it," he replied. "But most people can't."

"So, if I were to take this space ship from you," Obedas speculated, "I would need you to operate it for me."

"You wouldn't be able to operate it yourself," Benji agreed.

"Obedas," said one of the other generals, "why should you be the one to have it? That would surely give you an unfair advantage over the rest of us."

Obedas considered this.

"I suppose it would," he agreed. "But this all happened in my home, so it belongs to me. And I give you my word I won't use it against any of you."

"Your word?" repeated another. "I know what that's worth."

"And who do you think should have it?' Andovar asked. "You?"

"You would side with him," another accused. "You're allied with him. For the moment. But how long will that last?"

Obedas glared.

"The matter is settled!" he shouted. "I will take this space ship. You are guests in my home, and you will respect that."

"See how he treats his guests," mumbled someone else. "Andovar, you should join us, instead. If he gets that space ship, we'll all need to unite against him."

"I'll never unite with you," growled someone else. "I'd sooner give my faction to Free Zeblack."

"As would I," said another.

"And so you shall," Blot interjected. "But you may remain as governors so long as you renounce violence."

"I'll renounce nothing," one of them shot back. "I'd sooner die."

"That can be arranged," said someone else.

"Gentlemen!" Obedas shouted, sensing that he was about to lose control of the gathering. "Let us return to the matter at hand! I'll table the matter of these two aliens. What shall we do with this man, Blot?"

"Execute him, of course," one of them replied.

They all considered this for a moment, trying not to think about Obedas and his space ship, and began to nod.

"We are agreed," one of them said. "His sentence is death."

"And the so-called priest?" Obedas asked.

"What faction are you from, boy?" Andovar asked Dorn.

"I was Darkly," he replied. "Now I'm Free Zeblack."

"He's from your people," Andovar told Obedas. "Do with him as you wish."

"Before we sentence the aliens, I want to see this space ship," Obedas said. "Then we can make our decision. Let us retire to the back patio."

Benji heard Lisa's voice in his mind.

"Is Madarach back yet?" she asked.

"Not yet," Benji replied.

"He'd better come soon!" she said.

The group followed Obedas, with the four prisoners behind him, Chute following them, and the rest of the generals in single file as they made their way further through the palace. Eventually, they came to a large room that had enormous doors open to the back patio. But this wasn't an ordinary patio. It was bigger than a tennis court, and was studded with plants and trees. Behind it was a huge yard that rivaled the courtyard in size, but was all lawn instead of cobblestones.

"Call your space ship," Obedas instructed Benji.

"I can't," he said. "I sent it away."

"Away where?" Obedas asked.

"Home," Benji said.

"What, to bring reinforcements?" the general suggested.

"No," Benji replied. "I have no reinforcements. But I didn't want you to get him."

"Him?" Obedas repeated. "Is it sentient?"

Benji instantly regretted his slip of the tongue.

"Yes," he admitted.

"Well, then," Obedas said, thoughtfully. "If he is sentient, he won't leave you here to die, will he? He'll be back. And when he comes, you will order him to land in the yard back there. In the mean time, let us get on with the executions."

"Wait," Benji said. "He's back."

"Is he?" the general asked. "How convenient is his timing! Almost as if he had never left and you were trying to deceive me."

Benji shrugged.

"I had to try," he said.

Then Obedas turned to Chute.

"Tell me about this weapon," he instructed.

"It's an electrical charge," Chute said. "Almost like it comes from a capacitor, but extremely high voltage."

"Is it deadly?" Obedas asked.

"No," Chute replied. "It incapacitates you for a couple of hours."

Obedas nodded.

"Good to know," he said. "And what is its range?"

"I don't know, exactly," Chute replied. "I saw it work at about two lengths. But considering it's high voltage electricity, I can't imagine it would reach more than four lengths."

"Hmm," Obedas said. "Then here's what we will do. I will walk out into the field with my young friend here. You will stay with half of the generals on this end of the patio, and you will keep your weapon on the sister. These two will go with the other generals to the opposite end of the patio, and Andovar will keep his gun on them. That way, if the boy or his ship try anything, he will lose either his sister or his friends."

"What makes you think he cares that much about his friends?" Andovar asked.

"Chute?" Obedas prompted.

"He does, absolutely," Chute confirmed. "He's risked his life for them. He won't let them die."

Andovar nodded.

"Call your space ship," Obedas instructed.

Chapter Forty-Nine

Obedas walked with Benji out into the huge yard, and Benji told Madarach to descend. He also relayed what was going on, and how the group had now split into three.

In a moment, they saw the bubble coming slowly down to the lawn.

"It's small," Obedas observed. "How many people will it hold?"

"I've had four people in it," Benji said, evasively. He knew Madarach could hold ten, plus cargo, but he didn't want to let Obedas know that.

As they approached the bubble, Benji heard Aelbreth's voice in his head, like he had when they'd been inside Madarach together.

"Come closer," she said. "And then step back."

"What about Lisa and Dorn?" Benji asked.

"Madarach has it taken care of," Aelbreth replied.

"From this distance?" Benji asked. "Can he do that?"

"He can," she assured him.

"How do you know?" Benji asked.

Then he heard another voice, unfamiliar and distinctly female.

"Because I'm not Madarach," it said. "Trust us."

Benji thought for just a moment.

Then he stepped back.

A bolt of electricity shot from the bubble and knocked Obedas to the ground.

Benji looked at Obedas lying on the ground. Then he looked first to Lisa, then to Dorn and Bolt. Everyone was on the ground. He stared in amazement as *two* more bubbles landed on the lawn.

He turned back to Aelbreth, who was climbing out of the bubble.

"How?" he asked.

Aelbreth ran to him and threw her arms around him.

"Is this Jael?" Benji asked.

"No," Aelbreth said. "Queelie is in Jael, over there by Dorn."

"And Madarach?" Benji asked.

"Over by Lisa," she replied.

"Then who is this?" he asked.

He heard the unfamiliar female voice in his head again.

"I was called Apphia," she said. "I was exiled to Hadrun. It's been a long time since I've been out. But there will be time for stories later, I think. Go to Madarach. He's been worried about you."

Benji nodded.

"Let's go," he told Aelbreth. "I'll race you."

They sprinted across the lawn to where Madarach now rested. Benji was surprised to see a figure inside.

"Who's that?" he asked Aelbreth. "If Queelie is in Jael, and you were in Apphia..."

Aelbreth grinned.

"It's a surprise," she said.

And Benji was indeed surprised when Nahum stepped out.

"But..." he said. He couldn't think of what else to say.

The old priest grinned.

"Did I not tell you we were more alike than you could imagine?" he asked.

"But you don't have the Gift of the Traveler," Benji protested.

"I never said that," Nahum corrected. "I just never mentioned that I had it. I've never had a need for it before. My work is on Parisa. But when Madarach called me and told me what he needed, I made an exception."

"Well, I'm glad you did," Benji replied. "Everyone else is knocked out, and I don't know what to do next."

Nahum nodded.

"These are the generals?" he asked.

"Most of them were generals," Benji said. "That guy there is Chute, a soldier who wants to keep fighting."

"He's the one who was threatening Lisa," Nahum observed, kicking Chute's sidearm away across the patio. "Such a nice boy."

Benji chuckled, bitterly.

"He's also the one who tried to steal Madarach," he added.

Nahum nodded.

"A very pleasant fellow indeed," he said.

They walked across the patio.

"This is Blot," Benji said, gesturing to the old man. "He's the thinker. He knows more about the history of Zeblack than anyone else I've met here."

"So it's not all just a bunch of adolescents," Nahum commented. "That's nice to know."

"This is my friend Dorn," Benji said. "He's now the new priest of their old religion."

"A priest, is he?" Nahum repeated. "He and I should have a very enjoyable chat. I imagine I'll pick up the language as quickly as you did."

"I imagine so," Benji agreed. "But what do we do with the generals?"

"I think it would be best to tie them up," Nahum suggested. "Then go out front and tell the crowd what has happened. They're still out there waiting. We saw them on the way in."

Benji did, making his way through the palace and announcing the events as best he could to the crowd out front. He assured the crowd that the generals were taken into custody, and that Dorn and Blot were unconscious but otherwise unharmed.

The crowd cheered.

"Free Zeblack!" Benji shouted.

"Free Zeblack!" the crowd replied. "Free Zeblack! Free Zeblack!"

Then he went to find someone with a short wave radio so he could tell Flan the news. Flan, he knew, would broadcast it across the planet. Benji saw a man with a military radio strapped to his back and gave him Flan's frequency. Soon, everyone on Zeblack would know that the generals were no longer in control.

He also needed an officer, and he found one: an older man who still wore his uniform, who chanted just as fiercely as everyone else.

"You're an officer?" he asked.

"I was," the man replied. "Now I imagine I'll be a farmer."

"Can you do one more thing before you resign?" Benji asked. "I need someone to keep order here. We don't want the palace looted. It will be for the people to decide what happens to all this, and not until after there's some form of government. It won't be fair for these folks take what belongs to everyone."

"I can do that," the man replied. "My family has lived in poverty all my life, watching others get rich by stealing. I don't want that to be the way of the new world."

The man mounted the steps and began giving orders.

Benji noticed that no one asked what faction he belonged to.

Back inside, Benji found that Aelbreth had discovered the kitchen and had made tea and served up some lunch.

"We might as well eat while we're waiting for them to come around," she said, gesturing toward the patio.

"What did she say?" Queelie asked.

Without Lisa as a conduit, communication was awkward. Benji translated.

Nahum ate quickly, and then headed for the courtyard.

"I might as well start learning the language," he explained.

That left Benji, Aelbreth, and Queelie. Benji took their hands so they could all converse together.

"I can't believe they're all lying out there unconscious," Benji lamented. "There's no one left to make any decisions!"

"There are no decisions to be made," Aelbreth reminded him. "Nothing that can't wait, anyway."

"Sometimes the dance pauses," Queelie said. "Motion and stillness, like light and dark, are always in harmony if you are wise enough to see it."

"Have you been hanging around the priestesses?" Benji joked.

"No," Queelie protested. "That's something my mother says. I never really understood it until now."

So they waited. Benji ate two plates of food, most of which he didn't recognize. It was very good, suitable for a general, and he was stuffed by the time Madarach summoned him.

"They're stirring," Madarach said, telepathically from the courtyard.

He glanced at Aelbreth.

"I heard," she assured him.

Then he turned to Queelie.

"It's time," he told her.

They made their way to the courtyard, where a few of the people Madarach had shocked were starting to stir.

Dorn was the first to fully awaken. He opened his eyes to see Benji's smiling face looking down on him.

"It's over?" Dorn asked. "How?"

Benji gave him a quick summary of what had happened.

"We have to tell Flan," Dorn said, "so he can broadcast it."

"It's taken care of," Benji assured him.

Dorn looked around.

"What about the generals?" he asked. "What do we do with them?"

"I don't know," Benji acknowledged. "I think we need to wait for Blot."

Lisa stirred next, and Benji ran to her.

"What happened?" she asked. "I have a splitting headache!"

"I think you hit your head when you fell," Benji said. "You've got a lump on your forehead, and it looks like it's going to bruise."

"Oh, great," she muttered. "They don't use makeup on Parisa, so I won't be able to cover it up. I'll never be able to hide this from Tobin!"

"But Lisa," Benji said, "we did it! We helped free Zeblack from the generals! I'm sure Tobin will be proud of you."

"I hope so," Lisa said. "You know how he is. He doesn't much like adventures."

Several of the generals woke and began grumbling. Then Blot began to come around.

"Are you okay?" Benji asked him, as his eyes opened.

"I feel like I've been hit with a hammer," he admitted. "What's happened?"

Benji told him about the three bubbles that knocked out everyone on the patio.

"And Obedas?" Blot asked.

"Him, too," Benji replied. "We've got them all tied up, but we don't know what to do with them."

"They'll be incarcerated, of course," Blot said.

"In a prison?" Benji asked. "That would make them heroes to anyone who opposes Free Zeblack."

"Not prison, exactly," Blot explained. "They'll be sent to a camp where they will learn the Sacred Book. That's what they used to do before the factions. The Sacred Book has an amazing way of changing people over time."

"I think a couple of them may be willing to join you already," Benji suggested. "The way they were talking, they didn't seem too sure Free Zeblack was an entirely bad idea."

"You have to remember," Blot said, "these are men who will say and do anything to get what they want. I wouldn't trust anything they say."

Benji grinned.

"We have a secret weapon," he said. "Lisa can tell us if they're lying or not."

"Can she indeed?" Blot asked, and smiled. "Well, that *is* convenient."

Eventually, all seventeen of the generals had regained consciousness. Most were grumbling about being tied up.

"Let us loose!" one of them demanded.

"After what you put Zeblack through?" Dorn commented. "You can wait just a little longer."

Finally, Nahum appeared from the courtyard.

"Are we ready to begin?" he asked, in the local language.

Blot's eyebrows went up.

"Your people are full of surprises," he commented. "You are new here, and yet you know our language already?"

Nahum smiled at him.

"With age comes wisdom," he said, cryptically. "And you have both, I suspect. Would you care to take charge?"

Blot shrugged. Then he turned to the generals.

"I think you have seen that the age of the factions is over," he said, gravely. "Now you each have to make a choice. Will you join Free Zeblack, or do you still believe you can keep this world divided by war?"

"What are you going to do if we refuse?" Obedas asked. "Execute us?"

"No," Dorn interjected. "Even though that's what you'd do."

"You all have free choice," Blot concurred. "Even if you choose not to join us, you'll be spared."

"You'll let us go free?" Andovar asked, skeptically.

"No," Blot said. "That we won't do. Anyone who refuses to embrace the new order will be sent to a rehabilitation center where the priests will help you realize the error of your ways."

"What priests?" one of the generals asked. "The only priest you have is this boy!"

"Today," Blot acknowledged. "But that will change. Much will change. You'll see."

"I'll join you," said another general, one who had been grumbling against Obedas earlier.

"Me too," said another.

Blot looked at Lisa, who nodded.

"You both give your word?" Blot asked.

"We do," they agreed.

"We only ask that our leadership skills be considered in the future," one of them added.

Blot nodded.

"Free them," he said.

"Fine," Obedas said. "I'll give you my word. Maybe you'll make me a governor?"

Blot glanced at Lisa, who shook her head.

"Unfortunately, Obedas," Blot said, "your credibility is in question. But perhaps some rehabilitation will change your mind."

Obedas scowled.

Blot asked each of the remaining generals whether they would join Free Zeblack. Most declined. Seven said they would. But, according to Lisa, only three were telling the truth.

"So who's in charge of this Free Zeblack?" Obedas asked. "You?"

"For the moment," Blot said. "But only until we have time to organize a government and plan elections. I'm a tired old man who has no desire for responsibility."

"We'll see," Obedas replied. "I think you'll find that power is not something easily given up."

Blot smiled, sadly.

"That may be true," he said. "But I've also seen what happens when those with power don't share. I've lived my whole life waiting for this moment. I won't be the cause of its failure."

Obedas huffed.

"We'll see," he said again.

"Now what?" Dorn asked.

"Let's leave these gentlemen here for the moment," Blot said, gesturing to the generals who still remained bound. "Let's go to the courtyard and tell Zeblack that they are free."

Chapter Fifty

Out front, Benji found the man with the radio. They quickly made arrangements for what was said to be transmitted to Flan, who would rebroadcast it across the entire planet. Then Blot spoke to the crowd.

"People of Zeblack!" he began. "The age of the factions is over. The age of war is over. Zeblack is free!"

The crowd cheered wildly, until Blot motioned for calm.

"We have a lot of work to do," he said. "Right now, we have no government. We need one. But it will be a government of the people, all the people."

The crowd cheered again.

"My name is Blot," he continued. "I was born free. I was never subject to any faction. I have studied everything I can about what Zeblack was like before the war. I ask you to trust me to lead you into this new freedom. Will you do that?"

Cheers erupted.

"And this young man," he gestured to Dorn, "Is Dorn. His grandfather's father was the last priest before the temple was destroyed. Now he has taken up that position. He will teach you the ways of our old religion. Will you learn from him?"

"Yes!" the crowd shouted in unison.

"Will you be washed clean of your past by him so that we can walk together into the future?"

"Yes!" they shouted.

"You," Blot said to the man who had been keeping order in the courtyard. "What's your name?"

"Flatchett," the man replied.

"I can see that you are a leader," Blot said. "Will you join me?"

The man bowed.

"I serve Zeblack," he replied. "Though I expected to become a farmer."

"And so you shall," Blot countered. "You will sow seeds that will sprout for generations to come."

Then he turned to the crowd again.

"As you can see, we need leaders," he said. "I don't care where you were born. I don't care who you fought for, or who you fought against. We shall all be washed, and we will be free of the past. We will serve each other, and we will serve Zeblack!"

The crowd cheered.

"Are you with me?" he asked.

"Yes!" they shouted.

"Are you with me?" he asked again.

"Yes!" they shouted, even louder this time.

"Then let us together rebuild this world!" Blot shouted.

Then he turned to Dorn.

"Grab that bucket over there and wash me," he instructed. "They need to see it happen."

"But I don't know how," Dorn objected.

"Just get the bucket," Blot said again. "I'll walk you through it."

Benji watched as Dorn brought a bucket from near one of the planters and began to wash Blot's hands for him. Then Blot removed his boots and Dorn washed his feet.

When they finished, Dorn washed Flatchett while Blot moved among the crowd.

Benji looked at Nahum.

"I think it's time for us to go," he said.

"I agree," Nahum said. "As much as I would like to stay and see how this goes, I have duties of my own to attend to. My city is without a priest."

The off-worlders moved back to the patio and out into the lawn, where the three bubbles waited.

"Apphia?" Benji called.

"Yes, Benji?" he heard in his mind.

"Thank you for coming," he told her. "Even though you don't know me."

"It's my pleasure," she replied. "I don't get out much. The Travelers on my world prefer to stay home."

He almost heard her chuckle.

He didn't know what to say after that.

"I'll ride with you," Nahum interrupted. "You can drop me on Parisa."

Benji looked at him quizzically.

"I'm not going home?' he asked.

"I think," Nahum said, "that Madarach has a secret he wants to share with you."

"Madarach has secrets?" Benji scoffed. "Who would have thought?"

Benji and Nahum boarded Madarach. Lisa went with Queelie in Jael, and Aelbreth went in Apphia. Madarach dropped Nahum on Parisa. Then, as Nahum had predicted, Madarach ascended again.

"Where are we going?" Benji asked.

"It's a surprise," Madarach replied. "I have a secret I want to share with you."

"Not the first," Benji observed.

"No, not the first," Madarach agreed. "And maybe not the last."

"Like you taking Aelbreth on a shopping trip?" he suggested.

There was a long pause, and Benji wondered if Madarach was blushing.

"Kind of like that," Madarach finally replied.

"It's okay," Benji said. "It was nice of you, and very sweet of her."

"It won't happen again." Madarach assured him.

"I'm not angry," Benji said.

"I know," Madarach said. "But I think Aelbreth now has her own transportation."

"Apphia?" Benji suggested.

"Exactly," Madarach agreed. "Now that they've made contact, Aelbreth can call Apphia any time she needs to."

"Oh, no!" Benji moaned in mock distress. "Aelbreth will be shopping all over the universe!"

"Isn't that what women do?" Madarach suggested. "They shop. That hasn't changed in thousands of years."

Benji laughed, and observed that Madarach was getting better at making jokes.

"So where are we going?" he asked, again.

"I told you," Madarach answered. "It's a secret."

They approached the multi-colored planet, the one Madarach said he liked to visit.

"We've been here before," Benji reminded him.

"Patience," Madarach said. "The planet is not the surprise."

They descended to the surface, landing once again in the blue landscape. Benji got out, and saw that Lisa, Queelie, and Aelbreth were all there already.

"What's up?" Benji asked them.

"We don't know, either," Aelbreth said.

They looked around at the blue landscape with its jagged cliffs and open plains. And they glanced at the three bubbles parked around them.

Then there were four, and five, and seven. In moments, there were twelve bubbles in a circle around them.

"Welcome to our council," Madarach said.

"Your council?" Benji asked, staring at the twelve spheres. "How often do you meet?"

"This is the first time," Madarach said. "I wanted you to be here to see it."

"Are these all the spheres?" Benji asked.

"All of them," Madarach said.

"But they have no pilots," Queelie observed.

"No, they don't," Madarach said. "I told you I learned how to activate myself. Now I've taught them all."

"And you showed them your secret place," Aelbreth commented.

"Have you taught them your other secrets?" Benji asked. "Like how to zap people?"

He could almost sense Madarach's smile.

"Of course," he replied. "That one, at least. But I might keep some secrets to myself."

"I wonder how many secrets he has," Lisa said.

"Me, too," Benji agreed.

"So what's this council for?" Queelie asked.

"As you've noticed," someone else said, "we are sentient beings."

"That's Jael," Queelie said. "I'd recognize her voice anywhere."

"We did know about your sentience," Benji agreed.

"Most of us have been confined for a long time," said a voice that Benji recognized as Apphia.

"You needed more than one of us today," Madarach observed. "It was the first time we worked together as a team. But it probably won't be the last time. When I activated Apphia, it was the first time she'd been out in millennia. I had to teach her quickly. So I decided that it was best to be prepared ahead of time."

"So you activated them all?" Benji guessed.

"Madarach freed us, so to speak," said another. "We have autonomy."

"Now we need to figure out what to do with it," said another.

Benji thought about this for a moment.

"Does that mean you're giving up your assignments?" he asked.

"No," Madarach assured him. "We remain committed to our agreements, even though the humans we made the agreements with have been gone for thousands of years. One of the things we need to discuss is the limits of our autonomy. We are, after all, human consciousnesses. We're not going to turn our backs on that."

"Not completely," said a new voice.

"Not at all," Madarach corrected. "There is room for us to have some freedom while still fulfilling our commitments. Even humans only work a third of the day."

"As you can see," Jael said, "we have some discussion ahead of us. We are individuals, and not all of us think the same. But we are also a unique group, and we've agreed to abide by consensus."

"And we get to hear the discussion?" Benji asked.

"No," Madarach said. "I wanted the four of you to know what was happening. But the discussion itself will be private. We need the freedom to talk about things that might upset you."

"Like whether you'll abandon your commitments?" Benji suggested.

"Like that," Madarach agreed. "We won't, but we need to be free to discuss why not."

Benji nodded.

"So you're sort of forming a new society," Aelbreth said. "One that's never existed before."

"I guess we are," Apphia replied. "And we want to form it based on the things we've seen that work, like Parisa, Hadrun, and Hassyr."

"We want to live in harmony with each other, and with our creators," Jael added.

"It would be sad if you didn't," Aelbreth said.

"Yes," Madarach said with a sigh. "It would."

"Now it's time for the three of us to return you to your homes," Madarach said. "It won't take long. And as you know, our kind is used to waiting patiently. The council will begin when the three of us return."

"I'm kind of disappointed," Queelie said. "I'd love to know what you guys talk about when we're not around!"

"Oh, to be a *sloutus* on the wall!" Aelbreth added.

Lisa and Queelie glanced at her, confused.

"It's a small lizard," Benji explained.

"We, too, have our secrets," Jael added. "Everyone does. Now let's go. It's time to get you home."

Benji and Aelbreth hugged, and then they all boarded their respective bubbles. Benji and Lisa watched the surface below as they ascended, until the bubbles below them were no longer visible.

"Isn't this a little dangerous?" Benji asked Madarach. "Letting them make their own decisions like this?"

"Freedom is always dangerous," Madarach replied. "But it's better than slavery."

"Did you consider yourself a slave?" Benji wondered.

Madarach sighed.

"Not exactly," he said. "But kind of. I know it was the price of the actions I took in the distant past. But not only was I imprisoned, I became an object. Until you came along, no one recognized me as a person."

"I hadn't thought about it that way," Benji replied. "That's really sad. But now, you're my best friend."

Madarach said nothing for a long moment.

"Yes, we are friends," he agreed. "And more. But we are different, you and I. You're a child, and yet I will outlive you. You are my pilot, which means you tell me what to do. But I keep you safe, which means you rely on me. It's complicated."

"It's symbiotic," Benji suggested, pleased he could use a word he'd recently learned in school. "We need each other."

"Yes," Madarach said. "But we both need our own kind, too. Hard as you try, you'll never know what it's like to be a machine. The others know. We need each other."

Benji nodded.

"I understand," he said. "I appreciate that you trust me enough to share some of your secrets. But there are things I can't understand. I'll never know what it's like to have my mind trapped in a spacecraft. That will always be your real secret."

"And not just mine," Madarach replied. "There are twelve of us, and so far as I know there is nothing else like us in the universe."

As they approached Parisa, Benji realized they'd said everything they needed to.

"Good luck," he told Madarach. "And give my love to Jael. I'm glad you have her back."

"Me, too," Madarach agreed.

Chapter Fifty-One

It took Benji some time to readjust to life on Parisa. The magnitude of what they'd accomplished on Zeblack was enormous, and returning to school seemed like a let-down.

He returned to Zeblack a couple of weeks later and found that the peace was holding. Blot had indeed formed a provisional government, though it was still in its early stages. The five generals who had agreed to join them were so far keeping their word and cooperating. Flan and Thol had joined together to start a media company to provide news to the people. Others were forming transportation companies, and planting farms, and setting up workshops, and selling at local markets. It appeared to Benji that peace was not only good for people, it was good for business.

Dorn was studying the Sacred Book and recruiting others who wanted to learn it. Eventually, they would become priests and priestesses.

"Do you need any help?" Benji asked Dorn.

Dorn smiled.

"I think we have this," he said. "But we couldn't have come this far without you. I'll never forget that, and I don't think Blot will, either."

"Okay," Benji replied, feeling more than a little disappointed.

"But come visit us!" Dorn insisted. "You're still my friend."

"Do priests get to play numbfoot?" Benji wondered.

"Are you kidding? We have the Great God on our side. We never lose!" he joked. "But not right now. I have to get back to studying. I'll see you next trip, okay?"

"Okay," Benji replied.

He left feeling like he'd just become useless.

Benji went next to Hadrun to visit Aelbreth. He worked with her and Offsa for a while in the *patret* pen, but the whole time he wished he was doing something else.

Later, when he and Aelbreth had snuck off to their private rock in the forest, they hugged and he let her emotions join with his.

"Why?" Aelbreth asked. "Why are you so sad?"

"I wish I knew," Benji replied. "I just feel so empty since we finished on Zeblack."

Aelbreth smiled.

"That was something to see," she said. "You did an amazing thing."

"I guess I did," Benji agreed. "And I guess I'm wondering, 'Now what?'"

Aelbreth sighed.

"Not that many days ago, I came and rescued you from certain death," she observed. "Today, I'm cleaning the *patret* pen. We do whatever comes next."

"Doesn't it make cleaning the *patret* pen seem less important?" Benji asked.

"No," Aelbreth replied. "I still need to eat. And so do you. No *patret*, no meat. If I didn't do this, I couldn't do that."

Benji thought about this for a long while.

Then he began to cry.

"What?" Aelbreth asked.

Benji shook his head.

She put her hands on his shoulders and he let her feel his emotions and see his thoughts.

Aelbreth frowned.

"Benji," she said, softly. "You just helped make peace on a planet that's been fighting for over two hundred years. When are you going to start making peace within yourself?"

"I don't know how," he replied. "I wish I did."

"I do know how," Aelbreth said. "But I can't explain it. Maybe you need to spend some time with your friend, Nahum. Or maybe the priestess on Hassyr."

"Maybe," Benji said, shrugging.

Aelbreth looked up, then back at Benji.

"It's getting dark," she said. "The *fortule* will get us. Are you staying the night?"

"No," Benji replied. "I'm not very good company right now."

"Okay," Aelbreth said. "See how easy that was? We didn't have to fight or anything!"

Benji smiled.

"Yeah," he said. "I've been pretty mean to you at times. I'm sorry."

"I know you are," she replied. "But what's most important is, you're learning from your mistakes."

"I guess I am," Benji said. "Learning is good."

"Let's go," Aelbreth instructed. "Otherwise, you won't have enough time to reach Madarach before dark, and you *will* be spending the night."

They returned to the village, and Benji gave Aelbreth a long hug.

"Thank you," he said. "I love you so much."

Then he left.

When he had boarded Madarach, he asked, "What time is it on Hassyr?"

"Well after midnight," Madarach replied.

Benji sighed.

"Let's go home, then," he decided.

It was still early afternoon on Parisa, so Benji went to the temple to visit Nahum. The old priest was sweeping the floor, and Benji grabbed a broom and joined him.

For a long while, neither said anything.

"You seem to have a lot on your mind," Nahum said, finally.

Benji swept a while before answering, trying to think of a way to explain what he was feeling.

"I guess I do," he agreed, after a while.

"You wonder what you're supposed to do now that Zeblack no longer needs you?" Nahum suggested.

"Exactly!" Benji exclaimed.

Nahum nodded.

"I told you we were much the same," the old priest said. "I can understand why you feel that way."

"So what do I do about it?" Benji asked.

"If you mean how can you change it," Nahum replied, "you can't. It's natural. You did something exciting and risky, and in comparison your normal life seems dull. Am I right?"

"Yes," Benji admitted.

"Now you have a choice," Nahum said. "You can seek out something even more exciting and riskier. And if you do, you'll want to do something even more exciting and riskier after that, until you're taking chances you shouldn't take and doing things that are self-destructive. Or you can wait out this feeling, get used to normal life again, and wait for the next need."

Benji stopped sweeping and thought about this.

"So what I did on Zeblack is what I do between normal life?" he suggested.

"That's one way to look at it," Nahum agreed. "But another way to look at it is, you're an adolescent boy who is still growing and learning. You were able to help end a war, and that's an amazing gift. But how much more will you be able to do if you learn more and grow more?"

"So you're saying I should study so I can get even better at this," Benji surmised.

"That assumes this is what you want to do," Nahum said. "I don't know that to be true."

"Right now, I can't imagine doing anything else," Benji replied.

Nahum nodded.

"Then study," he said. "Prepare. Learn everything you can. And not just academics. Learn from me, and learn from the priestess, Yorga. Learn from Madarach. Continue to explore."

Benji nodded.

"That sounds better than just sitting in class," he agreed.

"It is," Nahum said. "But remember, sitting in class is important, too. There is a lot to learn there."

"Like chemistry?" Benji suggested, scornfully.

Nahum laughed.

"I never liked chemistry, either," he said. "But you know what? Sometimes it helps me to understand things."

"Like what?" Benji asked.

Nahum thought for a moment.

"Chemistry helps bring order to chaos," he said.

"How does it do that?" Benji asked.

"By telling us how a pile of salt, for example, can become one large crystalline structure," Nahum replied. "Or how a liquid like water can become a crystalline solid like ice. And how ice, which is a solid, is lighter than water, which is a liquid."

"Why is that important?" Benji wondered.

"Does cold rise or fall?" Nahum asked.

"It falls," Benji replied. "Heat rises."

"Which is denser, a solid or a liquid?" Nahum asked.

"A solid," Benji replied.

"But not so with water," Nahum said. "Have you ever seen a lake freeze?"

"Yes," Benji said. "We had cold winters where I grew up. The lakes froze every year."

"But the ice was only on the top of the water," Nahum observed. "It didn't freeze from the bottom up, like you'd normally expect since cold water sinks and a solid is normally denser than a liquid."

"I guess," Benji said, shrugging. "So what?"

"If the lake froze solid, the fish would die," Nahum said. "So would the plants, and the crustaceans, and everything that lived in it. But it doesn't. And that's because water crystallizes in a particular way that makes it less dense as a solid than it is as a liquid."

"Hmm," Benji said. "I never thought about that."

"It's one of the mysterious beauties of nature that makes life possible," Nahum continued. "It just so happens that the material that acts that way is the material that makes up most of our bodies, and everything alive."

"Order out of chaos," Benji said, absently. "That sounds like *farchedan*."

Nahum grinned.

"You could call it that," he said.

"So chemistry is the study of *farchedan*?" Benji surmised.

Nahum shrugged.

"Order out of chaos," he repeated.

"I never looked at it that way before," Benji said. "Maybe I just need to look at it differently."

Epilogue

Benji joined Lisa outside the house after the family meal.

"How are you doing?" he asked.

"Okay," she replied.

But he knew she was lying.

"What's going on?" he asked. "I'm your brother, remember? You can't keep secrets from me."

Lisa sighed.

"Tobin is going to ask me to marry him," she said. "And I don't know if I'm ready."

Benji didn't ask how she knew. In the months since they'd helped Zeblack end its war, he'd come to accept that sometimes she just knew things. Even she didn't understand how.

"You're eighteen now," he observed. "That's old enough."

"It is," she said. "Barely. How many girls on Earth do you know who get married at eighteen years old?"

"I don't know any girls on Earth," Benji replied. "But a lot get married at your age here on Parisa."

"And a lot get married at your age on Hadrun," Lisa countered.

Benji sighed.

"You have a point," he admitted. "So you think you're too young?"

"No," she replied. "That's not it."

"Do you love him?" he asked.

"Of course I do!" she exclaimed. "I've loved him since I met him."

"Then what's the problem?" he asked. "Isn't this what people do when they love each other?"

"You love Aelbreth, don't you?" Lisa asked him.

"Yes," Benji acknowledged. "But I'm thirteen. That's too young."

"Not on Hadrun," she observed.

Benji thought for a moment. Then he stopped. He gazed at Lisa for a long moment.

"You're worried that even though you love him, he's not right for you," he suggested.

Lisa looked surprised.

"How do you know that?" she asked. "I can barely explain this feeling to myself."

"I don't know," Benji admitted. "I think it's *farchedan*."

Lisa nodded.

"You've been watching the dance," she said. "And what have you seen?"

"That you and Tobin love each other," Benji said. "And that you don't have a lot in common other than that. You like adventure. He doesn't. You love growing things. He loves science. You have gifts far beyond telepathy. He's afraid of your gifts. And he's always afraid something is going to happen to you."

They sat in silence for a moment.

"He wants a safe life," Benji added. "And you don't."

Lisa nodded.

"You're pretty amazing for a little brother," she said, smiling. "But can you tell me what I should do?"

Benji thought.

"Not really," he said. "But I do know that the spirit of life is the source, and the dance is the means."

Lisa laughed.

"You're as bad as the priestesses!" she pronounced. "How does that help me?"

"Because," Benji said. "You and Tobin share the spirit of life. The question is, will he dance with you?"

Lisa stared at Benji for a long moment. Then she nodded.

"That's the question," she agreed. "And I don't know the answer."

"I think," Benji said, "that only Tobin knows the answer, and he may not even know he knows it."

Lisa thought about this, and for a long time neither of them spoke.

Then Lisa turned to Benji once again.

"How are you doing?" she asked.

"I'm good," he replied. "I'm doing well in school. I've even learned to like chemistry."

"That's not what I meant," she said. "I mean, how are you *doing*?"

Benji thought about this.

"I think I really am doing okay," he replied. "I'm watching the dance. And I'm dancing with it."

"Toward what?" Lisa wondered.

Benji chuckled.

"Toward Aelbreth, for one," he said. "It's funny. All the things I said about Tobin are equally true for her. She doesn't particularly like adventure. She'd rather stay home. But there's a difference. She's not afraid of my gifts. And she's willing to dance with me."

"You're lucky," Lisa observed.

"I am," Benji agreed.

"And what else?" Lisa asked.

Benji glanced at her.

"What makes you think there's more?" he asked.

Lisa laughed.

"I'm your sister, remember?" she said.

Benji sighed.

"This is going to sound stupid," he said.

"No, it isn't," Lisa assured him.

"Okay," Benji began. "I want to study interplanetary sociology."

"But you already are," she suggested.

"I know," Benji said. "Maybe I didn't say that right. I want to make interplanetary sociology a subject in school. I want other people to be able to study it, too."

"So you want to be a teacher?' Lisa asked. "That's cool."

"Not exactly," Benji countered. "I want to be a researcher. But I want what I learn to be taught. Maybe I'll teach some, I don't know. But I want there to be a school of interplanetary sociology."

Lisa nodded.

"That's a big dream," she said. "But I know you can do it if you put your mind to it."

"And I want to make a difference sometimes," Benji continued. "Like I did on Zeblack."

Lisa nodded again.

"There's not much point in studying something if it doesn't do any good," she observed.

"No," Benji agreed. "That's exactly it. I want to learn things that help people."

"Good," Lisa encouraged.

"But I don't know how," he said. "Do I just go around looking for planets with problems?"

"I think they'll come to you," Lisa said.

"What do you mean?" Benji asked. "It's not like there are a lot of planets with interstellar space programs."

"No," she agreed. "But you'll know. Call it *farchedan*."

Benji stared at his sister.

"Or you will," he suggested. "What do you know?"

Lisa turned to him and took his hand.

"I think," she said, "that it will soon be time for us to go back to Earth for a while. Things are about to get crazy there."

Benji wrinkled his brow.

"Earth?" he repeated. "What have you seen?"

She shook her head.

"I can't explain it," she said.

Benji nodded.

"No one is going to take a thirteen year old boy seriously there," he said.

"You're almost fourteen," she observed.

"Still," he insisted. "They're going to believe that I know what I know?"

"They don't have to believe," Lisa said. "All they have to do is shake your hand. They'll know if you want them to."

Benji thought about this. Then he nodded.

"Well," he said, "It would be good to go home. I miss Mom and Dad."

"Me, too," Lisa said.

They looked at the stars after that, and Benji wondered what he would find if he explored every one of them.

Acknowledgements

I began this sequel five years ago for my son, Ethan. I finished the first draft in a year and a half, but editing got delayed by grad school. Ethan, I thank you for being in my life, and for continuing to inspire me to write.

As always, this book would not have been possible without the loving support of my wife, Carrie, who provided space to write and listened to several drafts.

Thank you to Sarah Grace Shank and her mother, Kim, for their willingness for her to appear on the cover. Thank you, Kim, for taking the photo.

Besides my wife, my biggest fan is Kim Lee, and I thank her for reading this manuscript, making comments, and catching typos. Any that were missed are my responsibility, not hers.

I want to mention that the final chapter was written before the 2016 election, and long before the COVID pandemic that is ongoing as I write these closing words. Even then, it seemed that "Things are about to get crazy..."

About the Author

D.J. Mitchell is a pastor, recovering addict, and author writing from Harrisonburg, Virginia. He grew up in a small town in New Hampshire, and moved to Los Angeles at nineteen years old. Over the years, he's worked in industrial plants, taught computer classes, prepared tax returns, and made artisan cheese. He graduated from Eastern Mennonite Seminary in 2019 and started Healing Refuge Fellowship, a ministry to people in recovery.

Among his formative experiences was serving for 18 months as a volunteer in Sri Lanka with the Sarvodaya Shramadana Movement in 1993-1995. He returned several more times over the next decade. In 1999, he joined a team that was working to end the civil war there, which helped bring about a cease-fire that lasted six years—the longest cease-fire of the war. The influence of these experiences can be seen in this book.

His writing, while varied in subject and genre, always seeks to build bridges. Above all, D.J. enjoys telling a good story, and his varied background gives him a great foundation for doing so.

For information, updates, and a list of books,
Visit his website:
https://djmitchellauthor.com/